Jane Austen's Emma for Teens

a simplified retelling of the classic original

Gerry Baird

Clearstone
Publishing

PREFACE

I first unknowingly encountered the story of Emma in the 1990's movie "Clueless." When I read the original Jane Austen book several years later, I was pleasantly surprised to discover that I was already familiar with the plotline and many of the characters. It is a timeless story, and unquestionably one of her greatest works.

To make this edition more accessible to a modern audience, I have broken long sentences into shorter ones, updated punctuation to improve clarity, and gently toned down the vocabulary while still honouring – to the degree possible – the author's intent. I have also, in certain cases, genericized references to very specific terms, such as the different types of carriages then in use. Words like *barouche* and *chaise-and-four* would have made perfect sense to Jane Austen's contemporaries, but as they serve no essential role in the plot they have been replaced in this version by the generic term "carriage." Most of the words in this book are Jane Austen's, and most remain exactly as she wrote them.

I am deeply indebted to David M. Shapard, who published "The Annotated Emma" (New York: Anchor, 2012). The valuable insights offered in this well-researched volume further expanded my knowledge and understanding of the words and world of Jane Austen.

If you enjoy this simplified retelling of Emma, you may also be interested in my simplified retelling of Pride and Prejudice: "Pride and Prejudice for Teens." It's available on Amazon in both Kindle and Paperback formats.

CHAPTER 1

Emma Woodhouse was beautiful, clever, and rich. She had a comfortable home, a happy disposition, and in her nearly twenty-one years in the world she had found very little to distress or upset her.

She was the youngest of the two daughters of a most affectionate, indulgent father, and had, due to her sister's marriage, been mistress of his house from a very early period. Her mother had died too long ago for her to have more than an indistinct memory of her caresses, and her place had been supplied by an excellent woman as governess, who had fallen little short of a mother in affection.

Miss Taylor had been in Mr. Woodhouse's family for sixteen years, less as a governess than a friend. She was very fond of both daughters, but particularly of Emma. Between *them* it was more like the closeness of sisters. Even before Miss Taylor had ceased to hold the office of governess, the mildness of her temper had hardly allowed her to impose any restraint; and the shadow of authority being now long passed away, they had been living together as friend and friend very mutually attached, and Emma doing just what she liked. She highly valued Miss Taylor's judgment, but was directed chiefly by her own.

The real disadvantages indeed of Emma's situation were the power of having rather too much her own way, and a tendency to think a little too well of herself. These were the disadvantages which threatened to spoil her many enjoyments. The danger, however, was at present so unperceived, that they did not by any means rank as misfortunes with her.

Sorrow came – a gentle sorrow – when Miss Taylor married. It was the loss of Miss Taylor's company which first brought grief. It was on the wedding day of this beloved friend that Emma first sat alone in mournful thought. The wedding over and the guests gone, her father and herself were left to dine together, with no prospect of a third to cheer a long evening. Her father went to bed after dinner, as usual, and she had then only to sit and think of what she had lost.

The event had every promise of happiness for her friend. Mr. Weston was a man of exceptional character, comfortable fortune, suitable age and pleasant manners. There was some satisfaction in considering with what self-denying, generous friendship she had always wished and promoted the match. But the absence of Miss Taylor would be felt every hour of every day. She recalled her past kindness – the kindness, the affection of sixteen years – how she had taught and how she had played with her from five years old – how she had devoted all her powers to entertain her – and how she had cared for her through the various illnesses of childhood. A large debt of gratitude was owing here; but their relationship during the last seven years, with its equal footing and perfect openness which had soon followed Isabella's marriage on their being left to each other, was yet a dearer, tenderer recollection. Miss Taylor had been a friend and companion such as few possessed: intelligent, well-informed, useful, gentle. Miss Taylor was particularly interested in Emma herself; in every pleasure, every scheme of hers. Emma could speak every thought to her as it arose, and Miss Taylor had such an affection for her that she never found fault.

How was Emma to bear the change? It was true that her friend was going only half a mile from them, but Emma was aware that great must be the difference between a Mrs. Weston only half a mile from them, and a Miss Taylor in the house. Though Emma had much to be grateful for, she was now in great danger of suffering from an overabundance of solitude. She dearly loved her father, but he was no companion for her. He could not be her equal in conversation, logical or playful.

The evil of the actual disparity in their ages (and Mr. Woodhouse had not married early) was much increased by his constitution and habits. Having had a nervous constitution all his life, without activity of mind or body, he was a much older man in ways than in years. Though everywhere beloved for the friendliness of his heart and his gentle temper, his talents could not have recommended him at any time.

Her sister was settled in London, only sixteen miles off, but this was far enough away to be beyond her daily reach. Many a long October and

November evening must be struggled through at Hartfield before Christmas brought the next visit from Isabella and her husband and their little children to fill the house and give her pleasant company again.

Highbury, the large and populous village to which Hartfield, in spite of its separate lawn and shrubberies and name, did really belong, afforded her no equals. The Woodhouses were first in importance there. All looked up to them. She had many acquaintances in the place, for her father was universally civil, but not one among them who could be accepted in lieu of Miss Taylor for even half a day. It was a melancholy change; and Emma could not but sigh over it and wish for impossible things, till her father awoke, and made it necessary to be cheerful. He was easily depressed and therefore required support. He was fond of everybody that he was used to, and hated to part with them; hated change of every kind. Matrimony, as the origin of change, was always disagreeable; and he was by no means yet reconciled to his own daughter's marrying, nor could ever speak of her but with compassion, though it had been entirely a match of affection. He was now obliged to part with Miss Taylor too; and from his habits of gentle selfishness and of being never able to suppose that other people could feel differently from himself, he felt that Miss Taylor had done as sad a thing for herself as for them, and would have been a great deal happier if she had spent all the rest of her life at Hartfield. Emma smiled and chatted as cheerfully as she could, to keep him from such thoughts; but when tea came, it was impossible for him not to say exactly as he had at dinner,

"Poor Miss Taylor! I wish she were here again. What a pity it is that Mr. Weston ever thought of her!"

"I cannot agree with you, papa; you know I cannot. Mr. Weston is such a good-humoured, pleasant, excellent man, that he thoroughly deserves a good wife. You would not have had Miss Taylor live with us forever when she might have a house of her own?"

"A house of her own! But where is the advantage of a house of her own? This is three times as large."

"How often we shall be going to see them, and they coming to see us! We shall be always meeting! *We* must begin, we must go and pay our wedding visit very soon."

"My dear, how am I to get so far? Randalls is such a distance. I could not walk half so far."

3

"No, papa, nobody thought of your walking. We must go in the carriage to be sure."

"The carriage! But James will not like to put the horses to use for such a short distance; and where are the poor horses to be while we are paying our visit?"

"They are to be put into Mr. Weston's stable, papa. You know we have settled all that already. We talked it all over with Mr. Weston last night. And as for James, you may be very sure he will always like going to Randalls, because of his daughter's being housemaid there. I only doubt whether he will ever take us anywhere else. That was your doing, papa. You got Hannah that good place. Nobody thought of Hannah till you mentioned her — James is so obliged to you!"

"I am very glad I did think of her. It was very lucky, for I would not have had poor James think himself slighted upon any account; and I am sure she will make a very good servant. She is a civil, well-spoken girl; I have a high opinion of her. Whenever I see her, she always curtseys and asks me how I am doing, in a very pretty manner. I am sure she will be an excellent servant, and it will be a great comfort to poor Miss Taylor to have somebody around her that she is used to seeing. Whenever James goes over to see his daughter, you know, she will be hearing of us. He will be able to tell her how we all are."

Emma spared no exertions to maintain this happier flow of ideas, and hoped, by the help of backgammon, to get her father tolerably through the evening, and be attacked by no regrets but her own. The backgammon table was placed, but a visitor immediately afterwards walked in and made it unnecessary.

Mr. Knightley, a sensible man of about thirty-seven or thirty-eight, was not only a very close friend of the family, but particularly connected with it as the elder brother of Isabella's husband. He lived about a mile from Highbury, was a frequent visitor and always welcome, and at this time more welcome than usual, as coming directly from their mutual connections in London. He had returned to a late dinner after some days absence, and now walked up to Hartfield to say that all were well in Brunswick-square. It was a happy circumstance and animated Mr. Woodhouse for some time. Mr. Knightley had a cheerful manner which always did him good; and his many inquiries after "poor Isabella" and her children were answered most satisfactorily. When this was over, Mr. Woodhouse gratefully observed,

"It is very kind of you, Mr. Knightley, to come out at this late hour to call upon us. I am afraid you must have had a shocking walk."

JANE AUSTEN'S EMMA FOR TEENS

"Not at all, sir. It is a beautiful, moonlight night; and so mild that I must draw back from your large fire."

"But you must have found it very damp and dirty. I do not want you to catch cold."

"Dirty, sir! Look at my shoes. Not a speck on them."

"Well! That is quite surprising, for we have had a great deal of rain here. It rained dreadfully hard for half an hour, while we were at breakfast. I wanted them to put off the wedding."

"By the way – I have not wished you joy. Being pretty well aware of what sort of joy you must both be feeling, I have been in no hurry with my congratulations. But I hope it all went well. How was the wedding? Who cried most?"

"Ah! Poor Miss Taylor! 'Tis a sad business."

"Poor Mr. and Miss Woodhouse, if you please; but I cannot possibly say 'poor Miss Taylor. ' I have a great regard for you and Emma; but when it comes to the question of dependence or independence! At any rate, it must be better to have only one to please, than two."

"Especially when *one* of those two is such a fanciful, troublesome creature!" said Emma playfully. "That is what you have in your head, I know – and what you would certainly say if my father were not by."

"I believe it is very true, my dear, indeed," said Mr. Woodhouse with a sigh. "I am afraid I am sometimes very fanciful and troublesome."

"My dearest papa! You do not think I could mean *you*, or suppose Mr. Knightley to mean *you*. What a horrible idea! Oh, no! I meant only myself. Mr. Knightley loves to find fault with me you know – in a joke – it is all a joke. We always say whatever we like to one another."

Mr. Knightley, in fact, was one of the few people who could see faults in Emma Woodhouse, and the only one who ever told her of them. Though this was not particularly agreeable to Emma herself, she knew it would be much less so to her father. She did not want him to suspect such a circumstance as her not being thought perfect by everybody.

"Emma knows I never flatter her," said Mr. Knightley; "but I meant no reflection on anybody. Miss Taylor has had two persons to please; she will now have but one."

"Well," said Emma, willing to let it pass, "you want to hear about the wedding, and I shall be happy to tell you, for we all behaved charmingly. Everybody was punctual, everybody in their best dress. Not a tear, and hardly a long face to be seen. We all felt that we were going to be only half a mile apart, and were sure of meeting every day."

"Dear Emma bears everything so well," said her father. "But, Mr. Knightley, she is really very sorry to lose poor Miss Taylor, and I am sure she *will* miss her more than she thinks."

Emma turned away her head, divided between tears and smiles.

"It is impossible that Emma should not miss such a companion," said Mr. Knightley. "We should not like her as well as we do, sir, if we could suppose it. But she knows how much the marriage is to Miss Taylor's advantage; she knows how very acceptable it must be at Miss Taylor's time of life to be settled in a home of her own, and therefore cannot allow herself to feel as much pain as pleasure. Every friend of Miss Taylor must be glad to see her so happily married."

"And you have forgotten one matter of joy to me," said Emma, "and a very considerable one — that I made the match myself. I made the match, you know, four years ago; and to have it take place, and be proved in the right, when so many people said Mr. Weston would never marry again, is a great comfort to me."

Mr. Knightley shook his head at her. Her father fondly replied, "Ah! My dear, I wish you would not make matches and foretell things, for whatever you say always comes to pass. Pray do not make any more matches."

"I promise you to make none for myself, papa; but I must, indeed, for other people. It is the greatest amusement in the world! And after such success, you know! Everybody said that Mr. Weston would never marry again. Oh dear, no! Mr. Weston, who had been a widower so long, and who seemed so perfectly comfortable without a wife, so constantly occupied either in his business in town or among his friends here, always welcomed wherever he went, always cheerful — Mr. Weston need not spend a single evening in the year alone if he did not desire it. Oh, no! Mr. Weston certainly would never marry again. Some people even talked of a promise to his wife on her death-bed, and others of the son and the uncle not letting him. All manner of solemn nonsense was spoken about the subject, but I believed none of it. Ever since the day (about four years ago) that Miss Taylor and I met with him in Broadway-lane, when, because it began to drizzle, he darted away with so much gallantry and borrowed two umbrellas for us from Farmer Mitchell's, I made up my mind on the subject. I planned the match from that hour; and when such success has blessed me in this instance, dear papa, you cannot think that I shall give up matchmaking."

"I do not understand what you mean by 'success,'" said Mr. Knightley. "Success supposes endeavour. Your time has been properly and delicately spent, if you have been endeavouring for the last four years to bring about this marriage. A worthy employment for a young lady's mind! But if, which I rather imagine, your making the match, as you call it, means only your planning it, your saying to yourself one idle day, 'I think it would be a very good thing for Miss Taylor if Mr. Weston were to marry her,' and saying it again to yourself every now and then afterwards, – why do you talk of success? What is there to be proud of? You made a lucky guess; and *that* is all that can be said."

"And have you never known the pleasure and triumph of a lucky guess? I pity you. I thought you cleverer – for depend upon it, a lucky guess is never merely luck. There is always some skill in it. And as to my poor word 'success,' which you quarrel with, I do not know that I am so entirely without any claim to it. You have drawn two pretty pictures – but I think there may be a third – a something between the do-nothing and the do-all. If I had not promoted Mr. Weston's visits here, and given many little encouragements, and smoothed many little matters, it might not have come to anything after all. I think you must know Hartfield enough to comprehend that."

"A straightforward, open-hearted man like Weston, and a rational woman like Miss Taylor, may be safely left to manage their own concerns. You are more likely to have done harm to yourself, than good to them, by interference."

"Emma never thinks of herself, if she can do good to others," rejoined Mr. Woodhouse, understanding but a part of what was spoken. "But, my dear, pray do not make any more matches. They are silly things, and break up one's family circle grievously."

"Only one more, papa; only for Mr. Elton. Poor Mr. Elton! You like Mr. Elton, papa, – I must look for a wife for him. There is nobody in Highbury who deserves him – and he has been here a whole year, and has fitted up his house so comfortably that it would be a shame to have him single any longer – and I thought when he was joining their hands today he looked so very much as if he would like to have the same kind office done for him! I think very well of Mr. Elton, and this is the only way I have of doing him a service."

"Mr. Elton is a very good kind of young man to be sure, and I have a great regard for him. But if you want to show him any attention, my dear, ask him to come and dine with us some day. That will be a much better thing. I dare say Mr. Knightley will be so kind as to join us."

"With a great deal of pleasure, sir, at any time," said Mr. Knightley laughing. "And I agree with you entirely that it will be a much better thing. Invite him to dinner, Emma, and help him to the best of the fish and the chicken, but leave him to choose his own wife. Depend upon it, a man of twenty-six or twenty-seven can take care of himself."

CHAPTER 2

Mr. Weston was a native of Highbury, born of a respectable family which for the last two or three generations had been rising into gentility and property. He had received a good education, but upon acquiring sufficient wealth he had ceased the homely pursuits in which his brothers were engaged. He instead satisfied an active cheerful mind and social temper by entering into the militia of his country.

Captain Weston was a general favourite, and while in the course of his military life he had been introduced to one Miss Churchill, of a great Yorkshire family. She fell in love with him, and nobody was surprised except her brother and his wife, who had never seen him, and who were unimpressed by his limited wealth and connections.

Miss Churchill, however, being old enough to make the decision for herself, and with the full command of her fortune, entered into the marriage. It took place to the infinite mortification of Mr. and Mrs. Churchill, who immediately disowned her. The marriage did not produce much happiness. Mrs. Weston ought to have found more in it, for she had a husband whose warm heart and sweet temper made him think everything due to her in return for the great goodness of being in love with him. While she had the strength of character to pursue her own will in spite of her brother, she had not enough to refrain from unreasonable regrets at that brother's unreasonable anger. She missed the luxuries of her former home, and while they lived beyond their income it was nothing in comparison to Enscombe. She did not cease to love her husband, but she wanted at once to be the wife of Captain Weston, and Miss Churchill of Enscombe.

Captain Weston, who had been considered, especially by the Churchills, as having married exceptionally well, became rather poorer at the last than he had been at first. When his wife died after three years of marriage, he was left with a child to raise. From this expense, however, he was soon relieved. The boy had been the means of a sort of reconciliation, and Mr. and Mrs. Churchill, having no children of their own, nor any other young creature of equal kindred to care for, offered to take the whole charge of the little Frank soon after her decease. Some reluctance the widower father may be supposed to have felt, but as they were overcome by other considerations, the child was given up to the care and the wealth of the Churchills, and he had only his own comfort to seek and his own situation to improve as he could.

A complete change of life became desirable. He left the militia and engaged in trade, having brothers already established in London. It was a position which brought just employment enough. He had still a small house in Highbury, where most of his leisure days were spent, and between useful occupation and the pleasures of society the next eighteen or twenty years of his life passed cheerfully away. He had, by that time, earned enough to secure the purchase of a little estate adjoining Highbury, which he had always longed for – enough to marry a woman without a dowry such as Miss Taylor, and to live according to the wishes of his own friendly and social manner.

It was now some time since he had begun to think about a possible marriage to Miss Taylor, but he was determined not to propose till he could purchase Randalls. He had gone steadily on, with these objects in view, till they were accomplished. He had made his fortune, bought his house, obtained his wife, and was beginning a new period of existence with every probability of greater happiness than in any yet passed through. He had never been an unhappy man; his own temper had secured him from that, even in his first marriage. But his second must show him how delightful a wise and truly amiable woman could be, and must give him the pleasantest proof of its being a great deal better to choose than to be chosen, to excite gratitude rather than to feel it.

He had only himself to please in his choice, for his fortune was his own. As to Frank, it had become so avowed an adoption as to have him assume the name of Churchill on coming of age, and it appeared that he would become his uncle's heir. It was most unlikely, therefore, that he should ever want his father's assistance. His father had no worrisome thoughts on the matter. The aunt was an unpredictable woman, and governed her husband entirely; but it was not in Mr. Weston's nature to imagine that any whim could be strong enough to affect one so dear, and, as he believed, so deservedly dear. He saw his son every year in London, and was proud of him. His fond report of him as a very fine young man had made Highbury feel a sort of pride in him, too. He was looked on as sufficiently belonging to the place to make his merits and prospects a kind of common concern.

Mr. Frank Churchill was one of the treasures of Highbury, and a lively curiosity to see him prevailed, though the compliment was so little returned that he had never been there in his life. His coming to visit his father had been often talked of but never achieved.

Now, upon his father's marriage, it was very generally proposed, as a most proper attention, that the visit should take place. There was not a dissenting vote on the subject, either when Mrs. Perry drank tea with Mrs. and Miss Bates, or when Mrs. and Miss Bates returned the visit. Now was the time for Mr. Frank Churchill to come among them, and the hope strengthened when it was understood that he had written to his new stepmother on the occasion. For a few days, every morning visit in Highbury included some mention of the handsome letter Mrs. Weston had received. "I suppose you have heard of the handsome letter Mr. Frank Churchill had written to Mrs. Weston? I understand it was a very handsome letter, indeed. Mr. Woodhouse told me of it. Mr. Woodhouse saw the letter, and he says he never saw such a handsome letter in his life."

It was, indeed, a highly prized letter. Mrs. Weston had, of course, formed a very favourable idea of the young man. Such a pleasing attention was an irresistible proof of his great good sense, and a most welcome addition to every source and every expression of congratulation which her marriage had already secured. She felt that she was a most fortunate woman. She knew that at times she must be missed at Hartfield, and could not think, without pain, of Emma's losing a single pleasure, or suffering an hour's sadness, from the desire for her companionableness. But dear Emma was of no feeble character; she was more equal to her situation than most girls would have been, and had sense and energy and spirits that might be hoped would bear her well and happily through its little difficulties. And then there was such comfort in the very easy distance of Randalls from Hartfield and in Mr. Weston's disposition and circumstances, which would make the approaching winter no hindrance to their spending half the evenings of the week together.

Her situation was altogether the subject of hours of gratitude to Mrs. Weston, and there were very few moments of regret. Her satisfaction, which was really much *more* than satisfaction, and her cheerful enjoyment was so apparent that Emma, as well as she knew her father, was sometimes taken by surprise at his being still able to pity "poor Miss Taylor." When they left her at Randalls in the centre of every domestic comfort, or saw her go away in the evening attended by her pleasant husband to a carriage of her own, it seemed there was nothing to pity. But never did she go without Mr. Woodhouse's giving a gentle sigh, and saying:

"Ah! Poor Miss Taylor. She would be very glad to stay." There was no recovering Miss Taylor – nor much likelihood of ceasing to pity her: but a few weeks brought some alleviation to Mr. Woodhouse. The compliments of his neighbours were over; he was no longer provoked by being wished joy at so sorrowful an event; and the wedding cake, which had been a great distress to him, was all eaten up. His own stomach could bear nothing rich, and he could never believe other people to be different from himself. What was unwholesome to him, he regarded as unfit for anybody; and he had, therefore, earnestly tried to persuade them not to have any wedding cake at all. When that effort failed, he tried to prevent anybody's eating it. He had even consulted Mr. Perry, the apothecary, on the subject. Mr. Perry was an intelligent, gentlemanlike man, whose frequent visits were one of the comforts of Mr. Woodhouse's life. Upon being applied to, he could not but acknowledge that wedding cake might certainly disagree with many – perhaps with most people, unless taken moderately. With such an opinion in confirmation of his own, Mr. Woodhouse hoped to influence every visitor of the newly-married pair; but still the cake was eaten, and there was no rest for his benevolent nerves till it was all gone.

There was a strange rumour in Highbury of all the little Perrys being seen with a slice of Mrs. Weston's wedding cake in their hands, but Mr. Woodhouse would never believe it.

CHAPTER 3

Mr. Woodhouse was fond of company in his own way, and he liked very much to have his friends come to see him. From his long residence at Hartfield, his good nature, his fortune, his house, and his daughter, he could orchestrate the visits of his own little circle as he liked. He spent very little time with any families beyond that circle. His horror of late hours and large dinner parties made him unfit for any but those who would visit him on his own terms. Fortunately for him, Highbury, including Randalls, and Donwell Abbey, where Mr. Knightley lived, include many such persons. Not unfrequently, through Emma's persuasion, he had some of the chosen and the best to dine with him, but evening parties were what he preferred, and, unless he fancied himself at any time unequal to company, there was scarcely an evening in the week in which Emma could not make up a card table for him.

Real, long-standing regard brought the Westons and Mr. Knightley. Mr. Elton, a young man living alone without liking it, came for the privilege of exchanging any vacant evening of his own blank solitude for the elegancies and society of Mr. Woodhouse's drawing room and the smiles of his lovely daughter.

After these came a second set, among the most frequent of whom were Mrs. and Miss Bates and Mrs. Goddard, three ladies almost always at the service of an invitation from Hartfield. They were fetched and carried home so often that Mr. Woodhouse thought it no hardship for either James or the horses. Had it taken place only once a year, it would have been a grievance.

Mrs. Bates, the widow of a former clergyman of Highbury, was too old for almost anything but tea and cards. She lived with her single daughter in very humble circumstances, and was considered with all the regard and respect which a harmless old lady in such a state can excite. Her daughter enjoyed a most uncommon degree of popularity for a woman neither young, pretty, rich, nor married. Miss Bates had never boasted either beauty or cleverness. Her youth had passed without distinction, and her middle life was devoted to the care of a failing mother and the effort to make a small income go as far as possible. And yet she was a happy woman, and a woman whom no one named without goodwill. It was her own universal goodwill and contented temper which worked such wonders. She loved everybody, was interested in everybody's happiness, was quick to point out everybody's merits, thought herself a most fortunate creature, and was surrounded with blessings in such an excellent mother and so many good neighbours and friends and a home that lacked nothing. The simplicity and cheerfulness of her nature, and her contented and grateful spirit, commended her to everybody and were sources of happiness to herself. She was a great talker upon matters of little consequence, full of trivial communications and harmless gossip. This exactly suited Mr. Woodhouse.

Mrs. Goddard was the mistress of a school, not an establishment which professed, in long sentences of refined nonsense, to combine the acquisition of liberal accomplishments with elegant morality upon new principles and new doctrines – and where young ladies for enormous pay might be coaxed out of health and into vanity – but a real, honest, old-fashioned boarding school. It was a place where a reasonable quantity of accomplishments was sold at a reasonable price, and where girls might be sent to be out of the way and stumble into a little education, without any danger of coming back prodigies. Mrs. Goddard's school had a good reputation – and very deservedly, for Highbury was reckoned a particularly healthy spot. She had an ample house and garden, gave the children plenty of wholesome food, let them run about a great deal in the summer, and made sure their health was looked after in every season. It was no wonder that a train of twenty young girls now walked after her to church. She was a plain, motherly kind of woman, who had worked hard in her youth and now thought herself entitled to the occasional tea visit. Having formerly owed much to Mr. Woodhouse's kindness, she felt his particular claim on her to leave her neat parlour whenever she could and win or lose a few sixpences by his fireside.

These were the ladies whom Emma found herself very frequently able to collect, and happy was she, for her father's sake, that they were so willing, though, as far as she was herself concerned, it was no remedy for the absence of Mrs. Weston. She was delighted to see her father look comfortable, and was very much pleased with herself for contriving things so well. But the quiet conversation of three such women made her feel that every evening so spent was indeed one of the long evenings she had fearfully anticipated.

As she sat one morning, looking forward to exactly such a close of the present day, a note was brought from Mrs. Goddard requesting, in most respectful terms, to be allowed to bring Miss Smith with her. It was a most welcome request, for Miss Smith was a girl of seventeen whom Emma knew very well by sight and had long felt an interest in, on account of her beauty. A very gracious invitation was returned, and the evening was no longer dreaded by the fair mistress of the mansion.

Harriet Smith was the illegitimate daughter of somebody who had placed her, several years back, at Mrs. Goddard's school, and who had lately raised her from the condition of student to that of boarder. This was all that was generally known of her history, and she had recently returned from a long visit in the country to some young ladies who had been at school there with her.

She was a very pretty girl, and her beauty happened to be of a sort which Emma particularly admired. She was short, with fine blue eyes, light hair, regular features, and a look of great sweetness. Before the end of the evening, Emma was as much pleased with her behavior as her looks, and she was quite determined to continue the acquaintance.

She was not struck by anything remarkably clever in Miss Smith's conversation, but she found her altogether very engaging – not inconveniently shy, not unwilling to talk – showing so proper and becoming a deference, seeming so pleasantly grateful for being admitted to Hartfield, and so genuinely impressed by the appearance of everything that she must have good sense and deserve encouragement. Encouragement would be given. Those soft blue eyes and all those natural graces should not be wasted on the inferior society of Highbury and its connections. The friendships she had already formed were unworthy of her. Those from whom she had just parted, though very good sort of people, must be doing her harm. They were a family of the name of Martin, whom Emma well knew by character, as renting a large farm of Mr. Knightley, and residing in the parish of Donwell. She knew Mr. Knightley thought highly of them, but they must be coarse and unpolished, and very unfit to be the friends of a girl who needed only a little more knowledge and elegance to be quite perfect. *She* would notice her; she would improve her; she would detach her from her bad acquaintance, and introduce her into good society; she would form her opinions and her manners. It would be an interesting, and certainly a very kind undertaking; highly becoming her own situation in life, her leisure, and her influence.

She was so busy in admiring those soft blue eyes, in talking and listening, and forming all these schemes, that the evening flew by at an unusually quick pace. The supper table, which always closed such parties, was all set out and ready, and moved forward to the fire, before she was aware.

Upon such occasions, poor Mr. Woodhouse's feelings were in sad conflict. He loved to see the tablecloth laid, because it had been the fashion of his youth; but his conviction of suppers being very unwholesome made him rather sorry to see anything put on it. While his hospitality would have welcomed his visitors to everything, his care for their health made him grieve that they would eat.

A small basin of thin gruel, such as the one placed before him, was all that he could recommend, though he might constrain himself, while the ladies were comfortably clearing the nicer things, to say:

"Mrs. Bates, let me propose your trying one of these eggs. An egg boiled very soft is not unwholesome. Serle understands boiling an egg better than anybody. I would not recommend an egg boiled by anybody else – but you need not be afraid – they are very small, you see – one of our small eggs will not hurt you. Miss Bates, let Emma help you to a *little* bit of tart – a *very* little bit. Ours are all apple tarts. You need not be afraid of unwholesome preserves here. I do not advise the custard. Mrs. Goddard, what say you to *half* a glass of wine? A *small* half glass – put into a tumbler of water? I do not think it could disagree with you."

Emma allowed her father to talk, but supplied her visitors in a much more satisfactory style. On the present evening, she had the particular pleasure in sending them away happy. The happiness of Miss Smith was quite equal to her intentions. Miss Woodhouse was so great a personage in Highbury that the prospect of the introduction had given as much panic as pleasure – but the humble, grateful, little girl went off with highly gratified feelings, delighted with the kindness with which Miss Woodhouse had treated her all evening.

CHAPTER 4

Almost immediately, Harriet Smith was a regular Hartfield visitor. Quick and decided in her ways, Emma lost no time in inviting, encouraging, and telling her to come very often. As their acquaintance increased, so did their satisfaction with each other. As a walking companion, Emma had very early foreseen how useful she might find her. In that respect the loss of Mrs. Weston had been particularly felt. Her father never went beyond the shrubbery, and since Mrs. Weston's marriage her exercise had been too much confined. She had ventured once alone to Randalls, but it was not pleasant; and a Harriet Smith, therefore, whom she could summon at any time to a walk, would be a valuable addition to her privileges. But in every respect as she saw more of her, she approved of her, and was further justified in all her kind designs.

Harriet certainly was not clever, but she had a sweet, docile, grateful disposition. She was totally free from conceit, and only desired to be guided by anyone she looked up to. Her inclination for good company, and power of appreciating what was elegant and clever, showed that there was no lack of taste, though strength of understanding must not be expected. Altogether she was quite convinced of Harriet Smith's being exactly the young friend she wanted – exactly the something which her home required. Such a friend as Mrs. Weston was out of the question. Two such could never be granted. Two such she did not want. It was quite a different sort of thing – a sentiment distinct and independent. Mrs. Weston was the object of a regard, which had its basis in gratitude and esteem. Harriet would be loved as one to whom she could be useful.

Her first attempts at usefulness were in an endeavour to find out who her parents were; but Harriet did not know. She was ready to tell everything in her power, but on this subject questions were vain. Emma was obliged to imagine what she liked – but she could never believe that in the same situation *she* should not have discovered the truth. Harriet had no such designs. She had been satisfied to hear and believe just what Mrs. Goddard chose to tell her, and looked no farther.

Mrs. Goddard, and the teachers, and the girls, and the affairs of the school in general, were common subjects of conversation – and but for her acquaintance with the Martins of Abbey-Mill-Farm, they must have been the whole. But the Martins occupied her thoughts a good deal. She had spent two very happy months with them, and now loved to talk of the pleasures of her visit and describe the many comforts and wonders of the place. Emma encouraged her talkativeness – amused by such a picture of another set of beings. She enjoyed the youthful simplicity which could speak with so much exultation of Mrs. Martin's having "*two* parlours, two very good parlours indeed; one of them quite as large as Mrs. Goddard's drawing-room; and of her having an upper maid who had lived five-and-twenty years with her; and of their having eight cows, two of them Alderneys, and one a little Welch cow, a very pretty little Welch cow, indeed; and of Mrs. Martin's saying, as she was so fond of it, it should be called *her* cow; and of their having a very handsome summer house in their garden, where some day next year they were all to drink tea – a very handsome summer house, large enough to hold a dozen people."

For some time she was amused, without thinking beyond the immediate cause; but as she came to understand the family better, other feelings arose. She had taken up a wrong idea, believing it was a mother and daughter, a son and son's wife, who all lived together. For it appeared that the Mr. Martin, who bore a part in the narrative, and was always mentioned with approval for his great good-nature in doing something or other, was a single man. There was no young Mrs. Martin, no wife in the case; and Emma began to suspect danger to her poor little friend from all this hospitality and kindness. If she were not taken care of, she might be required to sink herself forever.

With this notion, her questions increased in number and meaning, and she particularly led Harriet to talk more of Mr. Martin. Harriet was very ready to speak of the share he had in their moonlight walks and merry evening games, and dwelt a good deal upon his being so very good-humoured and obliging. "He had gone three miles out of his way one day, in order to bring her some walnuts, because she had said how fond she was of them – and in everything else he was so very obliging! He brought his shepherd's son into the parlour one night to sing to her. She was very fond of singing. He could sing a little himself. She believed he was very clever, and understood everything. He had a very fine flock, and while she was with them, he had been bid more for his wool than anybody in the area. She believed everybody spoke well of him. His mother and sisters were very fond of him. Mrs. Martin had told her one day (and there was a blush as she said it), that it was impossible for anybody to be a better son; and therefore she was sure whenever he married he would make a good husband. Not that she *wanted* him to marry. She was in no hurry at all."

"Well done, Mrs. Martin!" thought Emma. "You know *exactly* what you are doing."

"And when she had come away, Mrs. Martin was so very kind as to send Mrs. Goddard a beautiful goose: the finest goose Mrs. Goddard had ever seen. Mrs. Goddard had dressed it on a Sunday, and asked all the three teachers, Miss Nash, and Miss Prince, and Miss Richardson, to eat with her."

"Mr. Martin, I suppose, is not a man of information beyond the line of his own business. He does not read?"

"Oh, yes! That is, no – I do not know – but I believe he has read a good deal – but not what you would think anything of. He reads the Agricultural Reports and some other books that lay in one of the window seats – but he reads all of *them* to himself. Sometimes in the evening, before we went to cards, he would read something aloud out of the Elegant Extracts – very entertaining. And I know he has read the Vicar of Wakefield. He never read the Romance of the Forest, nor the Children of the Abbey. He had never heard of such books before I mentioned them, but he is determined to get them now as soon as he can."

The next question was:

"What does Mr. Martin look like?"

"Oh! Not handsome – not at all handsome. I thought him very plain at first, but I do not think him so plain now. One does not, you know, after a time. But have you never seen him? He is in Highbury every now and then, and he is sure to ride through every week on his way to Kingston. He has passed you very often."

"That may be — and I may have seen him fifty times, but without having any idea of his name. A young farmer, whether on horseback or on foot, is the very last sort of person to raise my curiosity. Farmers are precisely the kind of people with whom I feel I cannot associate. If they were poor, I might hope to be useful to their families in some way or other. But a farmer can need none of my help, and is therefore in one sense as much above my notice as in every other he is below it."

"To be sure. Oh! Yes, it is not likely you should ever have observed him — but he knows you very well indeed — I mean by sight."

"I have no doubt of his being a very respectable young man. I know indeed that he is so; and as such wish him well. What do you imagine his age to be?"

"He was twenty-four the 8th of last June, and my birthday is the 23rd — just a fortnight and a day's difference! Which is very odd!"

"Only twenty-four. That is too young to marry. His mother is perfectly right not to be in a hurry. They seem very comfortable as they are, and if she were to take any pains to find someone for him to marry, she would probably regret it. Six years from now, if he could meet with a good sort of young woman in the same rank as his own, with a little money, it might be very desirable."

"Six years! Dear Miss Woodhouse, he would be thirty years old!"

"Well, and that is as early as most men can afford to marry, who are not born wealthy. Mr. Martin, I imagine, has to make his own fortune. Whatever money he might come into when his father died is likely all employed in his livestock. Though, with diligence and good luck, he may be rich in time, it is next to impossible that he should have achieved it yet."

"To be sure. But they live very comfortably. They have no indoor servant — otherwise they lack nothing; and Mrs. Martin talks of taking a boy another year."

"I wish you may not get into a scrape, Harriet, whenever he does marry — I mean, as to being acquainted with his wife. Though his sisters, from a superior education, are not to be altogether objected to, it does not follow that he might marry anybody at all fit for you to notice. The misfortune of your birth ought to make you particularly careful as to your associates. There can be no doubt of your being a gentleman's daughter, and you must support your claim to that station with everything in your power, or there will be plenty of people who would take pleasure in lowering you."

"Yes, to be sure – I suppose there are. But while I visit at Hartfield, and you are so kind to me, Miss Woodhouse, I am not afraid of what anybody can do."

"You understand the force of influence pretty well, Harriet; but I would have you so firmly established in good society, as to be independent even of Hartfield and Miss Woodhouse. I want to see you permanently well connected – and to that end it will be advisable to have as few odd acquaintances as possible. If you still live in this area when Mr. Martin marries, I wish you may not be drawn in, by your intimacy with the sisters, to be acquainted with the wife, who will probably be some mere farmer's daughter, without education."

"To be sure. Yes. Not that I think Mr. Martin would ever marry anybody that did not have *some* education – and been very well brought up. However, I do not mean to contradict your opinion – I am sure I shall not wish for the acquaintance of his wife. I shall always have a great regard for the Miss Martins, especially Elizabeth, and should be very sorry to give them up, for they are quite as well educated as me. But if he marries a very ignorant, vulgar woman, certainly it would be better if I did not visit her, if I can help it."

Emma watched her during this speech, and saw no alarming symptoms of love. The young man had been the first admirer, but she trusted there was no other hold, and that there would be no serious difficulty on Harriet's side to oppose any friendly arrangement of her own.

They met Mr. Martin the very next day, as they were walking on Donwell road. He was on foot, and after looking very respectfully at her, looked with most unfeigned satisfaction at her companion. Emma was not sorry to have such an opportunity of observation; and walking a few yards forward, while they talked together, soon made her quick eye sufficiently acquainted with Mr. Robert Martin. His appearance was very neat, and he looked like a sensible young man. But he had no other advantage, and when he came to be contrasted with gentlemen, she thought he must lose all the ground he had gained in Harriet's inclination. Harriet was not insensible of such things; she had voluntarily noticed her father's manners with admiration as well as wonder. Mr. Martin looked as if he did not know what manner was.

They remained but a few minutes together, as Miss Woodhouse must not be kept waiting, and Harriet then came running to her with a smiling face, and in a flutter of spirits, which Miss Woodhouse hoped very soon to compose.

"Only think of our happening to meet him! How very odd! It was quite a chance, he said, that he had not gone around by Randalls. He did not think we ever walked this road. He thought we walked towards Randalls most days. He has not been able to get the Romance of the Forest yet. He was so busy the last time he was at Kingston that he quite forgot it, but he goes again tomorrow. So very odd we should happen to meet! Well, Miss Woodhouse, is he like what you expected? What do you think of him? Do you think him so very plain?"

"He is very plain, undoubtedly – remarkably plain – but that is nothing compared with his entire lack of gentility. I had no right to expect much, and I did not expect much; but I had no idea that he could be so very rough, so totally without manners. I had imagined him, I confess, a degree or two nearer gentility."

"To be sure," said Harriet, in a mortified voice, "he is not as genteel as a real gentleman."

"I think, Harriet, since your acquaintance with us, you have been repeatedly in the company of such very real gentlemen that you must yourself be struck with the difference in Mr. Martin. At Hartfield you have had very good specimens of well educated, well-bred men. I should be surprised if, after seeing them, you could be in company with Mr. Martin again without perceiving him to be a very inferior creature – and rather wondering at yourself for having ever thought him at all agreeable before. Do not you begin to feel that now? I am sure you must have been struck by his awkward look and abrupt manner, and the uncouthness of his voice."

"Certainly, he is not like Mr. Knightley. He has not such a fine air and way of walking as Mr. Knightley. I see the difference plain enough. But Mr. Knightley is so very fine a man!"

"Mr. Knightley's air is so remarkably good, that it is not fair to compare Mr. Martin with *him*. You might not see one in a hundred, with *gentleman* so plainly written as in Mr. Knightley. But he is not the only gentleman you have been lately used to. What say you to Mr. Weston and Mr. Elton? Compare Mr. Martin with either of *them*. Compare their manner of carrying themselves, of walking, of speaking, of being silent. You must see the difference."

"Oh, yes! There is a great difference. But Mr. Weston is almost an old man. Mr. Weston must be between forty and fifty."

"Which makes his good manners more valuable. The older a person grows, Harriet, the more important it is that their manners should not be bad – the more glaring and disgusting any loudness, or coarseness, or awkwardness becomes. What is tolerable in youth is detestable in old age. Mr. Martin is now awkward and abrupt. What will he be at Mr. Weston's time of life?"

"There is no saying, indeed!" replied Harriet, rather solemnly.

"But there may be pretty good guessing. He will be a vulgar farmer – totally inattentive to appearances, and thinking of nothing but profit and loss."

"Will he, indeed? That will be very bad."

"How much his business engrosses him already, is very plain from the circumstance of his forgetting to inquire for the book you recommended. He was too concerned about the market to think of anything else – which is just as it should be. What has he to do with books? And I have no doubt that he *will* thrive and be a very rich man in time – and his being illiterate and coarse need not disturb *us*."

"It is a wonder that he did not remember the book," was all Harriet answered, speaking with a degree of grave displeasure which Emma thought might be safely left to itself. She therefore said no more for some time. Her next beginning was,

"In one respect, perhaps, Mr. Elton's manners are superior to Mr. Knightley's or Mr. Weston's. They have more gentleness. They might be more safely held up as a pattern. There is an openness, a quickness, almost a bluntness in Mr. Weston, which everybody likes in *him* because there is so much good-humour with it – but that would not do to be copied. Neither would Mr. Knightley's downright, decided, commanding sort of manner – though it suits *him* very well. His figure and look, and situation in life seem to allow it. But if any young man were to set about copying him, he would be insufferable. On the contrary, I think a young man might be very safely advised to take Mr. Elton as a model. Mr. Elton is good-humoured, cheerful, obliging, and gentle. He seems to me, to be grown particularly gentle of late. I do not know whether he has any design of ingratiating himself with either of us, Harriet, by additional softness, but it strikes me that his manners are softer than they used to be. If he means anything, it must be to please you. Did not I tell you what he said of you the other day?"

She then repeated some warm personal praise which she had drawn from Mr. Elton, and now did full justice to. Harriet blushed and smiled, and said she had always thought Mr. Elton very agreeable.

Mr. Elton was the very person fixed on by Emma for driving the young farmer out of Harriet's head. She thought it would be an excellent match, and only too desirable, natural, and probable, for her to have much merit in planning it. She feared it was what everybody else must think of and predict. It was not likely, however, that anybody should have thought of it before her, as it had entered her mind during the very first evening of Harriet's coming to Hartfield. The longer she considered it, the greater was her sense of its expediency. Mr. Elton's situation was most suitable, quite the gentleman himself, and without low connections — at the same time not of any family that could fairly object to the doubtful birth of Harriet. He had a comfortable home for her, and Emma imagined a very sufficient income. Though the vicarage of Highbury was not large, he was known to have some independent property. She thought very highly of him as a good-humoured, well-meaning, respectable young man, without any deficiency of useful understanding or knowledge of the world.

She had already satisfied herself that he thought Harriet a beautiful girl, which she trusted, with such frequent meetings at Hartfield, was foundation enough on his side. And on Harriet's side there could be little doubt that the idea of being preferred by him would have all the usual weight and efficacy. He was really a very pleasing young man, a young man whom any woman not too discriminating might like. He was reckoned very handsome; his person much admired in general, though not by her, there being a want of elegance of feature which she could not dispense with. But the girl who could be gratified by Robert Martin's riding about the country to get walnuts for her might very well be conquered by Mr. Elton's admiration.

CHAPTER 5

"I do not know what your opinion may be, Mrs. Weston," said Mr. Knightley, "of this new friendship between Emma and Harriet Smith, but I think it a bad thing."

"A bad thing! Do you really think it a bad thing? Why so?"

"I think they will neither of them do the other any good."

"You surprise me! Emma must do Harriet good: and by supplying her with a new object of interest, Harriet may be said to do Emma good. I have been seeing their growing friendship with the greatest pleasure. How very differently we feel! Not think they will do each other any good! This will certainly be the beginning of one of our quarrels about Emma, Mr. Knightley."

"Perhaps you think I am come on purpose to quarrel with you, knowing Weston to be out, and that you must still fight your own battle."

"Mr. Weston would undoubtedly support me, if he were here, for he thinks exactly as I do on the subject. We were speaking of it only yesterday, and agreeing how fortunate it was for Emma, that there should be such a girl in Highbury for her to associate with. Mr. Knightley, I shall not allow you to be a fair judge in this case. You are so used to living alone that you do not know the value of a companion. Perhaps no man can be a good judge of the comfort a woman feels in the society of another woman, after being used to it all her life. I can imagine your objection to Harriet Smith. She is not the superior young woman which Emma's friend ought to be. But on the other hand, as Emma wants to see her better informed, it will be an opportunity for her to read more herself. They can read together, and it will be good for them both."

"Emma has been meaning to read more ever since she was twelve years old. I have seen a great many lists of hers written at various times of books that she meant to read. And very good lists they were – very well chosen, and very neatly arranged – sometimes alphabetically. The list she drew up when only fourteen – I remember thinking it did her judgment so much credit, that I kept it for some time; and I dare say she may have made out a very good list now. But I am done expecting any course of steady reading from Emma. She will never submit to anything requiring industry and patience. Where Miss Taylor failed to stimulate, I may safely affirm that Harriet Smith will do nothing. You never could persuade her to read half as much as you wished. You know you could not."

"I dare say," replied Mrs. Weston, smiling, "that I thought so *then*; but since we have parted, I can never remember Emma's failing to do anything I wished."

"There is hardly any reason to recall a memory as *that*" – said Mr. Knightley, feelingly; and for a moment or two he paused. "But I," he soon added, "who have had no such charm thrown over my senses, must still see, hear, and remember. Emma is spoiled by being the cleverest of her family. At ten years old, she had the misfortune of being able to answer questions which puzzled her sister at seventeen. She was always quick and confident: Isabella slow and timid. And ever since she was twelve, Emma has been mistress of the house and of you all. In her mother she lost the only person able to manage her. "

"I should have been sorry, Mr. Knightley, to be dependent on *your* recommendation, had I left Mr. Woodhouse's family and needed another position; I do not think you would have spoken a good word for me to anybody. I am sure you always thought me unfit for the office I held."

"Yes," said he, smiling. "You are better placed *here*. Very fit for a wife, but not at all for a governess. But you were preparing yourself to be an excellent wife all the time you were at Hartfield. You might not have given Emma as complete an education as your abilities would seem to promise, but you were receiving a very good education from *her*. You learned to sacrifice your own will and do as you were told. If Weston had asked me to recommend him a wife, I should certainly have named Miss Taylor."

"Thank you. There will be very little merit in making a good wife to such a man as Mr. Weston."

"Why, to admit the truth, I am afraid life is far too easy for you now. We will not despair, however. Weston may grow cross from too much comfort, or his son may plague him."

"I hope *not*. It is not likely. No, Mr. Knightley, do not prophesy vexation from that quarter."

"Not I, indeed. I only name possibilities. I do not have Emma's genius for foretelling and guessing. I hope, with all my heart, the young man may be a Weston in merit, and a Churchill in fortune. But Harriet Smith − I have not finished talking about Harriet Smith. I think her the very worst sort of companion that Emma could possibly have. She knows nothing herself, and looks upon Emma as knowing everything. She is a flatterer in all her ways; and so much the worse, because it is not calculated. Her very ignorance is hourly flattery. How can Emma imagine she has anything to learn herself, while Harriet is presenting such a delightful inferiority? And as for Harriet, I will venture to say that *she* cannot gain by the acquaintance. Hartfield will only spoil her taste for all the other places she belongs to. She will grow just refined enough to be uncomfortable with those among whom birth and circumstances have placed her. I am much mistaken if Emma's doctrines will give her any strength of mind, or make her adapt herself rationally to her situation in life. They will only give her a little polish."

"I either depend more upon Emma's good sense than you do, or I am more anxious for her present comfort, for I cannot lament the acquaintance. How well she looked last night!"

"Oh! You would rather talk of her person than her mind, would you? Very well; I shall not attempt to deny Emma's being pretty."

"Pretty! Say beautiful rather. Can you imagine anything nearer perfect beauty than Emma altogether − face and figure?"

"I do not know what I could imagine, but I confess that I have seldom seen a face or figure more pleasing to me than hers. But I am a partial old friend."

"Such an eye! The true hazel eye − and so brilliant! Regular features, open countenance, with a complexion! Oh! What a bloom of full health, and such a perfect height and size; such a firm and upright figure. There is health, not merely in her bloom, but in her manner, her head, her glance. One hears sometimes of a child being "the picture of health." Now Emma always gives me the idea of being the complete picture of grown-up health. She is loveliness itself, Mr. Knightley, is she not?"

"I have not a fault to find with her person," he replied. "I think her all you describe. I love to look at her; and I will add this praise, that I do not think her personally vain. Considering how very beautiful she is, she appears to be little occupied with it. Her vanity lies in another place. Mrs. Weston, I am not to be talked out of my dislike of her friendship with Harriet Smith, or my dread of its doing them both harm."

"And I, Mr. Knightley, am equally firm in my confidence of its not doing them any harm. With all dear Emma's little faults, she is an excellent creature. Where shall we see a better daughter, or a kinder sister, or a truer friend? No, no; she has qualities which may be trusted. She will never lead anyone really wrong; she will make no lasting blunder. Where Emma errs once, she is in the right a hundred times."

"Very well, I will not plague you anymore. Emma shall be an angel, and I will keep my views to myself till Christmas brings John and Isabella. John loves Emma with a reasonable and therefore not a blind affection, and Isabella always thinks as he does; except when he is not quite frightened enough about the children. I am sure of having their agreeing with me."

"I know that you all love her really too well to be unjust or unkind; but forgive me, Mr. Knightley, for taking the liberty (I consider myself, you know, as having somewhat of the privilege of speech that Emma's mother might have had) of hinting that I do not think any possible good can arise from Harriet Smith's intimacy being made a matter of much discussion among you. Please excuse me, but supposing any little inconvenience may be apprehended from the friendship, it cannot be expected that Emma, accountable to nobody but her father should put an end to it. It has been so many years my role to give advice that you cannot be surprised, Mr. Knightley, at this little request."

"Not at all," cried he. "I am much obliged to you for it. It is very good advice, and it shall have a better fate than your advice has often found, for it shall be attended to."

"Mrs. John Knightley is easily alarmed, and might be made unhappy about her sister."

"Be satisfied," said he, "that I will not raise any outcry. I will keep my opinion to myself. I have a very sincere interest in Emma. There is an anxiety, a curiosity in what one feels for Emma. I wonder what will become of her!"

"So do I," said Mrs. Weston gently; "very much."

"She always declares she will never marry, which, of course, means just nothing at all. But I do not think she has ever met a man she cared for. It would not be a bad thing for her to be very much in love with a proper gentleman. I should like to see Emma in love, and in some doubt of a return; it would do her good. But there is nobody hereabouts to attach her, and she goes so seldom from home."

"There does, indeed, seem as little to tempt her to break her resolution, at present," said Mrs. Weston. "While she is so happy at Hartfield, I cannot wish her to be forming any attachment which might create such difficulties for poor Mr. Woodhouse. I do not recommend matrimony at present to Emma, though I mean no offense to the institution I assure you."

Part of her meaning was to conceal some favourite thoughts of her own and Mr. Weston's on the subject, as much as possible. There were wishes at Randalls respecting Emma's marriage, but it was not desirable to have them suspected. The quiet transition which Mr. Knightley soon afterwards made to "What does Weston think of the weather? Does he think it will rain?" convinced her that he had nothing more to say about Hartfield.

CHAPTER 6

Emma could not feel a doubt of having given Harriet's interest a proper direction, for she found her decidedly more aware than before of Mr. Elton's being a remarkably handsome man, with most agreeable manners. She was soon confident of creating as much liking on Harriet's side as there could be any occasion for. She was quite convinced of Mr. Elton's being on his way to falling in love, if not in love already. She had no concerns with regard to him. He talked of Harriet, and praised her so warmly, that she could not suppose anything lacking which a little time would not provide. His perception of the striking improvement of Harriet's manner, since her introduction at Hartfield, was one of the proofs of his growing attachment.

"You have given Miss Smith all that she required," said he. "You have made her graceful and confident. She was a beautiful creature when she came to you, but, in my opinion, the attractions you have added are infinitely superior to what she received from birth."

"I am glad you think I have been useful to her, but Harriet only needed a little guidance. She had all the natural grace of sweetness of temper and sincerity in herself. I have done very little."

"If it were admissible to contradict a lady," said the gallant Mr. Elton —

"I have perhaps given her a little more character, and have taught her to think on points which she had not thought about before," Emma continued.

"Exactly so; that is what principally strikes me. Skillful has been the hand."

"And great has been the pleasure. I never met with a disposition more truly amiable."

"I have no doubt of it." This was spoken with a sort of sighing animation, which seemed to indicate that he loved her. Emma was not less pleased another day with the manner in which he seconded a sudden wish of hers, to have Harriet's picture.

"Did you ever have your portrait painted, Harriet?" said she. "Did you ever sit for your picture?"

Harriet was on the point of leaving the room, and only stopped to say, with a very interesting naïveté –

"Oh! Dear, no, never."

No sooner was she out of sight than Emma exclaimed, "What an exquisite possession a good picture of her would be! I almost long to attempt her likeness myself. You do not know it, I dare say, but two or three years ago I had a great passion for painting portraits, and attempted several of my friends, and was thought to have a tolerable eye in general. But from one cause or another, I gave it up. But really, I could almost see myself doing it, if Harriet would sit for me. It would be such a delight to have her picture!"

"Let me encourage you," cried Mr. Elton. "It would indeed be a delight! Let me entreat you, Miss Woodhouse, to exercise so charming a talent on your friend's behalf. I know how excellent your drawings are. How could you suppose me ignorant? Is not this room rich in specimens of your landscapes and flowers? And has not Mrs. Weston some figure-pieces in her drawing-room, at Randalls?"

Yes, good man! thought Emma – but what has all that to do with portraits? You know nothing of drawing. Don't pretend to be in raptures about mine. Keep your raptures for Harriet's face. "Well, if you give me such kind encouragement, Mr. Elton, I believe I shall try what I can do. Harriet's features are very delicate, which makes a likeness difficult; and yet there is a peculiarity in the shape of the eye and the lines about the mouth which one ought to capture."

"Exactly so – The shape of the eye and the lines about the mouth – I have not a doubt of your success. Please, please attempt it. Since you will be the one doing it, it will indeed, to use your own words, be an exquisite possession."

"But I am afraid, Mr. Elton, Harriet will not like to sit. She thinks so little of her own beauty. Did not you observe her manner of answering me? How completely it meant, 'Why should my picture be drawn?'"

"Oh! Yes, I observed it, I assure you. It was not lost on me. But still I cannot imagine she could not be persuaded."

Harriet was soon back again, and the idea almost immediately proposed. She had no concerns which could stand many minutes against the earnest pressing of both the others. Emma wished to go to work immediately, and therefore produced the portfolio containing her various attempts at portraits, for not one of them had ever been finished, that they might decide together on the best size for Harriet. Her many beginnings were displayed. Miniatures, half-lengths, whole-lengths, pencil, crayon, and watercolours had been all tried in turn. She had always wanted to do everything, and had made more progress both in drawing and music than many might have done with as little effort as she was willing to make. She played and sang, and drew in almost every style; but steadiness had always been lacking, and in nothing had she approached the degree of excellence which she would have liked to have. She was not much deceived as to her own skill either as an artist or a musician, but she was not unwilling to have others deceived, or sorry to know that her reputation for accomplishment was often better than she deserved.

There was merit in every drawing – in the least finished, perhaps the most. Her style was spirited, but had there been much less, or had there been ten times more, the delight and admiration of her two companions would have been the same. They were both in ecstasies. A portrait pleases everybody; and Miss Woodhouse's performances must be exceptional.

"No great variety of faces for you," said Emma. "I had only my own family to study from. There is my father – another of my father – but the idea of sitting for his picture made him so nervous. that I could only take him by stealth. Neither of them are very accurate, therefore. Mrs. Weston again, and again, and again, you see. Dear Mrs. Weston! Always my kindest friend on every occasion. She would sit whenever I asked her. There is my sister, and really quite her own little elegant figure! And the face not unlike. I would have made a good likeness of her, if she would have sat longer, but she was in such a hurry to have me draw her four children that she would not. Then, here come all my attempts at three of those four children. There they are: Henry and John and Bella, from one end of the sheet to the other, and any one of them might do for any one of the rest. She was so eager to have them drawn that I could not refuse, but there is no making children of three or four years old stand still, you know. Nor can it be very easy to take any likeness of them, unless they are coarser featured than any mama's children ever were. Here is my sketch of the fourth, who was a baby. I drew him as he was sleeping on the sofa, and it is as strong a likeness as you would wish to see. He had nestled down his head most conveniently. I am rather proud of little George. The corner of the sofa is very good. Then here is my last" – unclosing a pretty sketch of a gentleman in small size, whole-length – "my last and my best – my brother-in-law, Mr. John Knightley. This was almost finished when I put it away and vowed I would never paint another portrait. I could not help being provoked, for after all my pains, Isabella's cold approbation of – 'Yes, it was a little similar – but to be sure it did not do him justice. '" We had had a great deal of trouble in persuading him to sit at all. It was altogether more than I could bear, and so I never did finish it, to have it apologized over to every morning visitor in Brunswick-square. As I said, I did then forswear ever drawing anybody again. But for Harriet's sake, or rather for my own, and as there are no husbands and wives in the case at present, I will break my resolution now."

Mr. Elton seemed very properly struck and delighted by the idea, and was repeating, "No husbands and wives in the case *at present* indeed, as you observe. Exactly so. No husbands and wives," with so much earnestness that Emma began to consider whether she had not better leave them alone together at once. But as she wanted to be drawing, the declaration must wait a little longer.

She had soon fixed on the size and sort of portrait. It was to be a whole-length in watercolours, like Mr. John Knightley's, and was destined to hold a very honourable station over the mantlepiece.

The sitting began, and Harriet, smiling and blushing, and afraid of not keeping her posture and expression, presented a very sweet mixture of youthful expression to the steady eyes of the artist. But there was no doing anything with Mr. Elton fidgeting behind her and watching every stroke. She gave him credit for stationing himself where he might gaze and gaze again without offence, but was really obliged to put an end to it and ask him to place himself elsewhere. It then occurred to her to employ him in reading.

"If he would be so good as to read to them, it would be a kindness indeed! It would amuse them immeasurably."

Mr. Elton was only too happy. Harriet listened, and Emma drew in peace. She must allow him to be still frequently coming to look; anything less would certainly have been too little in a lover. He was ready at the smallest stroke of the brush to jump up and see the progress, and be charmed. There was no being displeased with such an encourager, for his admiration made him discern a likeness almost before it was possible. She could not respect his eye, but his love and his deference were commendable.

The sitting was altogether very satisfactory; she was quite enough pleased with the first day's sketch to wish to go on. She had great confidence of its being in every way a pretty drawing, and of its filling its destined place with credit to them both – a standing memorial of the beauty of one, the skill of the other, and the friendship of both; with as many other agreeable associations as Mr. Elton's very promising attachment was likely to add.

Harriet was to sit again the next day, and Mr. Elton, just as he ought, asked permission to read to them again.

"By all means. We shall be most happy to consider you as one of the party."

The same civilities and courtesies, the same success and satisfaction, took place on the morrow, and accompanied the whole progress of the picture, which was rapid and happy. Everybody who saw it was pleased, but Mr. Elton was in continual raptures, and defended it through every criticism.

"You have made her too tall, Emma," said Mr. Knightley.

Emma knew that she had, but would not admit it, and Mr. Elton warmly added,

"Oh, no! certainly not too tall; not in the least too tall. Consider, she is sitting down – which naturally presents a different – which in short gives exactly the idea – and the proportions must be preserved, you know. "

"It is very pretty," said Mr. Woodhouse. "So prettily done! Just as your drawings always are, my dear. I do not know anybody who draws as well as you do. The only thing I do not thoroughly like is that she seems to be sitting out of doors, with only a little shawl over her shoulders – and it makes one think she must catch cold."

"But, my dear papa, it is supposed to be summer; a warm day in summer. Look at the tree."

"But it is never safe to sit out of doors, my dear."

"You, sir, may say anything," cried Mr. Elton, "but I must confess that I regard it as a most happy thought, the placing of Miss Smith out of doors. Any other setting would have been much less in character. The naïveté of Miss Smith's manners – and altogether – Oh, it is most admirable! I cannot keep my eyes from it. I never saw such a likeness."

The next thing wanted was to get the picture framed, and here were a few difficulties. It must be done immediately; it must be done in London; the order must go through the hands of some intelligent person whose taste could be depended on, and Isabella, the usual doer of all commissions, must not be applied to, because it was December, and Mr. Woodhouse could not bear the idea of her leaving her house in the fogs of December. But no sooner was the distress known to Mr. Elton than it was removed. His gallantry was always on the alert. "Might he be trusted with the commission, what infinite pleasure should he have in executing it! He could ride to London at any time. It was impossible to say how much he should be gratified by being employed on such an errand."

"He was too good! She could not endure the thought! – she would not give him such a troublesome office for the world" – this brought on the desired repetition of entreaties and assurances, and a very few minutes settled the business.

Mr. Elton was to take the drawing to London, choose the frame, and give the directions.

"What a treasure!" said he with a tender sigh as he received it.

"This man is almost too gallant to be in love," thought Emma. "He is an excellent young man, and will suit Harriet exactly."

CHAPTER 7

The very day of Mr. Elton's going to London produced a fresh occasion for Emma's services towards her friend. Harriet had been at Hartfield, as usual, soon after breakfast, and after a time had gone home to return again to dinner. She returned sooner than had been talked of, and with an agitated, hurried look, announced something extraordinary to have happened which she was longing to tell. Half a minute brought it all out. She had heard, as soon as she got back to Mrs. Goddard's, that Mr. Martin had been there an hour before, and finding she was not at home, nor particularly expected, had left a little package for her from one of his sisters, and gone away. On opening this package, she had actually found, besides the two songs which she had lent his sister Elizabeth to copy, a letter to herself; and this letter was from him, from Mr. Martin, and contained a direct proposal of marriage. "Who could have thought it! She was so surprised she did not know what to do. Yes, quite a proposal of marriage; and a very good letter, at least she thought so. And he wrote as if he really loved her very much – but she did not know – and so, she came as fast as she could to ask Miss Woodhouse what she should do." Emma was half ashamed of her friend for seeming so pleased and so doubtful.

"Upon my word," she cried, "the young man is determined not to lose anything for want of asking. He will connect himself well if he can."

"Will you read the letter?" cried Harriet. "Please do, I'd rather like it if you would."

Emma was not sorry to be so encouraged. She read, and was surprised. The style of the letter was much above her expectation.

JANE AUSTEN'S EMMA FOR TEENS

There were not merely no grammatical errors, but as a composition it would not have disgraced a gentleman. The language, though plain, was strong and sincere, and the sentiments it conveyed very much to the credit of the writer. It was short, but expressed good sense, warm attachment, generosity, good manners, even delicacy of feeling. She paused over it, while Harriet stood anxiously watching for her opinion, with a "Well, well," and was at last forced to add, "Is it a good letter? Or is it too short?"

"Yes, indeed, a very good letter," replied Emma rather slowly. "So good a letter, Harriet, that everything considered, I think one of his sisters must have helped him. I can hardly imagine the young man whom I saw talking with you the other day could express himself so well, if left quite to his own powers. And yet it is not the style of a woman; no, certainly, it is too strong and concise. No doubt he is a sensible man, and I suppose may have a natural talent for – thinks strongly and clearly – and when he takes a pen in hand, his thoughts naturally find proper words. It is so with some men. Yes, I understand the sort of mind. Vigorous, decided, with sentiments to a certain point, not coarse. A better written letter, Harriet (returning it), than I had expected."

"Well," said the still waiting Harriet, "and – and what shall I do?"

"What shall you do! In what respect? Do you mean with regard to this letter?"

"Yes."

"But what are you in doubt of? You must answer it of course – and speedily."

"Yes. But what shall I say? Dear Miss Woodhouse, do advise me."

"Oh, no, no! The letter had much better be all your own. You will express yourself very properly, I am sure. There is no danger of your not being intelligible, which is the most important thing. Your meaning must be unequivocal, and such expressions of gratitude and concern for the pain you are inflicting as propriety requires, will present themselves unbidden to *your* mind, I am persuaded. *You* need not be prompted to write with the appearance of sorrow for his disappointment."

"You think I ought to refuse him then?" said Harriet, looking down.

"Ought to refuse him! My dear Harriet, what do you mean? Are you in any doubt as to that? I thought – but I beg your pardon, perhaps I have been mistaken. I certainly have been misunderstanding you, if you feel in doubt as to the nature of your answer. I had imagined you were consulting me only as to the wording of it."

Harriet was silent. With a little reserve of manner, Emma continued:
"You mean to return a favourable answer, I gather."

"No, I do not; that is, I do not mean — What shall I do? What would you advise me to do? Please, dear Miss Woodhouse, tell me what I ought to do?"

"I shall not give you any advice, Harriet. I will have nothing to do with it. This is a point which you must settle with your own feelings."

"I had no notion that he liked me so very much," said Harriet, contemplating the letter. For a little while Emma persevered in her silence, but worrying that the bewitching flattery of that letter might be too powerful, she thought it best to say,

"I lay it down as a general rule, Harriet, that if a woman *wonders* if she should accept a man or not, she certainly ought to refuse him. If she can hesitate as to 'Yes,' she ought to say 'No' immediately. It is not a state to be safely entered into with doubtful feelings, with half a heart. I thought it my duty as a friend, and older than yourself, to say this much to you. But do not imagine that I want to influence you."

"Oh! No, I am sure you are a great deal too kind to — but if you would just advise me what I had best do — No, no, I do not mean that — As you say, one's mind ought to be quite made up — One should not be hesitating — It is a very serious thing. It will be safer to say 'No', perhaps. Do you think I had better say 'No?'"

"Not for the world," said Emma, smiling graciously, "would I advise you either way. You must be the best judge of your own happiness. If you prefer Mr. Martin to every other person; if you think him the most agreeable man you have ever been in company with, why should you hesitate? You blush, Harriet. Does anybody else occur to you at this moment under such a definition? Harriet, Harriet, do not deceive yourself. Do not be overcome by gratitude and compassion. At this moment, who are you thinking of?"

The symptoms were favourable. Instead of answering, Harriet turned away confused and stood thoughtfully by the fire. Though the letter was still in her hand, it was now mechanically twisted about without regard. Emma awaited the result with impatience, but not without strong hopes. At last, with some hesitation, Harriet said —

"Miss Woodhouse, as you will not give me your opinion, I must do as well as I can by myself; and I have now quite determined, and really almost made up my mind — to refuse Mr. Martin. Do you think I am right?"

"Perfectly, perfectly right, my dearest Harriet; you are doing just what you ought. While you were at all in suspense I kept my feelings to myself, but now that you are so completely decided I have no hesitation in approving. Dear Harriet, I find joy in this. It would have grieved me to lose your friendship, which must have been the consequence of your marrying Mr. Martin. While you were in the smallest degree wavering, I said nothing about it, because I would not influence; but it would have been the loss of a friend to me. I could not have visited Mrs. Robert Martin of Abbey-Mill Farm. Now I am secure of you forever."

Harriet had not surmised her own danger, but the idea of it struck her forcibly.

"You could not have visited me!" she cried, looking aghast. "No, to be sure you could not; but I never thought of that before. That would have been too dreadful! What an escape! Dear Miss Woodhouse, I would not give up the pleasure and honour of being your friend for anything in the world."

"Indeed, Harriet, it would have been a severe pang to lose you; but it must have been. You would have thrown yourself out of all good society. I must have given you up."

"Dear me! How should I ever have borne it! It would have killed me never to come to Hartfield again!"

"Dear affectionate creature! *You* banished to Abbey-Mill Farm! *You* confined to the society of the illiterate and vulgar all your life! I wonder how the young man could have the confidence to ask it. He must have a pretty good opinion of himself."

"I do not think he is conceited either, in general," said Harriet, her conscience opposing such censure. "At least he is very good natured, and I shall always feel much obliged to him, and have a great regard for – but that is quite a different thing from – and you know, though he may like me, it does not follow that I should – and certainly I must confess that since my visiting here I have seen people – and if one comes to compare them, person and manners, there is no comparison at all, *one* is so very handsome and agreeable. However, I do really think Mr. Martin a very amiable young man, and have a great opinion of him; and his being so much attached to me – and his writing such a letter – but as to leaving you, it is what I would not do upon any consideration."

"Thank you, thank you, my own sweet little friend. We will not be parted. A woman does not have to marry a man merely because she is asked, or because he is attached to her, and can write a tolerable letter."

"Oh! No – and it is but a short letter too."

Emma felt the bad taste of her friend, but let it pass with a "very true; and it would be a small consolation to her, for the clownish manner which might be offending her every hour of the day, to know that her husband could write a good letter."

"Oh! Yes, very. Nobody cares for a letter; it is better to be always happy with pleasant companions. I am quite determined to refuse him. But how shall I do it? What shall I say?"

Emma assured her there would be no difficulty in the answer, and advised its being written immediately, which was agreed to, in the hope of her assistance. Though Emma continued to protest against any assistance being needed, it was in fact given in the formation of every sentence. The looking over his letter again, in replying to it, had such a softening tendency, that it was particularly necessary to brace her up with a few decisive expressions. She was so very much concerned at the idea of making him unhappy, and thought so much of what his mother and sisters would think and say, and was so anxious that they should not think her ungrateful, that Emma believed if the young man had come in her way at that moment, he would have been accepted after all.

This letter, however, was written, and sealed, and sent. The business was finished, and Harriet was safe. She was rather depressed all evening, but Emma could allow for her amiable regrets, and sometimes relieved them by speaking of her own affection, sometimes by bringing forward the idea of Mr. Elton.

"I shall never be invited to Abbey-Mill again," was said in rather a sorrowful tone.

"Nor if you were, could I ever bear to part with you, my Harriet. You are a great deal too necessary at Hartfield, to be spared to Abbey-Mill."

"And I am sure I should never want to go there; for I am never happy but at Hartfield."

Sometime afterwards it was, "I think Mrs. Goddard would be very much surprised if she knew what had happened. I am sure Miss Nash would – for Miss Nash thinks her own sister very well married, and her husband is only a linen-draper."

"One should be sorry to see greater pride or refinement in the teacher of a school, Harriet. I dare say Miss Nash would envy you such an opportunity as this of being married. Even this conquest would appear valuable in her eyes. As to anything superior for you, I suppose she is quite in the dark. The attentions of a certain person can hardly be the gossip of Highbury yet. Hitherto I fancy you and I are the only people to whom his looks and manners have explained themselves."

Harriet blushed and smiled, and said something about wondering that people should like her so much. The idea of Mr. Elton was certainly cheering; but still, after a time, she was tender-hearted again towards the rejected Mr. Martin.

"Now he has got my letter," she said softly. "I wonder what they are all doing — whether his sisters know — if he is unhappy, they will be unhappy too. I hope he will not mind it so very much.

"Let us think of those among our absent friends who are more cheerfully employed," cried Emma. "At this moment, perhaps, Mr. Elton is showing your picture to his mother and sisters, telling how much more beautiful is the original, and after being asked for it five or six times, allowing them to hear your name, your own dear name."

"My picture! But he has left my picture in Bond Street."

"No, my dear little modest Harriet, depend upon it the picture will not be in Bond Street till just before he mounts his horse tomorrow. It is his companion all this evening, his solace, his delight. It opens his designs to his family, it introduces you among them, it diffuses through the party those pleasantest feelings of our nature, eager curiosity and warmth. How cheerful, how animated, how suspicious, how busy their imaginations all are!"

Harriet smiled again, and her smiles grew stronger.

CHAPTER 8

Harriet slept at Hartfield that night. For some weeks past she had been spending more than half her time there, and gradually getting to have a bedroom assigned to her. Emma judged it best in every respect, safest and kindest, to keep her with them as much as possible just at present. She was obliged to go the next morning for an hour or two to Mrs. Goddard's, but it was then to be settled that she should return to Hartfield for a visit of several days.

While she was gone, Mr. Knightley came and sat some time with Mr. Woodhouse and Emma, till Mr. Woodhouse, who had previously made up his mind to take a walk, was persuaded by his daughter not to defer it. Mr. Knightley, who had nothing of ceremony about him, was offering by his short, decided answers, an amusing contrast to the apologies and civil hesitations of the other as he prepared to leave.

"Well, I believe, if you will excuse me, Mr. Knightley, if you will not consider me as doing a very rude thing, I shall take Emma's advice and go out for a quarter of an hour. As the sun is out, I believe I had better take my walk while I can. I leave an excellent substitute in my daughter. Emma will be happy to entertain you. And, therefore, I think I will beg your excuse and take my winter walk."

"You cannot do better, sir."

"I would ask for the pleasure of your company, Mr. Knightley, but I am a very slow walker, and my pace would be tedious to you; and besides, you have another long walk before you, to Donwell Abbey."

"Thank you, sir, thank you. I am going this moment myself, and I think the sooner *you* go the better. I will fetch your coat and open the garden door for you."

Mr. Woodhouse at last was off; but Mr. Knightley, instead of being immediately off likewise, sat down again, seemingly inclined for more talk. He began speaking of Harriet, and speaking of her with more voluntary praise than Emma had ever heard before.

"I cannot rate her beauty as you do," said he, "but she is a pretty little creature, and I am inclined to think very well of her disposition. Her character depends upon those she is with, but in good hands she will become a sensible woman."

"I am glad you think so; and the good hands, I hope may not be lacking."

"Come," said he, "you are anxious for a compliment, so I will tell you that you have improved her. You have cured her of her school girl's giggle."

"Thank you. I should be mortified indeed if I did not believe I had been of some use; but it is not everybody who will bestow praise where they may. *You* do not often overpower me with it."

"You are expecting her again, you say, this morning?"

"Almost every moment. She has been gone longer already than she intended."

"Something has happened to delay her. Some visitors perhaps."

"Highbury gossips! Tiresome wretches!"

"Harriet may not consider everybody tiresome that you would."

Emma knew this was too true for contradiction, and therefore said nothing. He presently added, with a smile,

"I do not pretend to be able to predict times or places, but I must tell you that I have good reason to believe your little friend will soon hear of something to her advantage."

"Indeed! How so? Of what sort?"

"Of a very serious sort, I assure you." He was still smiling.

"Very serious! I can think of but one thing – Who is in love with her? Who makes you their confidant?"

Emma was more than half in hopes of Mr. Elton's having dropped a hint. Mr. Knightley was a sort of general friend and adviser, and she knew Mr. Elton looked up to him.

"I have reason to think," he replied, "that Harriet Smith will soon have an offer of marriage, and from a most exceptional quarter: Robert

Martin is the man. Her visit to Abbey-Mill, this summer, seems to have done his business. He is desperately in love and means to marry her."

"He is very obliging," said Emma, "but is he sure that Harriet means to marry him?"

"Well, he means to make her an offer then. Will that do? He came to the Abbey two evenings ago, to consult me about it. He knows I have a thorough regard for him and all his family. He came to ask me whether I thought it would be imprudent for him to be married so young; whether I thought her too young: in short, whether I approved his choice altogether. He had some concerns, perhaps, of her being considered (especially since *your* making so much of her) as in a line of society above him. I was very much pleased with all that he said. I never hear better sense from anyone than Robert Martin. He always speaks to the purpose; open, straightforward, and very well judging. He told me everything; his circumstances and plans, and what they all proposed doing in the event of his marriage. He is an excellent young man, both as son and brother. I had no hesitation in advising him to marry. He proved to me that he could afford it, and that being the case, I was convinced he could not do better. I praised the fair lady too, and altogether sent him away very happy. If he had never esteemed my opinion before, he would have thought highly of me then; and, I dare say, he left the house thinking me the best advisor a man ever had. This happened the night before last. Now, as we may fairly suppose, he would not allow much time to pass before he spoke to the lady, and as he does not appear to have spoken yesterday, it is not unlikely that he should be at Mrs. Goddard's to day; and she may be detained by a visitor, without thinking him at all a tiresome wretch."

" Mr. Knightley," said Emma, who had been smiling to herself through a great part of this speech, "how do you know that Mr. Martin did not speak yesterday?"

"Certainly," replied he, surprised, "I do not absolutely know it; but it may be inferred. Was not she with you the whole day?"

"Come," said she, "I will tell you something, in return for what you have told me. He did speak yesterday – that is, he wrote, and was refused."

This was obliged to be repeated before it could be believed; and Mr. Knightley actually looked red with surprise and displeasure, as he stood up in indignation, and said,

"Then she is a greater simpleton than I ever believed her. What is the foolish girl about?"

"Oh! To be sure," cried Emma, "it is always incomprehensible to a man that a woman should ever refuse an offer of marriage. A man always imagines a woman to be ready for anybody who asks her."

"Nonsense! A man does not imagine any such thing. But what is the meaning of this? Harriet Smith refuse Robert Martin? Madness, if it is so; but I hope you are mistaken."

"I saw her answer, nothing could be clearer."

"You saw her answer! You wrote her answer, too. Emma, this is your doing. You persuaded her to refuse him."

"And if I did, (which, however, I am far from admitting), I should not feel that I had done wrong. Mr. Martin is a very respectable young man, but I cannot admit him to be Harriet's equal; and am rather surprised indeed that he should have ventured to address her. By your account, he does seem to have had some concerns. It is a pity that they were ever got over."

"Not Harriet's equal!" exclaimed Mr. Knightley loudly and warmly; and with greater calmness added, a few moments afterwards, "No, he is not her equal indeed, for he is as much her superior in sense as in situation. Emma, your regard for that girl blinds you. What are Harriet Smith's claims, either of birth, nature or education, to any connection higher than Robert Martin? Her parentage is unknown, she likely has no dowry, and certainly no respectable relations. She is known only as a boarder at a common school. She is not a sensible girl, nor a girl of any intelligence. She has been taught nothing useful, and is too young and too simple to have acquired anything herself. At her age she can have no experience, and with her little wit, she is not very likely ever to have any that can be useful to her. She is pretty, and she is good tempered, and that is all. My only concern in advising the match was on his account, as being beneath him, and a bad connection for him. I felt, that as to fortune, in all probability he might do much better; and that as to a rational companion, he could not do worse. But I could not reason so to a man in love, and was willing to trust to there being no harm in her, to her having that sort of disposition, which, in good hands, like his, might be easily led aright and turn out very well. The advantage of the match I felt to be all on her side; and had not the smallest doubt (nor have I now) that there would be a general outcry about her extreme good luck. Even *your* satisfaction I made sure of. It crossed my mind immediately that you would not regret your friend's leaving Highbury, for the sake of her being settled so well. I remember saying to myself,

'Even Emma, with all her partiality for Harriet, will think this a good match.'"

"I cannot help wondering at your knowing so little of Emma as to say any such thing. What! Think a farmer, (and with all his sense and all his merit Mr. Martin is nothing more), a good match for my closest friend! Not regret her leaving Highbury for the sake of marrying a man whom I could never admit as an acquaintance of my own! I wonder you should think it possible for me to have such feelings. I assure you mine are very different. I must think your statement by no means fair. You are not just to Harriet's claims. They would be estimated very differently by others as well as myself. Mr. Martin may be the richest of the two, but he is undoubtedly her inferior as to rank in society. The sphere in which she moves is much above his. It would be a degradation."

"A degradation to illegitimacy and ignorance, to be married to a respectable, intelligent gentleman-farmer!"

"As to the circumstances of her birth, she is not to pay for the offence of others, by being held below the level of those with whom she is brought up. There can scarcely be a doubt that her father is a gentleman – and a gentleman of fortune. Her allowance is very generous; nothing has ever been withheld for her improvement or comfort. That she is a gentleman's daughter is undoubtable to me; that she associates with gentlemen's daughters, no one, I believe, will deny. She is superior to Mr. Robert Martin."

"Whoever might be her parents," said Mr. Knightley, "whoever may have had the charge of her, it does not appear to have been any part of their plan to introduce her into what you would call good society. After receiving a very indifferent education she is left in Mrs. Goddard's hands to make her own way in life; – to move, in short, in Mrs. Goddard's line, to have Mrs. Goddard's acquaintance. Her friends evidently thought this good enough for her; and it *was* good enough. She desired nothing better herself. Till you chose to turn her into a friend, her mind had no distaste for her social circle, nor any ambition beyond it. She was as happy as possible with the Martins in the summer. She had no sense of superiority then. If she has it now, you have given it to her. You have been no friend to Harriet Smith, Emma. Robert Martin would never have proceeded so far, if he had not felt persuaded of her liking him. "

It was most convenient to Emma not to make a direct reply to this claim; she chose rather to take up her own line of the subject again.

"You are a very good friend to Mr. Martin; but, as I said before, are unjust to Harriet. Harriet's claims to marry well are not so contemptible as you represent them. She is not a clever girl, but she has better sense than you are aware of, and does not deserve to have her understanding spoken of so slightingly. Waving that point, however, and supposing her to be, as you describe her, only pretty and good-natured, let me tell you, that in the degree she possesses them, they are not trivial recommendations to the world in general, for she is, in fact, a beautiful girl, and must be thought so by ninety-nine people out of an hundred. Till it appears that men are much more philosophical on the subject of beauty than they are generally supposed to be; till they do fall in love with well-informed minds instead of pretty faces, a girl with such loveliness as Harriet has a certainty of being admired and sought after, and of having the power of choosing from among many. Her good nature, too, is not so very slight a claim, comprehending, as it does, real, thorough sweetness of temper and manner, a very humble opinion of herself, and a great readiness to appreciate other people. I am very much mistaken if your sex in general would not think such beauty, and such temper, the highest claims a woman could possess."

"Upon my word, Emma, to hear you abusing the reason you have is almost enough to make me think so too. Better to be without sense than to misapply it as you do."

"To be sure!" cried she playfully. "I know *that* is the feeling of you all. I know that such a girl as Harriet is exactly what every man delights in – what at once bewitches his senses and satisfies his judgment. Oh! Harriet may pick and choose. Were you, yourself, ever to marry, she is the very woman for you. And is she, at seventeen, just entering into life, just beginning to be known, to be wondered at because she does not accept the first offer she receives? No – let her have time to look about her."

"I have always thought it a very foolish friendship," said Mr. Knightley presently, "though I have kept my thoughts to myself; but I now perceive that it will be a very unfortunate one for Harriet. You will puff her up with such ideas of her own beauty, and of what she has a claim to, that, in a little while, nobody within her reach will be good enough for her. Vanity working on a weak head produces every sort of mischief. Miss Harriet Smith may not find offers of marriage flow in so fast, though she is a very pretty girl. Men of sense, whatever you may choose to say, do not want silly wives. Men with family connections would not be very fond of marrying a girl of such obscurity – and most prudent men would be afraid of the inconvenience and disgrace they might be involved in, when the mystery of her parentage came to be revealed. Let her marry Robert Martin, and she is safe, respectable, and happy forever. But if you encourage her to expect to marry greatly, and teach her to be satisfied with nothing less than a man of consequence and large fortune, she may be a boarder at Mrs. Goddard's all the rest of her life – or, at least (for Harriet Smith is a girl who will marry somebody or other), till she grows desperate, and is glad to catch at the old writing master's son."

"We think so very differently on this point, Mr. Knightley, that there can be no use in discussing it. We shall only be making each other angrier. But as to my *letting* her marry Robert Martin, it is impossible. She has refused him, and so decidedly, I think, as must prevent any second proposal. She must abide by the evil of having refused him, whatever it may be; and as to the refusal itself, I will not pretend to say that I did not influence her a little. But I assure you there was very little for me or for anybody to do. His appearance is so much against him, and his manner so bad, that if she ever were disposed to favour him, she is not now. I can imagine that before she had seen anybody superior, she might have tolerated him. He was the brother of her friends, and he took pains to please her; and altogether, having seen nobody better (that must have been his greatest asset) she might not, while she was at Abbey-Mill, find him disagreeable. But the case is altered now. She knows now what gentlemen are; and nothing but a gentleman in education and manner has any chance with Harriet."

"Nonsense!" cried Mr. Knightley. "Robert Martin's manners have sense, sincerity, and good-humour to recommend them. His mind has more true gentility than Harriet Smith could understand."

Emma made no answer, and tried to look cheerfully unconcerned, but was really feeling uncomfortable and wanting him very much to be gone. She did not regret what she had done, and she still thought herself a better judge of such a point of female right and refinement than he could be. But yet she had a sort of habitual respect for his judgment in general, which made her dislike having it so loudly against her; and to have him sitting just opposite to her in angry state, was very disagreeable. Some minutes passed in this unpleasant silence, with only one attempt on Emma's side to talk of the weather, but he made no answer. He was thinking. The result of his thoughts appeared at last in these words –

Robert Martin has no great loss – if he can but think so; and I hope it will not be long before he does. Your views for Harriet are best known to yourself; but as you make no secret of your love of match-making, it is fair to suppose what views, and plans, and projects you have. As a friend I shall just hint to you that if Elton is the man, I think it will be all labour in vain."

Emma laughed and expressed disagreement. He continued,

"Depend upon it, Elton will not do. Elton is a very good sort of man, and a very respectable vicar of Highbury, but not at all likely to make an impractical match. He knows the value of a good income as well as anybody. Elton may talk sentimentally, but he will act rationally. He is as well acquainted with his own claims as you can be with Harriet's. He knows that he is a very handsome young man, and a great favourite wherever he goes. From his general way of talking in unreserved moments, when there are only men present, I am convinced that he means to marry well. I have heard him speak with great animation of a large family of young ladies that his sisters are friendly with, who all have twenty thousand apiece."

"I am very much obliged to you," said Emma, laughing again. "If I had set my heart on Mr. Elton's marrying Harriet, it would have been very kind to open my eyes; but at present I only want to keep Harriet to myself. I am done with match-making indeed. I could never hope to equal my own doings at Randalls. I shall quit while I am ahead."

"Good day to you," said he, rising and walking off abruptly. He was very upset. He felt the disappointment of the young man, and was mortified to have been the means of promoting it by the sanction he had given. The part which he was persuaded Emma had taken in the affair was provoking him exceedingly.

Emma remained in a state of vexation too; but there was more indistinctness in the causes of hers, than in his. She did not always feel so absolutely satisfied with herself, so entirely convinced that her opinions were right and her adversary's wrong, as Mr. Knightley. He walked off in more complete self-approval than he left for her. She was not so cast down, however, but that a little time and the return of Harriet were very adequate to restore her spirits. Harriet's staying away so long was beginning to make her uneasy. The possibility of the young man's coming to Mrs. Goddard's that morning, and meeting with Harriet and pleading his own cause, gave alarming ideas. The dread of such a failure after all became the primary concern. When Harriet appeared in very good spirits, and without having any such reason to give for her long absence, she felt a satisfaction which settled her feelings on the matter. She was convinced, that let Mr. Knightley think or say what he would, she had done nothing which woman's friendship and woman's feelings would not justify.

He had frightened her a little about Mr. Elton; but when she considered that Mr. Knightley could not have observed him as she had done, she was able to believe that he had rather said what he wished resentfully to be true than what he knew anything about. He certainly might have heard Mr. Elton speak with more openness than she had ever done, and Mr. Elton might not be of an impractical, inconsiderate disposition as to money matters. He might naturally be rather attentive than otherwise to them; but then, Mr. Knightley did not make due allowance for the influence of a strong passion at war with all interested motives. Mr. Knightley saw no such passion, and of course thought nothing of its effects. But she saw too much of it to feel a doubt of its overcoming any hesitations that a reasonable prudence might originally suggest.

Harriet's cheerful look and manner established hers: she came back, not to think of Mr. Martin, but to talk of Mr. Elton. Miss Nash had been telling her something, which she repeated immediately with great delight. Mr. Perry had been to Mrs. Goddard's to attend a sick child, and Miss Nash had seen him, and he had told Miss Nash that as he was coming back yesterday from Clayton Park, he had met Mr. Elton. He found to his great surprise that Mr. Elton was actually on his way to London, and not meaning to return till the morrow, though it was the card game night, which he had been never known to miss before. Mr. Perry had told him how unfortunate it was that he, their best player, would be absent, and tried very much to persuade him to put off his journey only one day. But it would not do; Mr. Elton had been determined to go on, and had said in a very particular way indeed, that he was going on business which he would not put off for anything in the world. He said something about a very enviable commission, and being the bearer of something exceedingly precious. Mr. Perry could not quite understand him, but he was very sure there must be a lady in the case, and he told him so. Mr. Elton only looked very conscious and smiling, and rode off in great spirits. Miss Nash had told her all this, and had talked a great deal more about Mr. Elton, and said, looking so very significantly at her, "that she did not pretend to understand what his business might be, but she only knew that any woman whom Mr. Elton could prefer, she should think the luckiest woman in the world; for, beyond a doubt, Mr. Elton had not his equal for handsomeness or agreeableness."

CHAPTER 9

Mr. Knightley might quarrel with her, but Emma could not quarrel with herself. He was so much displeased that it was longer than usual before he came to Hartfield again. When they did finally meet, his grave looks showed that she was not forgiven. She was sorry, but could not repent. On the contrary, her plans and proceedings were more and more justified, and further encouraged by the events of the next few days.

The picture, elegantly framed, arrived soon after Mr. Elton's return, and being hung over the mantle-piece of the common sitting room, he got up to look at it, and sighed out his half sentences of admiration just as he ought. As for Harriet's feelings, they were visibly forming themselves into as strong and steady an attachment as her youth and sort of mind admitted. Emma was soon perfectly satisfied of Mr. Martin's being remembered only as a contrast with Mr. Elton, and all advantage was on the side of the latter.

Her views of improving her little friend's mind by a great deal of useful reading and conversation had never yet led to more than a few first chapters, and the intention of going on tomorrow. It was much easier to chat than to study; much pleasanter to let her imagination range and work at Harriet's fortune than to be labouring to expand her knowledge or exercise it on sober facts. The only literary pursuit which engaged Harriet at present was the collecting and transcribing all the riddles of every sort that she could find into a thin notebook of hot-pressed paper, made up by her friend.

In this age of literature, such collections on a very grand scale are not uncommon. Miss Nash, head-teacher at Mrs. Goddard's, had written out at least three hundred. Harriet, who had taken the first hint of it from her, hoped, with Miss Woodhouse's help, to get a great many more. Emma assisted with her invention, memory and taste; and as Harriet wrote very prettily, it was likely to be a successful effort, in quality as well as quantity.

Mr. Woodhouse was almost as much interested in the business as the girls, and tried very often to recollect something worth their putting in. "So many clever riddles there used to be when he was young – he wondered he could not remember them! But he hoped he would in time." And it always ended in "Kitty, a fair but frozen maid."

His good friend Perry, too, whom he had spoken to on the subject, did not at present recollect anything of the riddle kind. But he had asked Perry to be on the watch, and as he went about so much, something, he thought, might come of it.

It was by no means his daughter's wish that the intellects of Highbury in general should be applied to. Mr. Elton was the only one whose assistance she asked. He was invited to contribute any really good enigmas, charades, or conundrums that he might recollect; and she had the pleasure of seeing him most intently at work with his recollections. At the same time, as she could perceive, he was most earnestly careful that nothing ungallant, nothing that did not breathe a compliment to women should pass his lips. They owed to him their two or three politest puzzles; and the joy and exultation with which at last he recalled, and rather sentimentally recited, that well-known charade –

My first doth affliction denote,
Which my second is destined to feel
And my whole is the best antidote
That affliction to soften and heal.

– made her quite sorry to acknowledge that they had transcribed it some pages ago already.

"Why will you not write one yourself for us, Mr. Elton? That is the only way to guarantee freshness; and nothing could be easier for you."

"Oh, no! He had never written, hardly ever, anything of the kind in his life. The stupidest fellow! He was afraid not even Miss Woodhouse" – he stopped a moment – "or Miss Smith could inspire him."

The very next day, however, produced some proof of inspiration. He visited for a few moments, just to leave a piece of paper on the table containing, as he said, a charade, which a friend of his had addressed to a young lady, the object of his admiration, but which, from his manner, Emma was immediately convinced must be his own.

"I do not offer it for Miss Smith's collection," said he. "Being my friend's, I have no right to expose it in any degree to the public eye, but perhaps you may not dislike looking at it."

The speech was more to Emma than to Harriet, which Emma could understand. There was deep consciousness about him, and he found it easier to meet her eye than her friend's. He was gone the next moment. After another moment's pause –

"Take it," said Emma, smiling and pushing the paper towards Harriet. "It is for you. "

But Harriet was in a tremor, and could not touch it; and Emma, never afraid to be first, was obliged to examine it herself.

CHARADE

My first displays the wealth and pomp of kings,
Lords of the earth! Their luxury and ease.
Another view of man, my second brings,
Behold him there, the monarch of the seas!

But, ah! United, what reverse we have!
Man's boasted power and freedom, all are flown;
Lord of the earth and sea, he bends a slave,
And woman, lovely woman, reigns alone.

Thy ready wit the word will soon supply,
May its approval beam in that soft eye!

She cast her eye over it, pondered, caught the meaning, read it through again to be quite certain, and then passing it to Harriet, sat happily smiling, and saying to herself, while Harriet was puzzling over the paper in confusion, "Very well, Mr. Elton, very well, indeed. I have read worse charades. *Courtship* – a very good hint. I give you credit for it. This is saying very plainly – 'Please, Miss Smith, give me leave to court you. Approve my charade and my intentions in the same glance.'

May its approval beam in that soft eye!

Harriet exactly. Soft is the very word for her eye — of all epithets, the most just that could be given.

Thy ready wit the word will soon supply —

Humph — Harriet's ready wit! All the better. A man must be very much in love indeed, to describe her so. Ah! Mr. Knightley, I wish you had the benefit of this; I think this would convince you. For once in your life you would be obliged to admit you were mistaken. An excellent charade indeed! And very much to the purpose. Things must change quickly now.

She was obliged to break off from these very pleasant observations, which were otherwise of a sort to run into great length, by the eagerness of Harriet's wondering questions.

"What can it be, Miss Woodhouse? What can it be? I have not an idea — I cannot guess it in the least. What can it possibly be? Do try to find it out, Miss Woodhouse. Do help me. I never saw anything so hard. Is it kingdom? I wonder who the friend was — and who could be the young lady! Do you think it is a good one? Can it be woman?"

And woman, lovely woman, reigns alone.

"Can it be Neptune?"

Behold him there, the monarch of the seas!

"Or a trident? Or a mermaid? Or a shark? Oh, no! Shark is only one syllable. It must be very clever, or he would not have brought it. Oh! Miss Woodhouse, do you think we shall ever find it out?"

"Mermaids and sharks! Nonsense! My dear Harriet, what are you thinking of? Where would be the use of his bringing us a charade made by a friend upon a mermaid or a shark? Give me the paper and listen."

My first displays the wealth and pomp of kings,
Lords of the earth! Their luxury and ease.

"That is *court*."

Another view of man, my second brings;
Behold him there, the monarch of the seas!

"That is *ship*; – plain as can be. Now for the cream. But ah! United, (*courtship*, you know), what reverse we have!"

Man's boasted power and freedom, all are flown.
Lord of the earth and sea, he bends a slave,
And woman, lovely woman, reigns alone.

"A very proper compliment! And then follows the application, which I think, my dear Harriet, you cannot find much difficulty in comprehending. Read it in comfort to yourself. There can be no doubt of its being written for you and to you."

Harriet could not long resist so delightful a persuasion. She read the concluding lines, and was all flutter and happiness. She could not speak. But she did not need to speak. It was enough for her to feel. Emma spoke for her.

"There is so pointed, and so particular a meaning in this compliment," said she, "that I cannot have a moment's doubt as to Mr. Elton's intentions. You are his object – and you will soon receive the completest proof of it. I thought it must be so. I thought I could not be so deceived; but now it is clear. The state of his mind is as clear and decided as my wishes on the subject have been ever since I knew you. Yes, Harriet, that's how long I have been wanting the very circumstance to happen which has happened. I am very happy. I congratulate you, my dear Harriet, with all my heart. This is an attachment which a woman may well feel pride in creating. This is a connection which offers nothing but good. It will give you everything that you want – respect, independence, a proper home – it will fix you in the centre of all your real friends, close to Hartfield and to me, and confirm our intimacy forever. This, Harriet, is an alliance which can never raise a blush in either of us."

"Dear Miss Woodhouse" – and "Dear Miss Woodhouse," was all that Harriet, with many tender embraces could articulate at first; but when they did arrive at something more like conversation, it was sufficiently clear to her friend that she saw, felt, anticipated, and remembered just as she ought. Mr. Elton's superiority had very ample acknowledgment.

"Whatever you say is always right," cried Harriet, "and therefore I suppose, and believe, and hope it must be so; but otherwise I could not have imagined it. It is so much beyond anything I deserve. Mr. Elton, who might marry anybody! There cannot be two opinions about *him*. He is so very superior. Only think of those sweet verses. Could they really be meant for me?"

"I cannot make a question, or listen to a question about that. It is a certainty. Receive it on my judgment. It is a sort of prologue to the play, a motto to the chapter; and it will be soon followed by a more direct declaration."

"It is a sort of thing which nobody could have expected. I am sure, a month ago, I could not have imagined it! The strangest things do take place!"

"When Miss Smiths and Mr. Eltons get acquainted – they do indeed. You and Mr. Elton are by situation called together; you belong to one another by every circumstance of your respective homes. Your marrying will be equal to the match at Randalls. There does seem to be a something in the air of Hartfield which gives love exactly the right direction, and sends it into the very channel where it ought to flow."

The course of true love never did run smooth –

"A Hartfield edition of Shakespeare would have a long note on that passage."

"That Mr. Elton should really be in love with me – me, of all people, who did not know him, to speak to him, only a few months ago! And he, the very handsomest man that ever was, and a man that everybody looks up to, quite like Mr. Knightley! His company so sought after, that everybody says he need not eat a single meal by himself if he does not choose it; that he has more invitations than there are days in the week. And so excellent in the Church! Miss Nash has written down all the texts he has ever preached from since he came to Highbury. Dear me! When I look back to the first time I saw him! How little did I think! The two Abbotts and I ran into the front room and peeped through the blind when we heard he was going by, and Miss Nash came and scolded us away, and stayed to look through herself; however, she called me back presently, and let me look too, which was very good-natured. And how handsome we thought he looked! He was arm in arm with Mr. Cole."

"This is an alliance which, whoever – whatever your friends may be, must be agreeable to them, provided at least they have common sense; and we are not to be addressing our conduct to fools. If they are anxious to see you *happily* married, here is a man whose amiable character gives every assurance of it. If they wish to have you settled in the same country and circle which they have chosen to place you in, here it will be accomplished; and if their only object is that you should, in the common phrase, be *well* married, here is the comfortable fortune, the respectable establishment, the rise in the world which must satisfy them."

"Yes, very true. How nicely you talk; I love to hear you. You understand everything. You and Mr. Elton are both so very clever. This charade! If I had studied a year, I could never have made anything like it."

"I thought he meant to try his skill, by his manner of declining it yesterday."

"I do think it is, without exception, the best charade I ever read."

"I never read one more to the purpose, certainly."

"It is as long again as almost all we have had before."

"I do not consider its length as particularly in its favour. Such things in general cannot be too short."

Harriet was too intent on the lines to hear. The most satisfactory comparisons were rising in her mind.

"It is one thing," said she, presently – her cheeks in a glow, "to have very good sense in a common way, like everybody else, and if there is anything to say, to sit down and write a letter, and say just what you must, in a short way; and another, to write verses and charades like this."

Emma could not have desired a more spirited rejection of Mr. Martin's prose.

"Such sweet lines!" continued Harriet, "these two last! But how shall I ever be able to return the paper, or say I have figured it out? Oh! Miss Woodhouse, what can we do about that?"

"Leave it to me. You do nothing. He will be here this evening, I dare say, and then I will give it back, and some nonsense or other will pass between us, and you won't need to say anything. Your soft eyes shall choose their own time for beaming. Trust to me."

"Oh! Miss Woodhouse, what a pity that I must not write this beautiful charade into my book! I am sure I have not got one half so good."

"Leave out the two last lines, and there is no reason why you should not write it into your book."

"Oh! but those two lines are–"

"The best of all. Granted, for private enjoyment; and for private enjoyment keep them. They are not at all the less written, you know, because you divide them. The couplet does not cease to be, nor does its meaning change. But take it away, and a very pretty gallant charade remains, fit for any collection. Depend upon it, he would not like to have his charade slighted. A poet in love must be encouraged. Give me the book, I will write it down, and then there can be no possible reflection on you."

Harriet submitted, though her mind could hardly separate the parts, so as to feel quite sure that her friend was not writing down a declaration of love. It seemed too precious an offering for any degree of publicity.

"I shall never let that book go out of my own hands," said she.

"Very well," replied Emma, "a most natural feeling; and the longer it lasts, the better I shall be pleased. But here is my father coming: you will not object to my reading the charade to him. It will be giving him so much pleasure! He loves anything of the sort, and especially anything that pays woman a compliment. He has the most tender spirit of gallantry towards us all! You must let me read it to him."

Harriet looked grave.

"My dear Harriet, you must not appear so self-conscious. You will betray your feelings and appear to affix more meaning, or even quite all the meaning which may be affixed to it. Do not be overpowered by such a little tribute of admiration. If he had been anxious for secrecy, he would not have left the paper while I was by; but he rather pushed it towards me than towards you. Do not let us be too solemn. He has encouragement enough to proceed, without our sighing out our souls over this charade."

"Oh! No – I hope I shall not be ridiculous about it. Do as you please."

Mr. Woodhouse came in, and very soon led to the subject again, by the recurrence of his very frequent inquiry of "Well, my dears, how does your book go on? Have you got anything fresh?"

"Yes, papa, we have something to read you, something quite fresh. A piece of paper was found on the table this morning (dropped, we suppose, by a fairy) containing a very pretty charade, and we have just copied it in."

She read it to him, just as he liked to have anything read, slowly and distinctly, and two or three times over, with explanations of every part as she proceeded. He was very much pleased, and, as she had foreseen, especially struck with the complimentary conclusion.

"Aye, that's very just, indeed, that's very properly said. Very true. "Woman, lovely woman." It is such a pretty charade, my dear, that I can easily guess what fairy brought it. Nobody could have written so prettily but you, Emma."

Emma only nodded, and smiled. After a little thinking, and a very tender sigh, he added —

"Ah! It is no difficulty to see who you take after! Your dear mother was so clever at all those things! If I had but her memory! But I can remember nothing; not even that particular riddle which you have heard me mention. I can only recollect the first stanza, and there are several.

Kitty, a fair but frozen maid,
Kindled a flame I yet deplore,
The hood-winked boy I called to aid,
Though of his near approach afraid,
So fatal to my suit before.

And that is all that I can recollect of it; but it is very clever all the way through. But I think, my dear, you said you had got it."

"Yes, papa, it is written out in our second page. We copied it from the Elegant Extracts. It was Garrick's, you know."

"Aye, very true. I wish I could recollect more of it."

Kitty, a fair but frozen maid.

"The name makes me think of poor Isabella; for she was very near being named Catherine after her grandma. I hope we shall have her here next week. Have you thought, my dear, where you shall put her — and what room there will be for the children?"

"Oh! Yes — she will have her own room, of course; the room she always has. And there is the nursery for the children, just as usual, you know. Why should there be any change?"

"I do not know, my dear — but it is so long since she was here! Not since last Easter, and then only for a few days. Mr. John Knightley's being a lawyer is very inconvenient. Poor Isabella! She is sadly taken away from us all! And how sorry she will be when she comes, not to see Miss Taylor here!"

"She will not be surprised, papa, at least."

"I do not know, my dear. I am sure I was very much surprised when I first heard she was going to be married."

"We must ask Mr. and Mrs. Weston to dine with us while Isabella is here."

"Yes, my dear, if there is time. But (in a very depressed tone), she is coming for only one week. There will not be time for anything."

"It is unfortunate that they cannot stay longer – but it seems a case of necessity. Mr. John Knightley must be in town again on the 28th, and we ought to be thankful, papa, that we are to have the whole time they can give to the country, that two or three days are not to be taken out for the Abbey. Mr. Knightley promises to give up his claim this Christmas – though you know it is longer since they were with him than with us."

"It would be very hard indeed, my dear, if poor Isabella were to be anywhere but at Hartfield."

Mr. Woodhouse could never allow for Mr. Knightley's claims on his brother, or anybody's claims on Isabella, except his own. He sat musing a little while, and then said,

"But I do not see why poor Isabella should be obliged to go back so soon, even though he will be leaving. I think, Emma, I shall try to persuade her to stay longer with us. "

"Ah! Papa – that is what you never have been able to accomplish, and I do not think you ever will. Isabella cannot bear to be without her husband."

This was too true for contradiction. Unwelcome as it was, Mr. Woodhouse could only give a submissive sigh. As Emma saw his spirits affected by the idea of his daughter's attachment to her husband, she immediately changed the subject.

"Harriet must give us as much of her company as she can while my brother and sister are here. I am sure she will be pleased with the children. We are very proud of the children, are not we, papa? I wonder which she will think the handsomest, Henry or John?"

"Aye, I wonder which she will. Poor little dears, how glad they will be to come. They are very fond of being at Hartfield, Harriet."

"I dare say they are, sir. I am sure I do not know who is not."

"Henry is a fine boy, but John is very like his mamma. Henry is the eldest. He was named after me, not after his father. John, the second, is named after his father. Some people are surprised, I believe, that the eldest was not, but Isabella would have him called Henry, which I thought very kind of her. And he is a very clever boy, indeed. They are all remarkably clever; and they have such good manners. They will come and stand by my chair, and say, 'Grandpapa, can you give me a bit of string?' Once Henry asked me for a knife, but I told him knives were only made for grandpapas. I think their father is too rough with them very often."

"He appears rough to you," said Emma, "because you are so very gentle yourself; but if you could compare him with other papas, you would not think him rough. He wishes his boys to be active and hardy. If they misbehave, he can give them a sharp word now and then; but he is an affectionate father. Certainly Mr. John Knightley is an affectionate father. The children are all fond of him."

"And then their uncle comes in, and tosses them up to the ceiling in a very frightful way!"

"But they like it, papa; there is nothing they like so much. It is such enjoyment to them, that if their uncle did not lay down the rule of their taking turns, whoever began would never give way to the other."

"Well, I cannot understand it."

"That is the case with us all, papa. One half of the world cannot understand the pleasures of the other."

Later in the morning, and just as the girls were going to separate in preparation for the regular four o'clock dinner, the author of their latest charade walked in again. Harriet turned away, but Emma could receive him with the usual smile. Her quick eye soon discerned in his the consciousness of having made a push – of having thrown a die; and she imagined he was come to see how it might turn up. His purported reason, however, was to ask whether Mr. Woodhouse's party could be made up in the evening without him, or whether he should be in the smallest degree necessary at Hartfield. If he were, everything else must give way; but otherwise his friend Cole had been saying so much about his dining with him – had made such a point of it, that he had promised him conditionally to come.

Emma thanked him, but could not allow him to disappoint his friend on their account; her father was sure to have enough players to join him. He re-urged – she re-declined; and he seemed then about to make his bow, when taking the paper from the table, she returned it.

"Oh! Here's the charade you were so obliging as to leave with us; thank you for sharing it with us. We admired it so much, that I have ventured to write it into Miss Smith's collection. Your friend will not take it amiss, I hope. Of course, I have not transcribed beyond the eight first lines."

Mr. Elton certainly did not very well know what to say. He looked rather doubtingly – rather confused; said something about "honour," glanced at Emma and at Harriet, and then seeing the book open on the table, took it up, and examined it very attentively. With the view of passing off an awkward moment, Emma smilingly said –

"You must make my apologies to your friend; but such a good charade must not be confined to one or two people. He may be sure of every woman's approval while he writes with such gallantry."

"I have no hesitation in saying," replied Mr. Elton, though hesitating a good deal while he spoke, "I have no hesitation in saying – at least, if my friend feels at all as *I* do – I have not the smallest doubt that, could he see his little verse honoured as *I* see it, (looking at the book again, and replacing it on the table), he would consider it as the proudest moment of his life."

After this speech, he was gone as soon as possible. Emma could not think it too soon; for with all his good and agreeable qualities, there was a sort of parade in his speeches which often made her want to laugh. She ran away to indulge the inclination, leaving the tender and sublime pleasure to Harriet.

CHAPTER 10

Though it was now the middle of December, there had not yet been any bad weather that prevented the young ladies from getting regular exercise. On the morrow, therefore, Emma had a charitable visit to pay to a poor sick family who lived a little way out of Highbury.

Their road to this detached cottage was down Vicarage-lane, which contained the blessed abode of Mr. Elton. A few inferior dwellings were first to be passed, and then, about a quarter of a mile down the lane rose the Vicarage. It was an old and not very good house, almost as close to the road as it could be. It had no advantage of situation; but it had been very much smartened up by the present proprietor. Such as it was, there could be no possibility of the two friends passing it without a slackened pace and observing eyes. Emma's remark was –

"There it is. There go you and your riddle-book one of these days." Harriet's was –

"Oh! What a sweet house! How very beautiful! There are the yellow curtains that Miss Nash admires so much."

"I do not often walk this way *now*," said Emma, as they proceeded, "but *then* there will be a reason, and I shall gradually get intimately acquainted with all the hedges, gates, and trees of this part of Highbury."

Harriet, she found, had never in her life been inside the Vicarage, and her curiosity to see it was so extreme, that Emma could only see it as a proof of love.

"I wish we could arrange it," said she; "but I cannot think of any ostensible reason for going in – no servant that I want to inquire about of his housekeeper, no message from my father."

She pondered, but could think of nothing. After a mutual silence of some minutes, Harriet thus began again –

"I do so wonder, Miss Woodhouse, that you should not be married, or going to be married! As charming as you are!"

Emma laughed, and replied,

"My being charming, Harriet, is not quite enough to convince me to marry. I must find other people charming – one other person at least. And I am not only not going to be married at present, but have very little intention of ever marrying at all."

"Ah! So you say; but I cannot believe it."

"I must see somebody very superior to anyone I have seen yet, to be tempted. Mr. Elton, you know, is out of the question, and I do *not* wish to see any such person. I would rather not be tempted. I cannot really change for the better. If I were to marry, I must expect to regret it."

"Dear me! It is so odd to hear a woman talk so!"

"I have none of the usual reasons women have to marry. Were I to fall in love, indeed, it would be a different thing! But I never have been in love; it is not my way, or my nature, and I do not think I ever shall. And, without love, I am sure I should be a fool to change a situation such as mine. Fortune I do not lack, and there is always something to keep me occupied. I believe few married women are half as much mistress of their husband's house as I am of Hartfield. And never, never could I expect to be so truly beloved and important, so always first and always right in any man's eyes as I am in my father's."

"But then, to be an old maid at last, like Miss Bates!"

"That is as formidable an image as you could present, Harriet. And if I thought I should ever be like Miss Bates! So silly – so satisfied – so smiling – so apt to tell everything relative to everybody about me, I would marry tomorrow. But between *us*, I am convinced there never can be any similarity, except in being unmarried."

"But still, you will be an old maid – and that's so dreadful!"

"But, Harriet, I shall not be a *poor* old maid; and it is poverty only which makes such a state contemptible to a generous public! A single woman with a very limited income must be a ridiculous, disagreeable, old maid! The proper sport of boys and girls. But a single woman of good fortune is always respectable, and may be as sensible and pleasant as anybody else. And the distinction is not quite as unfair as it appears at first; for a very narrow income has a tendency to contract the mind and sour the temper. Those who can barely live, and who live in a very small, and generally very inferior, society, may well be selfish and disagreeable. This does not apply, however, to Miss Bates; she is only too good natured and too silly to suit me. But, in general, she is very much liked by everybody, though single and poor. Poverty certainly has not contracted her mind: I really believe, if she had only a shilling in the world, she would be very likely to give away half of it; and nobody is afraid of her: that is a great charm."

"Dear me! But what shall you do? How shall you employ yourself when you grow old?"

"If I know myself, Harriet. Mine is an active, busy mind, with a great many independent resources. I do not perceive why I should be more in want of employment at forty or fifty than at twenty. Woman's usual occupations of eye and hand and mind will be as open to me then as they are now. If I draw less, I shall read more. If I give up music, I shall take up embroidery. And as for objects of interest, the absence of which is really the great evil to be avoided in *not* marrying, I shall be very well off, with all the children of a sister I love so much, to care about. There will be enough of them, in all probability, to supply every sort of sensation that declining life can require. There will be enough for every hope and every fear; and though my attachment to none can equal that of a parent, it suits my ideas of comfort better than what is warmer and blinder. My nephews and nieces: I shall often have a niece with me."

"Do you know Miss Bates' niece? That is, I know you must have seen her a hundred times – but are you acquainted?"

"Oh! Yes, we are always forced to be acquainted whenever she comes to Highbury. By the way, *that* is almost enough to change one's opinion of nieces in general. Heaven forbid that I should ever bore people half so much about all the Knightleys together as she does about Jane Fairfax. One is sick of the very name. Every letter from her is read forty times over. Her compliments to all friends go round and round again; and if she does but send her aunt a sewing pattern, or knit a pair of garters for her grandmother, one hears of nothing else for a month. I wish Jane Fairfax very well, but she tires me to death."

They were now approaching the cottage, and all idle topics were at an end. Emma was very compassionate, and the distresses of the poor were as sure of relief from her personal attention and kindness, her counsel and her patience, as from her purse. She understood their ways, could allow for their ignorance and their temptations, and had no romantic expectations of extraordinary virtue from those for whom education had done so little. She entered into their troubles with ready sympathy, and always gave her assistance with as much intelligence as goodwill. In the present instance, it was sickness and poverty together which she came to visit. After remaining there as long as she could give comfort or advice, she left the cottage with such an impression of the scene as made her say to Harriet, as they walked away,

"These are the sights, Harriet, to do one good. How trifling they make everything else appear! I feel now as if I could think of nothing but these poor creatures all the rest of the day; and yet, who can say how soon it may all vanish from my mind?"

"Very true," said Harriet. "Poor creatures! One can think of nothing else."

"And really, I do not think the impression will soon be over," said Emma, as she crossed the low hedge which ended the narrow, slippery path through the cottage garden, and brought them into the lane again. "I do not think it will." She stopped to look once more at all the outward wretchedness of the place, and recalled the still greater within.

"Oh! Dear, no," said her companion.

They walked on. The lane made a slight bend, and when that bend was passed, Mr. Elton was immediately in sight. He was so near as to give Emma time only to say farther,

"Ah! Harriet, here comes a very sudden trial of our stability in good thoughts. Well, (smiling), I hope it may be allowed that if compassion has produced relief to the sufferers, it has done all that is truly important. If we feel for the wretched, enough to do all we can for them, the rest is empty sympathy, only distressing to ourselves."

Harriet could just answer, "Oh! Dear, yes," before the gentleman joined them. The wants and sufferings of the poor family, however, were the first subject on meeting. He had been going to call on them. His visit he would now defer; but they had a very interesting talk about what could be done and should be done. Mr. Elton then turned back to accompany them.

"To run into each other on such an errand as this," thought Emma, "to meet in a charitable scheme. This will bring a great increase of love on each side. I should not wonder if it were to bring on the declaration. It probably would, if I were not here. I wish I were anywhere else."

Anxious to separate herself from them as far as she could, she soon afterwards took possession of a narrow footpath, a little raised on one side of the lane, leaving them together in the main road. But she had not been there two minutes when she found that Harriet's habits of dependence and imitation were bringing her up too, and that, in short, they would both be soon after her. This would not do; she immediately stopped, under pretence of having some alteration to make in the lacing of her boot, and stooping down in complete occupation of the footpath, begged them to walk on, and she would follow in half a minute. They did as they were asked, and by the time she judged it reasonable to be done with her boot, she had the comfort of further delay in her power. She was overtaken by a child from the cottage, setting out, according to orders, with her pitcher, to fetch broth from Hartfield. To walk by the side of this child, and talk to and question her, was the most natural thing in the world, or would have been the most natural, had she been acting just then without design; and by this means the others were still able to keep ahead, without any obligation of waiting for her. She gained on them, however, involuntarily; the child's pace was quick, and theirs rather slow. The two were evidently in a conversation which interested them. Mr. Elton was speaking with animation, Harriet was listening with a very pleased attention, and Emma, having sent the child on, was beginning to think how she might draw back a little more, when they both looked around and she was obliged to join them.

Mr. Elton was still talking, still engaged in some interesting detail; and Emma experienced some disappointment when she found that he was only giving his fair companion an account of yesterday's party at his friend Cole's, and that she had joined the conversation in time to hear about the Stilton cheese, the butter, the celery, the beets and the desserts.

"This would soon have led to something better of course," was her consoling reflection. "Anything is interesting to those who are in love, and anything will serve as an introduction to what is near the heart. If I could only have kept longer away!"

They now walked on together quietly, till within view of the vicarage, when a sudden resolution, of at least getting Harriet into the house, made her again find something very much amiss about her boot, and fall behind to arrange it once more. She then broke the lace off short, and dexterously throwing it into a ditch, was presently obliged to entreat them to stop and acknowledge her inability to put herself together so as to be able to walk home in tolerable comfort.

"Part of my lace is gone," said she, "and I do not know how I am to get on. I really am a most troublesome companion to you both, but I hope I am not often so ill-equipped. Mr. Elton, I must beg to stop at your house, and ask your housekeeper for a bit of ribbon or string, or anything that will help me keep my boot on."

Mr. Elton looked all happiness at this idea, and nothing could exceed his alertness and attention in conducting them into his house and endeavouring to make everything appear to advantage. The room they were taken into was the one he chiefly occupied, and behind it was another. The door between them was open, and Emma passed into it with the housekeeper to receive her assistance in the most comfortable manner. She was obliged to leave the door ajar as she found it, but she fully intended that Mr. Elton would close it. It was not closed however, it still remained ajar; but by engaging the housekeeper in incessant conversation, she hoped to make it possible for him to choose his own subject in the next room. For ten minutes she could hear nothing but herself. It could be drawn out no longer. She was then obliged to be finished and make her appearance.

The lovers were standing together at one of the windows. It had a most favourable view; and, for half a minute, Emma felt the glory of having schemed successfully. But it would not do; he had not come to the point. He had been most agreeable, most delightful; he had told Harriet that he had seen them go by, and had purposely followed them; other little gallantries and allusions had been dropped, but nothing serious.

"Cautious, very cautious," thought Emma. "He advances inch by inch, and will hazard nothing till he believes himself secure."

Still, however, though everything had not been accomplished by her ingenious device, she could not but flatter herself that it had been the occasion of much present enjoyment to both, and must be leading them forward to the great event.

CHAPTER 11

Mr. Elton must now be left to himself. It was no longer in Emma's power to arrange an increase in his happiness or speed the process of courting. The coming of her sister's family was so very near at hand that first in anticipation and then in reality it became henceforth her prime object of interest. During the ten days of their stay at Hartfield it was not to be expected — she did not herself expect — that anything beyond occasional assistance could be offered by her to the lovers. They might advance rapidly on their own, however, if they chose. She hardly wished to have more leisure for them. There are people, who the more you do for them, the less they will do for themselves.

Mr. and Mrs. Knightley, from having been longer than usual absent from Surrey, were exciting of course rather more than the usual interest. Till this year, every long vacation since their marriage had been divided between Hartfield and Donwell Abbey. But all the holidays of this autumn had been given to sea-bathing for the children, and it was therefore many months since they had been seen by their Surrey connections, or by Mr. Woodhouse. The latter could not be convinced to go as far as London, even for poor Isabella's sake; and he was consequently now most happy in anticipating this too short visit.

He thought much of the difficulties of the journey for her, and not a little of the fatigues of his own horses and coachman who were to bring some of the party the last half of the way. But his concerns were needless. The sixteen miles being happily accomplished, Mr. and Mrs. John Knightley, their five children, and their nursery-maids, all reached Hartfield in safety. The bustle and joy of such an arrival, the many to be talked to, welcomed, and encouraged, produced a noise and confusion which his nerves could not have borne for any other reason, nor have endured much longer even for this. But the ways of Hartfield and the feelings of her father were so respected by Mrs. John Knightley, that in spite of maternal concerns for the immediate enjoyment of her little ones, the children were never allowed to be a disturbance to him.

Mrs. John Knightley was a pretty, elegant little woman, of gentle, quiet manners, and a disposition remarkably amiable and affectionate. She was a devoted wife, a doting mother, and was also so tenderly attached to her father and sister that, but for these higher ties, a warmer love might have seemed impossible. She could never see a fault in any of them. She was not a woman of strong understanding or wit. And with this resemblance of her father, she inherited also much of his constitution. She was delicate in her own health, over-careful of that of her children, had many fears, and was as fond of her own Mr. Wingfield in town as her father could be of Mr. Perry. They were alike too, in a general benevolence of temper, and a strong habit of regard for every old acquaintance.

Mr. John Knightley was a tall, gentleman-like, and very clever man; rising in his profession, domestic, and respectable in his private character. But he had reserved manners which prevented his being generally pleasing, and he was capable of being sometimes out of humour. He was not an ill-tempered man, not so often unreasonably cross as to deserve such a reproach; but his temper was not his great perfection. Indeed, with such a worshipping wife, it was hardly possible that any natural defects in it should not be increased. He had all the clearness and quickness of mind which she lacked, and he could sometimes act ungracious, or say a severe thing. He was not a great favourite with his fair sister-in-law. Nothing wrong in him escaped her. She was quick in feeling the little injuries to Isabella which Isabella never felt herself. Perhaps she might have overlooked more had his manners been flattering to Isabella's sister, but they were only those of a calmly kind brother and friend, without praise and without blindness. But hardly any degree of personal compliment could have kept her from noticing that greatest fault of all in her eyes which he sometimes fell into, the lack of respectful forbearance towards her father. There he had not always the patience that could have been wished. Mr. Woodhouse's peculiarities sometimes provoked him to a sharp retort. It did not often happen; for Mr. John Knightley had really a great regard for his father-in-law, and generally a strong sense of what was due to him. But it was more often than Emma could completely forgive, especially as there was all the pain of worry frequently to be endured, though the offence came not. The beginning, however, of every visit displayed none but the most proper feelings. They had not been long seated and composed when Mr. Woodhouse, with a melancholy shake of the head and a sigh, called his daughter's attention to the sad change at Hartfield since she had been there last.

"Ah! My dear," said he. "Poor Miss Taylor — It is a grievous business!"

"Oh! Yes, sir," cried she with ready sympathy, "how you must miss her! And dear Emma too! What a dreadful loss to you both! I have been so grieved for you. I could not imagine how you could possibly do without her. It is a sad change indeed. But I hope she is well, sir."

"Pretty well, my dear — I hope — pretty well. I do not know but that the place agrees with her tolerably."

"And do you see her, sir, tolerably often?" asked Isabella in the mournful tone which just suited her father.

Mr. Woodhouse hesitated. "Not near so often, my dear, as I could wish."

"Oh! Papa, we have missed seeing them but one entire day since they married. Either in the morning or evening of every day, excepting one, have we seen either Mr. Weston or Mrs. Weston, and generally both, either at Randalls or here. As you may suppose, Isabella, most frequently here. They are very, very kind in their visits. Mr. Weston is really as kind as herself. Papa, if you speak in that melancholy way, you will be giving Isabella a false idea of us all. Everybody must be aware that Miss Taylor is missed, but everybody ought also to be assured that Mr. and Mrs. Weston do really prevent our missing her to the extent we ourselves anticipated — which is the exact truth."

"Just as it should be," said Mr. John Knightley, "and just as I hoped it was from your letters. Her wish of showing you attention could not be doubted, and his being so sociable makes it all easy. I have been always telling you, my love, that I had no idea of the change being so very material to Hartfield as you apprehended. Now that you have Emma's account, I hope you will be satisfied."

"Why to be sure," said Mr. Woodhouse, "yes, certainly — I cannot deny that Mrs. Weston, poor Mrs. Weston does come and see us pretty often — but then she is always obliged to go away again."

"It would be very hard upon Mr. Weston if she did not, papa. You quite forget poor Mr. Weston."

"I think, indeed," said John Knightley pleasantly, "that Mr. Weston has some little claim."

"Had it not been for the misery of her leaving Hartfield," said his wife, "I should never have thought of Miss Taylor but as the most fortunate woman in the world. And I believe Mr. Weston is one of the very best tempered men that ever existed. Excepting yourself and your brother, I do not know his equal for temper. I shall never forget his flying Henry's kite for him that very windy day last Easter — and ever since his particular kindness last September in writing that note, at twelve o'clock at night, on purpose to assure me that there was no scarlet fever at Cobham, I have been convinced there could not be a more feeling heart nor a better man in existence. If anybody can deserve him, it must be Miss Taylor."

"Where is Frank Churchill?" said John Knightley. "Has he been here on this occasion — or has he not?"

"He has not been here yet," replied Emma. "There was a strong expectation of his coming soon after the marriage, but it ended in nothing; and I have not heard him mentioned lately."

"But you should tell them of the letter, my dear," said her father. "He wrote a letter to poor Mrs. Weston, to congratulate her, and a very proper, handsome letter it was. She showed it to me. I thought it very well done indeed. Whether it was his own idea you know, one cannot tell. He is but young, and his uncle perhaps — "

"My dear papa, he is twenty-three. You forget how time passes."

"Twenty-three! Is he, indeed? Well, I could not have thought it; and he was but two years old when he lost his poor mother! Well, time does fly indeed! And my memory is very bad. However, it was an exceedingly good, pretty letter, and gave Mr. and Mrs. Weston a great deal of pleasure. I remember it was written from Weymouth, and dated Sept. 28th, and began, 'My dear Madam,' but I forget how it went on; and it was signed 'F. C. Weston Churchill.' I remember that perfectly."

"How very pleasing and proper of him!" cried the good-hearted Mrs. John Knightley. "I have no doubt of his being a most amiable young man. But how sad it is that he should not live at home with his father! There is something so shocking in a child's being taken away from his parents and natural home! I never can comprehend how Mr. Weston could part with him. To give up one's child! I really never could think well of anybody who proposed such a thing to anybody else."

"Nobody ever did think well of the Churchills, I believe," observed Mr. John Knightley coolly. "But you need not imagine Mr. Weston to have felt what you would feel in giving up Henry or John. Mr. Weston is rather an easy, cheerful tempered man, than a man of strong feelings. He takes things as he finds them, and makes enjoyment of them somehow, depending, I suspect, much more upon socializing for his comforts. That is, upon the power of eating and drinking, and playing whist with his neighbours five times a week, than upon family affection, or anything that home affords."

Emma did not like the way he spoke about Mr. Weston, and had half a mind to contradict him; but she struggled, and let it pass. She would keep the peace if possible.

CHAPTER 12

Mr. Knightley was to dine with them – rather against the preference of Mr. Woodhouse, who did not like that anyone should share with him in Isabella's first day. Emma's sense of right however had decided it; and besides the courtesy that was owed to each brother, she had particular pleasure, from the circumstance of the recent disagreement between Mr. Knightley and herself, in procuring him the proper invitation.

She hoped they might now become friends again. She thought it was time to make up. Making up, perhaps, was not the right term. *She* certainly had not been in the wrong, and *he* would never admit that he had. Concession was out of the question; but it was time to appear to forget that they had ever quarrelled. She hoped it might rather assist the restoration of friendship, that when he came into the room she had one of the children with her – the youngest, a nice little girl about eight months old, who was now making her first visit to Hartfield, and very happy to be in her aunt's arms. It did help, for though he began with grave looks and short questions, he soon talked to them all in the usual way, and took the child out of her arms with perfect amiability. Emma felt they were friends again, and the conviction giving her at first great satisfaction, and then a little sauciness, she could not help saying, as he was admiring the baby,

"What a comfort it is, that we think alike about our nephews and nieces. As to men and women, our opinions are sometimes very different; but with regard to these children, I observe we never disagree."

"If you were as much guided by nature in your estimate of men and women, and as little under the power of imagination and whim in your dealings with them as you are with these children, we might always think alike."

"To be sure — our disagreements must always arise from my being in the wrong."

"Yes," said he, smiling "and for good reason. I was sixteen years old when you were born."

"A material difference then," she replied, "and no doubt you were much my superior in judgment at that period of our lives. But does not the lapse of twenty-one years bring our understandings a good deal nearer?"

"Yes — a good deal *nearer*."

"But still not near enough to give me a chance of being right if we think differently."

"I have still the advantage of you by sixteen years' experience, and by not being a pretty young woman and a spoiled child. Come, my dear Emma, let us be friends and say no more about it. Tell your aunt, little Emma, that she ought to set a better example than to be renewing old grievances, and that if she were not wrong before, she is now."

"That's true," she cried, "very true. Little Emma, grow up a better woman than your aunt. Be infinitely cleverer and not half so conceited. Now, Mr. Knightley, a word or two more, and I will be done. As far as good intentions went, we were *both* right, and I must say that no effects on my side of the argument have yet proved wrong. I only want to know that Mr. Martin is not very, very bitterly disappointed."

"A man cannot be more so," was his short, full answer.

"Ah! Indeed I am very sorry. Come, shake hands with me."

This had just taken place and with great cordiality when John Knightley made his appearance, and "How do you do, George?" and "John, how are you?" succeeded in the true English style, burying under a calmness the real attachment which would have led either of them, if required, to do everything for the good of the other.

The evening was filled with quiet conversation, as Mr. Woodhouse declined cards entirely for the sake of comfortable talk with his dear Isabella. The little party made two natural divisions: on one side he and his daughter, on the other the two Mr. Knightleys. Their subjects were totally distinct, or very rarely mixing, and Emma only occasionally joined in one or the other.

The brothers talked of their own concerns and pursuits, but principally of those of the elder, whose temper was the most communicative, and who was always the greater talker. As a magistrate, he had generally some point of law to consult John about, or, at least, some curious anecdote to give. And as a farmer, he had to tell what every field was to bear next year, and to give all such local information as could not fail of being interesting to a brother whose home it had equally been for most of his life, and whose attachments were strong. The plan of a drain, the change of a fence, the felling of a tree, and the destination of every acre for wheat, turnips, or spring corn, was entered into with as much equality of interest by John as his cooler manners rendered possible. If his willing brother ever left him anything to inquire about, his inquiries even approached a tone of eagerness.

While they were thus comfortably occupied, Mr. Woodhouse was enjoying a full flow of happy regrets and fearful affection with his daughter.

"My poor dear Isabella," said he, fondly taking her hand, and interrupting, for a few moments, her busy labours for her children, "How long it is, how terribly long since you were here! And how tired you must be after your journey! You must go to bed early, my dear – and I recommend a little gruel to you before you go. You and I will have a nice basin of gruel together. My dear Emma, could we all have a little gruel?"

Emma could not allow any such thing, knowing, as she did, that both the Mr. Knightleys were as unpersuadable on that point as herself. Therefore, two basins only were ordered. After a little more praise of gruel, with some wondering at its not being eaten every evening by everybody, he proceeded to say, with an air of grave reflection,

"It was an awkward business, my dear, you spending the autumn at South End instead of coming here. I never had much opinion of the sea air."

"Mr. Wingfield most strenuously recommended it, sir, or we would not have gone. He recommended it for all the children, but particularly for the weakness in little Bella's throat – both sea air and bathing."

"Ah, my dear, but Perry had many doubts about the sea doing her any good; and as to myself, I am perfectly convinced, though perhaps I never told you so before, that the sea is very rarely of use to anybody. I am sure it almost killed me once."

"Come, come," cried Emma, feeling this to be an unsafe subject, "I must beg you not to talk of the sea. It makes me envious and miserable;

I who have never seen it! My dear Isabella, I have not heard you make one inquiry after Mr. Perry yet; and he never forgets you."

"Oh! Good Mr. Perry, how is he, sir?"

"Why, pretty well; but not quite well. Poor Perry has issues of digestion, and he has not time to take care of himself – he tells me he has not time to take care of himself – which is very sad – but he is always wanted all around the county. I suppose there is not a man in such practice anywhere. But then, there is not so clever a man anywhere."

"And Mrs. Perry and the children, how are they? I have a great regard for Mr. Perry. I hope he will be visiting soon. He will be so pleased to see my little ones."

"I hope he will be here tomorrow, for I have a question or two to ask him about myself of some consequence. And, my dear, whenever he comes, you had better let him look at little Bella's throat."

"Oh! My dear sir, her throat is so much better that I have hardly any uneasiness about it. Either bathing has been of the greatest service to her, or else it is to be attributed to an excellent concoction of Mr. Wingfield's, which we have been applying at times ever since August."

"It is not very likely, my dear, that bathing should have been of use to her – "

"You seem to me to have forgotten Mrs. and Miss Bates," said Emma, "I have not heard one inquiry after them."

"Oh! The good Bateses. I am quite ashamed of myself, but you mention them in most of your letters. I hope they are quite well. Good old Mrs. Bates! I will call upon her tomorrow, and take my children. They are always so pleased to see my children. And that excellent Miss Bates! Such thorough worthy people! How are they doing, sir?"

"Why, pretty well, my dear, upon the whole. But poor Mrs. Bates had a bad cold about a month ago."

"How sorry I am! But colds were never as prevalent as they have been this autumn. Mr. Wingfield told me that he had never known them more general or heavy, except when there was an influenza epidemic."

"That has been a good deal the case, my dear; but not to the degree you mention. Perry says that colds have been very general, but not so heavy as he has very often known them in November. Perry does not call it altogether a sickly season."

"No, I do not know that Mr. Wingfield considers it *very* sickly except– "

"Ah! My poor dear child, the truth is, that in London it is always a sickly season. Nobody is healthy in London – nobody can be. It is a dreadful thing to have you forced to live there! So far off! And the air so bad!"

"No, indeed – *we* are not at all in a bad air. Our part of London is so very superior to most others! You must not include us with London in general, my dear sir. The neighbourhood of Brunswick Square is very different from almost all the rest. I would be unwilling, I confess, to live in any other part of town; there is hardly any other that I could be satisfied to have my children in. But Mr. Wingfield thinks the vicinity of Brunswick Square is decidedly the most favourable as to air."

"Ah! My dear, it is not like Hartfield. You make the best of it – but after you have been a week at Hartfield, you are all of you different creatures; you do not look like the same. Now I cannot say that I think you are any of you looking well at present."

"I am sorry to hear you say so, sir; but I assure you, excepting those little nervous headaches and palpitations which I am never entirely free from anywhere, I am quite well myself; and if the children were rather pale before they went to bed, it was only because they were a little more tired than usual, from their journey and the happiness of coming. I hope you will think better of how they look tomorrow; for I assure you Mr. Wingfield told me, that he did not believe he had ever sent us off altogether, in such good condition. I trust, at least, that you do not think Mr. Knightley looks ill," and she turned her eyes with affectionate anxiety towards her husband.

"Middling, my dear; I cannot agree with you. I think Mr. John Knightley very far from looking well."

"What is the matter, sir? Did you speak to me?" cried Mr. John Knightley, hearing his own name.

"I am sorry to find, my love, that my father does not think you are looking well; but I hope it is only from being a little fatigued. I could have wished, however, as you know, that you had seen Mr. Wingfield before you left home."

"My dear Isabella," exclaimed he, hastily, "please do not concern yourself about my looks. Be satisfied with doctoring and coddling yourself and the children, and let me do as I choose."

"I do not thoroughly understand what you were telling your brother," cried Emma, "about your friend Mr. Graham's intending to have a steward from Scotland to look after his new estate. But will it work? Or will the old prejudice be too strong?"

She talked in this way so long and successfully that, when forced to give her attention again to her father and sister, she had nothing worse to hear than Isabella's kind inquiry after Jane Fairfax – and Jane Fairfax, though no great favourite with her in general, she was at that moment very happy to assist in praising.

"That sweet, amiable Jane Fairfax!" said Mrs. John Knightley. "It is so long since I have seen her, except now and then for a moment accidentally in town! What happiness it must be to her good old grandmother and excellent aunt when she comes to visit them! I always regret excessively on dear Emma's account that she cannot be more at Highbury. But now that their daughter is married, I suppose Colonel and Mrs. Campbell will not be able to part with her at all. She would be such a delightful companion for Emma."

Mr. Woodhouse agreed to it all, but added –

"Our little friend Harriet Smith, however, is just such another pretty kind of young person. You will like Harriet. Emma could not have a better companion than Harriet."

"I am most happy to hear it, but Jane Fairfax is so very accomplished and superior, and exactly Emma's age."

This topic was discussed very happily, and others followed with similar harmony; but the evening did not close without a little return of agitation. The gruel came and supplied a great deal to be said – much praise and many comments – undoubting decision of its wholesomeness. But, unfortunately, among the failures which the daughter had to relate, the most recent and therefore most prominent was in her own cook at South End. She was a young woman who never had been able to understand what she meant by a basin of nice smooth gruel: thin, but not too thin. As often as she had wished for and asked for it, she had never been able to get anything tolerable. Here was a dangerous opening.

"Ah!" said Mr. Woodhouse, shaking his head and fixing his eyes on her with tender concern. The sound in Emma's ear expressed, "Ah! There is no end of the sad consequences of your going to South End. It does not bear talking of." And for a little while she hoped he would not talk of it, and that a silent rumination might suffice to restore him to the relish of his own smooth gruel. After an interval of some minutes, however, he began with –

"I shall always be very sorry that you went to the sea this autumn, instead of coming here."

"But why should you be sorry, sir? I assure you, it did the children a great deal of good."

"And, moreover, if you had to go to the sea, it would have been better if it had not been to South End. South End is an unhealthy place. Perry was surprised to hear you had decided upon South End."

"I know there is such an idea with many people, but indeed it is quite a mistake, sir. We all had our health perfectly well there, and never found the least inconvenience from the mud. Mr. Wingfield says it is entirely a mistake to suppose the place unhealthy, and I am sure he may be depended on, for he thoroughly understands the nature of the air, and his own brother and family have been there repeatedly."

"You should have gone to Cromer, my dear, if you went anywhere. Perry spent a week at Cromer once, and he holds it to be the best of all the sea-bathing places. A fine open sea, he says, and very pure air. And, from what I understand, you might have had lodgings there quite away from the sea – a quarter of a mile off – very comfortable. You should have consulted Perry."

"But, my dear sir, the difference of the journey, only consider how great it would have been. A hundred miles, perhaps, instead of forty."

"Ah, my dear, as Perry says, where health is at stake, nothing else should be considered; and if one is to travel, there is little difference between forty miles and a hundred. Better not move at all, better stay in London altogether than travel forty miles to get into a worse air. This is just what Perry said. It seemed to him a very ill-judged measure."

Emma's attempts to stop her father had been vain, and when he had reached such a point as this, she could not wonder at her brother-in-law's speaking out.

"Mr. Perry," said he, in a voice of very strong displeasure, "would do as well to keep his opinion till it is asked for. Why does he make it any business of his, to wonder at what I do? At my taking my family to one part of the coast or another? I may be allowed, I hope, the use of my judgment as well as Mr. Perry. I want his advice no more than his drugs." He paused, and growing cooler in a moment, added, with only sarcastic dryness, "If Mr. Perry can tell me how to convey a wife and five children a distance of a hundred and thirty miles with no greater expense or inconvenience than a distance of forty, I should be as willing to prefer Cromer to South End as he could himself."

"True, true," cried Mr. Knightley, "very true. That's a consideration, indeed. But John, as to what I was telling you of my idea of moving the path to Langham, of turning it more to the right that it may not cut through the home meadows, I cannot conceive any difficulty. I should not attempt it, if it were to be the means of inconvenience to the Highbury people. But if you call to mind exactly the present line of the path – The only way of proving it, however, will be to turn to our maps. I shall see you at the Abbey tomorrow morning I hope, and then we will look them over, and you shall give me your opinion."

Mr. Woodhouse was rather agitated by such harsh reflections on his friend Perry, to whom he had, in fact, though unconsciously, been attributing many of his own feelings and expressions. But the soothing attentions of his daughters gradually removed the present evil, and the immediate alertness of one brother, and better recollections of the other, prevented any renewal of it.

CHAPTER 13

There could hardly be a happier creature in the world than Mrs. John Knightley, in this short visit to Hartfield, going about every morning among her old friends with her five children, and talking over what she had done every evening with her father and sister. She had nothing to wish for, but that the days did not pass so swiftly. It was a delightful visit.

In general, their evenings were less engaged with friends than their mornings, but one dinner engagement could not be avoided. Mr. Weston would not take no for an answer; they must all dine at Randalls one day. Even Mr. Woodhouse was persuaded to think it a positive thing, preferable to a division of the party.

How they were all to be conveyed, he would have made a difficulty if he could, but as his son and daughter's carriage and horses were actually at Hartfield, he was not able to make more than a simple question in that regard. It hardly amounted to a doubt; nor did it take Emma long to convince him that they might find room in one of their carriages for Harriet also.

Harriet, Mr. Elton, and Mr. Knightley were the only persons invited to meet them. The hours were to be early, and the numbers few, Mr. Woodhouse's habits and inclination being consulted in everything.

The evening before this great event (for it was a very great event that Mr. Woodhouse should dine out, on the 24th of December) had been spent by Harriet at Hartfield, and she had gone home with a cold. Emma visited her the next day and found her not well enough to go to Randalls. She was very feverish and had a bad sore throat. Mrs.

Goddard was full of care and affection. Mr. Perry was talked of, and Harriet herself was too ill and low to resist the authority which excluded her from this delightful engagement, though she could not speak of her loss without many tears.

Emma sat with her as long as she could, to attend her during Mrs. Goddard's unavoidable absences, and raise her spirits by representing how much Mr. Elton would be disappointed when he heard of her state. She left her at last tolerably comfortable, in the hopes of his having a most comfortless visit, and of their all missing her very much. She had not advanced many yards from Mrs. Goddard's door when she was met by Mr. Elton himself, evidently coming towards it. As they walked on slowly together in conversation about Harriet – of whom he, on the rumour of considerable illness, had been going to inquire – they were overtaken by Mr. John Knightley returning from the daily visit to Donwell. He was with his two eldest boys, whose healthy, glowing faces showed all the benefit of a country run. They joined company and proceeded together. Emma was just describing the nature of her friend's complaint – "a throat very much inflamed, with a great deal of heat about her, a quick low pulse, and she was sorry to find from Mrs. Goddard that Harriet often had very bad sore throats, and had frequently alarmed her with them." Mr. Elton exclaimed,

"A sore throat! I hope it is not infectious. Has Perry seen her? Indeed, you should take care of yourself as well as of your friend. Let me entreat you to run no risks. Why does not Perry see her?"

Emma, who was not really at all frightened herself, pacified his excess concerns with assurances of Mrs. Goddard's experience and care. But as there must still remain a degree of uneasiness which she could not wish to reason away, she added soon afterwards – as if quite another subject,

"It is so cold, so very cold – and looks and feels so very much like snow, that if it were to any other place or with any other party, I should really try not to go out today, and persuade my father not to venture. But as he has made up his mind, and does not seem to feel the cold himself, I do not like to interfere, as I know it would be so great a disappointment to Mr. and Mrs. Weston. But upon my word, Mr. Elton, you should certainly excuse yourself. You appear to me a little hoarse already, and when you consider what demand of voice and what fatigues tomorrow's sermon will bring, I think it would be no more than common prudence to stay at home and take care of yourself tonight."

Mr. Elton looked as if he did not know what answer to make, which was exactly the case, for though very much gratified by the kind care of such a fair lady, and not liking to resist any advice of hers, he had not really the least inclination to give up the visit. But Emma, too eager and busy in her own previous conceptions and views to hear him impartially, or see him with clear vision, was very well satisfied with his muttering acknowledgment of its being "very cold, certainly very cold," and walked on, rejoicing in having extricated him from Randalls, and secured him the power of sending to inquire after Harriet every hour of the evening.

"You do quite right," said she. "We will make your apologies to Mr. and Mrs. Weston."

But hardly had she spoken when she found her brother was civilly offering a seat in his carriage, if the weather were Mr. Elton's only objection, and Mr. Elton actually accepted the offer with much prompt satisfaction. It was a done thing; Mr. Elton was to go, and never had his broad handsome face expressed more pleasure than at this moment; never had his smile been stronger, nor his eyes more exulting than when he next looked at her.

"Well," said she to herself, "this is most strange! After I had given him an opportunity to decline, to choose to go into company and leave Harriet ill behind! Most strange indeed! But there is, I believe, in many men, especially single men, such an inclination – such a passion for dining out. A dinner engagement is so high on the list of their pleasures, their employments, their dignities, almost their duties, that anything gives way to it, and this must be the case with Mr. Elton. He was a most valuable, amiable, pleasing young man undoubtedly, and very much in love with Harriet; but still, he cannot refuse an invitation, he must dine out whenever he is asked. What a strange thing love is! He can see ready wit in Harriet, but will not dine alone for her."

Soon afterwards, Mr. Elton left them, and she could not but do him the justice of feeling that there was a great deal of sentiment in his manner of naming Harriet at parting; in the tone of his voice while assuring her that he should call at Mrs. Goddard's for news of her fair friend, the last thing before he prepared for the happiness of meeting her again, when he hoped to be able to give a better report; and he sighed and smiled in a way that left the balance of approval much in his favour.

After a few minutes of entire silence between them, John Knightley began with –

"I never in my life saw a man more intent on being agreeable than Mr. Elton. It is downright labour to him where ladies are concerned. With men, he can be rational and unaffected, but when he has ladies to please he will stop at nothing."

"Mr. Elton's manners are not perfect," replied Emma, "but where there is a wish to please, one ought to overlook a great deal. Where a man does his best with only moderate abilities, he will have the advantage over negligent superiority. There is such perfect good temper and good will in Mr. Elton as one cannot but value."

"Yes," said Mr. John Knightley presently, with some slyness, "he seems to have a great deal of good-will towards *you*."

"Me!" she replied with a smile of astonishment. "Are you imagining me to be Mr. Elton's object?"

"Such an imagination has crossed me, I must admit, Emma; and if it never occurred to you before, you may as well take it into consideration now."

"Mr. Elton in love with me! What an idea!"

"I do not say it is so; but you would do well to consider whether it is so or not, and to regulate your behaviour accordingly. I think your manners to him encouraging. I speak as a friend, Emma. You had better look about you, and ascertain what you do, and what you mean to do."

"I thank you, but I assure you that you are quite mistaken. Mr. Elton and I are very good friends, and nothing more." She walked on, amusing herself in the consideration of the blunders which often arise from a partial knowledge of circumstances, of the mistakes which people of high pretensions to judgment are forever falling into; and not very well pleased with her brother-in-law for imagining her blind and ignorant, and in need of advice. He said no more.

Mr. Woodhouse had so completely made up his mind to go to the dinner party, that in spite of the increasing coldness he seemed to have no intention of changing his mind. He went with his eldest daughter in his own carriage, with less apparent consciousness of the weather than either of the others; too full of the wonder of his own going, and too well wrapped up to feel the cold. The weather, however, was severe, and by the time the second carriage was in motion, a few flakes of snow were finding their way down.

Emma soon saw that her companion was not in a good mood. The preparing and the going abroad in such weather, were disagreeable to Mr. John Knightley. He anticipated nothing in the visit that could be at all worth the cost; and the whole of their drive to the Vicarage was spent by him in expressing his discontent.

"A man," said he, "must have a very good opinion of himself when he asks people to leave their own fireside, and encounter such a day as this, for the sake of coming to see him. He must think himself a most agreeable fellow; I could not do such a thing. It is the greatest absurdity – actually snowing at this moment! The folly of not allowing people to be comfortable at home, and the folly of people's not staying comfortably at home when they can! If we were obliged to go out on such an evening as this, by any call of duty or business, what a hardship we should deem it. Yet here we are, probably with rather thinner clothing than usual, setting forward voluntarily, without excuse, in defiance of the voice of nature, which tells man to stay at home. Here we are setting forth to spend five dull hours in another man's house, with nothing to say or to hear that was not said and heard yesterday, and may not be said and heard again tomorrow. Going in dismal weather, to return probably in worse; four horses and four servants taken out for nothing but to convey five idle, shivering creatures into colder rooms and worse company than they might have had at home."

Emma did not find herself equal to give the pleased assent, which no doubt he was in the habit of receiving, to emulate the "Very true, my love," which must have been usually administered by his travelling companion. But she had resolution enough to refrain from making any answer at all. Though she could not be complying, she dreaded being quarrelsome. Her heroism reached only to silence. She allowed him to talk, and wrapped herself up, without opening her lips.

They arrived. The carriage turned, the step was let down, and Mr. Elton, spruce, black, and smiling, was with them instantly. Emma thought with pleasure of some change of subject. Mr. Elton was all obligation and cheerfulness; he was so very cheerful in his civilities indeed, that she began to think he must have received a different account of Harriet from what had reached her. She had sent while dressing, and the answer had been, "Much the same – not better."

"*My* report from Mrs. Goddard's," said she presently, "was not as pleasant as I had hoped. 'Not better,' was *my* answer."

His face lengthened immediately; and his voice was the voice of sentiment as he answered: –

"Oh! No – I am grieved to find – I was on the point of telling you that when I called at Mrs. Goddard's door, which I did the very last thing before I returned to dress, I was told that Miss Smith was not better, by no means better, rather worse. Very much grieved and concerned – I had flattered myself that she must be better after as the medicine I knew had been given in the morning."

Emma smiled and answered – "My visit was of use to her, I hope; but not even I can charm away a sore throat; it is a most severe cold indeed. Mr. Perry has been with her, as you probably heard."

"Yes – I imagined – that is – I did not – "

"He has been used to her having these complaints, and I hope tomorrow morning will bring us both a better report. But it is impossible not to feel uneasiness. Such a sad loss to our party today!"

"Dreadful! Exactly so, indeed. She will be missed every moment."

This was very proper; the sigh which accompanied it was really estimable, but it should have lasted longer. Emma was rather in dismay when only half a minute afterwards he began to speak of other things, and in a voice of the greatest enjoyment.

"What an excellent device," said he, "the use of a sheepskin for carriages. How very comfortable they make it; impossible to feel cold with such precautions. The contrivances of modern days indeed have rendered a gentleman's carriage perfectly complete. One is so fenced and guarded from the weather, that not a breath of air can find its way unpermitted. Weather becomes absolutely of no consequence. It is a very cold afternoon – but in this carriage, we know nothing of the matter. It has even started snowing."

"Yes," said John Knightley, "and I think we shall have a good deal of it."

"Christmas weather," observed Mr. Elton. "Quite seasonable; and extremely fortunate we may think ourselves that it did not begin yesterday, and prevent this day's party, for Mr. Woodhouse would hardly have ventured had there been much snow on the ground; but now it is of no consequence. This is quite the season indeed for friendly meetings. At Christmas, everybody wants their friends around them, and people think little of even the worst weather. I was snowed in at a friend's house once for a week. Nothing could be pleasanter. I went for only one night, and could not get away till a week had passed."

Mr. John Knightley looked as if he did not comprehend the pleasure, but said only, coolly –

"I cannot wish to be snowed in for a week at Randalls."

At another time, Emma might have been amused, but she was too much astonished now at Mr. Elton's spirits for other feelings. Harriet seemed quite forgotten in the expectation of a pleasant party.

"We are sure of excellent fires," continued he, "and everything in the greatest comfort. Charming people, Mr. and Mrs. Weston. Mrs. Weston indeed is much beyond praise, and he is exactly what one values: so hospitable, and so fond of society. It will be a small party, but where small parties consist of the right people, they are perhaps the most agreeable of any. Mr. Weston's dining room does not accommodate more than ten comfortably; and for my part, I would rather, under such circumstances, fall short by two than exceed by two. I think you will agree with me, (turning with a soft air to Emma), I think I shall certainly have your agreement, though Mr. Knightley perhaps, from being used to the large parties of London, may not quite enter into our feelings."

"I know nothing of the large parties of London, sir – I never dine with anybody."

"Indeed! (In a tone of wonder and pity), I had no idea that the law had been so great a slavery. Well, sir, the time must come when you will be paid for all this, when you will have little labour and great enjoyment."

"My first enjoyment," replied John Knightley, as they passed through the gate, "will be to find myself safe at Hartfield again."

CHAPTER 14

Some change of countenance was necessary for each gentleman as they walked into Mrs. Weston's drawing room. Mr. Elton had to compose his joyous looks, and Mr. John Knightley had to cover his ill-humour. Mr. Elton had to smile less, and Mr. John Knightley more, to fit them for the occasion. Emma only might be as nature prompted, and show herself just as happy as she was. To her, it was real enjoyment to be with the Westons. Mr. Weston was a great favourite, and there was not a creature in the world to whom she spoke with such unreserve, as to his wife. There was no one else to whom she related with such conviction of being listened to and understood, of being always interesting and always intelligible, the little affairs, arrangements, perplexities and pleasures of her father and herself. She could tell nothing of Hartfield, in which Mrs. Weston had not an active concern. And half an hour's uninterrupted communication of all those little matters on which the daily happiness of life depends was one of the first gratifications of each. The very sight of Mrs. Weston, her smile, her touch, her voice brought joy to Emma, and she determined to think as little as possible of Mr. Elton's oddities, or of anything else unpleasant, and enjoy all that was enjoyable to the utmost.

The misfortune of Harriet's cold had been pretty well discussed before her arrival. Mr. Woodhouse had been safely seated long enough to tell the story of it, besides all the story of his own and Isabella's coming, and of Emma's being to follow, when the others appeared, and Mrs. Weston, who had been almost wholly engrossed by her attentions to him, was able to turn away and welcome her dear Emma.

Emma's project of forgetting Mr. Elton for a while made her rather sorry to find, when they had all taken their places, that he was close to her. The difficulty was great of driving his strange insensibility towards Harriet from her mind while he not only sat at her elbow, but was smilingly addressing her upon every occasion. Instead of forgetting him, his behaviour was such that she could not avoid wondering, "Can it really be as my brother imagined? Can it be possible for this man to be beginning to transfer his affections from Harriet to me? Absurd and insufferable!" Yet he would be so anxious for her being perfectly warm, would be so interested about her father, and so delighted with Mrs. Weston; and at last would begin talking of her drawings with so much zeal and so little knowledge as seemed terribly like a would-be lover, and made it some effort with her to preserve her good manners. For her own sake she could not be rude; and for Harriet's, in the hope that all would yet turn out right, she was even positively civil. But it was an effort, especially as something was going on amongst the others, in the most overpowering period of Mr. Elton's nonsense, which she particularly wished to listen to. She heard enough to know that Mr. Weston was giving some information about his son. She heard the words "my son," and "Frank," and "my son," repeated several times over; and from a few other half-syllables very much suspected that he was announcing an early visit from his son. But before she could quiet Mr. Elton, the subject was so completely past that any reviving question from her would have been awkward.

Now, in spite of Emma's resolution of never marrying, there was something in the name, in the idea of Mr. Frank Churchill, which always interested her. She had frequently thought – especially since his father's marriage with Miss Taylor – that if she *were* to marry, he was the very person to suit her in age, character and condition. He seemed by this connection between the families quite to belong to her. She could not but suppose it to be a match that everybody who knew them must think of. That Mr. and Mrs. Weston did think of it, she was very strongly persuaded; and though not meaning to be convinced by him, or by anybody else, to give up a situation which she believed more filled with good than any she could change it for, she had a great curiosity to see him, and a decided intention of finding him pleasant. She wanted to be liked by him to a certain degree, and found a sort of pleasure in the idea of their being coupled in their friends' imaginations.

With such sensations, Mr. Elton's attentions were dreadfully ill-timed; but she had the comfort of appearing very polite, while feeling very cross – and of thinking that the rest of the visit could not possibly pass without bringing forward the same information again, or the substance of it, from Mr. Weston. So it proved, for when happily released from Mr. Elton, and seated by Mr. Weston at dinner, he made use of the very first opportunity to say to her –

"We want only two more to be just the right number. I would like to see two more here, – your pretty little friend, Miss Smith, and my son – and then I would say we were quite complete. I believe you did not hear me telling the others in the drawing room that we are expecting Frank? I had a letter from him this morning, and he will be with us within two weeks."

Emma spoke with a very proper degree of pleasure, and agreed with him that the presence of Mr. Frank Churchill and Miss Smith would make their party quite complete.

"He has been wanting to come to us," continued Mr. Weston, "ever since September. Every letter has spoken of it, but he cannot command his own time. He has those to please who must be pleased, and who (between ourselves) are sometimes to be pleased only by a good many sacrifices. But now I have no doubt of seeing him here about the second week of January."

"What a very great pleasure it will be to you! And Mrs. Weston is so anxious to be acquainted with him that she must be almost as happy as you."

"Yes, she would be, but that she thinks there will be another delay. She does not count on his coming so much as I do, but she does not know those involved as well as I do. The case, you see, is – but this is quite between ourselves; I did not mention a syllable of it in the other room. There are secrets in all families, you know – The case is that a party of friends have been invited to pay a visit at Enscombe in January, and that Frank's coming depends upon their visit being postponed. If they are not delayed, he cannot come. But I know they will be, because it is a family that a certain lady of some consequence at Enscombe has a particular dislike to. Though it is thought necessary to invite them once every two or three years, the visits are always postponed when the time for them arrives. I have not the smallest doubt it. I am as confident of seeing Frank here before the middle of January as I am of being here myself. "I am disposed to side with you, Mr. Weston. If you think he will come, I shall think so too, for you know Enscombe."

"Yes – I have some right to that knowledge; though I have never been to the place in my life. She is an odd woman! But I never allow myself to speak ill of her, on Frank's account; for I do believe her to be very fond of him. I used to think she was not capable of being fond of anybody except herself, but she has always been kind to him (in her way – allowing for little whims and caprices, and expecting everything to be as she likes). And it is no small credit, in my opinion, to him, that he should receive such affection. Though I would not say it to anybody else, she has no more heart than a stone to people in general, and a devil of a temper."

Emma liked the subject so well that she began upon it to Mrs. Weston very soon after their moving into the drawing room: wishing her joy, yet observing that she knew the first meeting must make her rather anxious. Mrs. Weston agreed, but added that she should be very glad to know for certain that the first meeting would occur at the time talked of. " I cannot depend upon his coming, " said she "I cannot be as hopeful as Mr. Weston. I am very much afraid that it will all end in nothing. Mr. Weston, I dare say, has been telling you exactly how the matter stands?"

"Yes – it seems to depend upon nothing but the ill-humour of Mrs. Churchill, which I imagine to be the most certain thing in the world."

"Why, Emma!" replied Mrs. Weston, smiling. Then, turning to Isabella, she said, "You must know, my dear Mrs. Knightley, that we are by no means so sure of seeing Mr. Frank Churchill, in my opinion, as his father thinks. It depends entirely upon his aunt's spirits and pleasure; in short, upon her temper. To you – to my two daughters – I may speak the truth. Mrs. Churchill rules at Enscombe, and is a very odd-tempered woman. His coming now depends upon her being willing to spare him."

"Oh, Mrs. Churchill; everybody knows Mrs. Churchill," replied Isabella. " I am sure I never think of that poor young man without the greatest compassion. To be constantly living with an ill-tempered person must be dreadful. It is what we happily have never known anything of, but it must be a life of misery. What a blessing that she never had any children! Poor little creatures, how unhappy she would have made them!"

Emma wished she had been alone with Mrs. Weston. She would then have heard more: Mrs. Weston would speak to her with a degree of unreserve which she would not hazard with Isabella. But at present there was nothing more to be said. Mr. Woodhouse very soon followed them into the drawing room. To be sitting long after dinner was a confinement that he could not endure. Neither wine nor conversation meant anything to him, and gladly did he move to those with whom he was always comfortable.

While he talked to Isabella, however, Emma found an opportunity of saying –

"And so you do not consider this visit from your son as by any means certain. I am sorry for it. The introduction must be unpleasant, whenever it takes place. The sooner it could be over, the better."

"Yes; and every delay makes one more fearful of other delays. Even if this family, the Braithwaites, are put off, I am still afraid that some excuse may be found for disappointing us. I cannot bear to imagine any reluctance on his side, but I am sure there is a great wish on the Churchills' to keep him to themselves. There is jealousy. They are jealous even of his regard for his father. In short, I can feel no certainty of his coming, and I wish Mr. Weston were less hopeful."

"He ought to come," said Emma. "If he could stay only a couple of days, he ought to come; and one can hardly conceive a young man's not having it in his power to do as much as that. A young *woman*, if she falls into bad hands, may be kept at a distance from those she wants to be with; but one cannot comprehend a young *man's* being under such restraint as to not be able to spend a week with his father, if he chooses."

"One ought to be at Enscombe, and know the ways of the family, before one decides upon what he can do," replied Mrs. Weston. "One ought to use the same caution, perhaps, in judging the conduct of any individual of any family; but Enscombe, I believe, certainly must not be judged by general rules. She is so very unreasonable, and everything gives way to her."

"But she is so fond of him; he is so very great a favourite. Now, according to my idea of Mrs. Churchill, it would be most natural, that while she makes no sacrifice for the comfort of the husband, to whom she owes everything, she should frequently be governed by the nephew, to whom she owes nothing at all."

"My dearest Emma, do not pretend, with your sweet temper, to understand a bad one, or to lay down rules for it. I have no doubt of his having, at times, considerable influence; but it may be perfectly impossible for him to know beforehand *when* it will be."

Emma listened, and then coolly said, "I shall not be satisfied unless he comes."

"He may have a great deal of influence on some points," continued Mrs. Weston, "and on others, very little: and among those, it is but too likely, may be this very circumstance of his leaving them to visit us."

CHAPTER 15

Mr. Woodhouse was soon ready for his tea, and when he had finished drinking it he was quite ready to go home. It was as much as his three companions could do to explain away his notice of the lateness of the hour before the other gentlemen appeared. Mr. Weston was chatty and cheerful, and disliked early separations of any sort; but at last the drawing room party did receive an addition. Mr. Elton, in very good spirits, was one of the first to walk in. Mrs. Weston and Emma were sitting together on a sofa. He joined them immediately, and with scarcely an invitation seated himself between them.

Emma, in good spirits too, from the amusement afforded by the expectation of Mr. Frank Churchill, was willing to forget his recent improprieties, and be as well satisfied with him as before. Since he made Harriet his very first subject, she was ready to listen with most friendly smiles.

He professed himself extremely anxious about her fair friend – her fair, lovely, amiable friend. "Did she know? – had she heard anything about her, since their being at Randalls? He felt much anxiety – he must confess that the nature of her complaint alarmed him considerably." And in this style he talked on for some time very properly, altogether sufficiently awake to the terror of a bad sore throat; and Emma was quite pleased with him.

But at last there seemed an unfortunate turn; it seemed all at once as if he were more afraid of its being a bad sore throat on her account than on Harriet's. He was more anxious that she should escape the infection, than that there should be no infection. He began with great earnestness to entreat her to refrain from visiting the sick chamber again, for the present, to entreat her to *promise him* not to venture into such hazard till he had seen Mr. Perry and learned his opinion. Though she tried to laugh it off and bring the subject back into its proper course, there was no putting an end to his extreme solicitude about her. She was vexed. It did appear – there was no concealing it –like he was in love with her instead of Harriet; an inconstancy, if real, the most contemptible and abominable! And she had difficulty keeping her composure. He turned to Mrs. Weston to implore her assistance, "Would she not give him her support? Would not she add her persuasions to his, to convince Miss Woodhouse not to go to Mrs. Goddard's, till it was certain that Miss Smith's disorder was not contagious? He could not be satisfied without a promise – would not she give him her influence in obtaining it?"

"So concerned for others," he continued, "and yet so unworried about herself! She wanted me to nurse my cold by staying at home today, and yet will not promise to avoid the danger of catching a sore throat herself! Is this fair, Mrs. Weston? Judge between us. Have not I some right to complain? I am sure of your kind support and aid."

Emma saw Mrs. Weston's surprise at Mr. Elton's entreaties, which seemed to indicate a love interest. As for herself, she was too much provoked and offended to have the power of directly saying anything in response. She could only give him a look; but it was such a look as she thought must restore him to his senses. She then left the sofa, moving to a seat by her sister, and giving her all her attention.

She had not time to know how Mr. Elton took the reproof, so rapidly did another subject begin. For Mr. John Knightley now entered the room after examining the weather, and announced to them all that the ground was covered with snow, it was still snowing fast, and there was a strong drifting wind. He concluded with these words to Mr. Woodhouse:

"This will prove a spirited beginning of your winter engagements, sir. Something new for your coachman and horses to be making their way through a snowstorm."

Poor Mr. Woodhouse was silent with dread; but everybody else had something to say; everybody was either surprised or not surprised, and had some question to ask, or some comfort to offer. Mrs. Weston and Emma tried earnestly to cheer him and turn his attention from his son-in-law.

"I admired your resolution very much, sir," said he, "in venturing out in such weather, for of course you saw there would be snow very soon. Everybody must have seen the snow coming. I admired your spirit; and I dare say we shall get home very well. Another hour or two's snow can hardly make the road impassable; and we have two carriages. If *one* is blown over, there will be the other at hand. I dare say we shall be all safe at Hartfield before midnight."

Mr. Weston was confessing that he had known it to be snowing for some time, but had not said a word, lest it should make Mr. Woodhouse uncomfortable, and be an excuse for his hurrying away. As to there being any quantity of snow fallen or likely to fall to impede their return, that was a mere joke; he was afraid they would find no difficulty. He wished the road might be impassable, that he might be able to keep them all at Randalls; and with the utmost goodwill was sure that accommodation might be found for everybody.

"What is to be done, my dear Emma? What is to be done?" was Mr. Woodhouse's first exclamation, and all that he could say for some time. To her he looked for comfort; and her assurances of safety, her representation of the excellence of the horses, and of James, and of their having so many friends about them, revived him a little.

His eldest daughter's alarm was equal to his own. The horror of being stuck at Randalls, while her children were at Hartfield, was full in her imagination. Fancying the road to be now just passable for adventurous people, but in a state that admitted no delay, she was eager to have it settled that her father and Emma should remain at Randalls, while she and her husband set forward instantly through all the possible accumulations of drifted snow that might impede them.

"You had better order the carriage immediately, my love," said she. "I dare say we shall be able to get along, if we set off now; and if we do come to anything very bad, I can get out and walk. I am not at all afraid. I should not mind walking half the way. I could change my shoes, you know, the moment I got home."

"Walk home!" replied he. "You are not dressed for walking home, I dare say. It will be bad enough for the horses."

Isabella turned to Mrs. Weston for her approval of the plan. Mrs. Weston could only approve. Isabella then went to Emma; but Emma could not so entirely give up the hope of their being all able to get away. They were still discussing the point when Mr. Knightley, who had left the room immediately after his brother's first report of the snow, came back again, and told them that he had been out of doors to examine, and could answer for there not being the smallest difficulty in their getting home whenever they liked it, either now or an hour later. He had gone beyond the sweep – some way along the Highbury road. The snow was nowhere above half an inch deep – in many places hardly enough to whiten the ground. A very few flakes were falling at present, but the clouds were parting, and there was every appearance of its being soon over. He had seen the coachmen, and they both agreed with him in there being nothing to worry about.

To Isabella, the relief of such tidings was very great, and they were scarcely less acceptable to Emma on her father's account, who was immediately set as much at ease on the subject as his nervous constitution allowed. But the alarm that had been raised could not be appeased so as to admit of any comfort for him while he remained at Randalls. He was satisfied of there being no present danger in returning home, but no assurances could convince him that it was safe to stay; and while the others were variously arguing and recommending, Mr. Knightley and Emma settled it in a few brief sentences –

"Your father will not rest easy; why do not you go?"

"I am ready, if the others are."

"Shall I ring the bell?"

"Yes, do."

The bell was rung, and the carriages requested. A few minutes more, and Emma hoped to see one troublesome companion deposited in his own house, to get sober and cool, and the other recover his temper and happiness when this visit of hardship was over.

The carriages came, and Mr. Woodhouse was carefully attended to his own by Mr. Knightley and Mr. Weston. Not all that either could say could prevent some renewal of alarm at the sight of the snow which had actually fallen, and the discovery of a much darker night than he had been prepared for. "He was afraid they should have a very bad drive. He was afraid poor Isabella would not like it. And there would be poor Emma in the carriage behind. He did not know what they had better do. They must keep as much together as they could." James was talked to, and given a charge to go very slow and wait for the other carriage.

Isabella stepped in after her father; John Knightley, forgetting that he did not belong to their party, stepped in after his wife very naturally, so that Emma found, on being escorted and followed into the second carriage by Mr. Elton, that the door was to be shut on them, and that they were to be alone on the drive. It would not have been the awkwardness of a moment, it would have been rather a pleasure, prior to the suspicions of this very day. She could have talked to him of Harriet, and the three-quarters of a mile would have seemed but one. But now, she would rather it had not happened. She believed he had been drinking too much of Mr. Weston's good wine, and felt sure that he would be talking nonsense.

To restrain him as much as possible, by her own manners, she was immediately preparing to speak with exquisite calmness and gravity of the weather and the night; but scarcely had she begun, scarcely had they passed the front gate and joined the other carriage, than she found her subject cut off – her hand seized – her attention demanded, and Mr. Elton actually expressing his love for her. Availing himself of the precious opportunity, he declared sentiments which must be already well known, hoping – fearing – adoring – ready to die if she refused him; but flattering himself that his attachment and love and passion could not fail of having some effect, and in short, very much resolved on being seriously accepted as soon as possible. It really was so. Without hesitation – without apology – without any apparent reserve, Mr. Elton, the lover of Harriet, was professing himself *her* lover. She tried to stop him, but in vain; he went on, and said it all. Angry as she was, the thought of the moment made her resolve to restrain herself when she did speak. She felt that half this folly must be drunkenness, and therefore could hope that it might belong only to the passing hour. Accordingly, with a mixture of the serious and the playful, which she hoped would best suit his half and half state, she replied –

"I am very much astonished, Mr. Elton. This to *me*! You forget yourself – you take me for my friend – any message to Miss Smith I shall be happy to deliver; but no more of this to *me*, if you please."

"Miss Smith! Message to Miss Smith! What could you possibly mean?"

"Mr. Elton, this is the most extraordinary conduct! And I can account for it only in one way; you are not yourself, or you could not speak either to me, or of Harriet, in such a manner. Command yourself enough to say no more, and I will endeavour to forget it."

But Mr. Elton had only drunk wine enough to elevate his spirits, not at all to confuse his intellect. He perfectly knew his own meaning; and having warmly protested against her suspicion as most injurious, he acknowledged his wonder that Miss Smith should be mentioned at all, and resumed the subject of his own passion, pressing urgently for a favourable answer.

As she thought less of his drunkenness, she thought more of his inconstancy and presumption; and with less effort to be polite, replied,

"It is impossible for me to doubt any longer. You have made yourself too clear. Mr. Elton, my astonishment is much beyond anything I can express. After such behaviour, as I have witnessed during the last month, to Miss Smith — such attentions as I have been in the daily habit of observing — to be addressing me in this manner: this is an unsteadiness of character, indeed, which I had not supposed possible! Believe me, sir, I am far, very far, from gratified in being the object of such professions."

"Good heavens!" cried Mr. Elton. "What can be the meaning of this? Miss Smith! I never thought of Miss Smith in the whole course of my existence — never paid her any attentions, but as your friend: never cared whether she was dead or alive, but as your friend. If she has fancied otherwise, her own wishes have misled her, and I am very sorry — extremely sorry — but, Miss Smith, indeed! Oh! Miss Woodhouse! Who can think of Miss Smith, when Miss Woodhouse is near! No, upon my honour, there is no unsteadiness of character. I have thought only of you. I protest against having paid the smallest attention to anyone else. Everything that I have said or done, for many weeks past, has been with the sole view of marking my adoration of you. You cannot really, seriously, doubt it. No! I am sure you have seen and understood me."

It would be impossible to say what Emma felt, on hearing this, which of all her unpleasant sensations was strongest. She was too completely overpowered to be immediately able to reply: and two moments of silence being ample encouragement for Mr. Elton's hopeful state of mind, he tried to take her hand again, as he joyously exclaimed—

"Charming Miss Woodhouse! Allow me to interpret this interesting silence. It confesses that you have long understood me."

"No, sir," cried Emma. "It confesses no such thing. So far from having long understood you, I have been in a most complete error with respect to your views, till this moment. As to myself, I am very sorry that you should have been giving way to any feelings. Nothing could be farther from my wishes — your attachment to my friend Harriet — your pursuit of her, (pursuit, it appeared), gave me great pleasure, and I have been very earnestly wishing you success. But had I supposed that she was not your attraction to Hartfield, I should certainly have thought you judged ill in making your visits so frequent. Am I to believe that you have never sought to recommend yourself particularly to Miss Smith? That you have never thought seriously of her?"

"Never, madam," cried he, affronted, in his turn. "Never, I assure you. *I* think seriously of Miss Smith! Miss Smith is a very good sort of girl; and I should be happy to see her respectably settled. I wish her extremely well, and, no doubt, there are men who might not object to — everybody has their level. But as for myself, I am not, I think, quite so much at a loss. I need not so totally despair of an equal alliance, as to be addressing myself to Miss Smith! No, madam, my visits to Hartfield have been for yourself only; and the encouragement I received – "

"Encouragement! I give you encouragement! Sir, you have been entirely mistaken in supposing it. I have seen you only as the admirer of my friend. In no other light could you have been more to me than a common acquaintance. I am exceedingly sorry, but it is well that the mistake ends where it does. Had the same behaviour continued, Miss Smith might have been led into a misconception of your views; not being aware, probably, any more than myself, of the very great inequality which you are so sensible of. But, as it is, I hope the disappointment will not be lasting. I have no thoughts of matrimony at present."

He was too angry to say another word, and in this state of swelling resentment, and mutually deep mortification, they had to continue together a few minutes longer, for the fears of Mr. Woodhouse had confined them to a walking pace. If there had not been so much anger, there would have been desperate awkwardness. Without knowing when the carriage turned into Vicarage lane, or when it stopped, they found themselves, all at once, at the door of his house; and he was out before another syllable passed. Emma then felt it necessary to wish him a good night. The compliment was returned coldly and proudly; and, under indescribable irritation, she was then conveyed to Hartfield.

There she was welcomed with the utmost delight by her father, who had been trembling for the dangers of a solitary drive from Vicarage lane – turning a corner which he could never bear to think of – and in strange hands – a mere common coachman – not James. Mr. John Knightley, ashamed of his previous ill-humour, was now all kindness and attention; and so particularly solicitous for the comfort of her father, as to seem – if not quite ready to join him in a basin of gruel – perfectly sensible of its being exceedingly wholesome. The day was concluding in peace and comfort to all their little party, except herself. But her mind had never been in such commotion, and it took great effort to appear attentive and cheerful till the usual hour of separating allowed her the relief of quiet reflection.

CHAPTER 16

Her hair curled and the maid sent away, Emma sat down to think and be miserable. It was a wretched business, indeed! Such a reversal of everything she had been wishing for! Such a development of everything most unwelcome! Such a blow for Harriet! That was the worst of all. Every part of it brought pain and humiliation of some sort or other. But, compared with the evil to Harriet, all that was nothing. She would gladly have submitted to feel yet more mistaken — more in error — more disgraced by misjudgment, than she actually was, could the effects of her blunders have affected only herself.

"If I had not persuaded Harriet to like the man, I could have borne anything. Poor Harriet!"

How could she have been so deceived? He protested that he had never thought seriously of Harriet — never! She looked back as well as she could; but it was all confusion. She had taken up the idea, she supposed, and made everything bend to it. His manners, however, must have been wavering, or she could not have been so misled.

The picture! How eager he had been about the picture! And the charade! And a hundred other circumstances; how clearly they had seemed to point at Harriet. To be sure, the charade, with its "ready wit" — but then, the "soft eyes" — in fact it suited neither; it was a jumble without taste or truth. Who could have seen through such thick-headed nonsense?

Certainly she had often, especially recently, thought his manners to herself unnecessarily gallant; but she thought it a mere error of judgment, as proof that he had not always lived in the best society. With all the gentleness of his manners, true elegance was sometimes wanting. But, till this very day, she had never, for an instant, suspected it to mean anything but grateful respect to her as Harriet's friend.

To Mr. John Knightley was she indebted for her first idea on the subject, for the first start of its possibility. There was no denying that those brothers saw the situation more clearly than she had. She remembered what Mr. Knightley had said to her about Mr. Elton, the caution he had given, the conviction he had professed that Mr. Elton would never marry indiscreetly. She blushed to think how much truer a knowledge of his character had been there shown than any she had reached herself. It was dreadfully mortifying; but Mr. Elton was proving himself, in many respects, the very reverse of what she had believed him. He was proud, assuming, conceited; very full of his own interests, and little concerned about the feelings of others.

Contrary to the usual course of things, Mr. Elton's wanting to pay his addresses to her had sunk him in her opinion. His professions and his proposals did him no service. She thought nothing of his attachment, and was insulted by his hopes. He wanted to marry well, and having the arrogance to raise his eyes to her, pretended to be in love; but she was perfectly easy as to his not suffering any disappointment that she need be concerned about. There had been no real affection either in his language or manners. Sighs and fine words had been given in abundance; but she could hardly devise any set of expressions, or fancy any tone of voice, less aligned with real love. She need not trouble herself to pity him. He only wanted to aggrandize and enrich himself; and if Miss Woodhouse of Hartfield, the heiress of thirty thousand pounds, were not quite so easily obtained as he had believed, he would soon try for Miss Somebody Else with twenty, or with ten.

But, that he should talk of encouragement, should consider her as aware of his views, accepting his attentions, meaning (in short), to marry him! Should suppose himself her equal in connection or mind! Look down upon her friend, so well understanding the variations of rank below him, and be so blind to what rose above, as to believe himself showing no presumption in addressing her! It was most provoking.

Perhaps it was not fair to expect him to feel how very much he was her inferior in talent, and all the elegancies of mind. The very lack of such equality might prevent his perception of it; but he must know that in fortune and influence she was greatly his superior. He must know that the Woodhouses had been settled for several generations at Hartfield, the younger branch of a very ancient family – and that the

Eltons had no such claims. The landed property of Hartfield certainly was inconsiderable, being but a sort of notch in the Donwell Abbey estate, to which all the rest of Highbury belonged. But their fortune, from other sources, was such as to make them scarcely secondary to Donwell Abbey itself, in every other kind of consequence. The Woodhouses had long held a high place in the neighbourhood which Mr. Elton had first entered not two years ago, to make his way as he could, without any alliances but in trade, or anything to recommend him but his clerical position and his civility. But he had believed she was in love with him; that evidently must have been his belief; and after raving a little about the seeming inconsistency of gentle manners and a conceited head, Emma was obliged to stop and admit that her own behaviour to him had been so obliging, so full of courtesy and attention, as might warrant a man like Mr. Elton to believe himself a very decided favourite. If *she* had so misinterpreted his feelings, she had little right to wonder that *he*, with self-interest to blind him, should have mistaken hers.

The first error and the worst lay at her door. It was foolish and wrong to take so active a part in bringing any two people together. It was venturing too far, assuming too much, making light of what ought to be serious, a trick of what ought to be simple. She was quite concerned and ashamed, and resolved to do such things no more.

"Here have I," said she, "actually talked poor Harriet into being very much attached to this man. She might never have thought of him otherwise; and certainly never would have thought of him with hope, if I had not assured her of his attachment, for she is as modest and humble as I used to think him. Oh! That I had been satisfied with persuading her not to accept young Martin. There I was quite right. That was well done of me; but there I should have stopped, and left the rest to time and chance. I was introducing her into good society, and giving her the opportunity of pleasing someone worth having; I ought not to have attempted more. But now, poor girl, her peace is undone for some time. I have been but half a friend to her; and if she were *not* to feel this disappointment so very much, I am sure I have not an idea of anybody else who would be at all desirable for her. William Cox — Oh! No, I could not endure William Cox — a brash young lawyer."

She stopped to blush and laugh at her own relapse, and then resumed a more serious, more dispiriting consideration upon what had been, and might be, and must be. The distressing explanation she had to make to Harriet, and all that poor Harriet would be suffering, with the awkwardness of future meetings, the difficulties of continuing or discontinuing the acquaintance, of subduing feelings and concealing resentment were enough to occupy her in most unhappy reflections some time longer, and she went to bed at last with nothing settled but the conviction of her having erred most dreadfully.

To youth and natural cheerfulness like Emma's, though under temporary gloom at night, the return of day will hardly fail to bring return of spirits. The youth and cheerfulness of morning are a happy analogy; and if the distress be not poignant enough to keep the eyes unclosed, they will be sure to open to sensations of softened pain and brighter hope.

Emma got up on the morrow more disposed for comfort than she had gone to bed, more ready to see an end to the evil before her, and to depend on getting tolerably out of it.

It was a great consolation that Mr. Elton should not be really in love with her, or so particularly amiable as to make it shocking to disappoint him. Harriet's nature was not of that superior sort in which the feelings are most acute, and there was no reason for anybody to know what had passed except the three involved, and especially for her father's being given a moment's uneasiness about it.

These were very cheering thoughts; and the sight of a great deal of snow on the ground did her further service, for anything was welcome that might justify their all three being kept quite apart at present.

The weather was most favourable for her. Though it was Christmas-day, she could not go to church. Mr. Woodhouse would have been miserable had his daughter attempted it. The ground covered with snow, and the atmosphere in that unsettled state between frost and thaw, she was for many days a most honourable prisoner. No communication with Harriet possible except by note; no church for her on Sunday; and no need to find excuses for Mr. Elton's not visiting.

It was weather which might fairly confine everybody at home; and it was very pleasant to have her father so well satisfied with his being all alone in his own house, and to hear him say to Mr. Knightley, whom no weather could keep entirely from them, –

"Ah! Mr. Knightley, why do not you stay at home like poor Mr. Elton?"

These days of confinement would have been, but for her private perplexities, remarkably comfortable, as such seclusion exactly suited her brother-in-law, whose feelings must always be of great importance to his companions. He had so thoroughly cleared off his ill-humour at

Randalls that his amiableness never failed him during the rest of his stay at Hartfield. He was always agreeable and obliging, and speaking pleasantly of everybody. But with all the hopes of cheerfulness, and all the present comfort of delay, there was still such an evil hanging over her in the hour of explanation with Harriet, as made it impossible for Emma to be perfectly at ease.

CHAPTER 17

Mr. and Mrs. John Knightley were not detained long at Hartfield. The weather soon improved enough for those to move who must move. Mr. Woodhouse tried, as usual, to persuade his daughter to stay behind with all her children. But in the end, he was obliged to see the whole party set off, and returned to his lamentations over the destiny of poor Isabella; – which poor Isabella, passing her life with those she doted on, seeing their merits, blind to their faults, and always busy, might have been a model of right feminine happiness.

The evening of the very day on which they went brought a note from Mr. Elton to Mr. Woodhouse. It was a long, civil, ceremonious note, to say, with Mr. Elton's best compliments, "that he was proposing to leave Highbury the following morning in his way to Bath, where he planned to spend a few weeks with friends, and very much regretted the impossibility he was under, from various circumstances of weather and business, of taking a personal leave of Mr. Woodhouse, of whose friendly civilities he should ever retain a grateful sense – and had Mr. Woodhouse any requests, he should be happy to grant them."

Emma was most agreeably surprised. Mr. Elton's absence just at this time was the very thing to be desired. She admired him for arranging it, though she did not give him much credit for the manner in which it was announced. Resentment could not have been more plainly spoken than in a civility to her father, from which she was so pointedly excluded. She had not even a share in his opening compliments. Her name was not mentioned, and there was so striking a change in all this, and such an ill-judged solemnity of leave-taking in his grateful acknowledgments, as she thought, at first, could not escape her father's suspicion.

It did, however. Her father was quite taken up with the surprise of so sudden a journey, and his fears that Mr. Elton might never get safely to the end of it, and saw nothing extraordinary in his language. It was a very useful note, for it supplied them with fresh matter for thought and conversation during the rest of their lonely evening. Mr. Woodhouse talked over his concerns, and Emma was in the mood to persuade them away with all her usual attentiveness.

She now resolved to keep Harriet no longer in the dark. She had reason to believe her nearly recovered from her cold, and it was desirable that she should have as much time as possible for getting over Mr. Elton before the gentleman's return. She went to Mrs. Goddard's the very next day, to undergo the necessary penance of communication; and a severe one it was. She had to destroy all the hopes which she had been so industriously feeding, to confess that she was the one Mr. Elton preferred, and to acknowledge herself grossly mistaken and misjudging in all her ideas on the subject for the last six weeks.

The confession completely renewed her first shame, and the sight of Harriet's tears made her think that she would never be able to forgive herself.

Harriet bore the news very well, blaming nobody. She did not consider herself as having anything to complain of. The affection of such a man as Mr. Elton would have been too great a distinction. She never could have deserved him; and nobody but so partial and kind a friend as Miss Woodhouse would have thought it possible.

Her tears fell abundantly; but her grief was so truly sincere. Emma listened to her and tried to console her with all her heart and understanding – really for the time convinced that Harriet was the superior creature of the two, and that to resemble her would be more for her own welfare and happiness than all that sophistication or intelligence could do.

It was rather too late in the day to set about being simple-minded and ignorant; but she left her with every previous resolution confirmed of being humble and discreet, and repressing imagination all the rest of her life. Her second duty now, inferior only to her father's claims, was to promote Harriet's comfort, and endeavour to prove her own affection in some better method than by matchmaking. She got her to Hartfield, and showed her the most unvarying kindness, striving to occupy and amuse her with books and conversation, to drive Mr. Elton from her thoughts.

Time, she knew, must be allowed for this being thoroughly done; and she could suppose herself but a poor judge of such matters in general, and very inadequate to sympathize in an attachment to Mr. Elton in particular. But it seemed to her reasonable that at Harriet's age, and with the entire extinction of all hope, such a progress might be made towards a state of composure by the time of Mr. Elton's return, as to allow them all to meet again in passing, without any danger of betraying sentiments or increasing them.

Harriet did think him all perfection, and maintain the non-existence of anybody equal to him in person or goodness, and did, in truth, prove herself more resolutely in love than Emma had foreseen. But yet it appeared to her that an inclination of that sort, *unrequited*, could not last long.

If Mr. Elton, on his return, made his own indifference as obvious as she expected him to do, she could not imagine Harriet's persisting to place her happiness in the sight or the recollection of him.

Their being fixed in the same place was bad for each, for all three. Not one of them had the power of removal, or of effecting any material change of society. They must encounter each other, and make the best of it.

Harriet was further unfortunate in the tone of her companions at Mrs. Goddard's; Mr. Elton being the adoration of all the teachers and great girls in the school. It must be at Hartfield only that she could have any chance of hearing him spoken of with cooling moderation or sharp truth. Where the wound had been given, there must the cure be found if anywhere; and Emma felt that, till she saw her accepting the offered cure, there could be no true peace for herself.

CHAPTER 18

Mr. Frank Churchill did not come. When the time proposed drew near, Mrs. Weston's fears were justified in the arrival of a letter of excuse. For the present, he could not be spared, to his "very great mortification and regret; but still he looked forward with the hope of coming soon to Randalls."

Mrs. Weston was exceedingly disappointed – much more disappointed, in fact, than her husband, though she believed he would not come. But a hopeful temper, though forever expecting more good than occurs, soon begins to hope again. For half an hour Mr. Weston was surprised and sorry; but then he began to perceive that Frank's coming two or three months later would be a much better plan; better time of year; better weather; and that he would be able, without any doubt, to stay considerably longer with them than if he had come sooner.

These feelings rapidly restored his comfort, while Mrs. Weston foresaw nothing but a repetition of excuses and delays; and after all her concern for what her husband was to suffer, she suffered a great deal more herself.

Emma was not at this time in a state of spirits to care really about Mr. Frank Churchill's not coming, except as a disappointment at Randalls. The acquaintance at present had no charm for her. She wanted, rather, to keep to herself; but still, as it was desirable that she should appear, in general, like her usual self. So she took care to express as much interest in the circumstance, and enter as warmly into Mr. and

Mrs. Weston's disappointment, as might naturally belong to their friendship.

She was the first to announce it to Mr. Knightley; and exclaimed quite as much as was necessary, (or, being acting a part, perhaps rather more), at the conduct of the Churchills in keeping him away. She then proceeded to say a good deal more than she felt, of the advantage of such an addition to their confined society in Surrey; the pleasure of looking at somebody new, which the sight of him would have made; and ending with reflections on the Churchills again, found herself directly involved in a disagreement with Mr. Knightley. To her great amusement, she perceived that she was taking the other side of the argument from her real opinion.

"The Churchills are very likely at fault," said Mr. Knightley, coolly, "but I dare say he could come if he chose it."

"I do not know why you should say so. He wishes exceedingly to come, but his uncle and aunt will not spare him."

"I cannot believe that he cannot come, if he made a point of it. It is too unlikely for me to believe it without proof."

"How odd you are! What has Mr. Frank Churchill done to make you suppose him such an unnatural creature?"

"I am not supposing him at all an unnatural creature, in suspecting that he may have learned to be above his relations, and to care very little for anything but his own pleasure, from living with those who have always set that example for him. It is a great deal more natural than one could wish that a young man, brought up by those who are proud and selfish, should be proud and selfish too. If Frank Churchill had wanted to see his father, he would have contrived it between September and January. A man at his age – what is he? twenty-three? – cannot be without the means of doing as much as that. It is impossible."

"That's easily said by you, for you have always been your own master. You are the worst judge in the world, Mr. Knightley, of the difficulties of dependence. You do not know what it is to have tempers to manage."

"It is not to be conceived that a man of twenty-three should not have liberty of mind or manner to that degree. He cannot be short of money – he cannot be short of time. We know, on the contrary, that he has so much of both, that he is glad to get rid of them at the idlest haunts in the kingdom. We hear of him forever at some resort or other. A little while ago, he was at Weymouth. This proves that he can leave the Churchills."

"Yes, sometimes he can."

"And those times are whenever he thinks it worth his while; whenever there is any possibility of pleasure."

"It is very unfair to judge anybody's conduct, without an intimate knowledge of their situation. Nobody, who has not been in the interior of a family, can say what the difficulties of any individual of that family may be. We ought to be acquainted with Enscombe, and with Mrs. Churchill's temper, before we pretend to decide what her nephew can do. He may, at times, be able to do a great deal more than he can at others."

"There is one thing, Emma, which a man can always do, if he chooses, and that is his duty. It is Frank Churchill's duty to pay this attention to his father. He knows it to be so, by his promises and messages; but if he wished to do it, it might be done. A man who felt rightly would say at once, simply and resolutely, to Mrs. Churchill, 'Every sacrifice of mere pleasure you will always find me ready to make to your convenience; but I must go and see my father immediately. I know he would be hurt by my failing in such a mark of respect to him on the present occasion. I shall, therefore, set off tomorrow.' If he would say so to her at once, in a decisive manner, there would be no opposition made to his going."

"No," said Emma, laughing, "but perhaps there might be some made to his coming back again. Such language for a young man entirely dependent upon the kind wishes of his guardians to use! Nobody but you, Mr. Knightley, would imagine it possible. But you have not an idea of what is required in situations directly opposite to your own. Mr. Frank Churchill to be making such a speech as that to the uncle and aunt, who have brought him up, and are to provide for him! Standing up in the middle of the room, I suppose, and speaking as loud as he could! How can you imagine such conduct practical?"

"Depend upon it, Emma, a sensible man would find no difficulty in it. He would feel himself in the right; and the declaration – made, of course, as a man of sense would make it, in a proper manner – would do him more good, raise him higher, fix his interest stronger with the people he depended on, than all his attempts to please them. Respect would be added to affection. They would feel that they could trust him; that the nephew, who had done rightly by his father, would do rightly by them. For they know, as well as he does, as well as all the world must know, that he ought to pay this visit to his father. While they insist upon exerting their power to delay it, they are in their hearts not thinking the better of him for submitting to their whims. Respect for right conduct is felt by everybody. If he would act in this sort of manner, on principle, consistently, regularly, their little minds would bend to his."

"I rather doubt that. You are very fond of bending little minds; but where little minds belong to rich people in authority, I think they can become quite as unmanageable as great ones. I can imagine that if you, as you are, Mr. Knightley, were to be transported and placed all at once in Mr. Frank Churchill's situation, you would be able to say and do just what you have been recommending for him; and it might have a very good effect. The Churchills might not have a word to say in return; but then, you would have no habits of early obedience and long observance to break. To him who has, it might not be so easy to burst forth at once into perfect independence, and dismiss all their claims on his gratitude and regard. He may have as strong a sense of what would be right as you can have, without being as able under particular circumstances to act upon it."

"Then, it would not be so strong a sense. If it failed to produce equal exertion, it could not be an equal conviction."

"Oh! The difference of situation and habit! I wish you would try to understand what an amiable young man may be likely to feel in directly opposing those whom as child and boy he has been looking up to all his life."

"Your amiable young man is a very weak young man, if this is the first occasion of his carrying through a resolution to do right against the will of others. It ought to have been a habit with him by this time, of following his duty, instead of pleasing others. I can allow for the fears of the child, but not of the man. As he grew, he ought to have roused himself and shaken off all that was unworthy in their authority. He ought to have opposed the first attempt on their side to make him slight his father. Had he begun as he ought, there would have been no difficulty now."

"We shall never agree about him," cried Emma, "but that is nothing extraordinary. I have not the least idea of his being a weak young man; I feel sure that he is not. Mr. Weston would not be blind to folly, though in his own son; but he is very likely to have a more yielding, complying, mild disposition than would suit your notions of man's perfection. I dare say he has; and though it may cut him off from some advantages, it will secure him many others."

"Yes, all the advantages of sitting still when he ought to move, and of leading a life of mere idle pleasure, and believing himself extremely adept in finding excuses for it. He can sit down and write a fine flourishing letter, full of professions and falsehoods, and persuade himself that he has hit upon the very best method in the world of preserving peace at home and preventing his father's having any right to complain. His letters sicken me."

"Your feelings are singular. The letters seem to satisfy everybody else."

"I suspect they do not satisfy Mrs. Weston. They hardly can satisfy a woman of her good sense and quick feelings; standing in a mother's place, but without a mother's affection to blind her. It is on her account that attention to Randalls is doubly due, and she must doubly feel the omission. Had she been a person of consequence herself, he would have come, I dare say. Can you not think your friend tardy in paying these attentions? Do you suppose she does not often say all this to herself? No, Emma, your "amiable" young man can have very good manners, and be very agreeable; but he can have no delicacy towards the feelings of other people: nothing really amiable about him."

"You seem determined to think poorly of him."

"Me! Not at all," replied Mr. Knightley, rather displeased. "I do not want to think poorly of him. I should be as ready to acknowledge his merits as any other man; but I hear of none, except what are merely personal; that he is well grown and good looking, with smooth manners."

"Well, if he has nothing else to recommend him, he will be a treasure at Highbury. We do not often look upon fine young men, well-bred and agreeable. We must not be particular and ask for all the virtues in the bargain. Can you not imagine, Mr. Knightley, what a *sensation* his coming will produce? There will be but one subject throughout the parishes of Donwell and Highbury; but one interest – one object of curiosity; it will be all Mr. Frank Churchill; we shall think and speak of nobody else."

"You will excuse my being so much overpowered. If I find him capable of good conversation, I shall be glad to have his acquaintance; but if he is only a chattering fool, he will not occupy much of my time or thoughts."

"My idea of him is that he can adapt his conversation to the taste of everybody, and has the power as well as the wish of being universally agreeable. To you, he will talk of farming; to me, of drawing or music; and so on to everybody, having that general information on all subjects which will enable him to follow the lead or take the lead, just as propriety may require, and to speak extremely well on each; that is my idea of him."

"And mine," said Mr. Knightley, "is that if he turns out anything like it, he will be the most insufferable fellow breathing! What? At twenty-three to be the king of his company – the great man – the practised politician, who is to read everybody's character, and make everybody's talents bend to the display of his own superiority. To be dispensing his flatteries around, that he may make all appear like fools compared with himself! My dear Emma, your own good sense could not endure such a man when it came to the point."

"I will say no more about him," cried Emma. "You see the worst in everything. We are both prejudiced; you against, I for him; and we have no chance of agreeing till he is really here."

"Prejudiced! I am not prejudiced."

"But I am very much, and without being at all ashamed of it. My love for Mr. and Mrs. Weston gives me a decided prejudice in his favour."

"He is a person I never think of from one month's end to another," said Mr. Knightley, with a degree of vexation which made Emma immediately talk of something else, though she could not comprehend why he should be angry.

To take a dislike to a young man, only because he appeared to be of a different disposition from himself, was unworthy of him. With all the high opinion of himself, which she had often laid to his charge, she had never before for a moment supposed it could make him blind to the merits of another.

CHAPTER 19

Emma and Harriet had been walking together one morning, and, in Emma's opinion, been talking enough of Mr. Elton for that day. She could not think that Harriet's solace or her own penance required more; and she was therefore industriously ending the subject as they returned. But it burst out again when she thought she had succeeded, and after speaking some time of what the poor must suffer in winter, and receiving no other answer than a very plaintive – "Mr. Elton is so good to the poor!" she found something else must be done.

They were just approaching the house where Mrs. and Miss Bates lived. She determined to call upon them and seek safety in numbers. There was always sufficient reason for such an attention; Mrs. and Miss Bates loved to be visited, and she knew she was considered by the very few who presumed ever to see imperfection in her, as rather negligent in that respect, and as not contributing what she ought to increase their scanty comforts.

She had had many a hint from Mr. Knightley and some from her own heart, as to her deficiency – but none were equal to counteract the persuasion of its being very disagreeable, – a waste of time – tiresome women. This was added to the horror of being in danger of falling in with the second rate and third rate of Highbury, who were always calling on them, and therefore she seldom went near them. But now she made the sudden resolution of not passing their door without going in – observing, as she proposed to Harriet, that, as well as she could calculate, they were just now quite safe from any letter from Jane Fairfax.

The house belonged to people in business. Mrs. and Miss Bates occupied the drawing room floor; and there, in the very moderate sized apartment, which was all they had, the visitors were most cordially and even gratefully welcomed. The quiet, neat old lady, who with her knitting was seated in the warmest corner, offering to give up her place to Miss Woodhouse, and her more active, talking daughter, almost ready to overpower them with care and kindness, thanks for their visit, anxious inquiries after Mr. Woodhouse's health, cheerful communications about her mother's, and sweet-cake from the buffet: — "Mrs. Cole had just been there, intending to stay for ten minutes, and had been so good as to sit an hour with them. She had taken a piece of cake and been so kind as to say she liked it very much; and Miss Bates hoped Miss Woodhouse and Miss Smith would do them the favour to eat a piece too."

The mention of the Coles was sure to be followed by that of Mr. Elton. There was a social connection between them, and Mr. Cole had heard from Mr. Elton since his going away. Emma knew what was coming; they must have the letter over again, and settle how long he had been gone, and how much he was engaged in company, and what a favourite he was wherever he went, and how full the ball had been. She went through it very well, with all the interest and all the commendation that could be required, and always responding to prevent Harriet's being obliged to say a word.

This she had been prepared for when she entered the house; but meant, having once brought him up, to be no farther affected by any troublesome topic, and to wander at large amongst all the Mistresses and Misses of Highbury and their card-parties. She had not been prepared to have the subject of Jane Fairfax succeed Mr. Elton; but she jumped away from him at last abruptly to the Coles, to usher in a letter from her niece.

"Oh! yes — Mr. Elton, I understood — certainly as to dancing — Mrs. Cole was telling me that dancing at the rooms at Bath was — Mrs. Cole was so kind as to sit some time with us, talking of Jane; for as soon as she came in, she began inquiring after her, Jane is so very great a favourite there. Whenever she is with us, Mrs. Cole does not know how to show her kindness enough; and I must say that Jane deserves it as much as anybody can. And so she began inquiring after her directly, saying, 'I know you cannot have heard from Jane lately, because it is not her time for writing,' and when I immediately said, 'But indeed we have, we had a letter this very morning,' I do not know that I ever saw anybody more surprised. 'Have you, upon your honour!' said she. 'Well, that is quite unexpected. Do let me hear what she says.'"

Emma's politeness was at hand directly, to say, with smiling interest–

"Have you heard from Miss Fairfax so recently? I am extremely happy. I hope she is well?"

"Thank you. You are so kind!" replied the happily deceived aunt, while eagerly hunting for the letter. "Oh! here it is. I was sure it could not be far off; but I had put my sewing upon it, you see, without being aware, and so it was quite hidden, but I had it in my hand so very recently that I was almost sure it must be on the table. I was reading it to Mrs. Cole, and since she went away, I was reading it again to my mother, for it is such a pleasure to her – a letter from Jane – that she can never hear it often enough. I knew it could not be far off, and here it is, only just under my sewing – and since you are so kind as to wish to hear what she says; – but, first of all, I really must, in justice to Jane, apologise for her writing so short a letter – only two pages, you see, hardly two, and in general she fills the whole paper and crosses half. My mother often wonders that I can make it out so well. She often says, when the letter is first opened, 'Well, Hetty, now I think you will have your work cut out for you, trying to make sense of all that confusion' – don't you, ma'am? And then I tell her, I am sure she would contrive to make it out herself, if she had nobody to do it for her, every word of it – I am sure she would pore over it till she had made out every word. And, indeed, though my mother's eyes are not as good as they once were, she can see amazingly well still, with the help of spectacles. It is such a blessing! My mother's are really very good indeed. Jane often says, when she is here, 'I am sure, grandma, you must have had very strong eyes to see as you do, and so much fine needlework as you have done too! I only wish my eyes may last me as well.'"

All this spoken extremely fast obliged Miss Bates to stop for breath, and Emma said something very civil about the excellence of Miss Fairfax's handwriting.

"You are extremely kind," replied Miss Bates highly gratified; "you who write so beautifully yourself. I am sure there is nobody's praise that could give us so much pleasure as Miss Woodhouse's. My mother does not hear; she is a little deaf you know. Ma'am," addressing her, "do you hear what Miss Woodhouse is so obliging to say about Jane's handwriting?"

And Emma had the advantage of hearing her own silly compliment repeated twice over before the good old lady could comprehend it. She was pondering, in the meantime, upon the possibility, without seeming very rude, of making her escape from Jane Fairfax's letter, and had almost resolved on hurrying away directly under some flimsy excuse, when Miss Bates turned to her again and seized her attention.

"My mother's deafness is very trifling you see, just nothing at all. By only raising my voice, and saying anything two or three times over, she is sure to hear; but then she is used to my voice. But it is very remarkable that she should always hear Jane better than she does me. Jane speaks so distinctly! However, she will not find her grandma at all deafer than she was two years ago; which is saying a great deal at my mother's time of life. It really has been two years, you know, since she was here. We never were so long without seeing her before."

"Are you expecting Miss Fairfax here soon?"

"Oh, yes, next week."

"Indeed! That must be a very great pleasure."

"Thank you. You are very kind. Yes, next week. Everybody is so surprised; and everybody says the same obliging things. I am sure she will be as happy to see her friends at Highbury as they can be to see her. Yes, Friday or Saturday; she cannot say which, because Colonel Campbell will be wanting the carriage himself one of those days. So very good of them to send her the whole way! But they always do, you know. Oh, yes, Friday or Saturday next. That is what she writes about. That is the reason of her writing so unexpectedly, for we did not think we would hear from her until next Tuesday or Wednesday."

"Yes, so I imagined. I was afraid there could be little chance of my hearing anything of Miss Fairfax today."

"So obliging of you! No, we should not have heard, if it had not been for this particular circumstance, of her planning to come here so soon. My mother is so delighted, for she is to be three months with us at least. Three months, she says, as I am going to have the pleasure of reading to you. The case is, you see, that the Campbells are going to Ireland. Mrs. Dixon has persuaded her father and mother to come over and see her immediately. They had not intended to go over till the summer, but she is so impatient to see them again – for till she married, last October, she was never away from them so much as a week, which must make it very strange to be in different countries, and so she wrote a very urgent letter to her mother – or her father, I declare I do not know which it was, but we shall see presently in Jane's letter – wrote in

Mr. Dixon's name as well as her own, to encourage them to come over immediately, and they would meet them in Dublin, and take them back to their estate, Balycraig, a beautiful place, I fancy. Jane has heard a great deal of its beauty; from Mr. Dixon I mean – I do not know that she ever heard about it from anybody else; but it was very natural, you know, that he should like to speak of his own place while he was courting – and as Jane used to be very often walking out with them – for Colonel and Mrs. Campbell were very particular about their daughter's not walking out often with only Mr. Dixon, for which I do not at all blame them; of course she heard everything he might be telling Miss Campbell about his own home in Ireland. And I think she wrote us word that he had shown them some drawings of the place, views that he had taken himself. He is a most amiable, charming young man, I believe. Jane was longing to go to Ireland, from his account of things."

At this moment, an ingenious and animating suspicion entering Emma's brain with regard to Jane Fairfax, this charming Mr. Dixon, and the not going to Ireland. She said, with the insidious design of further discovery,

"You must feel it very fortunate that Miss Fairfax should be allowed to come to you at such a time. Considering the very particular friendship between her and Mrs. Dixon, you could hardly have expected her to be excused from accompanying Colonel and Mrs. Campbell."

"Very true, very true, indeed. The very thing that we have always been rather afraid of; for we should not have liked to have her at such a distance from us, for months at a time – not able to come if anything was to happen. But you see, everything turns out for the best. They want her (Mr. and Mrs. Dixon) excessively to come over with Colonel and Mrs. Campbell. Depend upon it, nothing can be more kind or pressing than their *joint* invitation, Jane says, as you will hear presently. Mr. Dixon does not seem in the least backward in any attention. He is a most charming young man. Ever since the service he rendered Jane at Weymouth, when they were out in that party on the water, and she, by the sudden whirling around of something or other among the sails, would have been dashed into the sea at once, and actually was all but gone, if he had not, with the greatest presence of mind, caught hold of her dress – (I can never think of it without trembling!) – but ever since that day, I have been so fond of Mr. Dixon!"

"In spite of all her friend's urgency, however, and her own wish of seeing Ireland, Miss Fairfax prefers devoting the time to you and Mrs. Bates?"

"Yes – entirely her own doing, entirely her own choice; and Colonel and Mrs. Campbell think she does quite right, just what they would recommend. Indeed, they particularly wish her to try her native air, as she has not been feeling well lately."

"I am concerned to hear of it. I think they judge wisely. But Mrs. Dixon must be very much disappointed. Mrs. Dixon, I understand, has no remarkable degree of personal beauty; is not, by any means, to be compared with Miss Fairfax."

"Oh, no. You are very obliging to say such things, but certainly not. There is no comparison between them. Miss Campbell always was absolutely plain – but extremely elegant and amiable."

"Yes, that of course."

"Jane caught a bad cold, poor thing! As long ago as the 7th November (as I am going to read to you), and has never been well since. A long time, is not it, for a cold to be upon her? She never mentioned it before, because she did not want to alarm us. Just like her! So considerate! But she is so far from well that her kind friends the Campbells think she had better come home, and try an air that always agrees with her. They have no doubt that three or four months at Highbury will entirely cure her – and it is certainly a great deal better that she should come here than go to Ireland if she is unwell. Nobody could nurse her back to health, the way we can."

"It appears to me the most desirable arrangement in the world."

"And so she is to come to us next Friday or Saturday, and the Campbells leave town in their way to Holyhead the Monday following, as you will find from Jane's letter. So sudden! You may guess, dear Miss Woodhouse, what a flurry it has thrown me in! If it was not for the drawback of her illness – but I am afraid we must expect to see her grown thin, and looking very unwell. I must tell you what an unlucky thing happened to me, as to that. I always make a point of reading Jane's letters through to myself first, before I read them aloud to my mother, you know, for fear of there being anything in them to distress her. Jane asked me to do it, so I always do. And so I began today with my usual caution, but no sooner did I come to the mention of her being unwell than I burst out quite frightened with, 'Bless me! Poor Jane is ill!' which my mother, being on the watch, heard distinctly, and was sadly alarmed at. However, when I read on, I found it was not nearly as bad as I thought at first; and I make so light of it now to her, that she does not think much about it. But I cannot imagine how I could be so off my guard! If Jane does not get well soon, we will call in Mr. Perry. The expense shall not be thought of; and though he is so generous, and so fond of Jane that I dare say he would not charge anything, we could not allow it to be so, you know. He has a wife and family to provide for, and is not to be giving away his time. Well, now that I have just given you a hint of what Jane writes about, we will turn to her letter, and I am sure she tells her own story a great deal better than I can tell it for her."

"I am afraid we must be running away," said Emma, glancing at Harriet and beginning to rise. "My father will be expecting us. I thought I could not stay for more than five minutes when I first entered the house. I merely called because I cannot pass the door without inquiring after Mrs. Bates; but I have been so pleasantly detained! Now, however, we must wish you and Mrs. Bates good morning."

And no effort to detain her succeeded. She regained the street — happy in this, that though much had been forced on her against her will, though she had in fact heard the whole substance of Jane Fairfax's letter, she had been able to escape the letter itself.

CHAPTER 20

Jane Fairfax was an orphan, the only child of Mrs. Bates' youngest daughter.

The marriage of Lieutenant Fairfax and Miss Jane Bates had had its day of fame and pleasure, but nothing now remained of it but the sad memory of him dying in action abroad and of his widow dying of grief and tuberculosis soon afterwards.

By birth Jane belonged to Highbury. At three years old, upon losing her mother, she became the property, the charge, and the consolation of her grandmother and aunt. There had seemed every probability of her being permanently situated there; of her being taught only what very limited means would allow, and of growing up with no advantages of connection or education. Fate had given her only a good understanding, a pleasing personality and warmhearted, well-meaning relations.

The compassionate feelings of a friend of her father changed her destiny. This was Colonel Campbell, who had very highly regarded Fairfax as an excellent officer and most deserving young man. In fact, he credited him for saving his life during a severe camp-fever. These were claims which he had not forgotten, though it was some years before his own return to England made it possible for him to provide any assistance. When he did return, he sought out the child and took notice of her. He was a married man, with only one living child, a girl about Jane's age. Jane became their guest, paying them long visits and becoming a favourite with all. Before she was nine years old, his daughter's great fondness for her, and his own wish of being a real friend, united to produce an offer from Colonel Campbell of undertaking the whole charge of her education. It was accepted, and from that period Jane had belonged to Colonel Campbell's family. She had lived with them entirely, only visiting her grandmother from time to time.

The plan was that she should be brought up to be a governess, since the very few hundred pounds which she inherited from her father made independence impossible. To provide for her otherwise was out of Colonel Campbell's power. Though his income was sizable, his fortune was moderate and must be all his daughter's. But by giving Jane an education, he hoped to supply the means of respectable subsistence hereafter.

Such was Jane Fairfax's history. She had fallen into good hands, known nothing but kindness from the Campbells, and been given an excellent education. Living constantly with right-minded and well-informed people, her heart and understanding had received every advantage of discipline and culture. Colonel Campbell's residence being in London, she had ample opportunity to develop her talents under the tutelage of first-rate masters. At eighteen or nineteen she was, as far as such an early age can be qualified for the care of children, ready to begin her new life, but she was too much beloved to be parted with. The sad day was put off. It was easy to say that she was still too young, and Jane remained with them, sharing, as another daughter, in all the rational pleasures of elegant society, and a judicious mixture of home and social amusements. The only drawback of this arrangement was the sobering suggestions of her own good understanding to remind her that all this might soon be over.

The affection of the whole family, the warm attachment of Miss Campbell in particular, was the more honourable from the circumstance of Jane's decided superiority both in beauty and ability. That nature had given it in feature could not be unseen by the young woman, nor could her stronger intellect be unnoticed by the parents. They continued together with undiminished regard however, till the marriage of Miss Campbell, who had engaged the affection of Mr. Dixon, a rich and agreeable young man.

This event had very recently taken place; too recently for any employment to be sought by her less fortunate friend. Jane had long resolved that twenty-one should be the age at which her search for a suitable situation would begin. The good sense of Colonel and Mrs. Campbell could not oppose such a resolution, though their feelings did. As long as they lived, no exertions would be necessary. Their home might be hers forever, and for their own comfort they would have retained her wholly. But this would be selfishness – what must eventually come may as well come soon. Perhaps they began to feel it might have been kinder and wiser to have resisted the temptation of any delay and spared her from a taste of such enjoyments of ease and leisure as must now be given up. Still, however, affection was glad to look for any reasonable excuse for not hastening the wretched moment. She had never been quite well since the time of their daughter's marriage, and till she should have completely recovered her usual strength, they must prevent her a little longer from engaging in her duties.

With regard to her not accompanying them to Ireland, her account to her aunt contained nothing but truth, though perhaps not the whole of it. She decided to spend the time of their absence in Highbury. It would be, perhaps, her last months of perfect liberty with those kind relations to whom she was so very dear. The Campbells, whatever might be their motives, approved the arrangement and said that they depended more on a few months spent in her native air for the recovery of her health than on anything else. Thus Highbury, instead of welcoming that perfect novelty which had been so long promised it – Mr. Frank Churchill – must put up for the present with Jane Fairfax, who could bring only the freshness of a two-year absence.

Emma was sorry to have to pay civilities to a person she did not like through three long months! She was forever doing more than she wished, and less than she ought. Why she did not like Jane Fairfax was a difficult question to answer. Mr. Knightley had once told her it was because she saw in her the really accomplished young woman which she wanted to be thought of herself. Though the accusation had been eagerly refuted at the time, there were moments of self-examination in which her conscience could not quite deny it. But she could never get acquainted with her. There was such coldness and reserve; such apparent indifference whether she pleased or not; and then, her aunt was such an eternal talker! And she was made such a fuss with by everybody! It had always been imagined that they were to be such good friends, because they were the same age. Everybody had supposed they must become fond of each other. These were her reasons for not liking her; she had no better.

It was a dislike so unjust – every supposed fault was so magnified by imagination – that she never saw Jane Fairfax the first time after any considerable absence without feeling guilty. Now, when the due visit was paid on her arrival, she was particularly struck with the very appearance and manners which for two whole years she had been deploring. Jane Fairfax was very elegant, and she had herself the highest value for elegance. Her height was just right, tall but not too tall; her figure was particularly graceful; her size was a most becoming medium between fat and thin, though she had a slight appearance of ill-health. Emma could not but feel all this; and then, her face – her features – there was more beauty in them all together than she had remembered. Her eyes were a deep grey, with dark eye-lashes and eye-brows. Her skin, which she had previously felt needed more colour, had a clearness and delicacy which really needed no fuller bloom. She could not help but admire the elegance which, whether of person or of mind, she saw so little in Highbury.

In short, she sat, during the first visit, and determined that she would dislike her no longer. When she took in her history, indeed, her difficult situation as well as her beauty, it seemed impossible to feel anything but compassion and respect. Upon the whole, Emma left her with such softened, charitable feelings, as made her look around in walking home and lament that Highbury afforded no young man worthy of giving Jane independence.

These were charming feelings, but not lasting. Before she had committed herself by any public profession of eternal friendship for Jane Fairfax, or done more towards a retraction of past prejudices and errors, than saying to Mr. Knightley, "She certainly is beautiful; she is better than beautiful!" Jane had spent an evening at Hartfield with her grandmother and aunt, and everything was returning to its usual state. Former provocations reappeared. The aunt was as tiresome as ever; more tiresome, because anxiety for Jane's health was now added to admiration of her abilities; and they had to listen to the description of exactly how little bread and butter she ate for breakfast, and how small a slice of mutton for dinner, as well as to see exhibitions of new caps and new workbags for her mother and herself; and Jane's offences rose again. They had music; Emma was obliged to play. The thanks and praise which necessarily followed appeared to be more out of obligation than true appreciation. Jane's performance was far superior. But throughout the evening she was so cold, so cautious! There was no getting at her real opinion. Wrapped up in a cloak of politeness, she was suspiciously reserved.

She was more reserved on the subject of Weymouth and the Dixons than anything else. She seemed determined to give no real insight into

Mr. Dixon's character or her own assessment of his company or the suitableness of the match. It was all vague approval and smoothness.

Similar reserve prevailed on other topics. She and Mr. Frank Churchill had been at Weymouth at the same time. It was known that they were a little acquainted, but not a syllable of real information could Emma extract as to what he truly was. "Was he handsome?" – "She believed he was reckoned a very fine young man." "Was he agreeable?" – "He was generally thought so." "Did he appear to be a sensible, intelligent young man?" – "At a watering-place, or in a common London acquaintance, it was difficult to say. Manners were all that could be safely judged, and she believed everybody found his manners pleasing." Emma could not forgive her.

CHAPTER 21

Emma could not forgive her, but Mr. Knightley, who had been of the party, had seen only proper attention and pleasing behaviour on each side. He was expressing his approval the next morning, being at Hartfield again on business with Mr. Woodhouse. He had thought her unjust to Jane in the past, and now had great pleasure in noticing an improvement.

"A very pleasant evening," he began, as soon as he had concluded his business with Mr. Woodhouse, "particularly pleasant. You and Miss Fairfax gave us some very good music. I do not know a more enjoyable state, sir, than sitting at one's ease to be entertained a whole evening by two such young women; sometimes with music and sometimes with conversation. I am sure Miss Fairfax must have found the evening pleasant, Emma. I was glad you made her play so much, for having no piano at her grandmother's, it must have been a real pleasure."

"I am happy you approved," said Emma, smiling, "but I hope I am not often deficient in what is due to guests at Hartfield."

"No, my dear," said her father instantly; "*that* I am sure you are not. There is nobody half so attentive and civil as you are. If anything, you are too attentive. The muffins last night – if they had been handed around once, I think it would have been enough."

"No," said Mr. Knightley, nearly at the same time, "you are not often deficient either in manner or comprehension. I think you understand me, therefore."

A mischievous look expressed, "I understand you well enough," but she said only, "Miss Fairfax is reserved."

"I always told you she was – a little, but you will soon overcome all that part of her reserve which ought to be overcome."

"You think her shy. I do not see it."

"My dear Emma," said he, moving from his chair into one close by her, "you are not going to tell me, I hope, that you did not have a pleasant evening."

"Oh, no! I was pleased with my own perseverance in asking questions, and amused to think how little information I obtained."

"I am disappointed," was his only answer.

"I hope everybody had a pleasant evening," said Mr. Woodhouse, in his quiet way. "I did. Once, I felt the fire rather too much, but then I moved back my chair a little, a very little, and it did not disturb me. Miss Bates was very chatty and good-humoured, as she always is, though she speaks rather too quickly. However, she is very agreeable, and Mrs. Bates too, in a different way. I like old friends, and Miss Jane Fairfax is a very pretty sort of young lady. She must have found the evening agreeable, Mr. Knightley, because she had Emma."

"True, sir, and Emma, because she had Miss Fairfax."

Emma saw his concern, and wishing to appease it, at least for the present, said, and with a sincerity which no one could question –

"She is a sort of elegant creature that one cannot keep one's eyes from. I am always watching her to admire, and I do genuinely pity her."

Mr. Knightley looked as if he were more gratified than he cared to express, and before he could make any reply, Mr. Woodhouse, whose thoughts were on the Bates', said –

"It is a great pity that they should be so poor! A great pity indeed. We have killed a pig, and Emma thinks of sending them a loin or a leg. I think we had better send the leg – do not you think so, my dear?"

"My dear papa, I sent the whole hind-quarter. I knew you would wish it. There will be the leg to be salted, you know, which is so very nice, and the loin to be prepared immediately in any manner they like."

"That's right, my dear, very right. I had not thought of it before, but that was the best way. They must not over-salt the leg; and then, if it is not over-salted, and if it is very thoroughly boiled, and eaten very moderately with a boiled turnip and a little carrot or parsnip, I do not consider it unwholesome."

"Emma," said Mr. Knightley presently, "I have a piece of news for you. You like news – and I heard something on my way here that I think will interest you."

"News! Oh! Yes, I always like news. What is it? Why do you smile so? Where did you hear it? At Randalls?"

He had time only to say,

"No, not at Randalls; I have not been near Randalls," when the door was thrown open, and Miss Bates and Miss Fairfax walked into the room. Full of thanks and full of news, Miss Bates knew not which to give first. Mr. Knightley soon saw that he had lost his moment, and not another syllable of communication would now escape him.

"Oh! My dear sir, how are you this morning? My dear Miss Woodhouse – I am quite overwhelmed. Such a beautiful hind-quarter of pork! You are too kind! Have you heard the news? Mr. Elton is going to be married."

Emma had not had time to think of Mr. Elton, and she was so completely surprised that she could not avoid a little start, and a little blush, at the mention of his name.

"There is my news – I thought it would interest you," said Mr. Knightley with a smile.

"But where could *you* hear it?" cried Miss Bates. "Where could you possibly hear it, Mr. Knightley? For it is not five minutes since I received Mrs. Cole's note – no, it cannot be more than five – or at least ten – for I had got my bonnet and jacket on, just ready to come out – I was only gone down to speak to Patty again about the pork – Jane was standing in the passage – were not you, Jane? For my mother was so afraid that we had not any salting-pan large enough. So I said I would go down and see, and Jane said, 'Shall I go down instead?' 'Oh! my dear,' said I – well, and just then came the note. A Miss Hawkins – that's all I know. A Miss Hawkins of Bath. But, Mr. Knightley, how could you possibly have heard it? For the very moment Mr. Cole told Mrs. Cole of it, she sat down and wrote to me. A Miss Hawkins–"

"I was with Mr. Cole on business an hour and half ago. He had just read Elton's letter as I was shown in, and handed it to me."

"Well! That is quite – I suppose there never was a piece of news more generally interesting. My dear sir, you really are too kind. My mother desires her very best compliments and regards, and a thousand thanks, and says you really quite spoil her."

"We consider our Hartfield pork," replied Mr. Woodhouse – "indeed it certainly is, so very superior to all other pork, that Emma and I cannot have a greater pleasure than – "

"Oh! my dear sir, as my mother says, our friends are only too good to us. If ever there were people who, without having great wealth themselves, had everything they could wish for, I am sure it is us. Well, Mr. Knightley, and so you actually saw the letter. Well – "

"It was short, merely to announce – but cheerful, of course." – Here was a sly glance at Emma. "The information was, as you state, that he was going to be married to a Miss Hawkins. I imagine it had just been settled upon."

"Mr. Elton going to be married!" said Emma, as soon as she could speak. "He will have everybody's wishes for his happiness."

"He is very young to settle," was Mr. Woodhouse's observation. "He had better not be in a hurry. He seemed to me very well off as he was. We were always glad to see him at Hartfield."

"A new neighbour for us all, Miss Woodhouse!" said Miss Bates, joyfully. "My mother is so pleased! She says she cannot bear to have the poor old Vicarage without a mistress. This is great news, indeed. Jane, you have never met Mr. Elton! No wonder that you have such a curiosity to see him."

Jane's curiosity did not appear of that absorbing nature as wholly to occupy her.

"No – I have never seen Mr. Elton," she replied. "Is he a tall man?"

"Who can answer that question?" cried Emma. "My father would say 'yes,' Mr. Knightley, 'no,' and Miss Bates and I would say that he is just the happy medium. When you have been here a little longer, Miss Fairfax, you will understand that Mr. Elton is the standard of perfection in Highbury, both in person and mind."

"Very true, Miss Woodhouse, so she will. He is the very best young man – But, my dear Jane, if you remember, I told you yesterday he was precisely the height of Mr. Perry. Miss Hawkins, I dare say, is a very lucky young woman. His extreme attention to my mother – wanting her to sit in the front pew, that she might hear better, for my mother is a little deaf, you know. Jane says that Colonel Campbell is a little deaf. He fancied bathing might be good for it – the warm bath – but she says it did him no lasting benefit. Colonel Campbell, you know, is quite our benefactor. And Mr. Dixon seems to be a very charming young man, quite worthy of him. It is such a happiness when good people get together – and they always do. Now, here will be Mr. Elton and Miss Hawkins; and there are the Coles, such very good people; and the Perrys – I suppose there never was a happier or a better couple than Mr. and Mrs. Perry. I say, sir," turning to Mr. Woodhouse, "I think there are few places with such society as Highbury. I always say, we are quite blessed in our neighbours. My dear sir, if there is one thing my mother loves better than another, it is pork – a roast loin of pork –"

"As to who, or what Miss Hawkins is, or how long he has been acquainted with her," said Emma, "nothing I suppose can be known. One feels that it cannot be a very long acquaintance. He has been gone only four weeks."

Nobody had any information to give, and after a few more wonderings, Emma said,

"You are silent, Miss Fairfax – but I hope you mean to take an interest in this news. You, who have been hearing and seeing so much of late on these subjects, who must have been so deep in the business on Miss Campbell's account – we shall not excuse your being indifferent about Mr. Elton and Miss Hawkins."

"When I have seen Mr. Elton," replied Jane, "I dare say I shall be interested. And as it is some months since Miss Campbell married, the impression may be a little worn off."

"Yes, he has been gone just four weeks, as you observe, Miss Woodhouse," said Miss Bates, "four weeks yesterday. A Miss Hawkins. Well, I had always rather fancied it would be some young lady hereabouts; not that I ever – Mrs. Cole once whispered to me – but I immediately said, 'No, Mr. Elton is a most worthy young man – but' – In short, I do not think I am particularly quick at those sorts of discoveries. I do not pretend to it. What is before me, I see. At the same time, nobody could wonder if Mr. Elton should have aspired – Miss Woodhouse lets me chatter on, so good-humouredly. She knows I would not offend for the world. How is Miss Smith doing? She seems quite recovered now. Have you heard from Mrs. John Knightley lately? Oh! Those dear little children. Jane, do you know I always think Mr. Dixon must be like Mr. John Knightley? I mean in person – tall, and with that sort of look – and not very talkative."

"Quite wrong, my dear aunt; there is no likeness at all."

"Very odd! But one never does form a true idea of anybody beforehand. One takes up a notion, and runs away with it. Mr. Dixon, you say, is not, strictly speaking, handsome."

"Handsome! Oh no – far from it – certainly plain. I told you he was plain."

"My dear, you said that Miss Campbell would not allow him to be plain, and that you yourself – "

"Oh! As for me, my judgment is worth nothing. I always think a person I like is good-looking. But I gave what I believed the general opinion when I called him plain."

"Well, my dear Jane, I believe we must be running away. The weather does not look good, and grandma will be uneasy. You are too obliging, my dear Miss Woodhouse; but we really must leave. This has been a most agreeable piece of news indeed. I shall just go around by Mrs. Cole's; but I shall not stop three minutes. And, Jane, you had better go home immediately – I would not have you out in a shower! We think her health is better already. Thank you, we do indeed. I shall not attempt calling on Mrs. Goddard, for I really do not think she cares for anything but *boiled* pork. When we prepare the leg it will be another thing. Good morning to you, my dear sir. Oh! Mr. Knightley is coming too. Well, that is so very – I am sure if Jane is tired, you will be so kind as to give her your arm. Mr. Elton, and Miss Hawkins. Good morning to you."

Emma, alone with her father, had half her attention wanted by him, while he lamented that young people would be in such a hurry to marry – and to marry strangers too – and the other half she could give to her own view of the subject. It was to herself an amusing and a very welcome piece of news, proving that Mr. Elton could not have suffered long after her rejection of him. But she was sorry for Harriet, who must feel it – and all that she could hope was, by giving her the news herself, it would save her from hearing it abruptly from others. It was now about the time that she was likely to visit. If she were to meet Miss Bates on her way! And upon its beginning to rain, Emma was obliged to expect that the weather would be detaining her at Mrs. Goddard's, and that the news would undoubtedly rush upon her without preparation.

The shower was heavy, but short, and it had not been over five minutes, when Harriet came in with just the heated, agitated look which hurrying thither with a full heart was likely to give. "Oh! Miss Woodhouse, what do you think has happened!" she said. As the blow was given, Emma felt that she could not now show greater kindness than in listening; and Harriet, unchecked, ran eagerly through what she had to tell. "She had set out from Mrs. Goddard's half an hour ago – she had been afraid it would rain – she had been afraid it would pour down every moment – but she thought she might get to Hartfield first – she had hurried on as fast as possible, but then, as she was passing by the house where a young woman was making up a gown for her, she thought she would just step in and see how it was coming along.

Though she did not seem to stay half a moment there, soon after she came out it began to rain, and she did not know what to do. So she ran on, as fast as she could, and took shelter at Ford's shop. And so, there she had sat, without an idea of anything in the world, for ten minutes, perhaps – when, all of a sudden, who should come in but Elizabeth Martin and her brother! Dear Miss Woodhouse! Only think. I thought I should have fainted. I did not know what to do. I was sitting near the door – Elizabeth saw me, but he did not; he was busy with the umbrella. I am sure she saw me, but she looked away and took no notice; and they both went to the far end of the shop; and I kept sitting near the door! Oh dear; I was so miserable! I am sure I must have been as white as my gown. I could not go away you know, because of the rain; but I did so wish myself anywhere in the world but there. Oh dear, Miss Woodhouse – well, at last he looked round and saw me; for instead of going on with their purchases, they began whispering to one another. I am sure they were talking of me; and I could not help thinking that he was persuading her to speak to me – (do you think he was, Miss Woodhouse?) – for presently she came forward – came quite up to me, and asked me how I was doing. She did not do any of it in the same way as before; I could see she was altered. But she seemed to *try* to be very friendly, and we shook hands, and stood talking sometime. But I do not know what I said – I was in such a state! I remember she said she was sorry we never saw each other anymore, which I thought almost too kind! Dear, Miss Woodhouse, I was absolutely miserable! By that time the rain was slowing, and I was determined that nothing should stop me from getting away – and then – only think! I found he was coming up towards me too – slowly you know, and as if he did not quite know what to do; and so he came and spoke, and I answered – and I stood for a minute, feeling awful, you know, one can't tell how; and then I took courage, and said it had stopped raining, and I must go; and so off I set; and I had not gone three yards from the door when he came after me, only to say, if I was going to Hartfield, he thought I had much better go round by Mr. Cole's stables, for I should find the shorter way quite flooded by this rain. Oh dear, I thought it would have been the death of me! So I said I was very much obliged to him: you know I could not do less; and then he went back to Elizabeth, and I came round by the stables – I believe I did – but I hardly knew where I was. Oh! Miss Woodhouse, I would rather it hadn't happened: and yet, you know, there was a sort of satisfaction in seeing him behave so pleasantly and so kindly. And Elizabeth, too! Oh, Miss Woodhouse, do talk to me and make me comfortable again."

Very sincerely did Emma wish to do so; but it was not immediately in her power. She was obliged to stop and think. She was not thoroughly comfortable herself. The young man's conduct, and his sister's, seemed the result of real feeling, and she could not but pity them. As Harriet described it, there had been an interesting mixture of wounded affection and genuine delicacy in their behaviour. But she had believed them to be well meaning, worthy people before; and what difference did this encounter make? It was folly to be disturbed by it. Of course, he must be sorry to lose her – they must all be sorry. Ambition, as well as love, had probably been wounded. They might all have hoped to rise by Harriet's acquaintance.

She exerted herself and did try to make her comfortable, by considering all that had passed as a mere trifle, and quite unworthy of being dwelt on.

"It might be distressing, for the moment," said she, "but you seem to have behaved extremely well; and it is over – and may never – can never, as a first meeting, occur again, and therefore you need not think about it."

Harriet said, "Very true," and that she "would not think about it," but still she talked of it – still she could talk of nothing else. Emma, at last, in order to put the Martins out of her head, was obliged to quickly tell the news which she had meant to give with so much tender caution. Though Harriet did not react as she might have done the day before, or an hour before, its interest soon increased; and before their first conversation was over, she had talked herself into all the sensations of curiosity, wonder and regret, pain and pleasure, as to this fortunate Miss Hawkins.

Emma learned to be rather glad that there had been such a meeting. It had helped to deaden the first shock, and she felt assured that the Martins could not accidentally cross her path. Since her refusal of the brother, the sisters had never been at Mrs. Goddard's, and a year might pass without their seeing each other again.

CHAPTER 22

Human nature is so well disposed towards the novel and interesting, that a young person who either marries or dies is sure of being kindly spoken of.

Miss Hawkins' name was first mentioned in Highbury only a week before, but somehow she was discovered to have every recommendation of person and mind. She was beautiful, elegant, highly accomplished, and perfectly amiable. When Mr. Elton himself arrived to triumph in his happy prospects, there was very little more for him to do than to tell her Christian name and say whose music she principally played.

Mr. Elton returned a very happy man. He had gone away rejected and mortified – disappointed in his hopes after a series of what had appeared to him very strong encouragement. He had gone away deeply offended, and he had come back happy and self-satisfied, eager and busy, caring nothing at all for Miss Woodhouse or Miss Smith.

The charming Augusta Hawkins, in addition to all the usual advantages of perfect beauty and merit, was in possession of a ten-thousand-pound fortune. Mr. Elton had not thrown himself away – he had gained a wealthy wife, and he had done so quite quickly. The lady had been so easily impressed – so sweetly disposed – had in short, been so very ready to have him, that vanity and practicality were equally contented.

He had caught both fortune and affection, and was just the happy man he ought to be; talking only of himself and his own concerns – expecting to be congratulated – ready to be laughed at – and, with cordial, fearless smiles, now talking to all the young ladies of the place to whom, a few weeks ago, he might have hesitated to show too much attention out of fear that they would perceive a romantic interest where none existed.

The wedding would be held as soon as the necessary preparations could be made. When he set out for Bath again, there was a general expectation that when he next entered Highbury he would bring his bride.

During his present short stay, Emma had barely seen him, but she saw enough to give her the impression that he was not improved by the pretension he now possessed. She was, in fact, beginning to wonder why she had ever thought him pleasing at all, and would have been thankful to be assured of never seeing him again. She wished him very well; but he gave her pain, and if he could live happily twenty miles off it would be most satisfying.

Of the lady, Emma thought very little. She was good enough for Mr. Elton, no doubt; accomplished enough for Highbury – beautiful enough to look plain, probably, by Harriet's side. As to connection, there Emma was perfectly easy. Setting aside the £10,000, it did not appear that she was at all Harriet's superior. She brought no name, no blood, no alliance. Miss Hawkins was the youngest of the two daughters of a Bristol merchant. Part of every winter she had been used to spend in Bath, but Bristol was her home – the very heart of Bristol, for though the father and mother had died some years ago, an uncle remained, and with him the daughter had lived. All the grandeur of the connection seemed dependent on the elder sister, who was *very well married* to a wealthy gentleman near Bristol.

Could she but have given Harriet her feelings about it all! She had talked her into love; but alas! she was not so easily to be talked out of it. The charm of an object to occupy the many vacancies of Harriet's mind was not to be talked away. He might be superseded by another, but nothing else, she feared, would cure her. Harriet was one of those, who, having once begun, would be always in love. And now, poor girl! She was considerably worse from this reappearance of Mr. Elton. She was always having a glimpse of him somewhere or other. Emma saw him only once; but two or three times every day Harriet was sure *just* to meet with him, or *just* to miss him, *just* to hear his voice, or see his shoulder. She was, moreover, perpetually hearing about him; for, except when at Hartfield, she was always among those who saw no fault in Mr. Elton, and found nothing as interesting as the discussion of his concerns. Every report, therefore, every guess – all that had already occurred, all that might occur in the arrangement of his affairs, was continually in agitation around her. Her regard was receiving strength by invariable praise of him, and her regrets kept alive, and feelings irritated by ceaseless repetitions of Miss Hawkins' happiness, and continual observation of, how much he seemed attached! His air as he walked by the house – the very sitting of his hat being all proof of how much he was in love!

Mr. Elton's engagement had cured Harriet of the agitation of meeting Mr. Martin. The unhappiness produced by the knowledge of that engagement had been a little put aside by Elizabeth Martin's calling at Mrs. Goddard's a few days afterwards. Harriet had not been at home, but a note had been prepared and left for her. Till Mr. Elton himself appeared, she had been much occupied by it, continually pondering over what could be done in return, and wishing to do more than she dared to confess. But Mr. Elton, in person, had driven away all such cares. While he stayed, the Martins were forgotten; and on the very morning of his setting off for Bath again, Emma, to dissipate some of the distress it occasioned, judged it best for her to return Elizabeth Martin's visit.

How that visit was to be acknowledged – what would be necessary – and what might be safest, had been a point of some doubtful consideration. Absolute neglect of the mother and sisters, when invited to come, would be ingratitude. It must not be: and yet the danger of a renewal of the acquaintance!

After much thinking, she could determine on nothing better than Harriet's returning the visit; but in a way that should convince them that it was to be only a formal acquaintance. She meant to take her in the carriage, leave her at the Abbey Mill while she drove a little farther, and call for her again so soon as to allow no time for dangerous recurrences of past intimacy.

She could think of nothing better: and though there was something in it which her own heart could not approve – something of ingratitude – it must be done, or what would become of Harriet?

CHAPTER 23

Harriet had little interest in visiting. Only half an hour before Emma called for her at Mrs. Goddard's, she had seen a trunk directed to The Rev. Philip Elton, White-Hart, Bath, being lifted into the butcher's cart. Everything in this world, excepting that trunk and the address, was consequently forgotten.

She went, however, and when they reached the farm, the sight of everything which had given her so much pleasure the autumn before, was beginning to revive her a little. When they parted, Emma observed her to be looking around with a sort of fearful curiosity. She therefore decided not to allow the visit to exceed the proposed quarter of an hour. She went on herself, to give that portion of time to an old servant who was married and settled in Donwell.

The quarter of an hour brought her punctually to the white gate again, and Miss Smith was with her without delay. She came alone down the gravel walk – a Miss Martin just appearing at the door and parting with her with ceremonious civility.

Harriet could not very soon give her a report. She was feeling too much; but at last Emma collected from her enough to understand the sort of meeting, and the sort of pain it was creating. She had seen only Mrs. Martin and the two girls. They had received her doubtingly, if not coolly, and nothing beyond the merest triviality had been talked of – till the end, when Mrs. Martin said, all of a sudden, that she thought Miss Smith was grown, and it had revealed a warmer manner. In that very room she had been measured last September, with her two friends. There were the penciled marks and notes on the wall by the window. *He* had done it. They all seemed to remember the day, the hour, the party, the occasion – to feel the same awareness, the same regrets – to be ready to return to the same good understanding; and they were just growing again like each other (Harriet, as Emma must suspect, as ready as the best of them to be cordial and happy), when the carriage reappeared, and all was over. The style of the visit, and the shortness of it, were then felt to be decisive. Fourteen minutes to be given to those with whom she had thankfully spent six weeks less than six months ago! Emma could not but picture it all, and feel how much they might resent, how naturally Harriet must suffer. It was a bad business. She would have given a great deal, or endured a great deal, to have had the Martins in a higher rank of life. But as it was, how could she have done otherwise? Impossible! She could not repent. They must be separated; but there was a great deal of pain in the process – so much to herself at this time that she soon felt the necessity of a little consolation, and resolved on going home by way of Randalls to procure it. Her mind was quite sick of Mr. Elton and the Martins. The refreshment of Randalls was absolutely necessary.

It was a good scheme, but on driving to the door they heard that "neither master nor mistress was at home;" they had both been out sometime; the man believed they were gone to Hartfield.

"This is too bad," cried Emma, as they turned away. "And now we shall just miss them; I do not know when I have been so disappointed." She leaned back in the corner to indulge her disappointment, or to reason it away; probably a little of both – such being the commonest process of a not ill-disposed mind. Presently the carriage stopped; she looked up. It was stopped by Mr. and Mrs. Weston, who were standing to speak to her. There was instant pleasure in the sight of them, and still greater pleasure was conveyed in sound, for Mr. Weston immediately accosted her with,

"How do you do? How do you do? We have been visiting with your father – glad to see him so well. Frank comes tomorrow – I had a letter this morning – we will see him tomorrow by dinner time – he is at Oxford today, and he comes for a whole fortnight; I knew it would be so. If he had come at Christmas, he could not have stayed three days; I was always glad he did not come at Christmas. Now we are going to have just the right weather for him, fine, dry, settled weather. Everything has turned out exactly as we could wish."

There was no resisting such news, no possibility of avoiding the influence of such a happy face as Mr. Weston's, confirmed as it all was by the words and the countenance of his wife. To know that *she* thought his coming certain was enough to make Emma consider it so, and sincerely did she rejoice in their joy. It was a most delightful reanimation of exhausted spirits. In the rapidity of half a moment's thought, she hoped Mr. Elton would now be talked of no more.

Mr. Weston gave her the history of the engagements at Enscombe which allowed his son to have an entire fortnight at his command, as well as the route and the method of his journey; and she listened, and smiled, and congratulated.

"I shall soon bring him over to Hartfield," said he, at the conclusion.

"We had better move on, my dear," said his wife. "We are detaining the girls."

"Well, well, I am ready," and turning again to Emma, "but you must not be expecting such a *very* fine young man; you have only had *my* account you know; I dare say he is really nothing extraordinary," though his own sparkling eyes at the moment spoke something very different.

Emma looked perfectly unconscious and innocent, and answered in a manner that revealed nothing.

"Think of me tomorrow, my dear Emma, about four o'clock," was Mrs. Weston's parting injunction; spoken with some anxiety, and meant only for her.

"Four o'clock! Depend upon it, he will be here by three," was Mr. Weston's quick amendment; and so ended a most satisfactory meeting. Emma's spirits were raised quite up to happiness, and James and his horses seemed not half so sluggish as before. When she looked at the hedges, she thought the elder at least must soon be coming out; and when she turned around to Harriet, she saw something like a look of spring, a tender smile even there.

"Will Mr. Frank Churchill pass through Bath as well as Oxford?" was a question, however, which she did not expect.

But neither geography nor tranquillity could come all at once, and Emma resolved that they should both come in time.

The morning of the awaited day arrived, and Mrs. Weston's faithful pupil did not forget either at ten, or eleven, or twelve o'clock, that she was to think of her at four.

"My dear, dear, anxious friend," said she to herself while walking downstairs from her own room, "always thinking of everybody's comfort but your own; I see you now in all your little fidgets, going again and again into his room to be sure that all is right." The clock struck twelve as she passed through the hall. "'Tis twelve, I shall not forget to think of you four hours hence; and by this time tomorrow, perhaps, or a little later, I may be thinking of the possibility of their all calling here. I am sure they will bring him soon."

She opened the parlour door and saw two gentlemen sitting with her father – Mr. Weston and his son. They had arrived only a few minutes before, and Mr. Weston had scarcely finished his explanation of Frank's being a day early, and her father was yet in the midst of his very civil welcome and congratulations, when she appeared to have her share of surprise, introduction, and pleasure.

The Frank Churchill so long talked of, so high in interest, was actually before her – he was presented to her, and she did not think too much had been said in his praise. He was a *very* good looking young man; height, air, manners, all were exceptional, and his countenance had a great deal of the spirit and liveliness of his father's; he looked quick and sensible. She felt immediately that she would like him; and there was a well-bred ease of manner, and a readiness to talk, which convinced her that he came intending to be acquainted with her.

He had reached Randalls the evening before. She was pleased with the eagerness to arrive which had made him alter his plan and travel earlier, later, and quicker, that he might gain half a day.

"I told you yesterday," cried Mr. Weston with exultation, "I told you all that he would be here before the time named. I remembered what I used to do myself. One cannot go slowly while on a journey; one cannot help getting on faster than one has planned; and the pleasure of coming in upon one's friends before the expected time is worth a great deal more than any little exertion it requires."

"It is a great pleasure when one can indulge in it," said the young man, "and since I was coming *home* it seemed fitting."

The word *home* made his father look on him with fresh happiness. Emma was sure that he knew how to make himself agreeable; the conviction was strengthened by what followed. He was very much pleased with Randalls, thought it a most admirably arranged house, would hardly allow it even to be very small, admired the walk to Highbury, Highbury itself, Hartfield still more, and professed himself to have always felt the sort of interest in the country which none but one's *own* country gives, and the greatest curiosity to visit it. That he should never have been able to indulge so amiable a feeling before passed suspiciously through Emma's brain; but still, if it were a falsehood, it was a pleasant one, and pleasantly handled. His manner had no sense of insincerity or exaggeration. He did really look and speak as if in a state of great enjoyment.

Their subjects in general were such as belong to a new acquaintance. On his side were the inquiries –

"Was she a horsewoman? Pleasant rides? Pleasant walks? Had they a large neighbourhood? Highbury, perhaps, afforded society enough? There were several very pretty houses in and about it. Was it a musical society?"

When satisfied on all these points, and their acquaintance accordingly advanced, he contrived to find an opportunity, while their two fathers were engaged with each other, of talking about his stepmother. He spoke of her with so much praise, so much warm admiration, so much gratitude for the happiness she brought to his father, and her very kind reception of himself, as was an additional proof of his knowing how to please. He did not advance a word of praise beyond what she knew to be thoroughly deserved by Mrs. Weston, but undoubtedly he could know very little of the matter. He understood what would be welcome; he could be sure of little else. "His father's marriage," he said, "had been the wisest measure. Every friend must rejoice in it; and the family from whom he had received such a blessing must be ever considered as having conferred the highest obligation on him."

He got as near as he could to thanking her for Miss Taylor's merits, without seeming quite to forget that in the common course of things it was to be rather supposed that Miss Taylor had formed Miss Woodhouse's character, than Miss Woodhouse Miss Taylor's. And at last he wound it all up with astonishment at the youth and beauty of her person.

"Elegant, agreeable manners, I was prepared for," said he, "but I confess that, considering everything, I had not expected more than a very tolerably well-looking woman of a certain age; I did not know that I was to find a pretty young woman in Mrs. Weston."

"You cannot see too much perfection in Mrs. Weston for my feelings," said Emma. "Were you to guess her to be *eighteen*, I should listen with pleasure; but *she* would be ready to quarrel with you for using such words. Don't let her imagine that you have spoken of her as a pretty young woman."

"I hope I should know better," he replied; "no, depend upon it, (with a gallant bow) that in speaking to Mrs. Weston I should understand whom I might praise without any danger of being thought extravagant in my terms."

Emma had no doubt that Mr. Weston was thinking about the possibility of her and Frank Churchill marrying. His quick eye she detected again and again glancing towards them with a happy expression; and even, when he might have determined not to look, she was confident that he was often listening. Her own father's perfect obliviousness to any thought of the kind was a most fortunate circumstance.

A reasonable visit paid, Mr. Weston began to move. "He must be going. He had business at the Crown about his hay, and a great many errands for Mrs. Weston at Ford's; but he need not hurry anybody else." His son rose immediately also, saying,

"As you are going farther on business, sir, I will take the opportunity of paying a visit which must be paid some day or other, and therefore may as well be paid now. I have the honour of being acquainted with a neighbour of yours, (turning to Emma), a lady residing in or near Highbury; a family of the name of Fairfax. I shall have no difficulty, I suppose, in finding the house; though Fairfax, I believe, is not the proper name – I should rather say Barnes, or Bates. Do you know any family of that name?"

"To be sure we do," cried his father. "Mrs. Bates – we passed her house – I saw Miss Bates at the window. True, true, you are acquainted with Miss Fairfax; I remember you knew her at Weymouth, and a fine girl she is. Call upon her, by all means."

"There is no necessity for my calling this morning," said the young man. "Another day would do as well; but there was that degree of acquaintance at Weymouth which – "

"Oh! go today, go today. Do not defer it. What is right to be done cannot be done too soon. And, besides, I must give you a hint, Frank; any want of attention to her *here* should be carefully avoided. You saw her with the Campbells when she was the equal of everybody she mixed with, but here she is with a poor old grandmother, who has barely enough to live on. If you do not call early it will be a slight."

The son looked convinced.

"I have heard her speak of the acquaintance," said Emma. "She is a very elegant young woman."

He agreed to it, but with so quiet a "Yes" as inclined her almost to doubt he meant it.

"If you were never particularly struck by her manners before," said she, "I think you will be today. You will see her to advantage; see her and hear her – no, I am afraid you will not hear her at all, for she has an aunt who never holds her tongue."

"You are acquainted with Miss Jane Fairfax, sir, are you?" said Mr. Woodhouse, always the last to make his way into a conversation. "Give me leave to assure you that you will find her a very agreeable young lady. She is staying here on a visit to her grandma and aunt, very worthy people; I have known them all my life. They will be extremely glad to see you, I am sure, and one of my servants shall go with you to show you the way."

"My dear sir, there is no need; my father can direct me."

"But your father is not going that far; he is only going to the Crown, quite on the other side of the street, and there are a great many houses. You might be very much at a loss, and it is a very dirty walk, unless you keep on the foot-path; but my coachman can tell you where you had best cross the street."

Mr. Frank Churchill still declined it, looking as serious as he could, and his father gave his hearty support by calling out, "My good friend, this is quite unnecessary; Frank knows a puddle of water when he sees it, and as to Mrs. Bates's, he may get there from the Crown in a hop, step and jump."

They were permitted to go alone; and with a cordial nod from one, and a graceful bow from the other, the two gentlemen took leave. Emma remained very well pleased with this beginning of the acquaintance.

CHAPTER 24

The next morning brought Mr. Frank Churchill again. He came with Mrs. Weston, to whom he seemed to take very cordially. He had been sitting with her, it appeared, most companionably at home, till her usual hour of exercise. On being desired to choose their walk, he immediately fixed on Highbury. "He did not doubt there being very pleasant walks in every direction, but if left to him, he should always choose the same. Highbury, that airy, cheerful, happy-looking Highbury, would be his constant attraction." Highbury, with Mrs. Weston, stood for Hartfield; and trusting it meant the same with him, they walked there directly.

Emma did not expect them, for Mr. Weston, who had called in for half a minute, in order to hear that his son was very handsome, knew nothing of their plans. It was an agreeable surprise to her, therefore, to see them walking up to the house together, arm in arm. She was wanting to see him again, and especially to see him in company with Mrs. Weston. Her entire opinion of him depended upon his treatment of his step-mother. If he were deficient there, nothing should make amends for it. But on seeing them together, she became perfectly satisfied. It was not merely the fine words or compliments he paid; nothing could be more proper or pleasing than his whole manner to her – nothing could more agreeably indicate his wish of considering her a friend and securing her affection. And there was time enough for Emma to form a reasonable judgment, as they spent the day together. They were all three walking about for an hour or two – first round the shrubberies of Hartfield, and afterwards in Highbury. He was delighted with everything and admired Hartfield sufficiently for Mr. Woodhouse's ear. He confessed his wish to be made acquainted with the whole village, and found something of interest much oftener than Emma could have supposed.

Some of the objects of his curiosity spoke very amiable feelings. He begged to be shown the house which his father had lived in so long, and which had been the home of his father's father. Then, remembering that an old woman who had cared for him was still living, he walked in quest of her cottage from one end of the street to the other.

Emma watched and decided that with such feelings as were now shown, he could not have been responsible for the many delays that kept him from visiting until now. This was no mere parade of insincere professions, and Mr. Knightley certainly had not done him justice.

Their first pause was at the Crown Inn, a small house where a couple of pair of post-horses were kept. His companions had not expected to be detained by any interest excited there, but in passing it they gave the history of the large room recently added. It had been built many years ago for a ballroom, and had at one time been in frequent use – but such brilliant days had long passed away, and now the highest purpose for which it was ever wanted was to accommodate a whist club. He was immediately interested. Its character as a ballroom caught him, and instead of passing on, he stopped for several minutes at the two superior sashed windows which were open, to look in and contemplate its capabilities, and lament that its original purpose should have ceased. They ought to have balls there at least every fortnight through the winter. Why had not Miss Woodhouse revived the former good old days of the room? She who could do anything in Highbury! The lack of proper families in the place, and the conviction that none beyond the place and its immediate area could be tempted to attend, were mentioned; but he was not satisfied. He could not be persuaded that so many good-looking houses as he saw around him could not furnish numbers enough for such a meeting. Even when particulars were given and families described, he was still unwilling to admit that the inconvenience of such a mixture would be of any concern. He argued like a young man very much bent on dancing, and Emma was rather surprised. He seemed to have all the life and spirit, cheerful feelings, and social inclinations of his father, and nothing of the pride or reserve of Enscombe.

At last he was persuaded to move on from the front of the Crown; and being now almost facing the house where the Bateses lodged,

Emma recollected his intended visit the day before, and asked him if he had paid it.

"Yes, oh yes!" he replied. I was just going to mention it. A very successful visit. I saw all the three ladies, and felt very much obliged to you for your preparatory hint. If the talking aunt had taken me quite by surprise, it must have been the death of me. As it was, I was only betrayed into paying a most unreasonable visit. Ten minutes would have been all that was necessary, perhaps all that was proper; and I had told my father I should certainly be at home before him, but there was no getting away, no pause. To my utter astonishment, I found, when he joined me there at last, that I had been actually sitting with them very nearly three quarters of an hour. The good lady had not given me the possibility of escape before."

"And how did you think Miss Fairfax looked?"

"Ill, very ill – that is, if a young lady can ever be allowed to look ill. But the expression is hardly admissible, Mrs. Weston, is it? Ladies can never look ill. And, seriously, Miss Fairfax is naturally so pale as almost always to give the appearance of ill health. A most deplorable lack of complexion."

Emma would not agree to this, and began a warm defence of Miss Fairfax's complexion. "It was certainly never brilliant, but she would not allow it to have a sickly hue in general; and there was a softness and delicacy in her skin which gave peculiar elegance to the character of her face." He listened with all due respect; acknowledged that he had heard many people say the same – but yet he must confess, that to him nothing could make amends for the lack of the fine glow of health. Where features were indifferent, a fine complexion gave beauty to them all; and where they were good, the effect was – fortunately he need not attempt to describe what the effect was.

"Well," said Emma, "there is no arguing about taste. At least you admire her, except her complexion."

He shook his head and laughed. "I cannot separate Miss Fairfax and her complexion."

"Did you see her often at Weymouth?"

At this moment they were approaching Ford's, and he hastily exclaimed, "Ha! This must be the very shop where everybody goes every day of their lives, as my father informs me. He comes to Highbury himself, he says, six days out of the seven, and always has business at Ford's. If it wouldn't inconvenience you, let us go in, that I may prove myself to belong to the place, to be a true citizen of Highbury. I must buy something at Ford's. I dare say they sell gloves?"

"Oh! Yes, gloves and everything. I do admire your patriotism. You will be adored in Highbury. You were very popular before you came, because you were Mr. Weston's son; but lay out half-a-guinea at Ford's, and your popularity will stand upon your own virtues."

They went in; and while the sleek, well-tied parcels were being brought down and displayed on the counter, he said – "But I beg your pardon, Miss Woodhouse, you were speaking to me, you were saying something at the very moment of this burst of my patriotism. And now that I understand your question, I must pronounce it to be a very unfair one. It is always the lady's right to decide on the degree of acquaintance. Miss Fairfax must already have given her account. I shall not commit myself by claiming more than she may choose to allow."

"Upon my word! you answer as discreetly as she could do herself. But her account of everything leaves so much to be guessed, she is so very reserved, so very unwilling to give the least information about anybody, that I really think you may say what you like of your acquaintance with her."

"May I indeed? Then I will speak the truth, and nothing suits me so well. I met her frequently at Weymouth. I had known the Campbells a little in town, and at Weymouth we were very much in the same set. Colonel Campbell is a very agreeable man, and Mrs. Campbell a friendly, warm-hearted woman. I like them all."

"You know Miss Fairfax's situation in life, that she is destined to be a governess?"

"Yes, I do."

"You are bringing up a sensitive subject, Emma," said Mrs. Weston smiling. "Remember that I was a governess once. Mr. Frank Churchill hardly knows how to respond when you speak of Miss Fairfax's situation in life. I will move a little farther off."

"I certainly do forget to think of *her*," said Emma, "as having ever been anything but my friend and my dearest friend."

He looked as if he fully understood and honoured such a sentiment.

When the gloves were bought and they had left the shop again, "Did you ever hear the young lady we were speaking of play?" said Frank Churchill.

"Ever hear her!" repeated Emma. "You forget how much she belongs to Highbury. I have heard her every year of our lives since we both began. She plays charmingly."

"You think so, do you? I wanted the opinion of someone who could really judge. She appeared to me to play well, that is, with considerable taste, but I know nothing of the matter myself. I am excessively fond of music, but without the smallest skill or right of judging anybody's performance. I have been used to hear hers admired. I remember one proof of her being thought to play well: a man, a very musical man, and in love with another woman – engaged to her – on the point of marriage – would yet never ask that other woman to sit down to the instrument, if the lady in question could sit down instead – never seemed to like to hear one if he could hear the other. That I thought, in a man of known musical talent, was some proof."

"Proof, indeed!" said Emma, highly amused. "Mr. Dixon is very musical, is he? We shall know more about them all, in half an hour, from you, than Miss Fairfax would have told us in half a year."

"Yes, Mr. Dixon and Miss Campbell were the persons; and I thought it a very strong proof."

"Certainly, very strong. How did Miss Campbell appear to like it?"

"It was her very particular friend, you know."

"Poor comfort!" said Emma, laughing. "One would rather have a stranger preferred than one's very particular friend; with a stranger, it might not recur again, but the misery of having a very particular friend always at hand, to do everything better than one does oneself! Poor Mrs. Dixon! Well, I am glad she is gone to settle in Ireland."

"You are right. It was not very flattering to Miss Campbell; but she really did not seem to feel it."

"So much the better, or so much the worse; I do not know which. But, be it sweetness or be it naivete in her, there was one person, I think, who must have felt it: Miss Fairfax herself. *She* must have felt the improper and dangerous distinction."

"As to that – I do not – "

"Oh! Do not imagine that I expect an account of Miss Fairfax's sensations from you, or from anybody else. They are known to no human being, I guess, but herself. But if she continued to play whenever she was asked by Mr. Dixon, one may guess what one chooses."

"There appeared such a perfectly good understanding among them all – " he began rather quickly, but checking himself, added, "however, it is impossible for me to say on what terms they really were – how it might all be behind the scenes. I can only say that there was smoothness outwardly. But you, who have known Miss Fairfax since childhood, must be a better judge of her character, and of how she is likely to conduct herself, than I can be."

"I have known her since childhood, undoubtedly; we have been children and women together, and it is natural to suppose that we should be well-acquainted, that we should have taken to each other whenever she visited her friends. But we never did. I hardly know how it happened; a little, perhaps, from that jealousy on my side which was bound to arise towards a girl as idolized as she always was by her aunt and grandmother. And then, her reserve! I never could attach myself to anyone so completely reserved."

"It is a most repulsive quality, indeed," said he. "Oftentimes very convenient, no doubt, but never pleasing. There is safety in reserve, but no attraction. One cannot love a reserved person."

"Not till the reserve ceases towards oneself; and then the attraction may be the greater. But I must be more desperate for a friend, or an agreeable companion, than I have yet been, to take the trouble of conquering anybody's reserve to procure one. Intimacy between Miss Fairfax and me is quite out of the question. I have no reason to think poorly of her – not the least – except that such extreme and perpetual cautiousness of word and manner, such a dread of giving a distinct idea about anybody, is apt to suggest suspicions of there being something to conceal."

He perfectly agreed with her, and after walking together so long, and thinking so much alike, Emma felt herself so well acquainted with him that she could hardly believe it was only their second meeting. He was not exactly what she had expected; less of the man of the world in some of his notions, less of the spoiled child of fortune, therefore better than she had expected. His ideas seemed more moderate – his feelings warmer. She was particularly struck by his manner of considering Mr. Elton's house, which, as well as the church, he would go and look at, and would not join them in finding much fault with. No, he could not believe it a bad house; not such a house as a man was to be pitied for having. If it were to be shared with the woman he loved, he could not think any man to be pitied for having that house. There must be ample room in it for every real comfort.

Mrs. Weston laughed, and said he did not know what he was talking about. Used only to a large house himself, and without ever thinking how many advantages and accommodations were attached to its size, he could be no judge of the privations inevitably belonging to a small one. But Emma, in her own mind, determined that he did know what he was talking about, and that he showed a very amiable inclination to settle early in life, and to marry, from worthy motives. No doubt he did perfectly feel that Enscombe could not make him happy, and that whenever he fell in love, he would willingly give up much of his wealth to be allowed an early marriage.

CHAPTER 25

Emma's very good opinion of Frank Churchill was a little shaken the following day when she heard he had gone to London merely to have his hair cut. A sudden urge seemed to have seized him at breakfast, and he had sent for a carriage and set off, intending to return for dinner. There was certainly no harm in his travelling sixteen miles and back on such an errand, but there was an air of vanity in it which she could not approve. It did not agree with the rationality, moderation and unselfishness which she had believed herself to discern in him yesterday. That Mrs. Weston did not like it was clear enough by her making no other comment than that "all young people have their little whims."

With the exception of this little indiscretion, Emma found that his visit hitherto had given her friend only warm feelings about him. Mrs. Weston was very ready to say how attentive and pleasant a companion he made himself – how much she saw to like in his manner altogether. He appeared to have a very open temper – certainly a very cheerful and lively one; she could observe nothing wrong in his notions, a great deal decidedly right. He spoke of his uncle with warm regard, was fond of talking of him – said he would be the best man in the world if he were left to himself; and though there was no being attached to the aunt, he acknowledged her kindness with gratitude, and seemed to mean always to speak of her with respect. This was all very promising; and, but for such an unfortunate fancy for having his hair cut, there was nothing to denote him unworthy of the distinguished honour which her imagination had given him. It was the honour, if not of being really in love with her, of being at least very near it, and saved only by her own indifference (for still her resolution held of never marrying). He had the honour, in short, of being supposed destined to marry her by all their joint acquaintance.

Mr. Weston added something to the account which must have some weight. He gave her to understand that Frank admired her extremely – thought her very beautiful and very charming. With so much to be said for him altogether, she found she must not judge him harshly. As Mrs. Weston observed, "all young people have their little whims."

One person, however, was not so kindly disposed towards the young Mr. Churchill: Mr. Knightley. He was told of the hair cut while at Hartfield. For a moment he was silent, but Emma heard him almost immediately afterwards say to himself, over a newspaper he held in his hand, "Humph! Just the trifling, silly fellow I took him for." She had half a mind to resent it, but an instant's observation convinced her that it was really said only to relieve his own feelings, and not meant to provoke. She therefore let it pass.

Although in one instance the bearers of bad tidings, Mr. and Mrs. Weston's visit this morning was in another respect particularly opportune. Something occurred while they were at Hartfield to make Emma want their advice. And, what was still more lucky, she wanted exactly the advice they gave.

This was the occurrence: the Coles had been settled some years in Highbury, and were very good sort of people – friendly and liberal; but, on the other hand, they were of low origin, in trade, and only moderately genteel. On their first coming into the country, they had lived in proportion to their income, quietly, keeping little company. But the last year or two had brought them a considerable increase of means – the house in town had yielded greater profits, and fortune in general had smiled on them. With their wealth, their views increased; their want of a larger house, their inclination for more company. They added to their house, to their number of servants, to their expenses of every sort; and by this time were, in fortune and style of living, second only to the family at Hartfield. Their love of socializing, and their new dining-room, gave everyone the idea that there would soon be many dinner parties. In fact, a few had already taken place. The regular and best families Emma could hardly suppose they would presume to invite – neither Donwell, nor Hartfield, nor Randalls. Nothing could tempt *her* to go, if they did. The Coles were very respectable in their way, but they ought to be taught that it was not for them to arrange the terms on which the superior families would visit them. This lesson, she very much feared, they would receive only from herself.

But she had made up her mind how to meet this presumption so many weeks before it appeared that when the insult came at last, it found her very differently affected. Donwell and Randalls had received their invitation, and none had come for her father and herself. Mrs. Weston's accounting for it with "I suppose they will not take the liberty with you; they know you do not dine out," was not quite sufficient. She felt that she should like to have had the power of refusal; and afterwards, as the party to be assembled there would consist precisely of those whose company was dearest to her, she thought she might have been tempted to accept. Harriet was to be there in the evening, and the Bateses. They had been speaking of it as they walked about Highbury the day before, and Frank Churchill had most earnestly lamented her absence. Might not the evening end in a dance? had been a question of his. The mere possibility of it acted as a further irritation on her spirits; and her being left in solitary grandeur, even supposing the omission to be intended as a compliment, was but poor comfort.

It was the arrival of this very invitation while the Westons were at Hartfield which made their presence so acceptable; for though her first remark, on reading it, was that "of course it must be declined," she so very soon proceeded to ask them what they advised her to do, that their advice for her going was most prompt and successful.

She owned that, considering everything, she was not absolutely against the idea. The Coles expressed themselves so properly – there was so much real attention in the manner of it – so much consideration for her father. "They would have solicited the honour earlier, but had been waiting the arrival of a folding-screen from London, which they hoped might keep Mr. Woodhouse from any draught of air, and therefore induce him the more readily to give them the honour of his company." Upon the whole, she was very persuadable; and it being briefly settled among themselves how it might be done without neglecting his comfort – Mr. Woodhouse was to be talked into his daughter's spending the whole evening away from him. As for *his* going, Emma did not wish him to think it possible; the hours would be too late, and the party too numerous.

"I am not fond of dinner parties," said he. "I never was. Neither is Emma. Late hours do not agree with us. I am sorry Mr. and Mrs. Cole should have done it. I think it would be much better if they would come in one afternoon next summer, and take their tea with us – stop by during their afternoon walk; which they might do, as our hours are so reasonable, and yet get home without being out in the damp of the evening. The dews of a summer evening are what I would not expose anybody to. However, as they are so very desirous to have dear Emma dine with them, and as you will both be there, and Mr. Knightley too, to take care of her, I cannot wish to prevent it, provided the weather is neither damp, nor cold, nor windy." Then turning to Mrs. Weston, with a look of gentle reproach – "Ah! Miss Taylor, if you had not married, you would have stayed at home with me."

"Well, sir," cried Mr. Weston, "as I took Miss Taylor away, it is incumbent on me to supply her place, if I can; and I will apply to Mrs. Goddard in a moment, if you wish it."

But the idea of anything to be done in a *moment*, was increasing, not lessening Mr. Woodhouse's agitation. The ladies knew better how to attend to it. Mr. Weston must be quiet, and everything deliberately arranged.

With this treatment, Mr. Woodhouse was soon composed enough for talking as usual. "He should be happy to see Mrs. Goddard. He had a great regard for Mrs. Goddard; and Emma should write a line, and invite her. James could take the note. But first of all, there must be an answer written to Mrs. Cole."

"You will make my excuses, my dear, as civilly as possible. You will say that I am quite an invalid, and go nowhere, and therefore must decline their obliging invitation; beginning with my *compliments*, of course. But you will do everything right. I need not tell you what is to be done. We must remember to let James know that the carriage will be needed on Tuesday. I shall have no fears for you with him. When you get there, you must tell him at what time you would have him come for you again; and you had better name an early hour. You will not like staying late. You will get very tired when tea is over."

"But you would not wish me to come away before I am tired, papa?"

"Oh! no, my love; but you will soon be tired. There will be a great many people talking at once. You will not like the noise."

"But, my dear sir," cried Mr. Weston, "if Emma comes away early, it will be breaking up the party."

"And no great harm if it does," said Mr. Woodhouse. "The sooner every party breaks up, the better."

"But you do not consider how it may appear to the Coles. Emma's going away directly after tea might be giving offence. They are good-natured people, and think little of their own claims; but still they must feel that anybody's hurrying away is no great compliment. Miss Woodhouse's doing it would be more noticed than any other person's in the room. You would not wish to disappoint and mortify the Coles, I am sure, sir; friendly, good sort of people as ever lived, and who have been your neighbours these *ten* years."

"No, upon no account in the world. Mr. Weston, I am much obliged to you for reminding me. I should be extremely sorry to be giving them any pain. I know what worthy people they are. My dear Emma, we must consider this. I am sure, rather than run the risk of hurting Mr. and Mrs. Cole, you would stay a little longer than you might wish. You will be perfectly safe, you know, among your friends."

"Oh, yes, papa. I have no fears at all for myself; and I should have no scruples of staying as late as Mrs. Weston, but on your account. I am only afraid of your sitting up for me. I am not afraid of your not being exceedingly comfortable with Mrs. Goddard. She loves piquet, you know; but when she is gone home, I am afraid you will be sitting up by yourself, instead of going to bed at your usual time – and the idea of that would entirely destroy my comfort. You must promise me not to stay up."

He did, on the condition of some promises on her side: such as that, if she came home cold, she would be sure to warm herself thoroughly; if hungry, that she would take something to eat; that her own maid should sit up for her; and that Serle and the butler should see that everything was safe in the house, as usual.

CHAPTER 26

Frank Churchill came back again, and if he was late for dinner, it was not known at Hartfield. Mrs. Weston was too anxious for his being a favourite with Mr. Woodhouse to betray any imperfection which could be concealed.

He came back, had had his hair cut, and laughed at himself with very good grace, but without seeming really at all ashamed of what he had done. He had no reason to wish his hair longer to conceal any facial features that might indicate embarrassment; no reason to wish the money unspent. He was quite as undaunted and as lively as ever, and after seeing him, Emma said to herself –

"I do not know whether it ought to be so, but certainly silly things do cease to be silly if they are done by sensible people. Wickedness is always wickedness, but folly is not always folly. It depends upon the character of those who handle it. Mr. Knightley, he is *not* a trifling, silly young man. If he were, he would have done this differently. He would either have gloried in the achievement, or been ashamed of it. No, I am perfectly sure that he is not trifling or silly."

With Tuesday came the agreeable prospect of seeing him again, and for a longer time than before; of judging of his general manners, and by inference, of the meaning of his manners towards herself. Of guessing how soon it might be necessary for her to feign indifference, and of wondering what the observations of all those might be who were now seeing them together for the first time.

She intended to enjoy the party, in spite of its being at Mr. Cole's, though without being able to forget that among the failings of Mr.

Elton, even in the days of his favour, none had disturbed her more than his habit of dining with Mr. Cole.

Her father's comfort was amply secured, Mrs. Bates as well as Mrs. Goddard being able to come. Her last pleasing duty before she left the house was to pay her respects to them as they sat together after dinner. While her father was fondly noticing the beauty of her attire, she made the two ladies all the amends in her power by helping them to large slices of cake and full glasses of wine. It was her way of protecting them against whatever unwilling self-denial her father's care of their constitution might have obliged them to practise during the meal. She had provided a plentiful dinner for them, and she hoped they would be allowed to eat it.

She followed another carriage to Mr. Cole's door and was pleased to see that it was Mr. Knightley's. The proprietor of Donwell Abbey kept no horses, as they were needed for farm work. In her opinion, he did not use his carriage as often as became the owner of such a large estate. She had an opportunity now of speaking her approbation while warm from her heart, for he stopped to give her a hand out of her carriage.

"This is coming as you should," she said, "like a gentleman. I am quite glad to see you."

He thanked her, observing, "How lucky that we should arrive at the same moment! For, if we had met first in the drawing-room, I doubt whether you would have discerned me to be more of a gentleman than usual."

"Perhaps not. There is always a look of consciousness when people come in a way which they know to be beneath them. You think you carry it off very well, I dare say, but with you it is a sort of bravado, an air of affected unconcern. I always observe it whenever I meet you under those circumstances. *Now* I shall really be very happy to walk into the same room with you."

"Nonsensical girl!" was his reply, but not at all in anger.

Emma had as much reason to be satisfied with the rest of the party as with Mr. Knightley. She was received with a cordial respect which could not but please, and given all the air of importance she could wish for. When the Westons arrived, their kindest looks of love, the strongest of admiration were for her, from both husband and wife. Their son approached her with a cheerful eagerness which marked her as his peculiar object, and at dinner she found him seated by her and, as she firmly believed, not without some contriving on his side.

The party was rather large, as it included one other family, a proper unobjectionable country family whom the Coles had the advantage of naming among their acquaintance, and the male part of Mr. Cox's family, the lawyer of Highbury. Others, such as Miss Bates, Miss Fairfax, and Miss Smith, would join the party later in the evening; but already, at dinner, they were too numerous for any subject of conversation to be general. While politics and Mr. Elton were talked over, Emma could give all her attention to the pleasantness of her neighbour. The first remote sound to which she felt herself obliged to attend was the name of Jane Fairfax. Mrs. Cole seemed to be relating something of her that was expected to be very interesting. She listened, and found it well worth listening to. Mrs. Cole was mentioning that she had been calling on Miss Bates, and as soon as she entered the room had been struck by the sight of a piano – a very elegant looking instrument – not a grand, but a large-sized square piano. This piano had arrived from Broadwood's the day before, to the great astonishment of both aunt and niece – entirely unexpected. At first, by Miss Bates' account, Jane herself was quite at a loss, quite bewildered to think who could possibly have ordered it – but now they were both perfectly satisfied that it could be from only one quarter – of course it must be from Colonel Campbell.

"One can suppose nothing else," added Mrs. Cole, "and I was only surprised that there could ever have been a doubt. But Jane, it seems, had a letter from them very recently, and not a word was said about it. She knows their ways best; but I should not consider their silence as any reason for their not meaning to make the present. They might choose to surprise her."

Mrs. Cole had many to agree with her; everybody who spoke on the subject was equally convinced that it must come from Colonel Campbell, and equally rejoiced that such a present had been made. There were enough ready to speak to allow Emma to think her own way, and still listen to Mrs. Cole.

"I declare, I do not know when I have heard anything that has given me more satisfaction! It always has quite hurt me that Jane Fairfax, who plays so delightfully, should not have an instrument. It seemed quite a shame, especially considering how many houses there are where fine instruments are simply gathering dust. It was but yesterday I was telling Mr. Cole, I really was ashamed to look at our new grand piano in the drawing-room, while I do not know one note from another, and our little girls, who are but just beginning, perhaps may never make anything of it. Yet there is poor Jane Fairfax, who is mistress of music, without an instrument, not even the pitifullest old spinet in the world, to amuse herself with. I was saying this to Mr. Cole but yesterday, and he quite agreed with me; only he is so particularly fond of music that he could not help indulging himself in the purchase, hoping that some of our good neighbours might be so obliging occasionally to put it to a better use than we can. That really is the reason why the instrument was bought – or else I am sure we ought to be ashamed of it. We are in great hopes that Miss Woodhouse may be prevailed upon to try it this evening."

Miss Woodhouse made the proper acquiescence, and finding that nothing more was to be learned from any communication of Mrs. Cole's, turned to Frank Churchill.

"Why are you smiling?" she asked him.

"Why are *you* smiling?"

"Me! I suppose I smile for pleasure at Colonel Campbell's being so rich and so generous. It is a thoughtful present."

"Very."

"I rather wonder that it was never made before."

"Perhaps Miss Fairfax has never been staying here so long before."

"Why didn't he just give her the use of their own instrument – which must now be shut up in London, untouched by anybody."

"That is a grand piano, and he might think it too large for Mrs. Bates' house."

"You may *say* what you choose – but your countenance testifies that your *thoughts* on this subject are very much like mine."

"I do not know. I rather believe you are giving me more credit than I deserve. I smile because you smile, and shall probably suspect whatever I find you suspect; but at present I do not see what there is to question. If Colonel Campbell is not the person, who can be?"

"What do you say to Mrs. Dixon?"

"Mrs. Dixon! Very true indeed. I had not thought of Mrs. Dixon. She must know as well as her father how acceptable an instrument would be. Perhaps the mode of it, the mystery, the surprise, is more like a young woman's scheme than an elderly man's. It is Mrs. Dixon I dare say. I told you that your suspicions would guide mine."

"If so, you must extend your suspicions and include *Mr.* Dixon as well."

"Mr. Dixon! Very true. Yes, I immediately perceive that it must be the joint present of Mr. and Mrs. Dixon. We were speaking the other day, you know, of his being an admirer of her playing."

"Yes, and what you told me in that regard confirmed an idea which I had entertained before. I do not mean to reflect upon the good intentions of either Mr. Dixon or Miss Fairfax, but I cannot help suspecting either that, after making his proposals to her friend, he had the misfortune to fall in love with *her*, or that he became conscious of a little attachment on her side. One might guess twenty things without guessing exactly the right; but I am sure there must be a particular cause for her choosing to come to Highbury instead of going with the Campbells to Ireland. Here, she must be leading a life of privation; there it would have been all enjoyment. As to the pretence of trying her native air, I look upon that as a mere excuse. In the summer, it might have passed; but what can anybody's native air do for them in the months of January, February, and March? Good fires and carriages would be much more to the purpose in most cases of delicate health. I do not require you to adopt all my suspicions, though you make so noble a profession of doing it, but I tell you honestly what they are."

"And, upon my word, they have an air of great probability. Mr. Dixon's preference of her music to his wife's I can answer for being very decided."

"And then, he saved her life. Did you ever hear of that? A water-party; and by some accident she nearly fell overboard. He caught her."

"He did. I was there – one of the party."

"Were you really? Well! But you observed nothing of course, for it seems to be a new idea to you. If I had been there, I think I should have made some discoveries."

"I dare say you would; but I saw nothing but the fact that Miss Fairfax was nearly dashed from the vessel and that Mr. Dixon caught her. It was the work of a moment. And though the consequent shock and alarm was very great – indeed I believe it was half an hour before any of us were comfortable again – yet that was too general a sensation for anything of peculiar anxiety to be observable. I do not mean to say, however, that you might not have made discoveries."

The conversation was here interrupted. They were called on to share in the awkwardness of a rather long interval between the courses, and obliged to be as formal and as orderly as the others. When the table was again set, when every corner dish was placed exactly right, Emma said,

"The arrival of this piano decides it for me. I wanted to know a little more, and this tells me quite enough. Depend upon it, we shall soon hear that it is a present from Mr. and Mrs. Dixon."

"And if the Dixons should absolutely deny all knowledge of it, we must conclude that it came from the Campbells."

"No, I am sure it is not from the Campbells. Miss Fairfax knows it is not from the Campbells, or they would have been guessed at first. She would not have been puzzled, had she dared fix on them. I may not have convinced you perhaps, but I am perfectly convinced myself that Mr. Dixon is involved in the business."

"Indeed you injure me if you suppose me unconvinced. Your reasonings carry my judgment along with them entirely. At first, while I supposed you satisfied that Colonel Campbell was the giver, I saw it only as paternal kindness, and thought it the most natural thing in the world. But when you mentioned Mrs. Dixon, I felt how much more probable that it should be the tribute of warm female friendship. And now I can see it in no other light than as an offering of love."

There was no occasion to press the matter farther. The conviction seemed real; he looked as if he felt it. She said no more, and other subjects took their turn. The rest of the dinner passed; the dessert followed, the children came in, and were talked to and admired. A few clever things were said, a few downright silly, but by much the larger proportion neither the one nor the other – nothing worse than everyday remarks and dull repetitions.

The ladies had not been long in the drawing room before the other ladies arrived. Emma watched the entrance of her own particular little friend; and if she could not exult in her dignity and grace, she could most heartily rejoice in that light, cheerful, unsentimental disposition which allowed her to still experience pleasure while in the midst of the pangs of disappointed affection. There she sat – and who would have guessed how many tears she had been lately shedding? To be in company, nicely dressed herself and seeing others nicely dressed, to sit and smile and look pretty, and say nothing, was enough for the happiness of the present hour. Jane Fairfax did look and move in a superior manner, but Emma suspected she might have been glad to trade places with Harriet, very glad to have purchased the mortification of having loved – yes, of having loved even Mr. Elton in vain – by the surrender of all the dangerous pleasure of knowing herself beloved by the husband of her friend.

In so large a party it was not necessary that Emma should approach her. She did not wish to speak of the piano; she felt too much in the secret herself to think the appearance of curiosity or interest fair, and therefore purposely kept at a distance. But by the others the subject was almost immediately introduced, and she saw the blush of consciousness with which congratulations were received, the blush of guilt which accompanied the name of "my excellent friend Colonel Campbell."

Mrs. Weston, kind-hearted and musical, was particularly interested by the circumstance, and Emma could not help being amused at her perseverance in dwelling on the subject. Having so much to ask and to say as to tone, touch, and pedal, totally unsuspicious of that wish of saying as little about it as possible, which she plainly read in the fair heroine's countenance.

They were soon joined by some of the gentlemen, and the very earliest was Frank Churchill. In he walked, the first and the handsomest; and after paying his compliments to Miss Bates and her niece, made his way directly to the opposite side of the circle, where sat Miss Woodhouse. Till he could find a seat by her, he would not sit at all. Emma divined what everybody present must be thinking. She was his object, and everybody must perceive it. She introduced him to her friend, Miss Smith, and, at convenient moments afterwards, heard what each thought of the other. "He had never seen so lovely a face, and was delighted with her naïveté."

Smiles of intelligence passed between her and the gentleman on first glancing towards Miss Fairfax; but it was most prudent to avoid speech. He told her that he had been impatient to leave the dining room – hated sitting long – was always the first to move when he could – that his father, Mr. Knightley, Mr. Cox, and Mr. Cole, were left very busy over parish business – that as long as he had stayed, however, it had been pleasant enough, as he found them in general a set of gentlemen-like, sensible men. He spoke so handsomely of Highbury altogether – thought it so abundant in agreeable families – that Emma began to feel she had taken the place for granted. She questioned him as to the society in Yorkshire, the extent of the neighbourhood about Enscombe, and the sort; and could make out from his answers that, as far as Enscombe was concerned, there was very little going on. Their visits were among a range of great families, none very near; and even when days were fixed, and invitations accepted, there was a good chance that Mrs. Churchill were not in health or spirits for going. They made a point of visiting no new person, and though he had his separate engagements, it was not without difficulty, without considerable effort, that he could get away, or spend an evening with a friend.

She saw that Enscombe could not satisfy, and that Highbury, taken in its best, might reasonably please a young man who had more seclusion at home than he liked. His importance at Enscombe was very evident. He did not boast, but it naturally betrayed itself that he had persuaded his aunt where his uncle could do nothing, and on her laughing and noticing it, he admitted that he believed (excepting one or two points) he could with time persuade her to anything. One of those points on which his influence failed, he then mentioned. He had wanted very much to go abroad – had been very eager indeed to be allowed to travel – but she would not hear of it. This had happened the year before. *Now*, he said, he was beginning to have no longer the same wish.

The unpersuadable point, which he did not mention, Emma guessed to be visiting his father.

"I have made a most wretched discovery," said he, after a short pause. "I have been here a week tomorrow – half my time. I never knew days could fly so fast. A week tomorrow! I have hardly begun to enjoy myself, and I have only just got acquainted with Mrs. Weston, and others! I hate to think of it."

"Perhaps you may now begin to regret that you spent one whole day, out of so few, in having your hair cut."

"No," said he, smiling, "that is no subject of regret at all. I have no pleasure in society unless I can believe myself fit to be seen."

The rest of the gentlemen being now in the room, Emma found herself obliged to turn from him for a few minutes and listen to Mr. Cole. When Mr. Cole had moved away, and her attention could be restored as before, she saw Frank Churchill looking intently across the room at Miss Fairfax, who was sitting exactly opposite.

"What is the matter?" said she.

He started. "Thank you for rousing me," he replied. "I believe I have been very rude; but really Miss Fairfax has done her hair in so odd a way – so very odd a way – that I cannot keep my eyes from her. I never saw anything like it! Those curls! This must be a fancy of her own. I see nobody else looking like her! I must go and ask her whether it is an Irish fashion. Shall I? Yes, I will – I declare I will – and you shall see how she takes it – whether she blushes."

He was gone immediately, and Emma soon saw him standing before Miss Fairfax, and talking to her; but as to its effect on the young lady, as he had improvidently placed himself exactly between them, exactly in front of Miss Fairfax, she could absolutely distinguish nothing.

Before he could return to his chair, it was taken by Mrs. Weston.

"This is the luxury of a large party," said she. "One can get near everybody, and say everything. My dear Emma, I am longing to talk to you. I have been making discoveries and forming plans, just like yourself, and I must tell them while the idea is fresh. Do you know how Miss Bates and her niece came here?"

"How! They were invited, were they not?"

"Oh! Yes – but how they were conveyed hither? The manner of their coming?"

"They walked, I conclude. How else could they come?"

"Very true. Well, a little while ago it occurred to me how very sad it would be to have Jane Fairfax walking home again late at night, especially since the nights are so cold now. And as I looked at her, though I never saw her appear to more advantage, it struck me that she might catch a cold. Poor girl! I could not bear the idea of it; so, as soon as Mr. Weston came into the room, I spoke to him about the carriage. You may guess how readily he came into my wishes; and having his approbation, I made my way directly to Miss Bates, to assure her that the carriage would be at her service before it took us home; for I thought it would be making her comfortable at once. Good soul! She was as grateful as possible, you may be sure. 'Nobody was ever so fortunate as herself!' – but with many, many thanks, – 'there was no occasion to trouble us, for Mr. Knightley's carriage had brought them, and was to take them home again.' I was quite surprised; very glad, I am sure, but really quite surprised. Such a very kind attention – and so thoughtful an attention! The sort of thing that so few men would think of. And, in short, from knowing his usual ways, I am very much inclined to think that it was for their accommodation the carriage was used at all. I do suspect he would not have had a pair of horses for himself, and that it was only as an excuse for assisting them."

"Very likely," said Emma, "nothing more likely. I know no man more likely than Mr. Knightley to do the sort of thing – to do anything really good-natured, useful, considerate, or benevolent. He is not a gallant man, but he is a very thoughtful one; and this, considering Jane Fairfax's ill health, would appear a case of charity to him. For an act of unostentatious kindness, there is nobody whom I would fix on more than on Mr. Knightley. I know he had horses today – for we arrived together, and I teased him about it, but he said not a word that could betray."

"Well," said Mrs. Weston, smiling, "you give him credit for more simple, disinterested benevolence in this instance than I do; for while Miss Bates was speaking, a suspicion darted into my head, and I have never been able to get it out again. The more I think of it, the more probable it appears. In short, I have made a match between Mr. Knightley and Jane Fairfax. See the consequence of keeping you company! What do you say to it?"

"Mr. Knightley and Jane Fairfax!" exclaimed Emma. "Dear Mrs. Weston, how could you think of such a thing? Mr. Knightley! Mr. Knightley must not marry! You would not have little Henry lose his inheritance? Oh! No, no, Henry must have Donwell. I cannot at all consent to Mr. Knightley's marrying; and I am sure it is not at all likely. I am amazed that you should think of such a thing."

"My dear Emma, I have told you what led me to think of it. I do not want the match – I do not want to injure dear little Henry – but the idea occurred to me because of circumstances. If Mr. Knightley really wished to marry, you would not have him refrain on Henry's account?"

"Yes, I would. I could not bear to have Henry replaced. Mr. Knightley marry! No, I have never had such an idea, and I cannot adopt it now. And Jane Fairfax, too, of all women!"

"Nay, she has always been a first favourite with him, as you very well know."

"But the impracticality of such a match!"

"I am not speaking of its practicality; merely its probability."

"I see no probability in it, unless you have any more evidence than what you mention. His good nature, his humanity would be quite enough to account for the horses. He has a great regard for the Bateses, you know, independent of Jane Fairfax – and he is always glad to show them attention. My dear Mrs. Weston, do not take to matchmaking. You do it very poorly. Jane Fairfax mistress of the Abbey! Oh! no, no; – every feeling revolts. For his own sake, I would not have him do so mad a thing."

"It may be imprudent – but it is not mad. Excepting inequality of fortune, and perhaps a little disparity of age, I can see nothing unsuitable."

"But Mr. Knightley does not want to marry. I am sure he has not the least idea of it. Do not put it into his head. Why should he marry? He is as happy as possible by himself; with his farm, and his sheep, and his library, and all the parish to manage. He is extremely fond of his brother's children and has no reason to marry, either to fill up his time or his heart."

"My dear Emma, as long as he thinks so, it is so; but if he really loves Jane Fairfax – "

"Nonsense! He does not care about Jane Fairfax. As far as love goes, I am sure he does not love her. He would do any good to her, or her family; but – "

"Well," said Mrs. Weston, laughing, "perhaps the greatest good he could do them would be to give Jane such a respectable home."

"If it would be good to her, I am sure it would not be to himself; a very shameful and degrading connection. How would he bear to have Miss Bates belonging to him? To have her haunting the Abbey, and thanking him all day long for his great kindness in marrying Jane? 'So very kind and obliging! But he always had been such a very kind neighbour!' And then fly off, through half a sentence, to her mother's old petticoat. 'Not that it was such a very old petticoat either – for still it would last a great while – and, indeed, she must thankfully say that their petticoats were all very strong.'"

"For shame, Emma! Do not imitate her. You amuse me against my conscience. And, upon my word, I do not think Mr. Knightley would be much disturbed by Miss Bates. Little things do not irritate him. She might talk on; and if he wanted to say anything himself, he would only talk louder, and drown out her voice. But the question is not whether it would be a bad connection for him, but whether he wishes it; and I think he does. I have heard him speak, and so must you, so very highly of Jane Fairfax! The interest he takes in her – his anxiety about her health – his concern that she should have no happier prospect than becoming a governess! I have heard him express himself so warmly on those points! Such an admirer of her performance on the piano, and of her voice! I have heard him say that he could listen to her forever. Oh, and I had almost forgotten one idea that occurred to me – this piano that has been sent her by somebody. Though we have all been so well satisfied to consider it a present from the Campbells, might it not be from Mr. Knightley? I cannot help suspect he's just the person to do it, even without being in love."

"Then it can be no argument to prove that he is in love. But I do not think it is at all a likely thing for him to do. Mr. Knightley does nothing mysteriously."

"I have heard him lamenting her having no instrument repeatedly; oftener than I should suppose such a circumstance would, in the common course of things, occur to him."

"Very well; and if he had intended to give her one, he would have told her so."

"There might be scruples of delicacy, my dear Emma. I have a very strong notion that it comes from him. I am sure he was particularly silent when Mrs. Cole told us of it at dinner."

"You take up an idea, Mrs. Weston, and run away with it; as you have many a time reproached me with doing. I see no sign of attachment — I believe nothing of the piano — and proof only shall convince me that Mr. Knightley has any thought of marrying Jane Fairfax."

They combated the point sometime longer in the same way; Emma rather gaining ground over the mind of her friend, for Mrs. Weston was the most used of the two to yield. Then a little bustle in the room showed them that tea was over, and the instrument in preparation. At the same moment, Mr. Cole approached to entreat Miss Woodhouse to do them the honour of trying it. Frank Churchill, of whom, in the eagerness of her conversation with Mrs. Weston, she had been seeing nothing, except that he had found a seat by Miss Fairfax, followed Mr. Cole, to add his very pressing entreaties. As in every respect it suited Emma best to lead, she gave a very proper acquiescence.

She knew the limits of her own abilities too well to attempt more than she could perform well. She lacked neither taste nor spirit in the little things which are generally acceptable, and could accompany her own voice well. One accompaniment to her song took her agreeably by surprise — Frank Churchill had joined her in singing. Her pardon was duly begged at the close of the song, and everything usual followed. He was accused of having a delightful voice, and a perfect knowledge of music; which was properly denied. He said he knew nothing of the matter, and had no singing voice at all. They sang together once more, and Emma then resigned her place to Miss Fairfax, whose performance, both vocal and instrumental, was infinitely superior to her own.

With mixed feelings, she seated herself at a little distance from those around the instrument to listen. Frank Churchill sang again. They had sung together once or twice, it appeared, at Weymouth. But the sight of Mr. Knightley among the most attentive soon drew away half of Emma's mind, and she fell into a train of thinking on the subject of Mrs. Weston's suspicions. Her objections to Mr. Knightley's marrying did not in the least subside. She could see nothing but misfortune in it. It would be a great disappointment to Mr. John Knightley; consequently, to Isabella. A real injury to the children; a most mortifying change, and material loss to them all. It would be a very great loss to her father's daily comfort; and, as to herself, she could not at all endure the idea of Jane Fairfax at Donwell Abbey. A Mrs. Knightley for them all to give way to! No – Mr. Knightley must never marry. Little Henry must remain the heir of Donwell.

Presently, Mr. Knightley looked back, and came and sat down by her. They talked at first only of the performance. His admiration was certainly very warm; yet she thought, but for Mrs. Weston, it would not have struck her as indicating anything more than general approbation. However, she began to speak of his kindness in conveying the aunt and niece; and though his answer was in the spirit of cutting the matter short, she believed it to indicate only his disinclination to dwell on any kindness of his own.

"I often feel concerned," said she, "that I dare not make *our* carriage more useful on such occasions. It is not that I am without the wish; but you know how impossible my father would deem it that James should go out of his way for such a purpose."

"Quite out of the question, quite out of the question," he replied; "but you must often wish it, I am sure." And he smiled with such seeming pleasure at the conviction, that she must proceed another step.

"This present from the Campbells," said she – "This piano is very kindly given."

"Yes," he replied, and without the smallest apparent embarrassment. "But they would have done better had they told her about it. Surprises are foolish things. The pleasure is not enhanced, and the inconvenience is often considerable. I should have expected better judgment in Colonel Campbell."

From that moment, Emma could have taken her oath that Mr. Knightley had had no involvement in giving the instrument. But whether he was entirely free from any particular attachment – whether there was no actual preference – remained a little longer doubtful. Towards the end of Jane's second song, her voice grew tired.

"That will do," said he, when it was finished, thinking aloud "You have sung quite enough for one evening; now, be quiet."

Another song, however, was soon begged for. "One more; they would not fatigue Miss Fairfax on any account, and would only ask for one more." And Frank Churchill was heard to say, "I think you could manage this without effort; the melody part is so trifling. The strength of the song falls on the second, and I can easily manage that part."

Mr. Knightley grew angry.

"That fellow," said he, indignantly, "thinks of nothing but showing off his own voice. This must not be." And touching Miss Bates, who at that moment passed near "Miss Bates, are you mad, to let your niece sing herself hoarse in this manner? Go and interfere. They have no mercy on her."

Miss Bates, in her real anxiety for Jane, could hardly stay even to be grateful before she stepped forward and put an end to all further singing. Here ceased the concert part of the evening, for Miss Woodhouse and Miss Fairfax were the only young lady performers; but soon (within five minutes) the proposal of dancing – originating nobody exactly knew where – was so effectually promoted by Mr. and Mrs. Cole that everything was rapidly clearing away to give proper space. Mrs. Weston was seated at the piano and began an irresistible waltz. Frank Churchill, coming up with most becoming gallantry to Emma, secured her hand and led her up to the top.

While waiting till the other young people could pair themselves off, Emma found time, in spite of the compliments she was receiving on her voice and her taste, to look about, and see what became of Mr. Knightley. This would be a trial for him. He was no dancer in general. If he were to be very alert in engaging Jane Fairfax now, it might give weight to Mrs. Weston's ideas. There was no immediate appearance. No; he was talking to Mrs. Cole – he was looking on unconcerned. Jane was asked by somebody else, and he was still talking to Mrs. Cole.

Emma had no longer any alarm for Henry; his interest was yet safe, and she led off the dance with genuine spirit and enjoyment. Not more than five couples could be mustered, but the rarity and the suddenness of it made it very delightful, and she found herself well matched in a partner. They were a couple worth looking at.

Two dances, unfortunately, were all that could be allowed. It was growing late, and Miss Bates became anxious to get home, on her mother's account. After some attempts, therefore, to be permitted to begin again, they were obliged to thank Mrs. Weston, look sorrowful, and be done.

"Perhaps it is just as well," said Frank Churchill, as he attended Emma to her carriage. "I must have asked Miss Fairfax, and her dancing would not have agreed with me after yours."

CHAPTER 27

Emma did not regret her decision to go to the Coles. The visit afforded her many pleasant recollections the next day; and all that she might be supposed to have lost on the side of dignified seclusion must be amply repaid in the splendour of popularity. She must have delighted the Coles – worthy people, who deserved to be made happy! And left a name behind her that would not soon be forgotten.

Perfect happiness, even in memory, is not common; and there were two points on which she was not quite easy. She doubted whether she had not transgressed by betraying her suspicions of Jane Fairfax's feelings to Frank Churchill. It was hardly right; but it had been so strong an idea that it had to be said, and his submission to all that she told was a compliment to her keen mind which made it difficult for her to be quite certain that she ought to have held her tongue.

The other circumstance of regret related also to Jane Fairfax; and there she had no doubt. She regretted the inferiority of her own playing and singing. She most heartily grieved over the idleness of her childhood – and sat down and practised vigorously for an hour and a half.

She was interrupted by Harriet's coming in, and if Harriet's praise could have satisfied her, she might soon have been comforted.

"Oh! If I could but play as well as you and Miss Fairfax!"

"Don't class us together, Harriet. My playing is no more like her playing than a candle is like sunshine."

"Oh! Dear, I think you play the best of the two. I think you play quite as well as she does. I am sure I had much rather hear you. Everybody last night said how well you played."

"Those who knew anything about it must have noticed the difference. The truth is, Harriet, that my playing is just good enough to be praised, but Jane Fairfax's is much beyond it."

"Well, I always shall think that you play quite as well as she does, or that if there is any difference nobody would ever find it out. Mr. Cole said how much taste you had; and Mr. Frank Churchill talked a great deal about your taste, and that he valued taste much more than execution."

"Ah! But Jane Fairfax has them both, Harriet."

"Are you sure? I saw she had execution, but I did not know she had any taste. Nobody talked about it. And I hate Italian singing. There is no understanding a word of it. Besides, if she does play so very well, you know, it is no more than she is obliged to do, in order to be a good governess. The Coxes were wondering last night whether she would be hired by a family of consequence. How did you think the Coxes looked?"

"Just as they always do — very shabby."

"They told me something," said Harriet rather hesitatingly, "but it is nothing important."

Emma was obliged to ask what they had told her, though fearful of its producing Mr. Elton.

"They told me that Mr. Martin dined with them last Saturday."

"Oh!"

"He came to their father upon some business, and he asked him to stay to dinner."

"Oh!"

"They talked a great deal about him, especially Anne Cox. I do not know what she meant, but she asked me if I thought I would go and stay there again next summer."

"It can certainly be none of her business."

"She said he was very agreeable the day he dined there. He sat by her at dinner. Miss Nash thinks either of the Coxes would be very glad to marry him."

"Very likely. I think they are, without exception, the most vulgar girls in Highbury."

Harriet had business at Ford's. Emma thought it most prudent to go with her. Another accidental meeting with the Martins was possible, and, in her present state, it would be dangerous.

Harriet, tempted by everything and swayed by half a word, was always very long making purchases; and while she was still looking over muslins and changing her mind, Emma went to the door for amusement. She watched Mr. Perry walking hastily by, Mr. William Cox letting himself in at the office door, Mr. Cole's carriage horses returning from exercise, and a stray letter-boy on an obstinate mule. When her eyes fell only on the butcher with his tray, a tidy old woman travelling homewards from the shops with her full basket, two dogs quarrelling over a dirty bone, and a string of dawdling children round the baker's window eyeing the gingerbread, she knew she had no reason to complain, and was amused enough. A mind lively and at ease can do with seeing nothing, and can see nothing that does not serve to entertain.

She looked down the Randalls road. The scene enlarged, and two persons appeared: Mrs. Weston and her son-in-law. They were walking into Highbury – to Hartfield, of course. They were stopping, however, first to see the Bateses, whose house was a little nearer Randalls than Ford's. They had all but knocked when Emma caught their eye. Immediately they crossed the road and came up to her. The agreeableness of yesterday's engagement seemed to give fresh pleasure to the present meeting. Mrs. Weston informed her that she was going to call on the Bateses in order to hear the new instrument.

"For my companion tells me," said she, "that I absolutely promised Miss Bates last night, that I would come this morning. I was not aware of it myself. I did not know that I had determined the day, but as he says I did, I am going now."

"And while Mrs. Weston pays her visit, I may be allowed, I hope," said Frank Churchill, "to join your party and wait for her at Hartfield, if you are going home."

Mrs. Weston was disappointed.

"I thought you meant to go with me. They would be very much pleased."

"Me! I should be quite in the way. But, perhaps – I may be equally in the way here. Miss Woodhouse looks as if she did not want me. My aunt always sends me off when she is shopping. She says I annoy her to death; and Miss Woodhouse looks as if she could almost say the same. What am I to do?"

"I am here on no business of my own," said Emma, "I am only waiting for my friend. She will probably be soon done, and then we shall go home. But you had better go with Mrs. Weston and hear the instrument."

"Well, if you advise it. But (with a smile), if Colonel Campbell should have employed a careless friend, and if it should prove to have poor tone, what shall I say? I shall be no support to Mrs. Weston. She might do very well by herself. A disagreeable truth would be palatable through her lips, but I am the wretchedest being in the world at a civil falsehood."

"I do not believe any such thing," replied Emma. "I am persuaded that you can be as insincere as your neighbours, when it is necessary; but there is no reason to call into question the quality of the instrument. Quite the opposite, if I understood Miss Fairfax's opinion last night."

"Do come with me," said Mrs. Weston, "if it is not very disagreeable to you. It need not detain us long. We will go to Hartfield afterwards. We will follow them to Hartfield. I really want you to join me. It will be felt so great an attention!"

He could say no more; and with the hope of Hartfield to reward him, returned with Mrs. Weston to Mrs. Bates's door. Emma watched them go in, then joined Harriet at the interesting counter, trying, with all the force of her own mind, to convince her that if she wanted plain muslin it was of no use to look at patterned; and that a blue ribbon, be it ever so beautiful, would still never match yellow. At last it was all settled.

Voices approached the shop – or rather one voice and two ladies; Mrs. Weston and Miss Bates met them at the door.

"My dear Miss Woodhouse," said the latter, "I am just running across to ask you to come and sit down with us a little while, and give us your opinion of our new instrument; you and Miss Smith. How do you do, Miss Smith? And I begged Mrs. Weston to come with me, that I might be sure of succeeding."

"I hope Mrs. Bates and Miss Fairfax are – "

"Very well, I am much obliged to you. My mother is delightfully well; and Jane caught no cold last night. How is Mr. Woodhouse? I am so glad to hear such a good account. Mrs. Weston told me you were here. Oh! then, said I, 'I must run across, I am sure Miss Woodhouse will allow me just to run across and entreat her to come in; my mother will be so very happy to see her.' 'Aye, pray do,' said Mr. Frank Churchill, 'Miss Woodhouse's opinion of the instrument will be worth having.' But, said I, I shall be more sure of succeeding if one of you will go with me. – 'Oh!'

said he, 'wait half-a-minute till I have finished my job.' For, would you believe it, Miss Woodhouse, there he is, in the most obliging manner in the world, fastening in the rivet of my mother's spectacles. The rivet came out, you know, this morning. So very obliging! – For my mother had no use of her spectacles – could not put them on. And, by the bye, everybody ought to have two pair of spectacles; they should indeed. Jane said so. I meant to take them over to John Saunders the first thing I did, but something or other hindered me all the morning; first one thing, then another, there is no saying what, you know. At one time Patty came to say she thought the kitchen chimney needed sweeping. Oh! said I, Patty do not come with your bad news to me. Here is the rivet of your mistress's spectacles out. Then the baked apples came home; Mrs. Wallis sent them by her boy. They are extremely civil and obliging to us, the Wallises, always – I have heard some people say that Mrs. Wallis can be uncivil and give a very rude answer, but we have never known anything but the greatest attention from them. And it cannot be for the value of our business now, for what is our consumption of bread, you know? Only three of us – besides dear Jane at present – and she really eats nothing – it makes such a shocking breakfast, you would be quite frightened if you saw it. I dare not let my mother know how little she eats, but about the middle of the day she gets hungry, and there is nothing she likes so well as these baked apples, and they are extremely wholesome, for I took the opportunity the other day of asking Mr. Perry; I happened to meet him in the street. Not that I had any doubt before – I have so often heard Mr. Woodhouse recommend a baked apple. I believe it is the only way that Mr. Woodhouse thinks the fruit thoroughly wholesome. We have apple dumplings, however, very often. Patty makes an excellent apple-dumpling. Well, Mrs. Weston, you have prevailed, I hope, and these ladies will oblige us."

Emma would be "very happy to wait on Mrs. Bates," and they did at last move out of the shop, with no further delay from Miss Bates than,

"How do you do, Mrs. Ford? I beg your pardon. I did not see you before. I hear you have a charming collection of new ribbons from town. Jane came back delighted yesterday. Thank ye, the gloves do very well – only a little too large about the wrist; but Jane is taking them in."

"What was I talking of?" said she, beginning again when they were all in the street.

Emma wondered what, of all the possible options, she would choose.

"I declare I cannot recollect what I was talking of. Oh! My mother's spectacles. So very obliging of Mr. Frank Churchill! 'Oh!' said he, 'I do think I can fasten the rivet; I like a job of this kind excessively.' Which you know showed him to be so very – Indeed I must say that, much as I had heard of him before and much as I had expected, he very far exceeds anything – I do congratulate you, Mrs. Weston, most warmly. He seems everything the fondest parent could – 'Oh!', said he, 'I can fasten the rivet. I like a job of that sort excessively.' I never shall forget his manner. And when I brought out the baked apples from the closet, and hoped our friends would be so very obliging as to take some, 'Oh!' said he, directly, 'these are the finest looking home-baked apples I ever saw in my life.' That, you know, was so very – And I am sure, by his manner, it was no mere flattery. Indeed, they are very delightful apples, and Mrs. Wallis does them full justice – only we do not have them baked more than twice, and Mr. Woodhouse made us promise to have them done three times – but Miss Woodhouse will be so good as not to mention it. The apples themselves are the very finest sort for baking, beyond a doubt; all from Donwell – some of Mr. Knightley's. He sends us a sack every year; and certainly there never was such a good apple anywhere as from one of his trees – I believe he has two. My mother says the orchard was always famous in her younger days. But I was really quite shocked the other day – for Mr. Knightley stopped by one morning, and Jane was eating these apples, and we talked about them and said how much she enjoyed them, and he asked whether we were running low. 'I am sure you must be,' said he, 'and I will send you another supply; for I have a great many more than I can ever use. William Larkins, my steward, let me keep a larger quantity than usual this year. I will send you some more before they go bad.' So I begged he would not – for really as to ours being gone, I could not absolutely say that we had a great many left – it was but half a dozen indeed; but they should be all kept for Jane, and I could not at all bear that he should be sending us more, as generous as he had been already. Jane said the same, and when he was gone, she almost quarrelled with me – No, I should not say quarrelled, for we never had a quarrel in our lives; but she was quite distressed that I had admitted the apples were so nearly gone; she wished I had made him believe we had a great many left. Oh! said I, my dear, I did say as much as I could. However, the very same evening William Larkins came over with a large basket of apples, the same sort of apples, a bushel at least, and I was very much obliged, and went down and spoke to William Larkins and said everything, as you may suppose. William Larkins is such an old acquaintance! I am always glad to see him. But, however, I found afterwards from Patty, that William said it was all the apples of *that* sort his master had; he had brought them all – and now his master had not one left to bake or boil. William did not seem to mind it himself, he was so pleased to think his master had sold so many; for William, you know, thinks more of his master's profit than anything; but Mrs. Hodges, he said, was quite displeased at their being all sent away. She could not bear that her master should not be able to have another apple-tart this spring. I would not have Mr. Knightley know anything about it for the world! He would be so very – I wanted to keep it from Jane's knowledge; but unluckily, I had mentioned it before I was aware."

Miss Bates had just finished talking as Patty opened the door, and her visitors walked upstairs pursued by the sounds of "Pray take care, Mrs. Weston, there is a step at the turning. Pray take care, Miss Woodhouse, ours is rather a dark staircase – rather darker and narrower than one could wish. Miss Smith, pray take care. Miss Woodhouse, I am quite concerned, I am sure you hit your foot. Miss Smith, the step at the turning."

CHAPTER 28

The appearance of the little sitting room as they entered was tranquillity itself. Mrs. Bates was slumbering on one side of the fire, Frank Churchill was at a table near her, occupied with her spectacles, and Jane Fairfax was standing with her back to them, intent on her piano.

Busy as he was, however, the young man was yet able to show a most happy countenance on seeing Emma again.

"This is a pleasure," said he, in rather a low voice, "coming at least ten minutes earlier than I had calculated. You find me trying to be useful; tell me if you think I shall succeed."

"What!" said Mrs. Weston, "Have not you finished it yet? You would not earn a very good livelihood repairing spectacles at this rate."

"I have not been working uninterruptedly," he replied. "I have been assisting Miss Fairfax in trying to make her instrument stand steadily. It was not quite firm; an unevenness in the floor, I believe. You see we have been wedging one leg with paper. This was very kind of you to be persuaded to come. I was almost afraid you would be hurrying home."

He contrived that she should be seated by him, and was sufficiently employed in selecting the best baked apple for her, and trying to make her help or advise him in his work, till Jane Fairfax was quite ready to sit down at the piano again. That she was not immediately ready, Emma did suspect to arise from the state of her nerves. She had not yet possessed the instrument long enough to touch it without emotion. Emma could not but pity such feelings, whatever their origin, and resolved never to expose them to her neighbour again.

At last Jane began, and though the first bars were feebly given, the powers of the instrument were gradually done full justice to. Mrs. Weston had been delighted before, and was delighted again; Emma joined her in all her praise, and the piano was pronounced to be altogether of the highest quality.

"Whoever Colonel Campbell might employ," said Frank Churchill, with a smile at Emma, "the person has not chosen ill. I heard a good deal of Colonel Campbell's taste at Weymouth; and the softness of the upper notes I am sure is exactly what he and *those with him* would particularly prize. I dare say, Miss Fairfax, that he either gave his friend very detailed directions, or wrote to Broadwood himself. Do you not think so?"

Jane did not look round. She was not obliged to hear. Mrs. Weston had been speaking to her at the same moment.

"It is not fair," said Emma in a whisper. "Mine was a random guess. Do not distress her."

He shook his head with a smile, and looked as if he had very little doubt and very little mercy. Soon afterwards he began again,

"How much your friends in Ireland must be enjoying your pleasure on this occasion, Miss Fairfax. I dare say they often think of you, and wonder which will be the day, the precise day of the instrument's arriving. Do you imagine Colonel Campbell knows the business to be going forward just at this time? Do you imagine it to be the consequence of an immediate commission from him, or that he may have sent only general instructions?"

He paused. She could not but hear; she could not avoid answering,

"Till I have a letter from Colonel Campbell," said she, in a voice of forced calmness, "I can imagine nothing with any confidence. It must be all conjecture."

"Conjecture – aye, sometimes one conjectures right, and sometimes one conjectures wrong. I wish I could guess how soon I shall make this rivet quite firm. What nonsense one talks, Miss Woodhouse, when hard at work, if one talks at all; real workmen, I suppose, hold their tongues, but we gentlemen labourers lack such focus. There, it is done. I have the pleasure, madam, (to Mrs. Bates), of restoring your spectacles, repaired for the present."

He was very warmly thanked both by mother and daughter; to escape a little from the latter, he went to the piano and begged Miss Fairfax, who was still sitting at it, to play something more.

"If you are very kind," said he, "it will be one of the waltzes we danced last night; let me live them over again. You did not enjoy them as I did; you appeared tired the whole time. I believe you were glad we danced no longer; but I would have given worlds – all the worlds one ever has to give – for another half hour."

She played.

"What felicity it is to hear a tune again which has made one happy! If I mistake not that was danced at Weymouth."

She looked up at him for a moment, coloured deeply, and played something else. He took some music from a chair near the piano, and turning to Emma, said,

"Here is something quite new to me. Do you know it? And here is a new set of Irish melodies. This was all sent with the instrument. Very thoughtful of Colonel Campbell, was not it? He knew Miss Fairfax could have no music here. I honour that part of the attention particularly; it shows it to have been so thoroughly from the heart. Nothing hastily done; nothing incomplete. True affection only could have prompted it."

Emma wished he would be less obvious, yet could not help being amused

Frank brought all the music to her, and they looked it over together. Emma took the opportunity of whispering,

"You speak too plainly. She must understand you."

"I hope she does. I would have her understand me. I am not in the least ashamed of my meaning."

"But really, I am half ashamed, and wish I had never spoken the idea."

"I am very glad you did, and that you communicated it to me. I have now a key to all her odd looks and ways. Leave shame to her. If she does wrong, she ought to feel it."

"She is not entirely without it, I think."

"I do not see much sign of it. She is playing *Robin Adair* at this moment – Mr. Dixon's favourite."

Shortly afterwards Miss Bates, passing near the window, saw Mr. Knightley on horseback not far off.

"Mr. Knightley I declare! I must speak to him if possible, just to thank him. I will not open the window here; it would give you all cold, but I can go into my mother's room you know. I dare say he will come in when he knows who is here. Quite delightful to have you all meet so! Our little room so honoured!"

She was in the adjoining chamber while she still spoke, and opening the window there, immediately called Mr. Knightley's attention, and every syllable of their conversation was as distinctly heard by the others as if it had passed within the same apartment.

"How do you do? How do you do? Very well, I thank you. So obliged to you for the carriage last night. We were just in time; my mother just ready for us. Pray come in; do come in. You will find some friends here."

So began Miss Bates, and Mr. Knightley seemed determined to be heard in his turn, for most resolutely and commandingly did he say,

"How is your niece, Miss Bates? I want to inquire after you all, but particularly your niece. How is Miss Fairfax? I hope she caught no cold last night. How is she today? Tell me how Miss Fairfax is."

And Miss Bates was obliged to give a direct answer before he would hear her in anything else.

"So obliged to you! So very much obliged to you for the carriage," she continued.

He cut her short with,

"I am going to Kingston. Can I do anything for you?"

"Oh! Dear, Kingston – are you? Mrs. Cole was saying the other day she wanted something from Kingston."

"Mrs. Cole has servants to send. Can I do anything for *you*?"

"No, I thank you. But do come in. Who do you think is here? Miss Woodhouse and Miss Smith; so kind as to call to hear the new piano. Do put up your horse at the Crown and come in."

"Well," said he in a deliberating manner, "for five minutes, perhaps."

"And here is Mrs. Weston and Mr. Frank Churchill too! Quite delightful. So many friends!"

"No, not now, I thank you. I could not stay two minutes. I must get on to Kingston as fast as I can."

"Oh! Do come in. They will be so very happy to see you."

"No, no, your room is full enough. I will call another day and hear the piano."

"Well, I am so sorry! Oh! Mr. Knightley, what a delightful party last night; how extremely pleasant. Did you ever see such dancing? Was not it delightful? Miss Woodhouse and Mr. Frank Churchill; I never saw anything equal to it."

"Oh! Very delightful indeed; I can say nothing less, for I suppose Miss Woodhouse and Mr. Frank Churchill are hearing everything that passes. And (raising his voice still more) I do not see why Miss Fairfax should not be mentioned too. I think Miss Fairfax dances very well; and Mrs. Weston is the very best country dance player, without exception, in England. Now, if your friends have any gratitude, they will say something pretty loudly about you and me in return; but I cannot stay to hear it."

"Oh! Mr. Knightley, one moment more; something of consequence – so shocked! Jane and I are both so shocked about the apples!"

"What is the matter now?"

"To think of your sending us all your remaining apples. You said you had a great many, and now you have not one left. We really are so shocked! Mrs. Hodges may well be angry. William Larkins mentioned it here. You should not have done it, indeed you should not. Ah! He is off. He never can bear to be thanked. But I thought he would have stayed now, and it would have been a pity not to have mentioned – Well, (returning into the room), I have not been able to succeed. Mr. Knightley cannot stop. He is going to Kingston. He asked me if he could do anything – "

"Yes," said Jane, "we heard his kind offers, we heard everything."

"Oh! Yes, my dear, I dare say you might, because you know the door was open, and the window was open, and Mr. Knightley spoke loudly. You must have heard everything to be sure. 'Can I do anything for you at Kingston?' said he, so I just mentioned – Oh! Miss Woodhouse, must you be going? You seem but just come; so very obliging of you."

Emma found it really time to be at home; the visit had already lasted long, and on examining watches, so much of the day was perceived to be gone that Mrs. Weston and her companion took leave also, and could allow themselves only to walk with the two young ladies to Hartfield gates before they set off for Randalls.

CHAPTER 29

It may be possible to go without dancing entirely. Instances have been known of young people passing many, many months successively, without being at any ball, and no material injury accrued either to body or mind. But when a beginning is made — when the felicities of rapid motion have once been felt — it must be a very obstinate person that does not ask for more.

Frank Churchill had danced once at Highbury, and longed to dance again; and the last half hour of an evening which Mr. Woodhouse was persuaded to spend with his daughter at Randalls was passed by the two young people in schemes on the subject. Frank's was the first idea; and his was the greatest zeal in pursuing it. The lady was the best judge of the difficulties, and the most solicitous for accommodation and appearance. But still she had inclination enough for showing people again how delightfully Mr. Frank Churchill and Miss Woodhouse danced.

His first proposition and request was that the dance begun at Mr. Cole's should be finished at Randalls — that the same party should be collected, and the same musicians engaged. Mr. Weston entered into the idea with thorough enjoyment, and Mrs. Weston most willingly undertook to play as long as they could wish to dance.

"You and Miss Smith, and Miss Fairfax, will be three, and the two Miss Coxes five," had been repeated many times over. "And there will be the two Gilberts, young Cox, my father, and myself, besides Mr. Knightley. Yes, that will be quite enough for pleasure. You and Miss Smith, and Miss Fairfax, will be three, and the two Miss Coxes five; and for five couples there will be plenty of room."

But soon it came to be on one side,

"But will there be enough room for five couples? I really do not think there will."

On another,

"And after all, five couples are not enough to make it worthwhile. Five couples are nothing, when one thinks seriously about it. It will not do to *invite* five couples. It can be allowable only as the thought of the moment."

Somebody said that *Miss* Gilbert was expected at her brother's, and must be invited with the rest. Somebody else believed *Mrs.* Gilbert would have danced the other evening, if she had been asked. A word was put in for a second young Cox; and at last, Mr. Weston naming one family of cousins who must be included, and another of very old acquaintance who could not be left out, it became a certainty that the five couples would be at least ten.

The doors of the two rooms were just opposite each other. "Might not they use both rooms, and dance across the passage?" It seemed the best scheme, but Emma said it would be awkward and Mrs. Weston would have no place to serve supper. Mr. Woodhouse opposed it earnestly, for reasons of health. It made him so very unhappy, indeed, that his views could convince no one.

"Oh! No," said he; "it would be extremely unwise. I could not bear it for Emma! Emma is not strong. She would catch a dreadful cold. So would poor little Harriet. So would you all. Mrs. Weston, you would be quite laid up; do not let them talk of such a wild thing. Pray do not let them talk of it. That young man (speaking lower) is very thoughtless. Do not tell his father, but that young man has been opening the doors very often this evening, and keeping them open very inconsiderately. He does not think of the draft. I do not mean to speak ill of him, but indeed he is quite inconsiderate!"

Mrs. Weston was sorry for such an accusation, and said everything in her power to explain it away. Every door was now closed, the passage plan given up, and the first scheme of dancing only in the room they were in resorted to again. With such goodwill on Frank Churchill's part, the space which a quarter of an hour before had been deemed barely sufficient for five couples was now endeavoured to be made into quite enough for ten.

"We were too liberal," said he. "We allowed unnecessary room. Ten couples may dance here very well."

Emma disagreed. "It would be a crowd — a sad crowd; and what could be worse than dancing without enough space to turn in?"

"Very true," he gravely replied, "it is very bad." But still he went on measuring, and still he ended with,

"I think there will be very tolerable room for ten couples."

"No, no," said she, "you are quite unreasonable. It would be dreadful to be standing so close! Nothing can be farther from pleasure than to be dancing in a crowd – and a crowd in a little room!"

"There is no denying it," he replied. "I agree with you exactly. A crowd in a little room – Miss Woodhouse, you have the art of giving pictures in a few words. Exquisite, quite exquisite! Still, however, having proceeded so far, one is unwilling to give the matter up. It would be a disappointment to my father – and altogether – I do not know that – I am rather of opinion that ten couples might dance here very well."

Emma perceived that the nature of his gallantry was a little self-willed, and that he would rather oppose than lose the pleasure of dancing with her; but she took the compliment, and forgave the rest.

Before the middle of the next day, he was at Hartfield, and he entered the room with such an agreeable smile as certified the continuance of the scheme. It soon appeared that he came to announce an improvement.

"Well, Miss Woodhouse," he almost immediately began, "your inclination for dancing has not been quite frightened away, I hope, by the terrors of my father's little rooms. I bring a new proposal on the subject – a thought of my father's, which waits only your approval to be acted upon. May I hope for the honour of your hand for the two first dances of this little projected ball, to be given not at Randalls, but at the Crown Inn?"

"The Crown!"

"Yes; if you and Mr. Woodhouse see no objection, and I trust you cannot, my father hopes his friends will be so kind as to visit him there. Better accommodations he can promise them, and not a less grateful welcome than at Randalls. It is his own idea. Mrs. Weston has no objection to it, provided you are satisfied. This is what we all feel. Oh! You were perfectly right! Ten couples, in either of the Randalls rooms, would have been insufferable! Dreadful! I felt how right you were the whole time, but was too anxious for securing *anything* that might have worked. Is not it a good change? You consent – I hope you consent?"

"It appears to me a plan that nobody can object to, if Mr. and Mrs. Weston do not. I think it admirable; and, as far as I can answer for myself, shall be most happy. Papa, do you not think it an excellent improvement?"

She was obliged to repeat and explain it, before it was fully comprehended; and then, being quite new, further representations were necessary to make it acceptable.

"No, he thought it very far from an improvement – a very bad plan – much worse than the other. A room at an inn was always damp and dangerous. If they must dance, they had better dance at Randalls. He had never been in the room at the Crown in his life – did not know the people who kept it. Oh! "No – a very bad plan. They would catch worse colds at the Crown than anywhere."

"I was going to observe, sir," said Frank Churchill, "that one of the great recommendations of this change would be the very little danger of anybody's catching cold – so much less danger at the Crown than at Randalls!"

"Sir," said Mr. Woodhouse, rather warmly, "I do not understand how the room at the Crown can be safer for you than your father's house."

"From the very circumstance of its being larger, sir. We shall have no occasion to open the windows at all – not once the whole evening; and it is that dreadful habit of opening the windows, which (as you well know, sir) does the mischief."

"Open the windows! Nobody could be so imprudent! I never heard of such a thing. Dancing with open windows! I am sure, neither your father nor Mrs. Weston (poor Miss Taylor that was) would suffer it."

"Ah! Sir – but a thoughtless young person will sometimes throw open a curtained window, without its being suspected. I have often known it done myself."

"Have you indeed, sir? Bless me! I never could have supposed it. But I am often astonished at what I hear. However, this does make a difference; and, perhaps, when we come to talk it over – but these sorts of things require a good deal of consideration. One cannot resolve upon them in a hurry. If Mr. and Mrs. Weston will be so obliging as to call here one morning, we may talk it over, and see what can be done."

"But, unfortunately, sir, my time is so limited – "

"Oh!" interrupted Emma, "there will be plenty of time for talking everything over. There is no hurry at all. If it can be contrived to be at the Crown, papa, it will be very convenient for the horses. They will be so near their own stable."

"So they will, my dear. That is a great thing. Not that James ever complains; but it is right to spare our horses when we can. "

"There, papa! Now you must be satisfied. And with our own dear Mrs. Weston, who is carefulness itself, as our hostess, all will be just as it should. Do you not remember what Mr. Perry said so many years ago, when I had the measles? 'If *Miss Taylor* undertakes to wrap Miss Emma up, you need not have any fears, sir.' How often I have heard you speak of it as such a compliment to her!"

"Aye, very true. Mr. Perry did say so. I shall never forget it. Poor little Emma! You were very bad with the measles; that is, you would have been very bad, but for Perry's great attention. He came four times a day for a week. The measles are a dreadful complaint. I hope whenever poor Isabella's little ones have the measles, she will send for Perry.

"My father and Mrs. Weston are at the Crown at this moment," said Frank Churchill, "I left them there and came on to Hartfield, impatient for your opinion, and hoping you might be persuaded to join them and give your advice on the spot. I was desired to say so from both. It would be the greatest pleasure to them, if you could allow me to attend you there. They can do nothing satisfactorily without you."

Emma was most happy to be called to such a council, and the two young people set off together without delay for the Crown. There were Mr. and Mrs. Weston, delighted to see her and receive her approval.

"Emma," said she, "this wallpaper is worse than I expected. Look! In places, you see, it is dreadfully dirty."

"My dear, you are too particular," said her husband. "You will see nothing of it by candlelight. It will be as clean as Randalls by candlelight. We never see anything of it on our club nights."

The ladies here probably exchanged looks which meant, "Men never know when things are dirty or not," and the gentlemen perhaps thought each to himself, "Women will have their little nonsenses and needless cares."

One perplexity, however, arose, which the gentlemen did not dismiss. It related to a supper-room. At the time of the ballroom's being built, suppers had not been served; and a small card room was the only addition. What was to be done? This card room would be wanted as a card room now; or, if cards were conveniently voted unnecessary, still it was too small for any comfortable supper. Another room of much better size might be secured for the purpose, but it was at the other end of the house, and a long, awkward passage must be gone through to reach it. This was a difficulty. Mrs. Weston was afraid of drafts for the young people in that passage, and neither Emma nor the gentlemen could tolerate the prospect of being miserably crowded at supper.

Mrs. Weston proposed having no regular supper; merely sandwiches set out in the little room; but that was decried as a wretched suggestion. A private dance without sitting down to supper was pronounced an infamous fraud upon the rights of men and women; and Mrs. Weston must not speak of it again. She then took another approach, and looking into the doubtful room, observed,

"I do not think it *is* so very small. We shall not be many, you know."

And Mr. Weston at the same time, walking briskly with long steps through the passage, was calling out,

"You talk a great deal of the length of this passage, my dear. It is a mere nothing after all; and not the least draft from the stairs."

"I wish," said Mrs. Weston, "one could know which arrangement our guests in general would like best. To do what would be most generally pleasing must be our object — if one could but tell what that would be."

"Yes, very true," cried Frank, "very true. You want your neighbours' opinions. I wholeheartedly agree. If one could ascertain what the chief of them — the Coles, for instance. They are not far off. Shall I call upon them? Or Miss Bates? She is still nearer. Suppose I go and invite Miss Bates to join us?"

"Well —" said Mrs. Weston rather hesitating, "if you think she will be of any use."

"You will get nothing to the purpose from Miss Bates," said Emma. "She will be all delight and gratitude, but she will tell you nothing. She will not even listen to your questions. I see no advantage in consulting Miss Bates."

"But she is so amusing, so extremely amusing! I am very fond of hearing Miss Bates talk. And I need not bring the whole family, you know."

Here Mr. Weston joined them, and on hearing what was proposed, gave it his decided approval. "Aye, go, Frank. Fetch Miss Bates, and let us end the matter at once. She will enjoy the scheme, I am sure; and I do not know a more proper person for showing us how to do away difficulties. Fetch Miss Bates, and her niece as well."

"I will endeavour to persuade them both to come." And away he went.

Long before he reappeared, attending the aunt and her elegant niece, Mrs. Weston, like a sweet-tempered woman and a good wife, had examined the passage again, and found it much less troublesome than she had supposed before – indeed very trifling; and here ended the difficulties of decision. All the rest, in speculation at least, was perfectly smooth. All the minor arrangements of table and chair, lights and music, tea and supper, made themselves; or were left as mere trifles to be settled at any time. Everybody invited was certain to come; Frank had already written to Enscombe to propose staying a few days beyond his fortnight, which could not possibly be refused. And a delightful dance it was to be.

Most cordially, when Miss Bates arrived, did she agree that it must. Her approval, at once warm and incessant, could not but please; and for another half-hour they were all walking to and fro between the different rooms, all in happy enjoyment of the future. The party did not break up without Emma's being positively secured for the two first dances by the hero of the evening, nor without her overhearing Mr. Weston whisper to his wife, "He has asked her, my dear. That's right. I knew he would!"

CHAPTER 30

One thing only was needed to make the prospect of the ball completely satisfactory to Emma – its being fixed for a day within the granted term of Frank Churchill's stay in Surrey. In spite of Mr. Weston's confidence, she could not think it so very impossible that the Churchills might not allow their nephew to remain a day beyond his fortnight. But this was not judged feasible. The preparations must take their time, nothing could be properly ready till the third week were entered on, and for a few days they must be planning, proceeding and hoping in uncertainty – at the risk of its being all in vain.

Enscombe, however, was gracious. His wish of staying longer evidently did not please; but it was not opposed. All was safe and prosperous, and as the removal of one concern generally makes way for another, Emma, being now certain of her ball, began to adopt as the next vexation Mr. Knightley's indifference about it. Either because he did not dance himself, or because the plan had been formed without his being consulted, he seemed resolved that it should not interest him. To her voluntary communications Emma could get no more approving reply than,

"Very well. If the Westons think it worthwhile to go to all this trouble for a few hours of noisy entertainment, I have nothing to say against it, but that they shall not choose pleasures for me. Oh! Yes, I must be there; I could not refuse; and I will try to stay awake; but I would rather be at home, looking over William Larkins's week's account; much rather, I confess. Pleasure in seeing dancing! Not I, indeed – I never look at it – I do not know who does. Fine dancing, I believe, like virtue, must be its own reward. Those who are standing by are usually thinking of something very different."

Alas! there was soon no leisure for quarrelling with Mr. Knightley. Two days of happiness were immediately followed by the overthrow of everything. A letter arrived from Mr. Churchill to urge his nephew's instant return. Mrs. Churchill was unwell – far too unwell to do without him; she had been in a very suffering state (so said her husband) when writing to her nephew two days before, though from her usual unwillingness to give pain, and constant habit of never thinking of herself, she had not mentioned it; but now she had grown worse, and must entreat him to set off for Enscombe without delay.

The substance of this letter was forwarded to Emma, in a note from Mrs. Weston, instantly. As to his going, it was inevitable. He must be gone within a few hours, though without feeling any real alarm for his aunt. He knew her illnesses; they never occurred but for her own convenience.

Mrs. Weston added, "that he could only allow himself time to hurry to Highbury, after breakfast, and take leave of the few friends there whom he could suppose to feel any interest in him; and that he might be expected at Hartfield very soon."

This wretched note was the finale of Emma's breakfast. When once it had been read, there was no doing anything, but to lament and complain. The loss of the ball – the loss of the young man – and all that the young man might be feeling! It was too wretched! Such a delightful evening as it would have been! Everybody so happy! And she and her partner the happiest! "I said it would be so," was the only consolation.

Her father's feelings were quite distinct. He thought principally of Mrs. Churchill's illness, and wanted to know how she was treated. As for the ball, it was shocking to have dear Emma disappointed; but they would all be safer at home.

Emma was ready for her visitor sometime before he appeared; but if this reflected at all upon his impatience, his sorrowful look when he did come might redeem him. He felt the going away almost too much to speak of it. His dejection was most evident. He sat really lost in thought for the first few minutes; and when rousing himself, it was only to say,

"Of all horrid things, saying goodbye is the worst."

"But you will come again," said Emma. "This will not be your only visit to Randalls."

"Ah! (shaking his head) – the uncertainty of when I may be able to return! I shall try for it with zeal! It will be the object of all my thoughts and cares! If my uncle and aunt go to town this spring – but they did not stir last spring – I am afraid it is a custom gone forever."

"Our poor ball must be quite given up."

"Ah! that ball! Why did we wait? Why not seize the pleasure at once? How often is happiness destroyed by preparation, foolish preparation! You told us it would be so. Oh! Miss Woodhouse, why are you always so right?"

"Indeed, I am very sorry to be right in this instance. I would much rather have been merry than wise."

"If I can come again, we will have our ball. My father depends on it. Do not forget your engagement."

Emma nodded graciously.

"Such a fortnight it has been!" he continued. "Every day more precious and more delightful than the day before! Every day making me less fit to bear my life at Enscombe. Happy are those who get to stay in Highbury!"

"As you do us such ample justice now," said Emma, laughing, "I will venture to ask whether you did not come a little doubtingly at first? Did we surpass your expectations? I am sure we did. I am sure you did not much expect to like us. You would not have been so long in coming, if you had had a pleasant idea of Highbury."

He laughed.

"And you must be off this very morning?"

"Yes; my father is to join me here. We shall walk back together, and I must be off immediately. I am almost afraid that every moment will bring him."

"Not five minutes to spare even for your friends Miss Fairfax and Miss Bates? How unlucky! Miss Bates's powerful, argumentative mind might have strengthened yours."

"Yes – I *have* called there; passing the door, I thought it better. It was a right thing to do. I went in for three minutes, and was detained by the absence of Miss Bates. She was out; and I felt it impossible not to wait till she came in. She is a woman that one may, that one *must* laugh at; but that one would not wish to slight. It was better to pay my visit, then" –

He hesitated, got up, walked to a window.

"In short," said he, "perhaps, Miss Woodhouse – I think you can hardly be quite without suspicion –"

He looked at her, as if wanting to read her thoughts. She hardly knew what to say. It seemed like he was about to declare his love for her, and she did not wish it. Forcing herself to speak, therefore, in the hope of preventing such a declaration, she calmly said,

"You were quite in the right; it was most natural to pay your visit, then – "

He was silent. She believed he was looking at her; probably reflecting on what she had said, and trying to understand the manner. She heard him sigh. It was natural for him to feel that he had *cause* to sigh. He could not believe her to be encouraging him. A few awkward moments passed, and he sat down again; and in a more determined manner said,

"It was something to feel that all the rest of my time might be given to Hartfield. My regard for Hartfield is most warm – "

He stopped again, rose again, and seemed quite embarrassed. He was more in love with her than Emma had supposed; and who can say how it might have ended, if his father had not made his appearance? Mr. Woodhouse soon followed; and Frank quickly regained his composure.

A very few minutes more, however, completed the present trial. Mr. Weston, always alert when business was to be done, said it was time to go, and the young man, though he might and did sigh, could not but agree, and rose to take leave.

"I shall hear about you all," said he; "that is my chief consolation. I shall hear of everything that is going on among you. I have engaged Mrs. Weston to correspond with me. She has been so kind as to promise it."

A very friendly shake of the hand, a very earnest "Goodbye," closed the speech, and the door had soon shut out Frank Churchill. Short had been the notice – short their meeting; he was gone, and Emma felt so sorry to part, and foresaw a great loss to their little society from his absence.

It was a sad change. They had been meeting almost every day since his arrival. Certainly his being at Randalls had given great liveliness to the last two weeks. The expectation of seeing him which every morning had brought, the assurance of his attentions, his manners! It had been a very happy fortnight, and forlorn must be the sinking from it into the common course of Hartfield days. To complete every other recommendation, he had *almost* told her that he loved her. What strength, or what constancy of affection he might be subject to, was another point; but at present she could not doubt his having a decidedly warm admiration, a conscious preference of herself. This persuasion, joined to all the rest, made her think that she *must* be a little in love with him, in spite of every previous determination against it.

"I certainly must," said she. "This sensation of listlessness and weariness, this disinclination to sit down and employ myself, this feeling of everything's being dull about the house! I must be in love; I should be the oddest creature in the world if I were not – for a few weeks at least. Well! I shall have many fellow-mourners for the ball, if not for Frank Churchill; but Mr. Knightley will be happy. He may spend the evening with his dear William Larkins now if he likes."

Mr. Knightley, however, showed no triumphant happiness. He could not say that he was sorry on his own account; his very cheerful look would have contradicted him if he had. But he said, and very steadily, that he was sorry for the disappointment of the others, and with considerable kindness added,

"You, Emma, who have so few opportunities of dancing. It is most unfortunate. Most unfortunate indeed."

It was some days before she saw Jane Fairfax, and when they did meet, she did not appear well. She had been suffering from a severe headache, which made her aunt declare that had the ball taken place, she did not think Jane could have attended it.

CHAPTER 31

Emma continued to entertain no doubt of her being in love. Her ideas only varied as to how much. At first, she thought it was a good deal; and afterwards, but little. She had great pleasure in hearing Frank Churchill talked of; and, for his sake, greater pleasure than ever in seeing Mr. and Mrs. Weston. She was very often thinking of him, and quite impatient for a letter, that she might know how he was, and what was the chance of his coming to Randalls again this spring. But, on the other hand, she could not admit herself to be unhappy, nor, after the first morning, to be less disposed for employment than usual. She was still busy and cheerful, and, pleasing as he was, she could yet imagine him to have faults. As she sat drawing or working, forming a thousand amusing schemes for the progress and close of their attachment, the conclusion of every imaginary declaration on his side was that she *refused him*. Their affection was always to subside into friendship. Everything tender and charming was to mark their parting; but still they were to part. When she became sensible of this, it struck her that she could not be very much in love. In spite of her previous determination never to leave her father, never to marry, a strong attachment certainly must produce more of a struggle than she could foresee in her own feelings.

"I do not find myself making any use of the word *sacrifice*," said she. "In not one of all my clever replies, my delicate negatives, is there any allusion to making a sacrifice. I do suspect that he is not really necessary to my happiness. So much the better. I certainly will not persuade myself to feel more than I do. I am quite enough in love. I should be sorry to be more."

She was equally contented with her view of his feelings.

"*He* is undoubtedly very much in love – everything indicates it – very much in love indeed! When he comes again, if his affection continues, I must be on my guard not to encourage it. It would be most inexcusable to do otherwise, as my own mind is quite made up. Not that I imagine he can think I have been encouraging him. Still, however, I must be on my guard. This is supposing his attachment continues; but I do not expect it will. I do not look upon him to be quite the sort of man – I do not count on his steadiness or constancy. His feelings are warm, but I can imagine them rather changeable. Every consideration of the subject, in short, makes me thankful that my happiness is not more deeply involved. I shall do very well again after a little while – and then it will be over; for they say everybody is in love once in their lives, and I shall have been let off easily."

When his letter to Mrs. Weston arrived, Emma read it with a degree of pleasure and admiration which made her at first shake her head over her own feelings, and then think she had undervalued their strength. It was a long, well-written letter, giving the particulars of his journey and of his feelings, expressing all the affection, gratitude, and respect which was natural and honourable, and describing everything exterior and local that could be supposed attractive, with spirit and precision. No suspicious flourishes now of apology or concern; it was the language of real feelings towards Mrs. Weston. The transition from Highbury to Enscombe, the contrast between the places in terms of social life was just enough touched on to show how keenly it was felt, and how much more might have been said but for the restraints of propriety. The charm of her own name was not missing. *Miss Woodhouse* appeared more than once, either with a compliment to her taste or a remembrance of what she had said. Compressed into the very lowest vacant corner were these words – "I had not a spare moment on Tuesday, as you know, for Miss Woodhouse's beautiful little friend. Pray make my excuses and adieus to her." This, Emma could not doubt, was all for herself. Harriet was remembered only from being *her* friend. His information about Enscombe was neither worse nor better than had been anticipated. Mrs. Churchill was recovering, and he dared not yet, even in his own imagination, plan a time for coming to Randalls again.

Gratifying as was the letter, its sentiments had not added any lasting warmth. She could still do without the writer, and he must learn to do without her. Her intentions were unchanged. Her resolution of refusal only grew more intriguing by the addition of a scheme for his subsequent consolation and happiness. His recollection of Harriet, and the words which clothed it, the "beautiful little friend," suggested to her the idea of Harriet's succeeding her in his affections. Was it impossible? No – Harriet undoubtedly was greatly his inferior in understanding; but he had been very much struck with the loveliness of her face and the warm simplicity of her manner. For Harriet, it would be advantageous and delightful indeed.

"I must not dwell upon it," said she. "I must not think of it. I know the danger of indulging such speculations. But stranger things have happened."

It was good to have a comfort in store on Harriet's behalf, though it might be wise not to think too much of it, for trouble was now at hand. As Frank Churchill's arrival had succeeded Mr. Elton's engagement in the conversation of Highbury, so now Mr. Elton's concerns were beginning again to be talked of. His wedding day was named. He would soon be among them again; Mr. Elton and his bride. There was hardly time to talk over the first letter from Enscombe before "Mr. Elton and his bride" was in everybody's mouth, and Frank Churchill was forgotten. Emma grew sick at the sound. She had enjoyed three weeks of happy exemption from Mr. Elton; and Harriet's mind, she had been willing to hope, had been lately gaining strength. With Mr. Weston's ball in view at least, there had been a great deal of insensibility to other things; but it was now too evident that she had not attained such a state of composure as could withstand the marriage itself.

Poor Harriet was in a flutter of spirits which required all the reasonings and soothings and attentions of every kind that Emma could give. Emma felt that she could not do too much for her, that Harriet had a right to all her patience; but it was hard work to be forever convincing without producing any effect. Harriet listened submissively, and said "it was very true – it was just as Miss Woodhouse described – it was not worthwhile to think about them – and she would not think about them any longer" – but no change of subject could avail, and the next half hour saw her as anxious and restless about the Eltons as before. At last Emma took another approach.

"Your allowing yourself to be so occupied and so unhappy about Mr. Elton's marrying, Harriet, is the strongest reproach you can make *me*. You could not give me a greater punishment for the mistake I made. It was all my doing, I know. I have not forgotten it, I assure you. It will be a painful reflection to me forever. Do not imagine me in danger of forgetting it."

Harriet felt this too much to utter more than a few words of eager exclamation. Emma continued,

"I would not ask you to cease talking of Mr. Elton for my sake alone. My being saved from pain is a very secondary consideration. I want you to save *yourself* from greater pain."

This appeal to her affections did more than all the rest. The idea of lacking gratitude and consideration for Miss Woodhouse, whom she really loved extremely, made her wretched for a while, and when the violence of grief was comforted away, it still remained powerful enough to prompt her to do what was right and support her in it very tolerably.

"You, who have been the best friend I ever had in my life – be ungrateful to you! Nobody is equal to you! I care for nobody as I do for you! Oh! Miss Woodhouse, how ungrateful I have been!"

Such expressions, assisted as they were by everything that look and manner could do, made Emma feel that she had never loved Harriet so well, nor valued her affection so highly before.

"There is no charm equal to tenderness of heart," said she afterwards to herself. "There is nothing to be compared to it. Warmth and tenderness of heart, with an affectionate, open manner, will beat all the clearness of head in the world, for attraction. I am sure it will. It is tenderness of heart which makes my dear father so generally beloved – which gives Isabella all her popularity. I do not have it; but I know how to prize and respect it. Harriet is my superior in all the charm and all the felicity it gives. Dear Harriet! I would not change you for the clearest-headed, best-judging female breathing. Oh! The reserve of a Jane Fairfax! Harriet is worth a hundred such: and for a wife – a sensible man's wife – it is invaluable. I mention no names; but happy is the man who trades Emma for Harriet!"

CHAPTER 32

Mrs. Elton was first seen at church: but curiosity could not be satisfied by a bride in a pew, and it must be left for the usual introductory visits which were then to be paid, to settle whether she was very pretty indeed, or only rather pretty, or not pretty at all.

Emma had feelings, less of curiosity than of pride or propriety, to make her resolve on not being the last to pay her respects. She made a point of Harriet's going with her, to get the worst of the business over with as soon as possible.

She could not enter the house again, could not be in the same room to which she had retreated three months ago, to lace up her boot, without *remembering*. A thousand vexatious thoughts came to her. Compliments, charades, and horrible blunders; and it was not to be supposed that poor Harriet should not be remembering, too; but she behaved very well, and was only rather pale and silent. The visit was of course short; and there was so much embarrassment and occupation of mind to shorten it, that Emma would not allow herself entirely to form an opinion of the lady, and on no account to give one, beyond her being "elegantly dressed and very pleasing."

She did not really like her. She would not be in a hurry to find fault, but she suspected that there was no elegance. Her person was rather good; her face not unpretty; but neither feature, nor voice, nor manner, were elegant. Emma thought at least it would turn out so.

As for Mr. Elton, his manners did not appear – but no, she would not permit a hasty or a witty word from herself about his manners. It was awkward at any time to be receiving wedding visits, and a man needed to be all grace to get through it. The woman was better off; she might have the assistance of fine clothes, and the privilege of bashfulness, but the man had only his own good sense to depend on. When she considered how peculiarly unlucky poor Mr. Elton was in being in the same room at once with the woman he had just married, the woman he had wanted to marry, and the woman whom he had been thought to marry, she must allow him to have the right to hide his unease behind a cloak of formality.

"Well, Miss Woodhouse," said Harriet when they had left the house, and after waiting in vain for her friend to begin, "Well, Miss Woodhouse (with a gentle sigh), what do you think of her? Is not she very charming?"

There was a little hesitation in Emma's answer.

"Oh! Yes – very – a very pleasing young woman."

"I think her beautiful, quite beautiful."

"Very nicely dressed, indeed; a remarkably elegant gown."

"I am not at all surprised that he should have fallen in love."

"Oh! No; there is nothing to surprise one at all. "

"I dare say," returned Harriet, sighing again, "I dare say she was very much attached to him."

"Perhaps; but it is not every man's fate to marry the woman who loves him best. Maybe Miss Hawkins wanted a home, and thought this the best offer she was likely to have."

"Yes," said Harriet earnestly, "and well she might, nobody could ever have a better. Well, I wish them happiness with all my heart. And now, Miss Woodhouse, I do not think I shall mind seeing them again. He is just as good as ever; but being married, you know, it is quite a different thing. No, indeed, Miss Woodhouse, you need not be afraid; I can sit and admire him now without any great misery. She does seem a charming young woman, just what he deserves. Happy creature! He called her 'Augusta' How delightful!"

When the visit was returned, Emma made up her mind. She could then see more and judge better. From Harriet's happening not to be at Hartfield, and her father's being present to talk with Mr. Elton, she had a quarter of an hour of the lady's conversation to herself. That quarter of an hour quite convinced her that Mrs. Elton was a vain woman, extremely well satisfied with herself, and thinking much of her own importance. She meant to shine and be very superior, but with manners which had been formed in a bad school. If not foolish, she was ignorant, and her society would certainly do Mr. Elton no good.

Harriet would have been a better match. If not wise or refined herself, she would have connected him with those who were; but Miss Hawkins, it might be fairly supposed from her conceit, had been the best of her own set. The rich brother-in-law near Bristol was the pride of the alliance

The very first subject after being seated was Maple Grove. The grounds of Hartfield were small in comparison, but neat and pretty; and the house was modern and well-built. Mrs. Elton seemed most favourably impressed by the size of the room, the entrance, and all that she could see or imagine. "Very like Maple Grove indeed! She was quite struck by the likeness! That room was the very shape and size of the morning-room at Maple Grove; her sister's favourite room." Mr. Elton was appealed to. "Was not it astonishingly like it? She could really almost fancy herself at Maple Grove."

"And the staircase – You know, as I came in, I observed how very like the staircase was; placed exactly in the same part of the house. I really could not help exclaiming! I assure you, Miss Woodhouse, it is very delightful to be reminded of a place I am so extremely partial to as Maple Grove. I have spent so many happy months there! (with a little sigh of sentiment). A charming place, undoubtedly. Everybody who sees it is struck by its beauty; but to me, it has been quite a home. Whenever you are transplanted, like me, Miss Woodhouse, you will understand how very delightful it is to find anything at all like what one has left behind. I always say this is quite one of the inconveniences of matrimony."

Emma made as slight a reply as she could; but it was fully sufficient for Mrs. Elton, who only wanted to be talking herself.

"So extremely like Maple Grove! And it is not merely the house; the grounds, I assure you, as far as I could observe, are strikingly alike. The laurels at Maple Grove stand very much in the same way – just across the lawn; and I had a glimpse of a fine large tree, with a bench round it, which made me feel so at home! My brother and sister will be enchanted with this place. People who have extensive grounds themselves are always pleased with anything in the same style."

Emma doubted the truth of this sentiment. She had a great idea that people who had extensive grounds themselves cared very little for the extensive grounds of anybody else; but it was not worthwhile to attack such an error, and therefore only said in reply,

"When you have seen more of this country, I am afraid you will think you have over-rated Hartfield. Surrey is full of beauties."

"Oh! Yes, I am quite aware of that. It is the garden of England, you know. Surrey is the garden of England."

"Yes; but we must not rest our claims on that distinction. Many counties, I believe, are called the garden of England, as well as Surrey."

"No, I fancy not," replied Mrs. Elton, with a most satisfied smile. "I never heard any county but Surrey called so."

Emma was silenced.

"My brother and sister have promised us a visit in the spring, or summer at latest," continued Mrs. Elton, "and that will be our time for exploring. While they are with us, we shall explore a great deal, I dare say. They will have their carriage, of course, which holds four perfectly; and therefore, without saying anything of *our* carriage, we should be able to explore the different beauties extremely well. When people come into a beautiful country of this sort, you know, Miss Woodhouse, one naturally wishes them to see as much as possible; and Mr. Suckling is extremely fond of exploring. We explored to King's-Weston twice last summer, in that way, most delightfully. You have many parties of that kind here, I suppose, Miss Woodhouse, every summer?"

"No; not immediately here. We are rather out of distance of the very striking beauties which attract the sort of parties you speak of, and we are a very quiet set of people, I believe; more disposed to stay at home than engage in schemes of pleasure."

"Ah! There is nothing like staying at home, for real comfort. Nobody can be more devoted to home than I am. Many a time my sister Selina has said, when she has been going to Bristol, 'I really cannot get this girl to move from the house. I absolutely must go in by myself, though I hate being stuck in the carriage without a companion; but Augusta, I believe, with her own good will, would never stir beyond the grounds.' Many a time she has said so; and yet I am no advocate for entire seclusion. I think, on the contrary, when people shut themselves up entirely from society, it is a very bad thing; and that it is much more advisable to mix in the world in a proper degree, without living in it either too much or too little. I perfectly understand your situation, however, Miss Woodhouse (looking towards Mr. Woodhouse). Your father's state of health must be a great drawback. Why does not he try Bath? Indeed, he should. Let me recommend Bath to you. I assure you I have no doubt of its doing Mr. Woodhouse good."

"My father tried it more than once, formerly; but without receiving any benefit. Mr. Perry, whose name, I dare say, is not unknown to you, does not conceive it would be at all more likely to be useful now."

"Ah! That's a great pity; for I assure you, Miss Woodhouse, where the waters do agree, it is quite wonderful the relief they give. In my Bath life, I have seen such instances of it! And it is so cheerful a place that it could not fail of being of use to Mr. Woodhouse's spirits, which, I understand, are sometimes much depressed. And as to its recommendations to *you*, I fancy I need not take much pains to dwell on them. The advantages of Bath to the young are pretty generally understood. It would be a charming introduction for you, who have lived so secluded a life; and I could immediately secure you some of the best society in the place. My particular friend, Mrs. Partridge, the lady I have always resided with when in Bath, would be most happy to show you any attentions, and would be the very person for you to go into public with."

It was as much as Emma could bear without being impolite. The idea of her being indebted to Mrs. Elton for what was called an *introduction* – of her going into public under the auspices of a friend of Mrs. Elton's. The dignity of Miss Woodhouse, of Hartfield, was sunk indeed!

She restrained herself, however, from any of the reproofs she could have given, and only thanked Mrs. Elton coolly, "But their going to Bath was quite out of the question; and she was not perfectly convinced that the place might suit her better than her father." And then, to prevent further outrage and indignation, changed the subject:

"I do not ask whether you are musical, Mrs. Elton. Upon these occasions, a lady's character generally precedes her; and Highbury has long known that you are a superior performer."

"Oh! No, indeed; I must protest against any such idea. A superior performer! Very far from it, I assure you. Consider from how partial a quarter your information came. I am dotingly fond of music – passionately fond – and my friends say I am not entirely devoid of taste; but as to anything else, upon my honour my performance is *mediocre* to the last degree. You, Miss Woodhouse, I well know, play delightfully. I assure you it has been the greatest satisfaction, comfort, and delight to me, to hear what a musical society I have joined. I absolutely cannot do without music. It is a necessity of life to me; and having always been used to a very musical society, both at Maple Grove and in Bath, it would have been a most serious sacrifice. I honestly said as much to Mr. E. when he was speaking of my future home, and expressing his fears lest the quietness of the neighbourhood should be disagreeable; and the inferiority of the house too – knowing what I had been accustomed to – of course he was not wholly without concern. When he was speaking of it in that way, I honestly said that *society* I could give up – parties, balls, plays – for I had no fear of seclusion. Blessed with so many resources within myself, it was not necessary to *me*. I could do very well without it. To those who had no resources it was a different thing; but my resources made me quite independent. And as to smaller-sized rooms than I had been used to, I really could not give it a thought. I hoped I was perfectly equal to any sacrifice of that description. Certainly I had been accustomed to every luxury at Maple Grove; but I did assure him that two carriages were not necessary to my happiness, nor were spacious apartments. 'But,' said I, 'to be quite honest, I do not think I can live without something of a musical society. I require nothing else; but without music, life would be a blank for me.'"

"We cannot suppose," said Emma, smiling, "that Mr. Elton would hesitate to assure you of there being a *very* musical society in Highbury; and I hope you will not find he has stretched the truth more than is forgivable, in consideration of the motive."

"No, indeed, I have no doubts at all in that regard. I am delighted to find myself in such a circle. I hope we shall have many sweet little concerts together. I think, Miss Woodhouse, you and I must establish a musical club, and have regular weekly meetings at your house, or ours. Will not it be a good plan? If *we* exert ourselves, I think others shall soon join us. Something of that nature would be particularly desirable for *me*, as an inducement to keep me in practice; for married women are but too apt to give up music."

"But you, who are so extremely fond of it – there can be no danger, surely."

"I should hope not; but really when I look round among my acquaintance, I tremble. Selina has entirely given up music – never touches the instrument – though she played sweetly. And the same may be said of Mrs. Jeffereys – Clara Partridge that was – and of the two Milmans, now Mrs. Bird and Mrs. James Cooper; and of more than I can enumerate. Upon my word, it is enough to put one in a fright. I used to be quite angry with Selina; but really, I begin to comprehend that a married woman has many things that require her attention. I believe I was half an hour this morning talking with my housekeeper."

"But everything of that kind," said Emma, "will soon be in so regular a routine – "

"Well," said Mrs. Elton, laughing, "we shall see."

Emma, finding her so determined to neglect her music, had nothing more to say; and, after a moment's pause, Mrs. Elton chose another subject.

"We have been visiting at Randalls," said she, "and found them both at home; and very pleasant people they seem to be. I like them extremely. Mr. Weston seems an excellent creature – quite a first-rate favourite with me already, I assure you. And *she* appears so truly good – there is something so motherly and kind-hearted about her. She was your governess?"

Mrs. Elton hardly waited for the affirmative before she went on.

"Having understood as much, I was rather astonished to find her so very lady-like! But she is really quite the gentlewoman."

"Mrs. Weston's manners," said Emma, "were always particularly good. Their propriety, simplicity, and elegance would make them the safest model for any young woman."

"And who do you think came in while we were there?"

Emma was quite at a loss. The tone implied some old acquaintance – and how could she possibly guess?

"Knightley!" continued Mrs. Elton. "Knightley himself! Was not it lucky? For, not being home when he called the other day, I had never seen him before; and of course, as so particular a friend of Mr. E.'s, I had a great curiosity. 'My friend Knightley' had been so often mentioned that I was really impatient to see him; and I must do my dear husband the justice to say that he need not be ashamed of his friend. Knightley is quite the gentleman. I like him very much. Decidedly, I think, a very gentleman-like man."

Happily, it was now time to be gone. They were off; and Emma could breathe.

"Insufferable woman!" was her immediate exclamation. "Worse than I had supposed. Absolutely insufferable! Knightley! I could not have believed it. Knightley! Never seen him in her life before, and call him Knightley! And discover that he is a gentleman! A little upstart, vulgar being, with her Mr. E., and her resources, and all her airs of pretension and under-bred finery. Actually to discover that Mr. Knightley is a gentleman! I doubt whether he will return the compliment, and discover her to be a lady. I could not have believed it! And to propose that she and I should unite to form a musical club! One would fancy we were bosom friends! And Mrs. Weston! Astonished that the person who had brought me up should be a gentlewoman! Worse and worse. I never met with her equal. Much beyond my hopes. Harriet is disgraced by any comparison. Oh! What would Frank Churchill say to her, if he were here? How angry and how diverted he would be! Ah! There I am thinking of him. Always the first person to be thought of!"

All this ran so glibly through her thoughts, that by the time her father had arranged himself, after the bustle of the Eltons' departure, and was ready to speak, she was very tolerably capable of attending.

"Well, my dear," he deliberately began, "considering we never saw her before, she seems a very pretty sort of young lady; and I dare say she was very much pleased with you. She speaks a little too quickly. A little quickness of voice there is which rather hurts the ear. But I do not like strange voices; and nobody speaks like you and poor Miss Taylor. However, she seems a very obliging, well-behaved young lady, and no doubt will make him a very good wife. Though I think he had better not have married. I made the best excuses I could for not having been able to visit on him and Mrs. Elton on this happy occasion; I said that I hoped I *would* in the course of the summer. But I ought to have gone before. Not to visit a bride is very bad manners. Ah! It shows what a sad invalid I am!"

"I dare say your apologies were accepted, sir. Mr. Elton knows you."

"Yes: but the young lady – a bride – I ought to have paid my respects to her if possible. It was being very deficient."

"But my dear papa, you are no friend to matrimony; and therefore why should you be so anxious to pay your respects to a *bride*? It is only encouraging people to marry if you make so much of them."

"No, my dear, I never encouraged anybody to marry, but I would always wish to pay every proper attention to a lady – and a bride, especially, is never to be neglected."

"Well, papa, if this is not encouragement to marry, I do not know what is. And I should never have expected you to be lending your sanction to such vanity."

"My dear, you do not understand me. This is a matter of mere common politeness and good-breeding, and has nothing to do with any encouraging people to marry."

Emma was done. Her father was growing agitated. Her mind returned to Mrs. Elton's offences, and long, very long, did they occupy her.

CHAPTER 33

Emma was not required, by any subsequent discovery, to retract her ill opinion of Mrs. Elton. Her observation had been pretty correct. She was self-important, presuming, familiar, ignorant, and ill-bred. She had a little beauty and a little accomplishment, but such poor judgment that she imagined herself coming with superior knowledge of the world to enliven and improve a country neighbourhood.

There was no reason to suppose Mr. Elton thought at all differently from his wife. He seemed not merely happy with her, but proud. He had the air of congratulating himself on having brought such a woman to Highbury. The greater part of her new acquaintance, disposed to commend, or not in the habit of judging, followed the lead of Miss Bates' goodwill and assumed that the bride must be as clever and as agreeable as she professed to be. Mrs. Elton's praise passed from one mouth to another as it ought to do, unimpeded by Miss Woodhouse, who readily continued her first contribution and talked with a good grace of her being "very pleasant and very elegantly dressed."

In one respect Mrs. Elton grew even worse than she had appeared at first. Her feelings altered towards Emma. Offended, probably, by the little encouragement which her proposals of friendship met with, she drew back in her turn and gradually became much more cold and distant. Though the effect was agreeable, the ill-will which produced it was necessarily increasing Emma's dislike. Her manners too – and Mr. Elton's – were unpleasant towards Harriet. They were sneering and negligent. Emma was, of course, the object of their joint dislike. When they had nothing else to say, it must be always easy to begin abusing

Miss Woodhouse; and the enmity which they dared not show in open disrespect to her found a broader vent in contemptuous treatment of Harriet.

Mrs. Elton took a great fancy to Jane Fairfax. She was not satisfied with expressing a natural and reasonable admiration, but wanted to assist and befriend her. About the third time of their meeting, Emma heard all Mrs. Elton's thoughts on the subject.

"Jane Fairfax is absolutely charming, Miss Woodhouse. I quite rave about Jane Fairfax. A sweet, interesting creature. So mild and ladylike – and with such talents! I assure you I think she has very extraordinary talents. I do not hesitate to say that she plays extremely well. I know enough of music to speak decidedly on that point. Oh! She is absolutely charming! You will laugh at my warmth, but upon my word; I talk of nothing but Jane Fairfax. Miss Woodhouse, we must exert ourselves and endeavour to do something for her. Such talents as hers must not be suffered to remain unknown. I dare say you have heard those charming lines of the poet,

'Full many a flower is born to blush unseen,
And waste its fragrance on the desert air.'

We must not allow them to be verified in sweet Jane Fairfax."

"I cannot think there is any danger of it," was Emma's calm answer, "and when you are better acquainted with Miss Fairfax's situation and understand what her home has been, with Colonel and Mrs. Campbell, you will not suppose that her talents can be unknown."

"Oh! But dear Miss Woodhouse, she is now in such seclusion, such obscurity, so thrown away. Whatever advantages she may have enjoyed with the Campbells are so palpably at an end! And I think she feels it. I am sure she does. She is very timid and silent. One can see that she feels the want of encouragement. I like her the better for it. I must confess it is a recommendation to me. I am a great advocate for timidity – and I am sure one does not often meet with it. But in those who are at all inferior, it is extremely prepossessing. Oh! I assure you, Jane Fairfax is a very delightful character, and interests me more than I can express."

"You appear to feel a great deal; but I am not aware how you or any of Miss Fairfax's acquaintance here, any of those who have known her longer than yourself, can show her any other attention than – "

"My dear Miss Woodhouse, a vast deal may be done by those who dare to act. You and I need not be afraid. If *we* set the example, many will follow it as far as they can; though all have not our situations. *We* have carriages to fetch and convey her home, and *we* live in a style which could not make the addition of Jane Fairfax, at any time, the least bit inconvenient. I shall certainly have her very often at my house, shall introduce her wherever I can, shall have musical parties to draw out her talents, and shall be constantly on the watch for an eligible situation. My acquaintance is so very extensive, that I have little doubt of hearing of something to suit her shortly. I shall introduce her, of course, very particularly to my brother and sister when they come to us. I am sure they will like her extremely; and when she gets a little acquainted with them, her fears will completely wear off, for there really is nothing in the manners of either but what is highly praiseworthy. I shall have her very often indeed while they are with me, and I dare say we shall sometimes find a seat for her in the carriage in some of our exploring parties."

"Poor Jane Fairfax!" thought Emma. "You do not deserve this. You may have done wrong with regard to Mr. Dixon, but this is a punishment beyond what you can have merited! The kindness and protection of Mrs. Elton! 'Jane Fairfax and Jane Fairfax.' Heavens!"

Emma did not have to listen to such things again – to any so exclusively addressed to herself – so distastefully decorated with a "dear Miss Woodhouse." The change on Mrs. Elton's side soon afterwards appeared, and she was left in peace – neither forced to be the very particular friend of Mrs. Elton, nor, under Mrs. Elton's guidance, the very active patroness of Jane Fairfax.

She looked on with some amusement. Miss Bates' gratitude for Mrs. Elton's attentions to Jane was in the first style of guileless simplicity and warmth. She was quite one of her worthies – the most amiable, affable, delightful woman – accomplished and gracious. Emma's only surprise was that Jane Fairfax should accept those attentions and tolerate Mrs. Elton as she seemed to do. She heard of her walking with the Eltons, sitting with the Eltons, spending a day with the Eltons! This was astonishing! She could not have believed it possible that the taste or the pride of Miss Fairfax could endure such society and friendship as the Vicarage had to offer.

"She is a riddle, quite a riddle!" said she. "To choose to remain here month after month, under privations of every sort! And now to choose the mortification of Mrs. Elton's notice and the shallowness of her conversation, rather than return to the companions who have always loved her with such real, generous affection."

Jane had come to Highbury supposedly for three months; the Campbells were gone to Ireland for that long. But now the Campbells had promised their daughter to stay at least till midsummer, and fresh invitations had arrived for her to join them there. According to Miss Bates – it all came from her – Mrs. Dixon had written most pressingly. Would Jane but go, means were to be found, servants sent, friends contrived – no travelling difficulty allowed to exist; but still she had declined it!

"She must have some motive, more powerful than appears, for refusing this invitation," was Emma's conclusion. "She must be under some sort of penance, inflicted either by the Campbells or herself. There is great fear, great caution, great resolution somewhere. She is *not* to be with the *Dixons*. The decree is issued by somebody. But why must she consent to be with the Eltons? Here is quite a separate puzzle."

Upon her speaking her wonder aloud on that part of the subject, before the few who knew her opinion of Mrs. Elton, Mrs. Weston ventured this apology for Jane.

"We cannot suppose that she has any great enjoyment at the Vicarage, my dear Emma – but it is better than being always at home. Her aunt is a good creature, but, as a constant companion, must be very tiresome. We must consider what Miss Fairfax leaves behind before we condemn her taste for what she goes to."

"You are right Mrs. Weston," said Mr. Knightley warmly, "Miss Fairfax is as capable as any of us of forming a just opinion of Mrs. Elton. Could she have chosen with whom to associate, she would not have chosen her. But (with a reproachful smile at Emma) she receives attentions from Mrs. Elton, which nobody else pays her."

Emma felt that Mrs. Weston was giving her a momentary glance; and she was herself struck by his warmth. With a faint blush, she presently replied,

"Such attentions as Mrs. Elton's, I should have imagined, would rather annoy than gratify Miss Fairfax. Mrs. Elton's invitations I should have imagined anything but inviting."

"I should not wonder," said Mrs. Weston, "if Miss Fairfax were to have been compelled by her aunt's eagerness in accepting Mrs. Elton's civilities for her. Poor Miss Bates may very likely have committed her niece and hurried her into a greater appearance of intimacy than her own good sense would have dictated, in spite of the very natural wish of a little change."

Both felt rather anxious to hear him speak again; and after a few minutes of silence, he said,

"Another thing must be taken into consideration – Mrs. Elton does not talk *to* Miss Fairfax as she speaks *of* her. As a general principle, you may be sure that Miss Fairfax awes Mrs. Elton by her superiority both of mind and manner; and that face-to-face Mrs. Elton treats her with all the respect which she has a claim to."

"I know how highly you think of Jane Fairfax," said Emma. Little Henry was in her thoughts, and a mixture of alarm and delicacy made her unsure what else to say.

"Yes," he replied, "anybody may know how highly I think of her."

"And yet," said Emma, beginning hastily, "and yet, perhaps, you may hardly be aware yourself how high it is. The extent of your admiration may take you by surprise some day or other."

Mr. Knightley was hard at work upon the lower buttons of his thick leather gaiters, and either the exertion of getting them together, or some other cause, brought the colour into his face, as he answered,

"That will never be, however, I can assure you. Miss Fairfax, I dare say, would not have me if I were to ask her; and I am very sure I shall never ask her."

Emma was pleased enough to exclaim,

"You are not vain, Mr. Knightley. I will say that for you."

He seemed hardly to hear her; he was thoughtful, and in a manner which showed him not pleased, soon afterwards said,

"So you have been thinking that I should marry Jane Fairfax."

"No indeed I have not. You have scolded me too much for matchmaking for me to presume to take such a liberty with you. What I said just now meant nothing. One says those sort of things, of course, without any idea of a serious meaning. Oh! No, upon my word I have not the smallest wish of your marrying Jane Fairfax or Jane anybody. You would not come in and sit with us in this comfortable way, if you were married."

Mr. Knightley was thoughtful again. The result of his reverie was, "No, Emma, I do not think the extent of my admiration for her will ever take me by surprise. I never had a thought of her in that way, I assure you."

And soon afterwards, "Jane Fairfax is a very charming young woman – but not even Jane Fairfax is perfect. She has a fault. She has not the open temper which a man would wish for in a wife."

Emma could not but rejoice to hear that she had a fault.

"Mrs. Weston, your argument carries the most weight with me. I can much more readily enter into the temptation of getting away from Miss Bates than I can believe in the triumph of Miss Fairfax's mind over Mrs. Elton. I have no faith in Mrs. Elton's acknowledging herself the inferior in thought, word, or deed; or in her being under any restraint beyond her own scanty rule of good-breeding. I cannot imagine that she will not be continually insulting her visitor with praise, encouragement, and offers of service; that she will not be continually detailing her magnificent intentions, from the procuring her a permanent situation to the including her in those delightful exploring parties which are to take place."

"Jane Fairfax has feeling," said Mr. Knightley. "I do not accuse her of lacking feeling. Her sensibilities, I suspect, are strong, and her temper excellent in its power of forbearance, patience, self-control; but it lacks openness. She is reserved, more reserved, I think, than she used to be, and I love an open temper."

"Well, Mrs. Weston," said Emma triumphantly when he left them, "what do you say now to Mr. Knightley's marrying Jane Fairfax?"

"Why really, dear Emma, I say that he is so very much occupied by the idea of *not* being in love with her, that I should not wonder if it were to end in his eventually being so."

CHAPTER 34

Everybody in and about Highbury who had ever visited Mr. Elton was disposed to pay him attention on his marriage. Dinner parties and evening parties were made for him and his lady; and invitations flowed in so fast that she had soon the pleasure of believing they were never to have a day without an invitation of some kind.

"I see how it is," said she. "I see what a life I am to lead among you. We really seem quite the fashion. If this is living in the country, it is nothing very to worry about. From Monday next to Saturday, I assure you we have not a disengaged day! A woman with fewer resources than I have need not have been concerned."

Her Bath habits made evening parties perfectly natural to her, and Maple Grove had given her a taste for dinners. She was a little shocked at the lack of two drawing rooms, at the poor attempt at cakes, and there being no ice in the Highbury card parties. Mrs. Bates, Mrs. Perry, Mrs. Goddard and others were a good deal behind hand in knowledge of the world, but *she* would soon show them how everything ought to be arranged. In the course of the spring she must return their civilities by one very superior party, in which her card tables should be set out with their separate candles and unbroken packs in the true style, and more waiters engaged for the evening than their own establishment could furnish, to carry round the refreshments at exactly the proper hour, and in the proper order.

Emma, in the meantime, could not be satisfied without a dinner at Hartfield for the Eltons. They must not do less than others, or they should be exposed to suspicions, and imagined capable of resentment.

A dinner there must be. After Emma had talked about it for ten minutes, Mr. Woodhouse felt no unwillingness, and only made the usual stipulation of not carving the meat himself, with the usual difficulty of deciding who should do it for him.

The persons to be invited required little thought. Besides the Eltons, it must be the Westons and Mr. Knightley, and it was hardly less inevitable that poor little Harriet must be asked to make the eighth; but this invitation was not given with equal satisfaction, and on many accounts Emma was particularly pleased by Harriet's begging to be allowed to decline it. "She would rather not be in *his* company more than she could help. She was not yet quite able to see him and his charming happy wife together without feeling uncomfortable. If Miss Woodhouse would not be displeased, she would rather stay at home." It was precisely what Emma would have wished, had she deemed it possible enough for wishing. She was delighted with the fortitude of her little friend — for fortitude she knew it was in her to give up being in company and stay at home. She could now invite the very person whom she really wanted to make the eighth, Jane Fairfax. Since her last conversation with Mrs. Weston and Mr. Knightley, her conscience had been bothering her, and she decided it was time to do her part for Jane Fairfax.

"Mr. Knightley's words were very true," said she, "and I have behaved very shamefully. Of the same age, and always knowing her, I ought to have been more her friend. She will never like me now. I have neglected her too long. But I will show her greater attention than I have done before."

Every invitation was successful, and they were all happy to come. However, a rather unlucky circumstance occurred. The two eldest little Knightleys were to pay their grandpa and aunt a visit of some weeks in the spring, and their papa now proposed bringing them, and staying one whole day at Hartfield — which one day would be the very day of this party. His professional engagements did not allow him to change his plans. Mr. Woodhouse considered eight persons at dinner together as the utmost that his nerves could bear — and here would be a ninth — and Emma apprehended that it would be a ninth very much out of humour.

She comforted her father better than she could comfort herself, by saying that though he certainly would make them nine, yet he always said so little, that the increase of noise would be very immaterial. She thought it in reality a sad occurrence for herself, to have his grave looks and reluctant conversation among the party.

The event was more favourable to Mr. Woodhouse than to Emma. John Knightley came; but Mr. Weston was unexpectedly summoned to town and must be absent on the very day. He might be able to join them later in the evening, but certainly not for dinner. Mr. Woodhouse was quite at ease; and seeing him so, with the arrival of the little boys and the philosophic composure of her brother on hearing his fate, removed the primary source of Emma's vexation.

The day came, the party were punctually assembled, and Mr. John Knightley seemed early to devote himself to the business of being agreeable. Instead of drawing his brother off to a window while they waited for dinner, he was talking to Miss Fairfax. Mrs. Elton, as elegant as lace and pearls could make her, he looked at in silence – wanting only to observe enough for Isabella's information – but Miss Fairfax was an old acquaintance and a quiet girl, and he could talk to her. He had met her before breakfast as he was returning from a walk with his little boys, when it had been just beginning to rain, and he now said to her,

"I hope you did not venture far, Miss Fairfax, this morning, or I am sure you must have been wet. *We* scarcely got home in time. I hope you turned around immediately."

"I only went to the post office," she replied, "and reached home before it was raining too hard. It is my daily errand. I always fetch the letters when I am here. It saves trouble, and is a something to get me out. A walk before breakfast does me good."

"Not a walk in the rain, I should imagine."

"No, but it wasn't raining when I set out."

Mr. John Knightley smiled, and replied,

"That is to say, you chose to have your walk, for you were not six yards from your own door when I had the pleasure of meeting you; and Henry and John had seen more drops than they could count long before. The post office has a great charm at one period of our lives. When you have lived to my age, you will begin to think letters are never worth going through the rain for."

There was a little blush, and then this answer,

"I must not hope to be ever situated as you are, in the midst of every dearest connection, and therefore I cannot expect that simply growing older should make me indifferent about letters."

"Indifferent! Oh! No – I never conceived you could become indifferent. Letters are no matter of indifference; they are generally a very positive curse."

"You are speaking of letters of business; mine are letters of friendship."

"I have often thought them the worse of the two," replied he coolly. "Business, you know, may bring money, but friendship hardly ever does."

"Ah! You are not serious now. I know Mr. John Knightley too well – I am very sure he understands the value of friendship as well as anybody. I can easily believe that letters mean very little to you, but it is not your being ten years older than myself which makes the difference. It is not age, but situation. You have everybody dearest to you always near you. I, probably, never shall again; and therefore, till I have outlived all my affections, a post office, I think, must always have power to draw me out, in worse weather than today."

"When I talked of your being altered by time, by the progress of years," said John Knightley, "I meant to imply the change of situation which time usually brings. I consider one as including the other. As an old friend, you will allow me to hope, Miss Fairfax, that ten years hence you may have as many concentrated objects of affection as I have."

It was kindly said, and very far from giving offence. A pleasant "thank you" seemed meant to laugh it off, but a blush, a quivering lip, a tear in the eye, showed that it was felt beyond a laugh. Her attention was now claimed by Mr. Woodhouse, who was paying his compliments to the ladies.

"I am very sorry to hear, Miss Fairfax, of your being out this morning in the rain. Young ladies should take care of themselves. Young ladies are delicate plants. They should take care of their health and their complexion. My dear, did you change your stockings?"

"Yes, sir, I did indeed; and I am very much obliged by your kind solicitude about me."

"My dear Miss Fairfax, young ladies are very sure to be cared for. I hope your good grandma and aunt are well. They are some of my very old friends. I wish my health allowed me to visit them more. You do us a great deal of honour today, I am sure. My daughter and I are both highly sensible of your goodness, and have the greatest satisfaction in seeing you at Hartfield."

The kind-hearted, polite old man then sat down and felt that he had done his duty, making every fair lady welcome and easy.

By this time, the walk in the rain had reached Mrs. Elton, and her disapproval now opened upon Jane.

"My dear Jane, what is this I hear? Going to the post office in the rain! This must not be, I assure you. You sad girl, how could you do such a thing? It is a sign I was not there to take care of you."

Jane very patiently assured her that she had not caught any cold.

"Oh! Do not tell *me*. You really are a very sad girl, and do not know how to take care of yourself. To the post office indeed! Mrs. Weston, did you ever hear the like? You and I must positively exert our authority."

"My advice," said Mrs. Weston kindly and persuasively, "I certainly do feel tempted to give. Miss Fairfax, you must not run such risks. Liable as you have been to severe colds, indeed you ought to be particularly careful, especially at this time of year. The spring I always think requires more than common care. Better wait an hour or two, or even half a day for your letters, than run the risk of bringing on your cough again. Yes, I am sure you are much too reasonable to do something like that again."

"Oh! She *shall not* do such a thing again," eagerly rejoined Mrs. Elton. "We will not allow her to do such a thing again" – and nodding significantly – "there must be some arrangement made, there must indeed. I shall speak to Mr. E. The man who fetches our letters every morning (one of our men, I forget his name) shall inquire for yours too and bring them to you. That will eliminate all difficulties you know; and from *us* I really think, my dear Jane, you can have no hesitation to accept such an accommodation."

"You are extremely kind," said Jane, "but I cannot give up my early walk. I am advised to be out of doors as much as I can. I must walk somewhere, and the post office is a destination; upon my word, I have scarcely ever had a bad morning before."

"My dear Jane, say no more about it. The thing is determined, that is (laughing affectedly) as far as I can presume to determine anything without the concurrence of my husband. But I do flatter myself, my dear Jane, that I carry some influence with him still. If I meet with no difficulties from that quarter, consider the point as settled."

"Excuse me," said Jane earnestly, "I cannot by any means consent to such an arrangement, so needlessly troublesome to your servant. If the errand were not a pleasure to me, it could be done, as it always is when I am not here, by my grandma's servant."

"Oh! My dear; but Patty already has so much to do! And it is a kindness to employ our men."

Instead of answering, Jane began speaking again to Mr. John Knightley.

"The post office is a wonderful establishment!" said she. "The regularity and dispatch of it! If one thinks of all that it has to do, and all that it does so well, it is really astonishing!"

"It is certainly very well regulated."

"So seldom that any negligence or blunder appears! So seldom that a letter, among the thousands that are constantly passing about the kingdom, is even carried wrong – and not one in a million, I suppose, actually lost! And when one considers the variety of handwriting that must be deciphered, it increases the wonder!"

"The clerks become experts with practice. They must begin with some quickness of sight and hand, and exercise improves them. If you want any further explanation," continued he, smiling, "they are paid for it. That is the key to a great deal of capacity. The public pays and must be served well."

The varieties of handwriting were further talked of, and the usual observations made.

"I have heard it asserted," said John Knightley, "that the same sort of handwriting often prevails in a family; and where the same master teaches, it is natural enough. But for that reason, I should imagine the likeness must be chiefly confined to the females, for boys have very little instruction of that sort after an early age, and must simply do the best they can. Isabella and Emma, I think, do write very much alike. I cannot always tell their writing apart."

"Yes," said his brother hesitatingly, "there is a likeness. I know what you mean – but Emma's handwriting is superior."

"Isabella and Emma both write beautifully," said Mr. Woodhouse; "and always did. And so does poor Mrs. Weston" – with half a sigh and half a smile at her.

"I never saw any gentleman's handwriting" – Emma began, looking also at Mrs. Weston; but stopped, on perceiving that Mrs. Weston was talking with someone else – and the pause gave her time to reflect, "Now, how am I going to bring him up? Am I unequal to speaking his name at once before all these people? Is it necessary for me to use any roundabout phrase? Your Yorkshire friend – your correspondent in Yorkshire – that would be the way, I suppose, if I were very direct. Yes, I can pronounce his name without the smallest distress."

Mrs. Weston was now paying attention and Emma began again – "Mr. Frank Churchill writes one of the best gentlemen's hands I ever saw."

"I do not admire it," said Mr. Knightley. "It is too small — lacks strength. It is like a woman's writing."

This was not agreed to by either lady. They defended him against such an accusation. "No, it by no means wanted strength — it was not a large hand, but very clear and certainly strong. Had not Mrs. Weston any letter with her to produce?" No, she had heard from him very recently, but having answered the letter, had put it away.

"If we were in the other room," said Emma, "if I had my writing desk, I am sure I could produce a specimen. I have a note of his. Do not you remember, Mrs. Weston, employing him to write for you one day?"

"He chose to say he was employed."

"Well, well, I have that note; and can show it after dinner to convince Mr. Knightley."

"Oh! When a gallant young man, like Mr. Frank Churchill," said Mr. Knightley drily, "writes to a fair lady like Miss Woodhouse, he will, of course, put forth his best."

Dinner was on the table. Mrs. Elton, before she could be spoken to, was ready; and before Mr. Woodhouse had reached her with his request to be allowed to walk her into the dining room, was saying —

"Must I go first? I really am ashamed of always leading the way."

Jane's insistence on fetching her own letters had not escaped Emma. She had heard and seen it all; and felt some curiosity to know whether the wet walk of this morning had produced any. She suspected that it *had*; that it would not have been so resolutely encountered but in full expectation of hearing from someone very dear, and that it had not been in vain. She thought there was an air of greater happiness than usual — a glow both of complexion and spirits.

She could have made an inquiry or two, as to the expedition and the expense of the Irish mail — but she abstained. She was quite determined not to utter a word that should hurt Jane Fairfax's feelings; and they followed the other ladies out of the room, arm in arm, with an appearance of goodwill highly becoming to the beauty and grace of each.

CHAPTER 35

When the ladies returned to the drawing room after dinner, Emma found it impossible to prevent their making two distinct parties. Mrs. Elton was engrossing Jane Fairfax in conversation and entirely ignoring Emma. She and Mrs. Weston were obliged to be almost always either talking together or silent together. Mrs. Elton left them no choice. Though much that passed between her and Jane was in a half-whisper, especially on Mrs. Elton's side, there was no avoiding knowledge of their principal subjects: the post office, catching cold, fetching letters, and friendship were long under discussion. Then a subject came up that must have been quite unpleasant to Jane – inquiries whether she had yet heard of any governess positions likely to suit her, and professions of Mrs. Elton's meditated intervention.

"It is already April!" said she, "I get quite anxious about you. June will soon be here."

"But I have never fixed on June or any other month – I have alluded only to finding something during this summer."

"But have you really heard nothing?"

"I have not even made any inquiry; I do not wish to make any yet."

"Oh! My dear, we cannot begin too early; you are not aware of the difficulty of procuring the most desirable situation."

"I not aware!" said Jane, shaking her head; "dear Mrs. Elton, who can have thought of it more than I have done?"

"But you have not seen as much of the world as I have. You do not know how many candidates there always are for the *good* situations. I saw a vast deal of that in the neighbourhood around Maple Grove. A cousin of Mr. Suckling, Mrs. Bragge, had so many applications; everybody was anxious to be in her family, for she moves in the first circle. Expensive wax candles in the schoolroom! You may imagine how desirable! Of all the houses in the kingdom, Mrs. Bragge's is the one I would most wish to see you in."

"Colonel and Mrs. Campbell are to be in town again by midsummer," said Jane, "I must spend some time with them; I am sure they will want it, and afterwards I may probably be glad to dispose of myself. But I would not wish you to take the trouble of making any inquiries at present."

"Trouble! I assure you, my dear Jane, the Campbells can hardly be more concerned about you than I am. I shall write to Mrs. Partridge in a day or two, and shall give her a strict charge to be on the lookout for anything eligible."

"Thank you, but I would rather you did not mention the subject to her; till the time draws nearer, I do not wish to be giving anybody trouble."

"But, my dear child, the time *is* drawing near. It is now April, and June, or say even July, is very near, with such business to accomplish before us. Your inexperience really amuses me! A situation such as you deserve, and your friends would require for you, is no everyday occurrence. It is not obtained at a moment's notice; indeed, indeed, we must begin inquiring immediately."

"Excuse me, ma'am, but this is by no means my intention; I make no inquiry myself, and should be sorry to have any made by my friends. When I am quite determined as to the time, I am not at all afraid of being long unemployed. There are places in London where inquiry would soon produce something that would do."

"Something that would do!" repeated Mrs. Elton. "Aye, *that* may suit your humble ideas of yourself; I know what a modest creature you are. But it will not satisfy your friends to have you taking up with any inferior, commonplace situation, in a family not moving in a certain circle, or able to command the elegances of life."

"You are very obliging, but as to all that, I am very indifferent; it does not matter to me if I am with the very rich. My mortifications, I think, would only be the greater; I should suffer more from comparison. A gentleman's family is all that I should want."

"I know you, I know you; you would settle for anything. But with your superior talents, you have a right to move in the first circle. Your musical knowledge alone would entitle you to name your own terms, have as many rooms as you like, and mix in the family as much as you chose. You must and shall be delightfully, honourably and comfortably settled before the Campbells or I have any rest."

"I am very serious in not wishing anything to be attempted at present for me," said Jane. "I am exceedingly obliged to you, Mrs. Elton, I am obliged to anybody who feels for me, but I am quite serious in wishing nothing to be done till the summer. For two or three months longer I shall remain where I am, and as I am."

"And I am quite serious too, I assure you," replied Mrs. Elton gaily, "in resolving to be always on the watch, and employing my friends to watch also, that nothing really unexceptionable may pass us."

In this style she went on; never thoroughly stopped by anything till Mr. Woodhouse came into the room. She then changed the subject, and Emma heard her saying in the same half-whisper to Jane,

"Here comes this dear old admirer of mine, I protest! Only think of his gallantry in coming away before the other men! What a dear creature he is; I assure you I like him excessively. I commend all that quaint, old-fashioned politeness, and fancy I am rather a favourite; he took notice of my gown. How do you like it? Selina's choice – nice, I think, but I do not know whether it is too extravagant. My natural taste is all for simplicity; a simple style of dress is so infinitely preferable to finery. But I am quite in the minority, I believe; few people seem to value simplicity of dress – show and finery are everything to them."

The whole party were but just reassembled in the drawing room when Mr. Weston made his appearance among them. He had returned to a late dinner, and walked to Hartfield as soon as it was over. The rest were glad to see him, but John Knightley was in mute astonishment. That a man who might have spent his evening quietly at home after a day of business in London should set off again and walk half-a-mile to another man's house, for the sake of being in company till bedtime, was a circumstance he could hardly comprehend. A man who had been in motion since eight o'clock in the morning, and might now have been still! Such a man, to leave the tranquillity and independence of his own fire, and on the evening of a cold, sleety April day rush out again into the world! Could he by a touch of his finger have instantly taken back his wife, there would have been a motive; but his coming would probably prolong rather than break up the party. John Knightley looked at him with amazement, then shrugged his shoulders, and said, "I could not have believed it even of *him*."

Mr. Weston meanwhile, perfectly unsuspicious of the indignation he was exciting, happy and cheerful as usual, was making himself agreeable among the rest. Having satisfied the inquiries of his wife as to his dinner, convincing her that none of all her careful directions to the servants had been forgotten, he was proceeding to a family communication. He gave her a letter, it was from Frank, and to herself; he had taken the liberty of opening it.

"Read it, read it," said he, "it will give you pleasure. Only a few lines – it will not take you long; read it to Emma."

The two ladies looked over it together; and he sat smiling and talking to them the whole time, in a voice a little subdued, but very audible to everybody.

"Well, he is coming, you see; good news, I think. What do you say to it? I always told you he would be here again soon, did I not? In London next week, you see – at the latest; most likely they will be there tomorrow or Saturday. As to Mrs. Churchill's illness, all nothing of course. But it is an excellent thing to have Frank among us again, as near as London. They will stay a good while when they do come, and he will be half his time with us. This is precisely what I wanted. Well, pretty good news, isn't it? Have you finished it? Has Emma read it all?"

Mrs. Weston was most comfortably pleased on the occasion. Her looks and words had nothing to restrain them. She was happy, she knew she was happy, and knew she ought to be happy. Her congratulations were warm and open; but Emma was a little occupied in weighing her own feelings, and trying to understand the degree of her agitation, which she rather thought was considerable.

Mr. Weston, however, too eager to be very observant, too communicative to want others to talk, was very well satisfied with what she did say, and soon moved away to make the rest of his friends happy by communicating what the whole room must have overheard already. It was good that he took everybody's joy for granted, or he might not have thought either Mr. Woodhouse or Mr. Knightley particularly delighted.

CHAPTER 36

"I hope I shall soon have the pleasure of introducing my son to you," said Mr. Weston.

Mrs. Elton, very willing to suppose a particular compliment intended her by such a hope, smiled most graciously.

"You have heard of Frank Churchill, I presume," he continued "and know him to be my son, though he does not bear my name."

"Oh! Yes, and I shall be very happy in his acquaintance. I am sure Mr. Elton will lose no time in visiting him; and we shall both have great pleasure in seeing him at the Vicarage."

"You are very obliging. Frank will be extremely happy, I am sure. He is to be in town next week, if not sooner. We have notice of it in a letter today. I met the letters on my way this morning, and seeing my son's hand, presumed to open it – though it was not directed to me – it was to Mrs. Weston. She is his principal correspondent, I assure you. I hardly ever get a letter."

"And so you absolutely opened what was directed to her! Oh! Mr. Weston (laughing affectedly) I must protest against that. A most dangerous precedent indeed! I beg you will not let your neighbours follow your example. Upon my word, I could not have believed it of you!"

"Aye, we men are sad fellows. You must take care of yourself, Mrs. Elton. This letter tells us – it is a short letter, written in a hurry, merely to give us notice – it tells us that they are all coming to London immediately, on Mrs. Churchill's account. She has not been well the whole winter, and thinks Enscombe too cold for her – so they are all to move southward without loss of time."

"Indeed! From Yorkshire, I think. Enscombe is in Yorkshire?"

"Yes, they are about 190 miles from London. A considerable journey."

"Yes, upon my word, very considerable. Sixty-five miles farther than from Maple Grove to London. But what is distance, Mr. Weston, to people of large fortune? You would be amazed to hear how my brother, Mr. Suckling, sometimes flies about. You will hardly believe me, but twice in one week he and Mr. Bragge went to London and back again with four horses."

"The inconvenient distance from Enscombe," said Mr. Weston, "is made worse by the fact that Mrs. Churchill has *supposedly* not been able to leave the sofa for a week. In Frank's last letter she complained, he said, of being too weak to get into her garden room without having both his arm and his uncle's! This, you know, betrays a great degree of weakness – but now she is so impatient to be in town, that she means to sleep only two nights on the road. Certainly, delicate ladies have very extraordinary constitutions, Mrs. Elton. You must acknowledge that."

"No, indeed, I shall acknowledge nothing. I always take the side of my own sex. You will find me a formidable antagonist on that point. I always stand up for women; and I assure you, if you knew how Selina feels with respect to sleeping at an inn, you would not wonder at Mrs. Churchill's making incredible exertions to avoid it. Selina says it is quite a horror to her. She always travels with her own sheets; an excellent precaution. Does Mrs. Churchill do the same?"

"Depend upon it, Mrs. Churchill does everything that any other fine lady ever did. Mrs. Churchill will not be second to any lady in the land for – "

Mrs. Elton eagerly interposed with,

"Oh! Mr. Weston, do not mistake me. Selina is no fine lady, I assure you. Do not run away with such an idea."

"Is she not? Then she is no model for Mrs. Churchill, who is as thorough a fine lady as anybody ever beheld."

Mrs. Elton began to think she had been wrong in objecting so warmly. It was by no means her object to have it believed that her sister was *not* a fine lady; she was considering in what way she had best retract, when Mr. Weston went on.

"Mrs. Churchill is not much in my good graces, as you may suspect; but this is quite between ourselves. She is very fond of Frank, and therefore I would not speak ill of her. Besides, she is out of health now; but *that* indeed, by her own account, she has always been. I would not say so to everybody, Mrs. Elton, but I have not much faith in Mrs. Churchill's illness."

"If she is really ill, why not go to Bath, Mr. Weston? To Bath, or to Clifton?"

"She has taken it into her head that Enscombe is too cold for her. The fact is, I suppose, that she is tired of Enscombe. She has now been a longer time stationary there than she ever was before, and she begins to want change. It is a secluded place. A fine place, but very secluded."

"Aye, like Maple Grove, I dare say. Nothing can stand more away from the road than Maple Grove. Such an immense wood all round it! You seem shut out from everything – in the most complete privacy. And Mrs. Churchill probably has not health or spirits like Selina to enjoy that sort of seclusion. Or, perhaps she may not have resources in herself to be qualified for a country life. I always say a woman cannot have too many resources – and I feel very thankful that I have so many myself as to be quite independent of society."

"Frank was here in February for a fortnight."

"So I have heard. He will find an *addition* to the society of Highbury when he comes again; that is, if I may presume to call myself an addition. But perhaps he may never have heard of there being such a creature in the world."

This was too loud a call for a compliment to be passed by, and Mr. Weston with very good grace, immediately exclaimed,

"My dear madam! Nobody but yourself could imagine such a thing possible. Not heard of you! I believe Mrs. Weston's letters lately have been full of very little else than Mrs. Elton."

He had done his duty and could return to talking of his son.

"When Frank left us," continued he, "it was quite uncertain when we might see him again, which makes this day's news doubly welcome. It has been completely unexpected. That is, *I* was convinced he would be here again soon, I was sure something favourable would turn up – but nobody believed me. He and Mrs. Weston were both dreadfully despondent. 'How could he contrive to come? And how could it be supposed that his uncle and aunt would spare him again?' And so forth – I always felt that something would happen in our favour; and so it has, you see. I have observed, Mrs. Elton, in the course of my life, that if things are going badly one month, they are sure to get better the next."

"Very true, Mr. Weston, perfectly true. It is just what I used to say to a certain gentleman who was courting me when, because things did not go quite right, did not proceed with all the rapidity which suited his feelings; he was ready to despair, and exclaim that he was sure at this rate it would be *May* before we were married! Oh! The pains I took to dispel those gloomy ideas and give him more cheerful views! The carriage – we had disappointments when the carriage was being built; one morning, I remember, he came to me quite in despair."

She was stopped by a slight fit of coughing, and Mr. Weston instantly seized the opportunity of going on.

"You were mentioning May. May is the very month which Mrs. Churchill has ordered herself to spend in some warmer place than Enscombe – in short, to spend in London; so that we have the agreeable prospect of frequent visits from Frank the whole spring – precisely the season of the year which one should have chosen for it. Spring days are almost at their longest; the weather is genial and pleasant, always inviting one out, and it is never too hot for exercise. When he was here before, we made the best of it; but there was a good deal of wet, damp, cheerless weather. There always is in February, you know, and we could not do half what we intended. Now will be the time. This will be complete enjoyment; and I do not know, Mrs. Elton, whether the uncertainty of our meetings, the sort of constant expectation there will be of his coming in today or tomorrow, and at any hour, may not be more friendly to happiness than having him actually in the house. I think it is so. I hope you will be pleased with my son. He is generally thought a fine young man, but do not expect a prodigy. Mrs. Weston's partiality for him is very great, and, as you may suppose, most gratifying to me. She thinks nobody equal to him."

"And I assure you, Mr. Weston, I have very little doubt that my opinion will be decidedly in his favour. I have heard so much praise of Mr. Frank Churchill. At the same time, it is fair to observe that I am one of those who always judge for themselves, and are by no means implicitly guided by others. I give you notice that as I find your son, so shall I judge him. I am no flatterer."

"I hope," he said, "I have not spoken too harshly of poor Mrs. Churchill. If she is truly ill I should be sorry to do her injustice; but there are some traits in her character which make it difficult for me to speak of her with the restraint I could wish. You cannot be ignorant, Mrs. Elton, of my connection with the family. Frank's mother would never have been slighted as she was but for her. Mr. Churchill has pride; but his pride is nothing compared to his wife's. His is a quiet, gentlemanlike sort of pride that would harm nobody, and only make him a little helpless and tiresome; but her pride is arrogance! And what makes it harder to bear is that she was nobody when he married her, barely the daughter of a gentleman; but ever since her being turned into a Churchill she has out-Churchilled them all in high and mighty claims."

"Only think! Well, that must be most provoking! I have quite a horror of upstarts. Maple Grove has given me a thorough disgust of people of that sort; for there is a family in that neighbourhood who are such an annoyance to my brother and sister from the airs they give themselves! Your description of Mrs. Churchill made me think of them. People of the name of Tupman, very recently settled there, and encumbered with many low connections, but giving themselves immense airs, and expecting to be on a footing with the old established families. A year and a half is the very utmost that they can have lived at West Hall; and how they got their fortune nobody knows. They came from Birmingham, which is not a place to promise much, you know, Mr. Weston. But nothing more is positively known of the Tupmans, though a good many things I assure you are suspected; and yet by their manners they evidently think themselves equal even to my brother, Mr. Suckling, who happens to be one of their nearest neighbours. It is quite disgraceful. Mr. Suckling, who has been eleven years a resident at Maple Grove, and whose father had it before him – I believe, at least – I am almost sure that old Mr. Suckling had completed the purchase before his death."

They were interrupted. Tea was being carried round, and Mr. Weston, having said all that he wanted, soon took the opportunity of walking away.

After tea, Mr. and Mrs. Weston and Mr. Elton sat down with Mr. Woodhouse to cards. The remaining five were left to themselves, and Emma doubted they would get along very well. Mr. Knightley did not seem interested in conversation. Mrs. Elton wanted to be noticed, but no one seemed to want to notice her. And Emma was herself in a worry of spirits which would have made her prefer being silent.

Mr. John Knightley proved more talkative than his brother. He was to leave them early the next day; and he soon began with –

"Well, Emma, I do not believe I have anything more to say about the boys; but you have your sister's letter. My explanation would be much more concise than hers, and probably not much in the same spirit; all that I have to recommend being comprised in, do not spoil them, and do not treat them with medicine."

"I rather hope to satisfy you both," said Emma, "for I shall do all in my power to make them happy, which will be enough for Isabella; and happiness must prohibit false indulgence and medicine."

"And if you find them troublesome, you must send them home again."

"That is rather unlikely. Do you think they will be too much trouble for us?"

"They may be too noisy for your father; or even may be some inconvenience to you, if your dinner engagements continue to increase as much as they have done lately."

"Increase!"

"Certainly; you must be sensible that the last half year has made a great difference in your way of life."

"Difference! No indeed I am not."

"There can be no doubt of your being much more often with company than you used to be. Witness this very time. Here am I come down for only one day, and you are engaged with a dinner party! When did it happen before, or anything like it? Your neighbourhood is growing, and you mix more with it. A little while ago, every letter to Isabella brought an account of fresh excitements; dinners at Mr. Cole's, or balls at the Crown. The difference which Randalls alone makes is very great."

"Yes," said his brother quickly, "it is Randalls that does it all."

"Very well; and as Randalls, I suppose, is not likely to have less influence than before, it strikes me as a possible thing, Emma, that Henry and John may be sometimes in the way. And if they are, I only beg you to send them home."

"No," cried Mr. Knightley, "that need not be the consequence. Let them be sent to Donwell. I shall certainly be able to care for them."

"Upon my word," exclaimed Emma, "you amuse me! I should like to know how many of all my numerous engagements take place without your being included; and why I am to be supposed in danger of being unable to care for the little boys. These engagements of mine – what have they been? Dining once with the Coles – and having a ball talked of, which never took place. I can understand you (nodding at Mr. John Knightley) – your good fortune in meeting with so many of your friends at once here, delights you too much to pass unnoticed. But you, (turning to Mr. Knightley), know how very, very seldom I am ever two hours from Hartfield, why you should foresee such a turn of events for me, I cannot imagine. And as to my dear little boys, I must say, that if aunt Emma has not time for them, I do not think they would fare much better with uncle Knightley, who is absent from home about five hours where she is absent one – and who, when he is at home, is either reading a book or settling his accounts."

Mr. Knightley seemed to be trying not to smile, and succeeded without difficulty, upon Mrs. Elton's beginning to talk to him.

CHAPTER 37

A very little quiet reflection was enough to satisfy Emma about the nature of her agitation on hearing this news of Frank Churchill. She was soon convinced that it was not for herself she was feeling at all apprehensive or embarrassed; it was for him. Her own attachment had really subsided into a mere nothing; it was not worth thinking of. But if he, who had undoubtedly been the most in love of the two, were to be returning with the same warmth of sentiment which he had taken away, it would be very distressing. If a separation of two months should not have cooled him, caution for him and for herself would be necessary. She did not intend to have her own affections entangled again, and it would be her primary goal to avoid any encouragement of his.

She wished she might be able to keep him from an absolute declaration of affection. That would be so very painful a conclusion of their present acquaintance! And yet, she could not help rather anticipating something decisive. She felt as if the spring would not pass without bringing a crisis, an event, a something to alter her present composed and tranquil state.

It was not very long, though rather longer than Mr. Weston had foreseen, before she had the power of forming some opinion of Frank Churchill's feelings. The Enscombe family were not in town quite as soon as had been imagined, but he was at Highbury very soon afterwards. He rode down for a couple of hours; he could not yet do more. He came from Randalls immediately to Hartfield, and she could then exercise all her quick observation and speedily determine how he was influenced. They met with the utmost friendliness. There could be no doubt of his great pleasure in seeing her. But she had an almost instant doubt of his caring for her as he had before, of his feeling the same tenderness in the same degree. She watched him closely. It was clear that he was less in love than he had been. Absence, with the conviction probably of her indifference, had produced this very natural and very desirable effect.

He was in high spirits; as ready to talk and laugh as ever, and seemed delighted to speak of his former visit. He was not calm; there was restlessness about him. But what decided her belief on the subject was his staying only a quarter of an hour, and hurrying away to make other calls in Highbury. "He had seen a group of old acquaintances in the street as he passed – he had not stopped, he would not stop for more than a word – but he had the vanity to think they would be disappointed if he did not call, and much as he wished to stay longer at Hartfield, he must hurry off."

She had no doubt as to his being less in love, but neither his agitated spirits, nor his hurrying away, seemed like a perfect cure. She was rather inclined to think it implied a dread of his beginning to love her again if he spent too much time with her.

This was the only visit from Frank Churchill in the course of ten days. He was often hoping, intending to come – but was always prevented. His aunt could not bear to have him leave her. Such was his own account at Randalls. That Mrs. Churchill was really ill was very certain; he had declared himself convinced of it, at Randalls. Though much might be imagined and exaggerated by her, he could not doubt, when he looked back, that she was in a weaker state of health than she had been half a year ago. He did not believe it to proceed from anything that care and medicine might not remove, but he could not be prevailed on by all his father's doubts to say that her complaints were entirely imaginary, or that she was as strong as ever.

It soon appeared that London was not the place for her. She could not endure its noise. Her nerves were under continual irritation and suffering; and by the ten days' end, her nephew's letter to Randalls communicated a change of plan. They were going to move immediately to Richmond. Mrs. Churchill had been recommended to the medical skill of an eminent person there. A ready-furnished house in a favourite spot was secured, and much benefit expected from the change.

Emma heard that Frank wrote in the highest spirits of this arrangement, and seemed most fully to appreciate the blessing of having two months before him of such near neighbourhood to many dear friends – for the house was taken for May and June. She was told that now he wrote with the greatest confidence of being often with them, almost as often as he could wish.

Emma saw how Mr. Weston understood these joyous prospects. He was considering her as the source of all the happiness they offered. She hoped it was not so. Two months must decide the question once and for all.

Mr. Weston's own happiness was indisputable. He was quite delighted. It was the very circumstance he could have wished for. Now it would be really having Frank in their neighbourhood. What were nine miles to a young man? An hour's ride. He would be always coming over. The difference in that respect of Richmond and London was enough to make the whole difference of seeing him always and seeing him never. Sixteen miles – nay, eighteen – it must be full eighteen to Manchester Street – was a serious obstacle. Were he ever able to get away, the day would be spent in coming and returning. There was no comfort in having him in London; he might as well be at Enscombe. But Richmond was the perfect distance for regular visiting.

One good thing was immediately brought to a certainty by this removal – the ball at the Crown. It had not been forgotten before, but it had been soon acknowledged pointless to attempt to fix a day. Now, however, it was absolutely to be; every preparation was resumed. Very soon after the Churchills had moved to Richmond, Frank sent a few lines to say that his aunt felt already much better for the change, and that he had no doubt of being able to join them for twenty-four hours at any given time.

Mr. Weston's ball was to be a real thing. A very few tomorrows stood between the young people of Highbury and happiness.

Mr. Woodhouse was resigned. The time of year lightened the evil to him. May was better for everything than February. Mrs. Bates was engaged to spend the evening at Hartfield, James had due notice, and he hoped that neither dear little Henry nor dear little John would have anything the matter with them while dear Emma was gone.

CHAPTER 38

No misfortune occurred again to prevent the ball. The day arrived, and after a morning of some anxious watching, Frank Churchill reached Randalls before dinner, and everything was safe.

No second meeting had yet occurred between him and Emma. The room at the Crown was to witness it; but it would not be a common meeting in a crowd. Mr. Weston had been so very earnest in his entreaties for her early arrival, for the purpose of taking her opinion as to the propriety and comfort of the rooms before any other persons came, that she could not refuse him. She must therefore spend some quiet interval in the young man's company, and she and Harriet drove to the Crown in good time.

Frank Churchill seemed to have been on the watch; and though he did not say much, his eyes declared that he meant to have a delightful evening. They all walked about together, to see that everything was as it should be. Within a few minutes were joined by the contents of another carriage, which Emma could not hear the sound of at first, without great surprise. "So unreasonably early!" she was going to exclaim; but she presently found that it was a family of old friends who were coming, like herself, by particular desire, to help Mr. Weston. They were so very closely followed by another carriage of cousins who had been entreated to come early with the same distinguishing earnestness, on the same errand, that it seemed as if half the company might soon be collected together for the purpose of preparatory inspection.

Emma perceived that her taste was not the only taste on which Mr. Weston depended, and felt that to be the favourite of a man who had so many confidantes was not the very first distinction on the scale of vanity. The whole party walked about, and looked, and praised again; and then, having nothing else to do, formed a sort of half circle round the fire.

Frank was standing by her, but not steadily; there was a restlessness, which showed a mind not at ease. He was looking about, he was going to the door, he was watching for the sound of other carriages, – impatient to begin, or afraid of being always near her.

Mrs. Elton was spoken of. "I think she must be here soon," said he. "I have a great curiosity to see Mrs. Elton, I have heard so much of her. It cannot be long, I think, before she comes."

A carriage was heard. He was on the move immediately; but coming back, said, "I am forgetting that I am not acquainted with her. I have never seen either Mr. or Mrs. Elton."

Mr. and Mrs. Elton appeared, and all the smiles and the proprieties passed.

"Where are Miss Bates and Miss Fairfax?" said Mr. Weston, looking about. "We thought you were to bring them."

They had forgotten. The carriage was sent for them now. Emma longed to know what Frank's first opinion of Mrs. Elton might be; how he was affected by the studied elegance of her dress, and her smiles of graciousness.

In a few minutes the carriage returned. Somebody talked of rain. "I will see that there are umbrellas, sir," said Frank to his father, and away he went. Mr. Weston was following, but Mrs. Elton detained him, to gratify him by her opinion of his son. So briskly did she begin that the young man himself, though by no means moving slowly, could hardly be out of hearing.

"A very fine young man indeed, Mr. Weston. You know I candidly told you I should form my own opinion, and I am happy to say that I am extremely pleased with him. I think him a very handsome young man, and his manners are precisely what I like and approve – so truly the gentleman, without the least conceit."

Mr. Weston thanked her and recollected that there were ladies just arriving to be attended to. With happy smiles he hurried away.

Mrs. Elton turned to Mrs. Weston. "I have no doubt of its being our carriage with Miss Bates and Jane. Our coachman and horses are so extremely quick! I believe we drive faster than anybody. What a pleasure it is to send one's carriage for a friend!"

Miss Bates and Miss Fairfax, escorted by the two gentlemen, walked into the room. As the door opened Miss Bates was heard to say,

"So very obliging of you! No rain at all. Nothing to signify. I do not care for myself. Quite thick shoes. And Jane declares – Well! (as soon as she was within the door) Well! This is brilliant indeed! This is admirable! Excellently contrived, upon my word. Nothing wanting. Could not have imagined it. So well lit. Jane, Jane, look – did you ever see anything like it?" – She was now met by Mrs. Weston. "Very well, I thank you, ma'am. I hope you are quite well. Very happy to hear it. So afraid you might have a headache! Seeing you pass by so often, and knowing how much trouble you must have. Delighted to hear it indeed. Ah! Dear Mrs. Elton, so obliged to you for the carriage! Excellent time. Jane and I quite ready. Did not keep the horses a moment. Most comfortable carriage. We have such wonderful neighbours. I said to my mother, 'Upon my word, ma'am – ' Thank you, my mother is remarkably well. Gone to Mr. Woodhouse's. I made her take her shawl – for the evenings are not warm – her large new shawl – Mrs. Dixon's wedding present. So kind of her to think of my mother! Bought at Weymouth, you know – Mr. Dixon's choice. There were three others, Jane says, which they hesitated about sometime. Colonel Campbell rather preferred an olive. My dear Jane, are you sure you did not wet your feet? It was but a drop or two, but I am so afraid – Oh! Mr. Frank Churchill, I must tell you my mother's spectacles have never been in fault since; the rivet never came out again. My mother often talks of your good nature. Does she not, Jane? Do not we often talk of Mr. Frank Churchill? Ah! Here's Miss Woodhouse. Dear Miss Woodhouse, how do you do? Very well I thank you, quite well. Upon my word, Miss Woodhouse, you do look – how do you like Jane's hair? Quite wonderful how she does her hair! Ah! Dr. Hughes I declare – and Mrs. Hughes. Must go and speak to Dr. and Mrs. Hughes for a moment. How do you do? How do you do? Very well, I thank you. This is delightful, is not it? Where's dear Mr. Richard? Oh! There he is. Don't disturb him. Much better employed talking to the young ladies. How do you do, Mr. Richard? I saw you the other day as you rode through the town – Mrs. Otway, I protest! And good Mr. Otway, and Miss Otway and Miss Caroline. Such a host of friends! And Mr. George and Mr. Arthur! How do you do? How do you all do? Quite well, I am much obliged to you. Never better. Don't I hear another carriage? Who can this be? Very likely the worthy Coles. Upon my word, this is charming to be standing among such friends! And such a noble fire! I am quite roasted. No coffee, I thank you, for me – never take coffee. A little tea if you please, sir. Oh! Here it comes. Everything so good!"

Frank Churchill returned to his station by Emma, and as soon as Miss Bates was quiet, she found herself necessarily overhearing the discourse of Mrs. Elton and Miss Fairfax, who were standing a little way behind her. After a good many compliments to Jane on her attire, compliments very quietly and properly taken, Mrs. Elton was evidently wanting to be complimented herself. "How do you like my gown? " she asked. "How do you like my trimming? My hair?" with many other relative questions, all answered with patient politeness. Mrs. Elton then said,

"Nobody can think less of dress and appearance in general than I do – but upon such an occasion as this, when everybody's eyes are so much upon me, and in compliment to the Westons – who I have no doubt are giving this ball chiefly to do me honour – I would not wish to be inferior to others. And I see very few pearls in the room except mine. So, Frank Churchill is a capital dancer, I understand. We shall see if our styles suit. A fine young man certainly is Frank Churchill. I like him very well."

At this moment, Frank again began talking so vigorously that Emma could not but imagine he had overheard his own praises, and did not want to hear more. The voices of the ladies were drowned out for a while, till another lull brought Mrs. Elton's tones again distinctly forward. Mr. Elton had just joined them, and his wife was exclaiming,

"Oh! You have found us at last, have you? I was this moment telling Jane I thought you would begin to be impatient."

"How do you like Mrs. Elton?" said Emma in a whisper.

"Not at all."

"You are ungrateful."

"I suppose I am." Then changing from a frown to a smile – "Where is my father? When are we to begin dancing?"

Emma could hardly understand him; he seemed in an odd humour. He walked off to find his father, but was quickly back again with both Mr. and Mrs. Weston. It had just occurred to Mrs. Weston that Mrs. Elton must be asked to begin the ball; that as a new bride she would expect it. This interfered with all their wishes of giving Emma that distinction. Emma heard the sad truth with fortitude.

"And what are we to do for a proper partner for her?" said Mr. Weston. "She will think Frank ought to ask her."

Frank turned instantly to Emma, to claim her former promise, and said he already had a dancing partner, which his father approved. It then appeared that Mrs. Weston was wanting *him* to dance with Mrs. Elton himself, and that their plan was to persuade him to do it, which was done pretty soon. Mr. Weston and Mrs. Elton led the way, Mr. Frank Churchill and Miss Woodhouse followed. Emma must submit to stand second to Mrs. Elton, though she had always considered the ball as particularly for her. It was almost enough to make her think of marrying.

Mrs. Elton had undoubtedly the advantage, at this time, in vanity completely gratified; for though she had intended to begin with Frank Churchill, Mr. Weston might be his son's superior. In spite of this little annoyance, however, Emma was smiling with enjoyment, delighted to see the respectable length of the set as it was forming, and to feel that she had so many hours of festivity before her. She was more disturbed by Mr. Knightley's not dancing than by anything else. There he was, among the onlookers, where he ought not to be; he ought to be dancing, not classing himself with the husbands, and fathers, and whist-players, who were pretending to feel an interest in the dance till their card tables were ready. He could not have appeared to greater advantage perhaps anywhere than where he had placed himself. His tall, firm, upright figure, among the bulky forms and stooping shoulders of the elderly men, was such as Emma felt must draw everybody's eyes; and, excepting her own partner, there was not one among the whole row of young men who could be compared with him. He moved a few steps nearer, and those few steps were enough to prove in how gentlemanlike a manner, with what natural grace, he must have danced, would he but take the trouble. Whenever she caught his eye, she forced him to smile; but in general he was looking grave. She wished he could love a ballroom, and Frank Churchill, better. He seemed often observing her. She must not flatter herself that he admired her dancing, but if he were criticising her behaviour, she did not feel afraid. There was nothing like flirtation between her and her partner. They seemed more like cheerful, easy friends than lovers. That Frank Churchill thought less of her than he had before was most certain.

The ball proceeded pleasantly. The anxious cares, the incessant attentions of Mrs. Weston, were not wasted. Everybody seemed happy; and the praise of it being delightful, which is seldom bestowed till after a ball is over, was repeatedly given. There was one, however, which Emma thought something of. The two last dances before supper were begun, and Harriet had no partner. She was the only young lady sitting down. Emma then saw Mr. Elton sauntering about. He would not ask

Harriet to dance if it were possible to be avoided: she was sure he would not – and she was expecting him every moment to escape into the card room.

Escape, however, was not his plan. The kind-hearted, gentle Mrs. Weston had left her seat to join him and say, "Do not you dance, Mr. Elton?" to which his prompt reply was, "Most readily, Mrs. Weston, if you will dance with me."

"Me! Oh no – I would get you a better partner than myself. I am no dancer."

"If Mrs. Gilbert wishes to dance," said he, "I shall have great pleasure, I am sure – for, though beginning to feel myself rather an old married man, and that my dancing days are over, it would give me very great pleasure at any time to dance with an old friend like Mrs. Gilbert."

"Mrs. Gilbert does not want to dance, but there is a young lady whom I should be very glad to see dancing – Miss Smith."

"Miss Smith! Oh! I had not observed. You are extremely obliging – and if I were not an old married man. But my dancing days are over, Mrs. Weston. You will excuse me. Anything else I should be most happy to do, at your command – but my dancing days are over."

Mrs. Weston said no more; and Emma could imagine with what surprise and mortification she must be returning to her seat. This was Mr. Elton! The amiable, obliging, gentle Mr. Elton. She looked round for a moment; he had joined Mr. Knightley at a little distance, and was arranging himself for settled conversation.

In another moment a happier sight caught her – Mr. Knightley leading Harriet to the set! Never had she been more surprised, seldom more delighted, than at that instant. She was all pleasure and gratitude, both for Harriet and herself, and longed to be thanking him. Though too distant for speech, her countenance said much, as soon as she could catch his eye again.

His dancing proved to be just what she had believed it, extremely good; and Harriet would have seemed almost too lucky, if it had not been for the cruel state of things before, and for the very complete enjoyment and very high sense of the distinction which her happy features announced.

Mr. Elton had retreated into the card room, looking (Emma trusted) very foolish. She did not think he was quite as hardened as his wife, though growing very like her; *she* spoke some of her feelings, by observing audibly to her partner,

"Knightley has taken pity on poor little Miss Smith! Very good-natured, I declare."

Supper was announced. The move began; and Miss Bates might be heard from that moment, without interruption, till her being seated at table and taking up her spoon.

"Jane, Jane, my dear Jane, where are you? Be careful, my dear. Mrs. Weston is afraid there will be drafts in the passage, though everything has been done – one door nailed up – quantities of matting. I ran home, as I said I should, to help grandma to bed, and got back again, and nobody noticed I was gone. I set off without saying a word, just as I told you. Grandma was quite well, had a charming evening with Mr. Woodhouse, a vast deal of chat, and backgammon. Tea was made downstairs, biscuits and baked apples and wine before she came away, amazing luck in some of her throws. She inquired a great deal about you, how you were amused, and who were your partners. 'Oh!' said I, 'I left her dancing with Mr. George Otway; she will love to tell you all about it herself tomorrow: her first partner was Mr. Elton, I do not know who will ask her next, perhaps Mr. William Cox.' Oh look, Mrs. Elton is going into the supper room; dear Mrs. Elton, how elegant she looks! Beautiful lace! Now we all follow her in turn. Quite the queen of the evening! Well, here we are at the passage. Two steps, Jane, watch for the two steps. Oh! no, there is but one. Well, I thought there were two. How very odd! I was convinced there were two, and there is but one. I never saw anything equal to the comfort and style – Candles everywhere. I was telling you of your grandma, Jane. There was a little disappointment. The baked apples and biscuits, excellent in their way, you know; but there was a delicate fricassee of sweetbread and some asparagus brought in at first, and good Mr. Woodhouse, not thinking the asparagus quite boiled enough, sent it all out again. Now there is nothing grandma loves better than sweetbread and asparagus – so she was rather disappointed, but we agreed we would not speak of it to anybody, for fear of its getting round to dear Miss Woodhouse, who would be so very much concerned! Well, this is brilliant! I am all amazement! Could not have supposed anything! Such elegance and profusion! I have seen nothing like it since – Well, where shall we sit? Where shall we sit? Anywhere, so that Jane is not in a draft. Where *I* sit does not matter. Dear Jane, how shall we ever remember half the dishes to tell grandma? Soup too! Bless me! It smells most excellent, and I cannot help beginning."

Emma had no opportunity of speaking to Mr. Knightley till after supper; but, when they were all in the ballroom again, her eyes invited him to come to her and be thanked. He was warm in his disapproval of Mr. Elton's conduct; it had been unpardonable rudeness.

"He aimed at wounding more than Harriet," said he. "Emma, why is he your enemy?"

He looked with smiling penetration; and, on receiving no answer, added, "Confess, Emma, that you did want him to marry Harriet."

"I did," replied Emma, "and neither he nor his wife can forgive me."

He shook his head; but there was a smile of indulgence with it, and he only said,

"I shall not scold you. I leave you to your own reflections."

"Can you trust me with such flatterers? Does my vain spirit ever tell me I am wrong?"

"Not your vain spirit, but your serious spirit. If one leads you wrong, I am sure the other tells you of it."

"I do admit being completely mistaken in Mr. Elton. There is a littleness about him which you discovered, and which I did not, and I was fully convinced of his being in love with Harriet. It was through a series of strange blunders!"

"And, in return for your acknowledging so much, I will do you the justice to say that you would have chosen for him better than he has chosen for himself. Harriet Smith has some first-rate qualities, which Mrs. Elton is totally without. A guileless, sincere girl — infinitely to be preferred by any man of sense and taste to such a woman as Mrs. Elton. I found Harriet more conversable than I expected."

Emma was extremely gratified. They were interrupted by the bustle of Mr. Weston calling on everybody to begin dancing again.

"Come Miss Woodhouse, Miss Otway, Miss Fairfax, what are you all doing? Come Emma, set an example for your companions. Everybody is lazy! Everybody is asleep!"

"I am ready," said Emma, "whenever I am wanted."

"Who are you going to dance with?" asked Mr. Knightley.

She hesitated a moment, and then replied, "With you, if you will ask me."

"Will you?" said he, offering his hand.

"Indeed I will, now that you have shown you can dance."

"When the need arises."

CHAPTER 39

This little exchange with Mr. Knightley gave Emma considerable pleasure. It was one of the agreeable recollections of the ball, which she walked about the lawn the next morning to enjoy. She was extremely glad they had come to such a good understanding respecting the Eltons, and that their opinions of both husband and wife were so much alike. His praise of Harriet, and his willingness to dance with her, were both peculiarly gratifying. The rude behavior of Mr. Elton, which for a few minutes had threatened to ruin the rest of her evening, had been the occasion of some of its highest satisfactions; and she looked forward to another happy result – the cure of Harriet's infatuation. From Harriet's manner of speaking of the circumstance before they left the ballroom, she had strong hopes. It seemed as if her eyes were suddenly opened, and she was able to see that Mr. Elton was not the superior creature she had believed him to be. The spell was broken, and Emma could harbour little fear of the pulse being quickened again by injurious kindness. With Harriet rational, Frank Churchill not too much in love, and Mr. Knightley not wanting to quarrel with her, how very happy a summer must be ahead for her!

She was not to see Frank Churchill this morning. He had told her that he could not allow himself the pleasure of stopping at Hartfield, as he was to be at home by the middle of the day. She did not regret it.

Having arranged all these matters, she was just turning to the house when the great iron gates opened, and two persons entered whom she had never less expected to see together: Frank Churchill, with Harriet leaning on his arm! A moment sufficed to convince her that something had happened. Harriet looked white and frightened, and he was trying to restore her spirits. They were all three soon in the hall, and Harriet immediately sinking into a chair fainted away.

A young lady who faints must be revived; questions must be answered, and surprises explained. Such events are very interesting, but the suspense of them cannot last long. A few minutes made Emma acquainted with the whole.

Miss Smith and Miss Bickerton, another parlour boarder at Mrs. Goddard's, who had also been at the ball, had walked out together and taken a road, the Richmond road, which had led them into danger. About half a mile beyond Highbury, making a sudden turn, and deeply shaded by elms on each side, it became for a considerable stretch very secluded. When the young ladies had advanced some way into it, they had suddenly perceived at a small distance before them, on a broader path of grass by the side, a party of gypsies. A child came towards them to beg, and Miss Bickerton, excessively frightened, gave a great scream, and calling on Harriet to follow her, ran up a steep bank, cleared a slight hedge at the top, and made her way by a shortcut back to Highbury. But poor Harriet could not follow. She had suffered very much from muscle cramps after dancing, and her first attempt to mount the bank brought on such a return of them as made her absolutely powerless. In this state, and exceedingly terrified, she had been obliged to remain.

How the gypsies might have behaved had the young ladies been more courageous cannot be certain; but such an invitation for attack could not be resisted. Harriet was soon surrounded by half a dozen children, headed by a stout woman and a large boy. She immediately promised them money, and taking out her purse, gave them a shilling and begged them not to ask for more. She was then able to walk, though but slowly, and was moving away – but her terror and her purse were too tempting, and she was followed by the whole gang, demanding more.

In this state Frank Churchill had found her. By a most fortunate chance his leaving Highbury had been delayed so as to bring him to her assistance at this critical moment. The pleasantness of the morning had induced him to walk for a bit, leaving his horses to meet him by another road a mile or two beyond Highbury. He had borrowed a pair of scissors the night before from Miss Bates, and had forgotten to return them. Therefore, he had been obliged to stop at her door and go in for a few minutes. He was later than he had intended; and being on foot, was unseen by the whole party till almost upon them. The terror which the woman and boy had been creating in Harriet was then returned to them. He had left them completely frightened; and Harriet, eagerly clinging to him, was hardly able to speak. She had just enough strength to reach Hartfield before she was quite overcome. It was his idea to bring her to Hartfield: he had thought of no other place.

Frank dared not stay longer than to see her well; these several delays left him not another minute to lose. Such an adventure as this – a fine young man and a lovely young woman thrown together in such a way, could hardly fail of suggesting certain romantic ideas to the coldest heart and the steadiest brain. So Emma thought, at least.

It was a very extraordinary thing! Nothing of the sort had ever occurred before to any young ladies in the place, within her memory; and now it had happened to the very person, and at the very hour, when the other very person was chancing to pass by to rescue her! It certainly was very extraordinary! And knowing, as she did, the favourable state of mind of each at this period, it struck her the more. He was wishing to get over his attachment to herself, and she was just recovering from her mania for Mr. Elton. It seemed as if everything united to promise the most interesting consequences. It was not possible that the occurrence should not leave the two of them thinking of each other.

In the few minutes' conversation which she had yet had with him, while Harriet had been partially insensible, he had spoken of her terror, her naïveté, her fervor as she seized and clung to his arm. At last, after Harriet's own account had been given, he had expressed his indignation at the abominable folly of Miss Bickerton in the warmest terms. Everything was to take its natural course, however. She would not stir a step, nor drop a hint. No, she had had enough of interference. There could be no harm in a scheme, a mere passive scheme. It was no more than a wish. Beyond it she would on no account proceed.

Emma's first resolution was to keep her father from the knowledge of what had passed, aware of the anxiety and alarm it would occasion: but she soon felt that concealment must be impossible. Within half an hour it was known all over Highbury. All the youth and servants in the place were soon in the happiness of frightful news. Last night's ball was nothing compared to the gypsies. Poor Mr. Woodhouse trembled as he sat, and, as Emma had foreseen, would scarcely be satisfied without their promising never to go beyond the shrubbery again. It was some comfort to him that many inquiries after himself and Miss Woodhouse (for his neighbours knew that he loved to be inquired after), as well as

Miss Smith, were coming in during the rest of the day. He had the pleasure of returning for answer that they were all very much affected – which, though not exactly true, Emma would not contradict.

The gypsies themselves left in a hurry, and the whole story soon dwindled into a matter of little importance except to Emma and her nephews. Henry and John asked their aunt every day for the story of Harriet and the gypsies, and set her right if she varied in the slightest from her original account.

CHAPTER 40

A very few days had passed after this adventure, when Harriet came one morning to Emma with a small parcel in her hand, and after sitting down and hesitating, thus began:

"Miss Woodhouse – if you have a moment – I have something that I should like to tell you – a sort of confession to make – and then, you know, it will be over."

Emma was a good deal surprised; but begged her to speak. There was a seriousness in Harriet's manner which prepared her, quite as much as her words, for something out of the ordinary.

"It is my duty, and I am sure it is my wish," she continued, "to keep no secrets from you on this subject. As I am happily quite an altered creature in *one respect*, it is very fit that you should have the satisfaction of knowing it. I do not want to say more than is necessary – I am too much ashamed of having held on as I have done, and I dare say you understand me."

"Yes," said Emma, "I hope I do."

"How I could so long a time admire him! " cried Harriet, warmly. "It seems like madness! I can see nothing at all extraordinary in him now. I do not care whether I meet him or not, and indeed I would go any distance round to avoid him. But I do not envy his wife in the least; I neither admire her nor envy her, as I have done, and I think her very ill-tempered and disagreeable. However, I assure you, Miss Woodhouse, I wish her no evil. No, let them be ever so happy together, it will not give me another moment's pang: and to convince you that I have been speaking truth, I am now going to destroy what I ought to have destroyed long ago (blushing as she spoke). It is my particular wish to do it in your presence, that you may see how rational I have become. Cannot you guess what this parcel holds?" said she, with a conscious look.

"Indeed, I cannot. Did he ever give you anything?"

"No – I cannot call them gifts; but they are things that I have valued very much."

She held the parcel towards her, and Emma read the words *most precious treasures* on the top. Her curiosity was greatly excited. Harriet unfolded the parcel, and she looked on with impatience. Within was a pretty little box, which Harriet opened: it was lined with the softest cotton; but, excepting the cotton, Emma saw only a small bandage.

"Now," said Harriet, "you *must* remember."

"No, I do not."

"Dear me! I should not have thought it possible you could forget what passed in this very room involving this bandage, one of the very last times we ever met in it! It was but a very few days before I had my sore throat – just before Mr. and Mrs. John Knightley came; I think the very evening. Do you not remember his cutting his finger with your new penknife, and your recommending a bandage? But as you did not have one, and knew I did, you desired me to supply him; and so I took mine out and cut him a piece; but it was a great deal too large, and he cut it smaller, and kept playing sometime with what was left, before he gave it back to me. And so then, in my nonsense, I could not help making a treasure of it. I put it by never to be used, and looked at it now and then as a great treat."

"My dearest Harriet!" cried Emma, putting her hand before her face, and jumping up. "I remember it all now; all, except your saving this: I knew nothing of that till this moment – but the cutting the finger, and my recommending a bandage, and saying I had none! Oh! My sins, my sins! I had plenty all the while in my pocket! One of my senseless tricks! I deserve to be under a continual blush all the rest of my life. Well," (sitting down again), "go on; what else?"

"You really had bandages? I am sure I never suspected it, you did it so naturally."

"And so you actually saved this piece for his sake!" said Emma, recovering from her state of shame and feeling divided between wonder and amusement. And secretly she added to herself, "Lord bless me! When should I ever have thought of putting by in cotton a piece of bandage that Frank Churchill had been playing with! I never was equal to this."

"Here," resumed Harriet, turning to her box again, " is something still more valuable. I mean that *has been* more valuable, because this did really once belong to him."

Emma was quite eager to see this superior treasure: it was the end of an old pencil.

"This was really his," said Harriet. "Do you not remember one morning? No, I dare say you do not. One morning — I forget exactly the day — he wanted to make a note in his pocketbook. Mr. Knightley had been telling him something about brewing spruce beer, and he wanted to put it down; but when he took out his pencil, it was too small, so you lent him another, and this was left upon the table as good for nothing. But I kept my eye on it; and, as soon as I dared, I put it in my pocket, and never parted with it again from that moment."

"I do remember it," cried Emma, "I perfectly remember it. Talking about spruce beer. Oh! Yes. Mr. Knightley and I both saying we liked it, and Mr. Elton's seeming resolved to learn to like it too. I perfectly remember it. Mr. Knightley was standing just here, was he not? I have an idea he was standing just here."

"Ah! I do not know. I cannot recollect. It is very odd, but I cannot recollect. Mr. Elton was sitting here, I remember, much about where I am now."

"Well, go on."

"Oh! That's all. I have nothing more to show you, or to say, except that I am now going to throw them both in the fire, and I wish you to see me do it."

"My poor dear Harriet! Have you actually found happiness in treasuring up these things?"

"Yes, but I am quite ashamed of it now, and wish I could forget as easily as I can burn them. It was very wrong of me, you know, to keep any remembrances, after he was married. I knew it was — but had not strength enough to part with them."

"And when," thought Emma, "will there be a beginning of Mr. Churchill?"

She had soon afterwards reason to believe that the beginning was already made. About a fortnight after the encounter with the gypsies, Emma said, in the course of some trivial chat, "Well, Harriet, whenever you marry I would advise you to do so and so" — and thought no more of it, till after a minute's silence she heard Harriet say in a very serious tone, "I shall never marry."

"Never marry! This is a new resolution."

"It is one that I shall never change, however."

After another short hesitation, "I hope it does not proceed from – I hope it is not because of Mr. Elton?"

"Mr. Elton indeed!" cried Harriet indignantly. "Oh! no" – and Emma could just catch the words, "so superior to Mr. Elton!"

She then took a longer time for consideration. Should she let it pass, and seem to suspect nothing? Perhaps Harriet might think her cold or angry if she did. She believed it would be wiser for her to say and know at once, all that she meant to say and know. Plain dealing was always best. She was decided, and thus spoke –

"Harriet, I will not pretend to be in doubt of your meaning. Your resolution, or rather your expectation of never marrying, results from an idea that the person whom you might prefer, would be too greatly your superior in situation to think of you. Is it not so?"

"Oh! Miss Woodhouse, believe me I have not the presumption to suppose – indeed I am not so mad. But it is a pleasure to me to admire him at a distance, and to think of his infinite superiority to all the rest of the world, with the gratitude, wonder, and veneration, which are so proper."

"I am not at all surprised at you, Harriet. The service he rendered you was enough to warm your heart."

"Service! Oh! It was such an inexpressible obligation! The very recollection of it, and all that I felt at the time, when I saw him coming – his noble look, and my wretchedness before. Such a change! In one moment, such a change! From perfect misery to perfect happiness."

"It is very natural. It is natural, and it is honourable. Yes, honourable, I think, to choose so well and so gratefully. But that it will be a fortunate preference is more than I can promise. I do not advise you to give way to it, Harriet. I do not by any means engage for its being returned. Perhaps it will be wisest to check your feelings while you can: at any rate, do not let them carry you far, unless you are persuaded of his liking you. Be observant of him. Let his behaviour be your guide. I give you this caution now, because I shall never speak to you again on the subject. I am determined against all interference. Henceforward I know nothing of the matter. Let no name ever pass our lips. We were very wrong before; we will be cautious now. He is your superior, no doubt, and there do seem objections and obstacles of a very serious nature; but yet, Harriet, more wonderful things have taken place, there have been matches of greater disparity. But take care of yourself. I would not have you too hopeful; though, however it may end, be assured that your raising your thoughts to *him*, is a mark of good taste which I shall always know how to value."

Harriet kissed her hand in silent and submissive gratitude. Emma was very decided in thinking such an attachment no bad thing for her friend. Its tendency would be to raise and refine her mind – and it must be saving her from the danger of degradation.

CHAPTER 41

In this state of schemes, and hopes, and connivance, June opened upon Hartfield. To Highbury in general it brought no material change. The Eltons were still talking of a visit from the Sucklings of Maple Grove; and Jane Fairfax was still at her grandmother's. As the return of the Campbells from Ireland was again delayed, and August, instead of June, fixed for it, she was likely to remain there two months longer, provided at least she were able to defeat Mrs. Elton's activity in her service, and save herself from being hurried into a governess situation against her will.

Mr. Knightley, who, for some reason best known to himself, had certainly taken an early dislike to Frank Churchill, was only growing to dislike him more. He began to suspect him of some double dealing in his pursuit of Emma. That Emma was his object appeared indisputable. Everything declared it; his own attentions, his father's hints, his mother-in-law's guarded silence; words, conduct, discretion, and indiscretion, told the same story. But while so many thought him devoted to Emma, and Emma herself thought him partial to Harriet, Mr. Knightley began to suspect him of some inclination towards Jane Fairfax. He could not understand it; but there were symptoms of understanding between them — he thought so at least — symptoms of admiration on his side, which, having once observed, he could not persuade himself to think entirely void of meaning, however he might wish to escape any of Emma's errors of imagination. *She* was not present when the suspicion first arose. He was dining with the Randalls' family, and Jane, at the Eltons'; and he had seen a look, more than a single look, at Miss Fairfax, which, from the admirer of Miss Woodhouse, seemed somewhat out of place. When he was again in their company, he could not help remembering what he had seen; nor could he avoid observations which brought him yet stronger suspicion of there being something of a private liking between Frank Churchill and Jane.

He had walked up one day after dinner, as he very often did, to spend his evening at Hartfield. Emma and Harriet were going to walk; and he joined them. On returning, they fell in with a larger party, who, like themselves, judged it wisest to take their exercise early, as the weather threatened rain. Mr. and Mrs. Weston and their son, Miss Bates and her niece, who had accidentally met, were now among them. On reaching Hartfield gates, Emma, who knew it was exactly the sort of visiting that would be welcome to her father, pressed them all to go in and drink tea with him. The Randalls' party agreed to it immediately; and after a pretty long speech from Miss Bates, which few persons listened to, she also found it possible to accept dear Miss Woodhouse's most obliging invitation.

As they were turning into the grounds, Mr. Perry passed by on horseback. The gentlemen spoke of his horse.

"By the way," said Frank Churchill to Mrs. Weston presently, "what became of Mr. Perry's plan of getting a carriage?"

Mrs. Weston looked surprised, and said, "I did not know that he ever had any such plan."

"Nay, I heard it from you. You wrote me word of it three months ago."

"Me! Impossible!"

"Indeed, you did. I remember it perfectly. You mentioned that it was certainly to be very soon. Mrs. Perry had told somebody, and was extremely happy about it. It was owing to his wife's persuasion, as she thought his being out in bad weather did him a great deal of harm. You must remember it now?"

"Upon my word, I never heard of it till this moment."

"Never! Really, never? Bless me! How could it be? I must have dreamt it – but I was completely persuaded – Miss Smith, you walk as if you were tired. You will not be sorry to find yourself at home."

"What is this? What is this?" cried Mr. Weston, "about Perry and a carriage? Is Perry going to get a carriage, Frank? I am glad he can afford it. You had it from himself, had you?"

"No, sir," replied his son, laughing, "I seem to have had it from nobody. Very odd! I really was persuaded of Mrs. Weston's having mentioned it in one of her letters to Enscombe, many weeks ago, with all these particulars; but as she declares she never heard a syllable of it before, of course it must have been a dream. I am a great dreamer. I dream of everybody at Highbury when I am away; and when I have gone through my particular friends, then I begin dreaming of Mr. and Mrs. Perry."

"It is odd, though," observed his father, "that you should have had such a regular connected dream about people whom it was not very likely you should be thinking of at Enscombe. Perry's getting a carriage! And his wife's persuading him to do it, out of care for his health – just what will happen, I have no doubt, sometime or other; only a little premature. What an air of probability sometimes runs through a dream! Well, Frank, your dream certainly shows that Highbury is in your thoughts when you are absent. Emma, you are a great dreamer, I think?"

Emma was out of hearing. She had hurried on before her guests to prepare her father for their appearance, and was beyond the reach of Mr. Weston's hint.

"Why, to tell the truth," cried Miss Bates, who had been trying in vain to be heard the last two minutes, "if I must speak on this subject, there is no denying that Mr. Frank Churchill might have – I do not mean to say that he did not dream it – I am sure I have sometimes the oddest dreams in the world – but if I am questioned about it, I must acknowledge that there was such an idea last spring; for Mrs. Perry herself mentioned it to my mother, and the Coles knew of it as well as ourselves – but it was quite a secret, known to nobody else, and only thought about for three days. Mrs. Perry was very anxious that he should have a carriage, and came to my mother in great spirits one morning because she thought she had prevailed. Jane, don't you remember grandma's telling us of it when we got home? I forget where we had been walking to – very likely to Randalls; yes, I think it was to Randalls. Mrs. Perry was always particularly fond of my mother – indeed I do not know who is not – and she had mentioned it to her in confidence; she had no objection to her telling us, of course, but it was not to go beyond. From that day to this, I never mentioned it to a soul that I know of. At the same time, I will not positively answer for my having never dropped a hint, because I know I do sometimes pop out a thing before I am aware. I am a talker, you know; I am rather a talker; and now and then I have let a thing escape me which I should not. I am not like Jane; I wish I were. I will answer for it, *she* never betrayed the least thing in the world. Where is she? Oh! Just behind. I perfectly remember Mrs. Perry's coming. Extraordinary dream indeed!"

They were entering the hall. Mr. Knightley's eyes had preceded Miss Bates's in a glance at Jane. From Frank Churchill's face, where he thought he saw confusion suppressed or laughed away, he had involuntarily turned to hers; but she was indeed behind, and too busy with her shawl. Mr. Weston had walked in. The two other gentlemen waited at the door to let her pass. Mr. Knightley suspected in Frank Churchill the determination of catching her eye – he seemed to be watching her intently – in vain, however, as Jane passed between them into the hall and looked at neither.

There was no time for a further remark or explanation. Mr. Knightley must take his seat with the rest around the large modern circular table which Emma had recently procured, and which none but Emma could have had power to place there and persuade her father to use, instead of the smaller table on which two of his daily meals had, for forty years, been crowded. Tea passed pleasantly, and nobody seemed in a hurry to leave.

"Miss Woodhouse," said Frank Churchill, after examining a table behind him, which he could reach as he sat, "have your nephews taken away their box of letters? It used to stand here. Where is it? This is a sort of dull-looking evening that ought to be treated rather as winter than summer. We had great amusement with those letters one morning. I want to see if I can stump you again."

Emma was pleased with the thought; and producing the box, the table was quickly scattered over with letters, which no one seemed so much disposed to employ as their two selves. They were rapidly forming words for each other, or for anybody else who would join them. The quietness of the game made it particularly suited to Mr. Woodhouse, who had often been distressed by the more animated sort which Mr. Weston had occasionally introduced, and who now sat happily occupied in lamenting, with tender melancholy, over the departure of the "poor little boys," or in fondly pointing out, as he took up any stray letter near him, how beautifully Emma had written it.

Frank Churchill placed a mixed-up word before Miss Fairfax. She gave a slight glance round the table, and applied herself to it. Frank was next to Emma, Jane opposite them – and Mr. Knightley so placed as to see them all. It was his object to see as much as he could, with as little apparent observation. The word was discovered, and with a faint smile pushed away. If meant to be immediately mixed with the others, and buried from sight, she should have looked on the table instead of looking just across, for it was not mixed; and Harriet, eager after every fresh word, and finding out none, directly took it up, and fell to work. She was sitting by Mr. Knightley, and turned to him for help. The word was *blunder*; and as Harriet exultingly proclaimed it, there was a blush on Jane's cheek. Mr. Knightley connected it with the dream; but how it could all be was beyond his comprehension. There seemed to be some great secret being kept from him. Disingenuousness double-dealing met him at every turn. These letters were but the vehicle for gallantry and trick. It was child's play, chosen to conceal a deeper game on Frank Churchill's part.

With great indignation did he continue to observe him; with great alarm and distrust, to observe also his two oblivious companions. He saw a short word prepared for Emma, and given to her with a look sly and demure. He saw that Emma had soon made it out, and found it highly entertaining, though it was something which she judged it proper to appear to censure; for she said, "Nonsense! For shame!" He heard Frank Churchill next say, with a glance towards Jane, "I will give it to her – shall I?" and as clearly heard Emma opposing it with eager laughing warmth. "No, no, you must not; you shall not, indeed."

It was done however. This gallant young man, who seemed to love without feeling, and to recommend himself without complaisance, directly handed over the word to Miss Fairfax, and with a particular degree of civility entreated her to study it. Mr. Knightley's excessive curiosity to know what this word might be made him seize every possible moment for darting his eye towards it, and it was not long before he saw it to be *Dixon*. Jane Fairfax's perception seemed to accompany his; her comprehension was certainly more equal to the covert meaning, the superior intelligence, of those five letters so arranged. She was evidently displeased; looked up, and seeing herself watched, blushed more deeply than he had ever perceived her, and saying only, "I did not know that proper names were allowed," pushed away the letters with even an angry spirit. She then looked resolved to be engaged by no other word that could be offered. Her face was averted from those who had made the attack, and turned towards her aunt.

"Aye, very true, my dear," cried the latter, though Jane had not spoken a word, "I was just going to say the same thing. It is time for us to be going indeed. The evening is closing in, and grandma will be looking for us. My dear sir, you are too obliging. We really must wish you goodnight."

Jane's alertness in moving proved her as ready as her aunt had conceived. She was immediately up, and wanting to leave the table; but so many were also moving, that she could not get away; and Mr. Knightley thought he saw another collection of letters anxiously pushed towards her, and resolutely swept away by her unexamined. She was afterwards looking for her shawl – Frank Churchill was looking also: it was growing darker outside, and the room was in confusion; how they parted, Mr. Knightley could not tell.

He remained at Hartfield after all the rest, his thoughts full of what he had seen; so full that when the candles came to assist his observations, he must – yes, he certainly must, as a friend – an anxious friend – give Emma some hint, ask her some question. He could not see her in a situation of such danger without trying to preserve her. It was his duty.

"Pray, Emma," said he, "may I ask in what lay the great amusement, the poignant sting of the last word given to you and Miss Fairfax? I saw the word, and am curious to know how it could be so very entertaining to the one, and so very distressing to the other."

Emma was extremely confused. She could not endure giving him the true explanation; for though her suspicions were by no means removed, she was really ashamed of having ever imparted them.

"Oh!" she cried in evident embarrassment, "It all meant nothing; a mere joke among ourselves."

"The joke," he replied gravely, "seemed confined to you and Mr. Churchill."

He had hoped she would speak again, but she did not. She would rather busy herself about anything than speak. He sat a little while in doubt. A variety of evils crossed his mind. Interference – fruitless interference. Emma's confusion, and the acknowledged intimacy, seemed to declare her affection engaged. Yet he would speak. He owed it to her, to risk anything that might be involved in an unwelcome interference, rather than her welfare; to encounter anything, rather than the remembrance of neglect in such a cause.

"My dear Emma," said he at last, with earnest kindness, "do you think you perfectly understand the degree of acquaintance between the gentleman and lady we have been speaking of?"

"Between Mr. Frank Churchill and Miss Fairfax! Oh! Yes, perfectly. Why do you make a doubt of it?"

"Have you never at any time had reason to think that he admired her, or that she admired him?"

"Never, never!" she cried with a most open eagerness "Never, for the twentieth part of a moment, did such an idea occur to me. And how could it possibly come into your head?"

"I have lately imagined that I saw symptoms of attachment between them; certain expressive looks, which I did not believe were meant to be public."

"Oh! You amuse me excessively. I am delighted to find that you can let your imagination wander – but it will not do – very sorry to check you in your first attempt – but indeed it will not do. There is no affection between them, I do assure you; and the appearances which have caught you have arisen from some peculiar circumstances; feelings rather of a totally different nature. It is impossible exactly to explain – there is a good deal of nonsense in it – but the part which is capable of being communicated is that they are as far from any attachment or admiration for one another as any two beings in the world can be. That is, I *presume* it to be so on her side, and I can *answer* for its being so on his. I will answer for the gentleman's indifference."

She spoke with a confidence which staggered, with a satisfaction which silenced, Mr. Knightley. She was in happy spirits, and would have prolonged the conversation, wanting to hear the particulars of his suspicions. But he found he could not be useful, and his feelings were too much irritated for talking. He soon afterwards took a hasty leave, and walked home to the coolness and solitude of Donwell Abbey.

CHAPTER 42

After being long fed with hopes of a speedy visit from Mr. and Mrs. Suckling, the Highbury world was obliged to endure the mortification of hearing that they could not possibly come till the autumn. In the daily exchange of news, they must be again restricted to the other topics with which for a while the Sucklings' coming had been united. There were the last accounts of Mrs. Churchill, whose health seemed every day to supply a different report, and the situation of Mrs. Weston, whose happiness it was to be hoped might eventually be as much increased by the arrival of a child.

Mrs. Elton was very much disappointed. It was the delay of a great deal of pleasure. Her introductions and recommendations must all wait, and every projected party be only talked of. So she thought at first; but a little consideration convinced her that everything need not be put off. Why should not they explore to Box Hill though the Sucklings did not come? They could go there again with them in the autumn. It was settled that they should go to Box Hill. That there was to be such a party had been long generally known. Emma had never been to Box Hill; she wished to see what everybody found so well worth seeing, and she and Mr. Weston had agreed to choose some fine morning and drive there. Two or three more were to be allowed to join them, and it was to be done in a quiet way, infinitely superior to the picnic parade of the Eltons and Sucklings.

This was so very well understood between them that Emma could not but feel some surprise, and a little displeasure, on hearing from Mr. Weston that he had been proposing to Mrs. Elton, as her brother and sister had failed her, that the two parties should unite and go together. Mrs. Elton had very readily agreed to it, so it was to be, if Emma had no objection. Now, as her objection was nothing but her very great dislike of Mrs. Elton, of which Mr. Weston must already be perfectly aware, it was not worth mentioning again. It could not be done without criticising him, which would be giving pain to his wife; and she found herself therefore obliged to consent to an arrangement which she would have done a great deal to avoid. Every feeling was offended, and her outward composure masked a deep frustration regarding the unmanageable goodwill of Mr. Weston's temper.

"I am glad you approve of what I have done," said he very comfortably. "But I thought you would. Such schemes as these are nothing without numbers. One cannot have too large a party. A large party secures its own amusement. And she is a good-natured woman after all. One could not leave her out."

Emma denied none of it aloud, and agreed to none of it in private.

It was now the middle of June, and the weather quite nice. Mrs. Elton was growing impatient to name the day, and settle with Mr. Weston as to pigeon-pies and cold lamb, when a lame carriage-horse threw everything into sad uncertainty. It might be weeks, it might be only a few days, before the horse was usable, but no preparations could be made, and it was all melancholy stagnation. Mrs. Elton's resources were inadequate to such an attack.

"Is not this most vexatious, Knightley?" she cried. "And such weather for exploring! These delays and disappointments are troublesome indeed. What are we to do? The summer will soon be gone at this rate, and nothing done. Before this time last year, I assure you we had had a delightful exploring party from Maple Grove to Kings Weston."

"You could explore Donwell," replied Mr. Knightley. "That may be done without horses. Come, and eat my strawberries. They are ripening fast."

If Mr. Knightley did not begin seriously, he was obliged to proceed so, for his proposal was caught at with delight; and the "Oh! I should like it of all things," was spoken of with great joy. Donwell was famous for its strawberry beds, which added to the enticement of the invitation: but no enticement was necessary; cabbage beds would have been enough to tempt the lady, who only wanted to go somewhere. She promised him again and again to come – though he had no doubts of her intention to do so – and was extremely gratified by such a proof of friendship, such a distinguishing compliment as she chose to consider it.

"You may depend upon me," said she. "I certainly will come. Name your day, and I will come. You will allow me to bring Jane Fairfax?"

"I cannot name a day," said he, "till I have spoken to some others whom I would wish to meet you."

"Oh! Leave all that to me. I will bring friends with me."

"I hope you will bring Elton," said he; "but I will not trouble you to give any other invitations."

"Oh! But it is my party. Leave it all to me. I will invite your guests."

"No," he calmly replied, "there is but one married woman in the world whom I can ever allow to invite what guests she pleases to Donwell, and that one is – "

"Mrs. Weston, I suppose," interrupted Mrs. Elton, rather mortified.

"No – Mrs. Knightley; and, till she comes along, I will manage such matters myself."

"Ah! You are an odd creature!" she cried, satisfied to have no one preferred to herself. "You may say what you like, but I shall bring Jane with me – Jane and her aunt. The rest I leave to you. I have no objections at all to meeting the Hartfield family. I know you are attached to them."

"You certainly will meet them if I can prevail; and I shall call on Miss Bates in my way home."

"That's quite unnecessary; I see Jane every day. But you may do as you wish. It is to be a morning scheme, you know, Knightley; quite a simple thing. I shall wear a large bonnet, and bring one of my little baskets hanging on my arm. Probably my basket with the pink ribbon. Nothing can be more simple, you see. And Jane will have a basket as well. We will walk about your gardens and gather the strawberries ourselves, and sit under trees; and whatever else you may like to provide. It is to be all out of doors; a table spread in the shade, you know. Everything as natural and simple as possible. Is that not your idea?"

"Not quite. My idea of the simple and the natural will be to have the table spread in the dining-room. The nature and the simplicity of gentlemen and ladies, with their servants and furniture, I think is best observed by meals indoors. When you are tired of eating strawberries in the garden, there shall be cold meat in the house."

"Well, as you please; only don't go to too much trouble. And, by the way, can I or my housekeeper be of any use to you with our opinion?

Pray be sincere, Knightley. If you wish me to talk to Mrs. Hodges, or to inspect anything – "

"I have not the least wish for it, thank you."

"Well – but if any difficulties should arise, my housekeeper is extremely clever."

"I will answer for it that mine thinks herself just as clever, and would spurn anybody's assistance."

"I wish we had a donkey. The thing would be for us all to come on donkeys: Jane, Miss Bates, and me – and my dear husband walking by. I really must talk to him about purchasing a donkey. In a country life, I conceive it to be necessary; for, let a woman have ever so many resources, it is not possible for her to be always shut up at home. Very long walks, you know, are not always desirable – in summer there is dust, and in winter there is dirt."

"You will not find either between Donwell and Highbury. Donwell lane is never dusty, and now it is perfectly dry. Come on a donkey, however, if you prefer it. You can borrow Mrs. Cole's. I would wish everything to be as much to your taste as possible."

"That I am sure you would. Indeed, I do you justice, my good friend. Under your peculiar sort of dry, blunt manner, I know you have the warmest heart. Believe me, Knightley, I am fully sensible of your attention to me in the whole of this scheme. You have hit upon the very thing to please me."

Mr. Knightley had another reason for avoiding a table in the shade. He wished to persuade Mr. Woodhouse, as well as Emma, to join the party, and he knew that Mr. Woodhouse would not enjoy sitting down out of doors to eat. He must not, under the pretence of a morning drive, and an hour or two spent at Donwell, be made miserable.

He was invited on good faith, and he did consent. He had not been at Donwell for two years. "Some very fine morning, he, and Emma, and Harriet, could go very well; and he could sit still with Mrs. Weston while the dear girls walked about the gardens. He did not suppose they could be damp now, in the middle of the day. He should like to see the old house again exceedingly, and should be very happy to meet Mr. and Mrs. Elton, and any other of his neighbours. He could not see any objection at all to his, and Emma's, and Harriet's, going there some very fine morning. He thought it very well done of Mr. Knightley to invite them; very kind and sensible, and much cleverer than eating outside. He was not fond of picnics."

Mr. Knightley was fortunate in everybody's most ready concurrence. The invitation was everywhere so well received that it seemed as if, like Mrs. Elton, they were all taking the scheme as a particular compliment to themselves. Emma and Harriet professed very high expectations of pleasure from it. Mr. Weston, unasked, promised to get Frank over to join them, if possible; a proof of approbation and gratitude which could have been dispensed with. Mr. Knightley was then obliged to say that he should be glad to see him; and Mr. Weston lost no time in writing, and spared no arguments to convince him to come.

In the meanwhile, the lame horse recovered so fast that the party to Box Hill was again under happy consideration; and at last Donwell was settled for one day, and Box Hill for the next, the weather appearing exactly right.

Under a bright mid-day sun in mid-June, Mr. Woodhouse was safely conveyed in his carriage, with one window down; and in one of the most comfortable rooms in the abbey, especially prepared for him by a fire all the morning, he was happily placed, quite at his ease, ready to talk with pleasure of what had been achieved, and advise everybody to come and sit down. Mrs. Weston, who seemed to have walked there on purpose to be tired, and sit all the time with him, remained, when all the others were invited or persuaded out, his patient listener and sympathizer.

It was so long since Emma had been at the Abbey that as soon as she was satisfied of her father's comfort, she was glad to leave him, and look around her. Eager to refresh and correct her memory with more particular observation, more exact understanding of a house and grounds which must ever be so interesting to her and all her family.

She felt all the honest pride and complacency which her alliance with the present and future proprietor could fairly warrant, as she viewed the respectable size and style of the building. Its ample gardens stretched down to meadows washed by a stream, and she admired its abundance of timber. The house was larger than Hartfield, and totally unlike it, covering a good deal of ground, with many comfortable and one or two elegant rooms. It was just what it ought to be, and Emma felt an increasing respect for it, as the residence of a family of such true gentility. Some faults of temper John Knightley had; but Isabella had connected herself well. These were pleasant feelings, and Emma walked about and indulged them till it was necessary to do as the others did, and collect round the strawberry beds. The whole party were assembled, excepting Frank Churchill, who was expected every moment from Richmond. Mrs. Elton, with her large bonnet and her basket, was very ready to lead the way in gathering, accepting, or talking – strawberries, and only strawberries, could now be thought or spoken of. "The best fruit in England – everybody's favourite – always wholesome. These the finest beds and finest sorts. – Delightful to gather for one's self – the only way of really enjoying them. Morning decidedly the best time – never tired – every sort good – price of strawberries in London – abundance about Bristol – Maple Grove – cultivation – beds when to be renewed – gardeners thinking exactly different – no general rule – gardeners never to be put out of their way – delicious fruit – only too rich to be eaten much of – inferior to cherries – currants more refreshing – only objection to gathering strawberries the stooping – glaring sun – tired to death – could bear it no longer – must go and sit in the shade."

Such, for half an hour, was the conversation, interrupted only once by Mrs. Weston, who came out, in her solicitude after her son-in-law, to inquire if he had come; and she was a little uneasy. She had some fears of his horse.

Seats in the shade were found; and now Emma was obliged to overhear what Mrs. Elton and Jane Fairfax were talking of. A job as governess, a most desirable one, was in question. Mrs. Elton had received notice of it that morning, and was in raptures. It was not with Mrs. Suckling, it was not with Mrs. Bragge, but in felicity and splendour it fell short only of them: it was with a cousin of Mrs. Bragge, an acquaintance of Mrs. Suckling, a lady known at Maple Grove. Delightful, charming, superior, first circles, spheres, lines, ranks, everything: and Mrs. Elton was wild to have the offer closed with immediately. On her side, all was warmth, energy, and triumph; and she positively refused to accept her friend's refusal, though Miss Fairfax continued to assure her that she would not at present engage in anything, citing the same motives which she had brought forward before. Still Mrs. Elton insisted on being authorized to write an acceptance. How Jane could bear it at all was astonishing to Emma. She did look vexed, she did speak warmly – and at last, with a decision of action unusual to her, proposed a removal. "Should not they walk? Would not Mr. Knightley show them the gardens – all the gardens? She wished to see the whole extent." The determination of her friend seemed more than she could bear.

It was hot; and after walking some time over the gardens in a scattered, dispersed way, scarcely any three together, they followed one another to the delicious shade of a broad short avenue of lime trees, which stretched beyond the garden at an equal distance from the river. It led to nothing; nothing but a view at the end over a low stone wall with high pillars, which seemed intended to give the appearance of an approach to the house. It was a charming walk, and the view which closed it was extremely pretty. The considerable slope, at nearly the foot of which the Abbey stood, gradually acquired a steeper form beyond its grounds. At half a mile distant was a bank of considerable abruptness and grandeur, well clothed with wood; and at the bottom of this bank, favourably placed and sheltered, rose the Abbey-Mill Farm, with meadows in front, and the river making a close and handsome curve around it.

In this walk, Emma and Mr. Weston found all the others assembled; and towards this view she immediately perceived Mr. Knightley and Harriet quietly leading the way. Mr. Knightley and Harriet! It was an odd combination; but she was glad to see it. There had been a time when he would have scorned her as a companion, and turned from her with little ceremony. Now they seemed to be in pleasant conversation. There had been a time also when Emma would have been sorry to see Harriet in a spot so near the Abbey-Mill Farm; but now she feared it not. It might be safely viewed with all its appendages of prosperity and beauty, its rich pastures, spreading flocks, and apple orchard. She joined them at the wall, and found them more engaged in talking than in looking around. He was giving Harriet information as to modes of agriculture. They reached Emma and took a few turns together along the walk. The shade was most refreshing, and Emma found it the pleasantest part of the day.

They next removed to the house; they must all go in and eat. They were all seated and busy, and still Frank Churchill did not come. Mrs. Weston looked, and looked in vain. His father would not admit his uneasiness, and laughed at her fears; but she could not be cured of wishing that he would part with his black mare. He had accepted the invitation with more than common certainty. "His aunt was so much better, that he had not a doubt of getting over to them." Mrs. Churchill's state, however, as many were ready to remind her, was liable to such sudden variation as might disappoint her nephew in the most reasonable hope; and Mrs. Weston was at last persuaded to believe, or to say, that it must be by some attack of Mrs. Churchill that he was prevented from coming. Emma looked at Harriet while the point was under consideration; she behaved very well and betrayed no emotion.

The light meal was over, and the party were to go out once more to see what had not yet been seen: the old Abbey fish-ponds; perhaps get as far as the clover, which was to be begun cutting on the morrow, or, at any rate, have the pleasure of being hot, and growing cool again. Mr. Woodhouse, who had already taken his little round in the highest part of the gardens, where no damps from the river were imagined even by him, stirred no more; and his daughter resolved to remain with him, that Mrs. Weston might be persuaded away by her husband to the exercise and variety which her spirits seemed to need.

Mr. Knightley had done all in his power for Mr. Woodhouse's entertainment. Books of engravings, drawers of medals, cameos, corals, shells, and every other family collection within his cabinets, had been prepared for his old friend, to while away the morning; and Mr. Woodhouse had been exceedingly well amused. Mrs. Weston had been showing them all to him, and now he would show them all to Emma. Before this second looking over was begun, however, Emma walked into the hall for the sake of a few moments' free observation of the entrance and ground-plot of the house, and was hardly there, when Jane Fairfax appeared, coming quickly in from the garden, and with a look of escape. Little expecting to meet Miss Woodhouse so soon, there was a start at first; but Miss Woodhouse was the very person she was in quest of.

"Will you be so kind," said she, "when I am missed, as to say that I am gone home? I am going this moment. My aunt is not aware how late it is, nor how long we have been absent; but I am sure we shall be wanted, and I am determined to go immediately. I have said nothing about it to anybody. It would only be giving trouble and distress. Some are gone to the ponds, and some to the lime walk. Till they all come in I shall not be missed; and when they do, will you have the goodness to say that I am gone?"

"Certainly, if you wish it; but you are not going to walk to Highbury alone?"

"Yes; what should hurt me? I walk fast. I shall be at home in twenty minutes."

"But it is too far, indeed it is, to be walking quite alone. Let my father's servant go with you. Let me order the carriage. It can be round in five minutes."

"Thank you, thank you – but on no account. I would rather walk. And for *me* to be afraid of walking alone! I, who may so soon have to guard others!"

She spoke with great agitation; and Emma very feelingly replied, "That can be no reason for your being exposed to danger now. I must order the carriage. The heat even would be danger. You are fatigued already."

"I am," she answered, "I am fatigued; but it is not the sort of fatigue – quick walking will refresh me. Miss Woodhouse, we all know at times what it is to be wearied in spirits. Mine, I confess, are exhausted. The greatest kindness you can show me will be to let me have my own way, and only say that I am gone when it is necessary."

Emma had not another word to oppose. She watched her safely off with the zeal of a friend. Her parting look was grateful; and her parting words, "Oh! Miss Woodhouse, the comfort of being sometimes alone!" seemed to burst from an over-taxed heart, and to describe somewhat of the continual endurance to be practised by her, even towards some of those who loved her best.

"Such a home, indeed! Such an aunt!" said Emma, as she turned back into the hall again. "I do pity her. And the more sensibility she betrays of their just horrors, the more I shall like her."

Jane had not been gone a quarter of an hour, and they had only accomplished some views of St. Mark's Place, Venice, when Frank Churchill entered the room. Emma had not been thinking of him, she had forgotten to think of him, but she was very glad to see him. Mrs. Weston would be at ease. The black mare was blameless; *they* were right who had named Mrs. Churchill as the cause. He had been detained by a temporary increase of illness in her; and he had quite given up every thought of coming, till very late. Had he known how hot a ride he should have, and how late, with all his hurry, he must be, he believed he should not have come at all. The heat was excessive; he had never suffered anything like it – almost wished he had stayed at home – nothing killed him like heat – he could bear any degree of cold, but heat was intolerable. He sat down at the greatest possible distance from the slight remains of Mr. Woodhouse's fire.

"You will soon be cooler, if you sit still," said Emma.

"As soon as I am cooler I shall go back again. Indeed, I could not really be spared; but such a point had been made of my coming! You will all be going soon I suppose; the whole party is breaking up. I met *one* as I came – Madness in such weather! Absolute madness!"

Emma listened, and looked, and soon perceived that Frank Churchill's state might be best defined by the expressive phrase of being out of humour. Some people were always cross when they were hot.

Such might be his constitution; and as she knew that eating and drinking were often the cure of such incidental complaints, she recommended his taking some refreshment.

"No; he should not eat. He was not hungry; it would only make him hotter." In two minutes, however, he relented in his own favour; and muttering something about spruce beer, walked off. Emma returned all her attention to her father, saying in secret –

"I am glad I am done being in love with him. I should not like a man who is so soon discomposed by a hot morning. Harriet's sweet easy temper will not mind it."

He was gone long enough to have had a very comfortable meal, and came back all the better – grown quite cool, and, with good manners, able to draw a chair close to them, take an interest in their employment; and regret, in a reasonable way, that he should be so late. He was not in his best spirits, but seemed to be trying to improve them; and, at last, he made himself talk nonsense very agreeably. They were looking over views of Switzerland.

"As soon as my aunt gets well, I shall go abroad," said he. "I shall never be easy till I have seen some of these places. You will have my sketches, sometime or other, to look at."

"That may be – but not by sketches in Switzerland. You will never go to Switzerland. Your uncle and aunt will never allow you to leave England."

"They may be induced to join me. A warm climate may be prescribed for her. I have more than half an expectation of our all going abroad. I assure you I have. I feel a strong persuasion, this morning, that I shall soon be abroad. I ought to travel. I am tired of doing nothing. I want a change. I am serious, Miss Woodhouse, whatever your penetrating eyes may fancy – I am sick of England, and would leave it tomorrow if I could."

"You are sick of prosperity and indulgence. Cannot you invent a few hardships for yourself, and be content to stay?"

"Sick of prosperity and indulgence! You are quite mistaken. I do not look upon myself as either prosperous or indulged. I am thwarted in everything material. I do not consider myself at all a fortunate person."

"You are not quite as miserable, though, as when you first came. Go and eat and drink a little more, and you will do very well. Another slice of cold meat, another drink of wine and water, will make you nearly on par with the rest of us."

"No – I shall not stir. I shall sit by you. You are my best cure."

"We are going to Box Hill tomorrow; you will join us. It is not Switzerland, but it will be something for a young man so much in want of a change. You will stay, and go with us?"

"No, certainly not; I shall go home in the cool of the evening."

"But you may come again in the cool of tomorrow morning."

"No – It will not be worthwhile. If I come, I shall be cross."

"Then pray stay at Richmond."

"But if I do, I shall be crosser still. I can never bear to think of you all there without me."

"These are difficulties which you must settle for yourself. Choose your own degree of crossness. I shall press you no more."

The rest of the party were now returning, and all were soon collected. With some there was great joy at the sight of Frank Churchill; others took it very composedly. But there was a very general distress and disturbance on Miss Fairfax's disappearance being explained. With a short final arrangement for the next day's scheme, they parted. Frank Churchill's disinclination to exclude himself increased so much that his last words to Emma were,

"Well; if *you* wish me to stay, and join the party, I will."

She smiled her acceptance; and nothing less than a summons from Richmond was to take him back before the following evening.

CHAPTER 43

They had a very fine day for Box Hill, and there was every indication that it would be a pleasant party. Emma and Harriet went together; Miss Bates and her niece, with the Eltons, and the gentlemen on horseback. Mrs. Weston remained with Mr. Woodhouse. Seven miles were travelled in expectation of enjoyment, and everybody had a burst of admiration on first arriving; but they separated too much into different groups. The Eltons walked together, Mr. Knightley took charge of Miss Bates and Jane, and Emma and Harriet were with Frank Churchill. Mr. Weston tried, in vain, to make them harmonize better. It seemed at first an accidental division, but it never materially varied.

At first it was downright dull to Emma. She had never seen Frank Churchill so silent and withdrawn. He said nothing worth hearing – looked without seeing – admired without intelligence – listened without knowing what she said. While he was so dull, it was no wonder that Harriet should be dull likewise, and they were both insufferable.

When they all sat down it was better; to her taste a great deal better, for Frank Churchill grew talkative and happy, making her his first object. Every distinguishing attention that could be paid, was paid to her. To amuse her, and be agreeable in her eyes, seemed all that he cared for – and Emma, glad to be enlivened, not sorry to be flattered, was happy and easy too, and gave him friendly encouragement. In her own estimation, it meant nothing, though in the judgment of most people looking on it must have had such an appearance as no English word but flirtation could very well describe. "Mr. Frank Churchill and Miss Woodhouse flirted together excessively." They were laying themselves open to that very phrase – and to having it sent off in a letter to Maple Grove by one lady, to Ireland by another. Not that Emma was overcome by any real happiness; it was rather because she felt less happy than she had expected. She laughed because she was disappointed; and though she liked him for his attentions, and thought them all, whether in friendship, admiration, or playfulness, extremely judicious, they were not winning back her heart. She still intended him for her friend.

"How much I am obliged to you," said he, "for telling me to come today! If it had not been for you, I would certainly have lost all the happiness of this party. I had quite determined to go away again."

"Yes, you were very cross; and I do not know what about, except that you were too late for the best strawberries. I was a kinder friend than you deserved. But you were humble. You begged hard to be commanded to come."

"Don't say I was cross. I was fatigued. The heat overcame me."

"It is hotter today."

"Not to my feelings. I am perfectly comfortable today."

"You are comfortable because you are under command."

"Your command? Yes."

"Perhaps I intended you to say so, but I meant self-command. You had, somehow or other, broken bounds yesterday, and run away from your own management; but today you are got back again – and as I cannot be always with you, it is best to believe your temper under your own command rather than mine."

"It comes to the same thing. I can have no self-command without a motive. You order me, whether you speak or not. And you can be always with me. You are always with me."

"Dating from three o'clock yesterday. My perpetual influence could not begin earlier, or you would not have been so much out of humour before."

"Three o'clock yesterday! That is your date. I thought I had seen you first in February."

"Your gallantry is really unanswerable. But (lowering her voice) nobody speaks except ourselves, and it is rather too much to be talking nonsense for the entertainment of seven silent people."

"I say nothing of which I am ashamed," replied he. "I saw you first in February. Let everybody on the Hill hear me if they can. Let my accents swell to Mickleham on one side, and Dorking on the other. I saw you first in February." And then whispering – "Our companions are excessively dull. What shall we do to rouse them? Any nonsense will serve. They *shall* talk. Ladies and gentlemen, I am ordered by Miss Woodhouse (who, wherever she is, presides) to say that she desires to know what you are all thinking of."

Some laughed, and answered good-humouredly. Miss Bates said a great deal. Mrs. Elton swelled at the idea of Miss Woodhouse's presiding, and Mr. Knightley's answer was the most distinct.

"Is Miss Woodhouse sure that she would like to hear what we are all thinking of?"

"Oh! no, no" cried Emma, laughing as carelessly as she could – "Upon no account in the world. It is the very last thing I would stand the brunt of just now. Let me hear anything rather than what you are all thinking of. I will not say quite all. There are one or two, perhaps, (glancing at Mr. Weston and Harriet) whose thoughts I might not be afraid of knowing."

"It is a sort of thing," cried Mrs. Elton emphatically, "which *I* should not have thought myself privileged to inquire into. Though, perhaps, as the *chaperone* of the party – *I* never was in any circle – exploring parties – young ladies – married women – "

Her mutterings were chiefly to her husband; and he murmured, in reply,

"Very true, my love, very true. Exactly so, indeed – quite unheard of – but some ladies say anything. Better pass it off as a joke. Everybody knows what is due to *you*."

"It will not do," whispered Frank to Emma, "they are most of them offended. I will attack them with more skill. Ladies and gentlemen, I am ordered by Miss Woodhouse to say that she waves her right of knowing exactly what you may all be thinking of, and only requires something very entertaining from each of you, in a general way. Here are seven of you, besides myself, (who, she is pleased to say, is very entertaining already) and she only demands from each of you either one thing very clever, be it prose or verse, original or repeated – or two things moderately clever – or three things very dull indeed, and she intends to laugh heartily at them all."

"Oh! Very well," exclaimed Miss Bates, "then I need not be uneasy. 'Three things very dull indeed.' That will just do for me, you know. I shall be sure to say three dull things as soon as ever I open my mouth, shan't I? (looking round with the most good-humoured expectation of everybody's assent) Do not you all think I shall?"

Emma could not resist. "Ah! Ma'am, but there may be a difficulty. Pardon me, but you will be limited as to number – only three at once."

Miss Bates, deceived by the mock ceremony of her manner, did not immediately catch her meaning; but, when she realized it, a slight blush showed that it caused her pain.

"Ah! Well – to be sure. Yes, I see what she means, (turning to Mr. Knightley), and I will try to hold my tongue. "

"I like your plan," cried Mr. Weston. "Agreed, agreed. I will do my best."

"Come, sir, pray let me hear what you have to say," Emma encouraged.

"I doubt it's being very clever myself," said Mr. Weston. "It is too matter-of-fact, but here it is. What two letters of the alphabet are there that express perfection?"

"What two letters! Express perfection! I am sure I do not know."

"Ah! You will never guess. You," (to Emma), "I am certain, will never guess. I will tell you. M. and A. Em-ma. Do you understand?"

Understanding and gratification came together. It might be a very indifferent piece of wit; but Emma found a great deal to laugh at and enjoy in it, and so did Frank and Harriet. It did not seem to touch the rest of the party equally, and Mr. Knightley gravely said,

"This explains the sort of clever thing that is wanted, and Mr. Weston has done very well for himself; but he has set a high standard for everyone else. *Perfection* should not have come quite so soon."

"Oh! For myself, I protest I must be excused," said Mrs. Elton. "*I* really cannot attempt – I am not at all fond of the sort of thing. These things are fine at Christmas, when one is sitting round the fire; but quite out of place, in my opinion, when one is exploring about the country in summer. Miss Woodhouse must excuse me. I am not one of those who have witty things at everybody's service. I do not pretend to be a wit. I have a great deal of vivacity in my own way, but I really must be allowed to judge when to speak and when to hold my tongue. Pass us, if you please, Mr. Churchill. Pass Mr. E., Knightley, Jane and myself. We have nothing clever to say – not one of us."

Mr. Elton then added,

"*I* have nothing to say that can entertain Miss Woodhouse, or any other young lady. An old married man – quite good for nothing. Shall we walk, Augusta?"

"Yes, please. I am really tired of exploring so long on one spot. Come, Jane, take my other arm."

Jane declined it, however, and the husband and wife walked off. "Happy couple!" said Frank Churchill, as soon as they were out of hearing: "How well they suit one another! Very lucky – marrying as they did, upon an acquaintance formed only in a public place! They only knew each other, I think, a few weeks in Bath! Peculiarly lucky! For as to any real knowledge of a person's disposition that Bath, or any public place, can give – it is all nothing; there can be no knowledge. It is only by seeing women in their own homes, among their own friends and family, just as they always are, that you can form any just judgment. Short of that, it is all guess and luck – and will generally be bad luck. How many a man has committed himself on a short acquaintance, and rued it all the rest of his life!"

Miss Fairfax, who had seldom spoken before, except among her own confederates, spoke now. "Such things do occur, undoubtedly." She was stopped by a cough. Frank Churchill turned towards her to listen.

"You were speaking," said he, gravely. She recovered her voice.

"I was only going to observe, that though such unfortunate circumstances do sometimes occur both to men and women, I cannot imagine them to be very frequent. A hasty and imprudent attachment may arise – but there is generally time to recover from it afterwards. I would be understood to mean, that it can be only weak, irresolute characters (whose happiness must be always at the mercy of chance,) who will allow an unfortunate acquaintance to become a lasting oppression."

He made no answer; merely looked, and bowed in submission, and soon afterwards said, in a lively tone,

"Well, I have so little confidence in my own judgment, that whenever I marry, I hope somebody will choose my wife for me. Will you? (turning to Emma). Will you choose a wife for me? I am sure I should like anybody fixed on by you. You provide for the family, you know, (with a smile at his father). Find somebody for me. I am in no hurry. Adopt her, educate her."

"And make her like myself."

"By all means, if you can."

"Very well. I undertake the commission. You shall have a charming wife."

"She must be very lively, and have hazel eyes. I care for nothing else. I shall go abroad for a couple of years – and when I return, I shall come to you for my wife. Remember."

Emma was in no danger of forgetting. It was a commission to touch every favourite feeling. Would not Harriet be the very creature described? Hazel eyes excepted, two years more might make her all that he wished. He might even have Harriet in his thoughts at the moment; who could say? Referring the education to her seemed to imply it.

"Now, ma'am," said Jane to her aunt, "shall we join Mrs. Elton?"

"If you please, my dear. I am quite ready. I was ready to have gone with her, but this will do just as well. We shall soon catch up. There she is — no, that's somebody else. That's one of the ladies in the Irish car party, not at all like her. Well, I declare — "

They walked off, followed in half a minute by Mr. Knightley. Mr. Weston, his son, Emma, and Harriet, only remained; and the young man's spirits now rose to a pitch almost unpleasant. Even Emma grew tired at last of flattery and merriment, and wished herself rather walking quietly about with any of the others, or sitting almost alone in tranquil observation of the beautiful views beneath her. The arrival of the carriages was a joyful sight, and even the bustle of collecting and preparing to depart, and the solicitude of Mrs. Elton to have *her* carriage first, were gladly endured, in the prospect of the quiet drive home. Such another scheme, composed of so many ill-assorted people, she hoped never to be a part of again.

While waiting for the carriage, she found Mr. Knightley by her side. He looked around, as if to see that no one were near, and then said,

"Emma, I must once more speak to you as I have before: a privilege rather endured than allowed, perhaps, but I must still use it. I cannot see you acting wrongly without saying something. How could you be so unfeeling to Miss Bates? How could you be so offensive in your wit to a woman of her character, age, and situation? Emma, I had not thought it possible."

Emma recollected, blushed, was sorry, but tried to laugh it off.

"Nay, how could I help saying what I did? Nobody could have helped it. It was not so very bad. I dare say she did not understand me."

"I assure you she did. She felt your full meaning. She has talked of it since. I wish you could have heard how she talked of it. I wish you could have heard her honouring your patience, in being able to pay her such attentions, as she was forever receiving from yourself and your father, when her company must be so irksome."

"Oh!" cried Emma, "I know there is not a better creature in the world: but you must admit that what is good and what is ridiculous are most unfortunately blended in her."

"They are blended," said he, "I acknowledge; and, were she prosperous, I could allow much for the occasional prevalence of the ridiculous over the good. Were she a woman of fortune, I would leave every harmless absurdity to take its chance. Were she your equal in situation – but, Emma, consider how far this is from being the case. She is poor; she has sunk from the comforts she was born to; and, if she lives to old age, must probably sink more. Her situation should secure your compassion. It was badly done, indeed! You, whom she had known from an infant, whom she had seen grow up from a period when her notice was an honour, to have you now, in thoughtless spirits, and the pride of the moment, laugh at her, humble her – and before her niece, too – and before others, many of whom (certainly *some*) would be entirely guided by *your* treatment of her. This is not pleasant to you, Emma – and it is very far from pleasant to me; but I must, I will tell you truths while I can, satisfied with proving myself your friend by very faithful counsel, and trusting that you will sometime or other do me greater justice than you can do now."

While they talked, they were advancing towards the carriage; it was ready, and before she could speak again, he had handed her in. He had misinterpreted the feelings which had kept her face averted, and her tongue motionless. They were combined only of anger against herself, mortification, and deep concern. She had not been able to speak; and, on entering the carriage, sunk back for a moment overcome – then reproaching herself for having taken no leave, making no acknowledgement, parting in apparent sullenness, she looked out with voice and hand eager to show a difference; but it was just too late. He had turned away, and the horses were in motion. She continued to look back, but in vain; and soon, with what appeared unusual speed, they were half way down the hill, and everything left far behind. She was vexed beyond what could have been expressed – almost beyond what she could conceal. Never had she felt so agitated, mortified, or grieved at any circumstance in her life. She was most forcibly struck. The truth of what he had said there was no denying. She felt it in her heart. How could she have been so brutal, so cruel to Miss Bates? How could she have exposed herself to such ill opinion in anyone she valued? And how could she suffer him to leave her without expressing one word of gratitude?

Time did not compose her. As she reflected more, she seemed but to feel it more. She never had been so depressed. Happily, it was not necessary to speak. There was only Harriet, who seemed not in spirits herself, tired and very willing to be silent; and Emma felt the tears running down her cheeks almost all the way home, without taking any trouble to check them, unusual as they were.

CHAPTER 44

The wretchedness of the Box Hill debacle was in Emma's thoughts all the evening. How it might be considered by the rest of the party, she could not tell. They, in their different homes, and their different ways, might be looking back on it with pleasure; but in her view it was the worst morning she had ever spent. A whole evening of backgammon with her father, normally not her favorite pastime, was pure joy by comparison, for she was giving up the sweetest hours of the twenty-four to his comfort. As a daughter, she hoped she was not entirely heartless. She hoped no one could have said to her, "How could you be so unfeeling to your father? I must, I will tell you truths while I can." If future attention to Miss Bates could do away the past, she might hope to be forgiven. She had been often remiss; her conscience told her so. Remiss, perhaps, more in thought than outward manner; scornful and ungracious. But it should be so no more. In the warmth of true contrition, she would call upon her the very next morning, and it should be the beginning, on her side, of a regular, equal, kindly interaction.

She was just as determined when the morrow came, and went early, that nothing might prevent her. It was not unlikely, she thought, that she might see Mr. Knightley on her way; or, perhaps, he might come in while she was paying her visit. She had no objection. She would not be ashamed of the appearance of penitence so justly and truly hers. Her eyes were towards Donwell as she walked, but she did not see him.

"The ladies were all at home." She had never rejoiced at the sound before, nor ever before entered the passage, nor walked up the stairs, with any wish of giving pleasure, or of deriving it, except in subsequent ridicule.

There was a bustle on her approach; a good deal of moving and talking. She heard Miss Bates's voice, something was to be done in a hurry. The maid looked frightened and awkward; hoped she would be pleased to wait a moment, and then ushered her in too soon. The aunt and niece seemed both to be escaping into the adjoining room. Jane she had a distinct glimpse of, looking extremely ill; and, before the door had shut them out, she heard Miss Bates saying, "Well, my dear, I shall *say* you are lying down upon the bed, and I am sure you are ill enough."

Poor old Mrs. Bates, civil and humble as usual, looked as if she did not quite understand what was going on.

"I am afraid Jane is not feeling very well," said she, "but I do not know; they *tell* me she is well. I dare say my daughter will be here presently, Miss Woodhouse. I hope you find a chair. I wish Hetty had not gone. I am very little able – Have you a chair, ma'am? Sit where you like, I am sure she will be here presently."

Emma seriously hoped she would. She had a moment's fear of Miss Bates keeping away from her. But Miss Bates soon came – "Very happy and obliged" – but Emma's conscience told her that there was not the same cheerfulness as before. A very friendly inquiry after Miss Fairfax, she hoped, might lead the way to a return of old feelings. The result seemed immediate.

"Ah! Miss Woodhouse, how kind you are! I suppose you have heard – and are come to give us joy. This does not seem much like joy, indeed, in me – (twinkling away a tear or two) – but it will be very trying for us to part with her, after having had her so long, and she has a dreadful headache just now, writing all the morning – such long letters, you know, to be written to Colonel Campbell, and Mrs. Dixon. 'My dear,' said I, 'you will blind yourself' – for tears were in her eyes perpetually. One cannot wonder, one cannot wonder. It is a great change; and though she is amazingly fortunate – such a position, I suppose, as no young woman before ever got on first going out – do not think us ungrateful, Miss Woodhouse, for such surprising good fortune – (again dispersing her tears) – but, poor dear soul! If you were to see what a headache she has. When one is in great pain, you know one cannot feel any blessing quite as it may deserve. She is as low as possible. To look at her, nobody would think how delighted and happy she is to have secured such a situation. You will excuse her not coming to you – she is not able – she is gone into her own room – I want her to lie down upon the bed. 'My dear,' said I, 'I shall say you are laid down upon the bed,' but she is not; she is walking about the room. But, now that she has written her letters, she says she shall soon be well. She will be extremely sorry to miss seeing you, Miss Woodhouse, but your kindness will excuse her. You were kept waiting at the door – I was quite ashamed – but somehow there was a little bustle – for it so happened that we had not heard the knock, and till you were on the stairs, we did not know anybody was coming. 'It is only Mrs. Cole,' said I, 'depend upon it. Nobody else would come so early.' "Well,' said she, 'it must be borne sometime or other, and it may as well be now.' But then Patty came in, and said it was you. 'Oh!' said I, 'it is Miss Woodhouse: I am sure you will like to see her.' – 'I can see nobody,' said she; and up she got, and went away; and that was what made us keep you waiting – and extremely sorry and ashamed we were. 'If you must go, my dear,' said I, 'you must, and I will say you are laid down upon the bed.'"

Emma was most sincerely interested. Her heart had been long growing kinder towards Jane; and this picture of her present sufferings acted as a cure of every former ungenerous suspicion, and left her nothing but pity. The remembrance of the less just and less gentle sensations of the past obliged her to admit that Jane might very naturally prefer Mrs. Cole or any other steady friend over herself. She spoke as she felt, with earnest regret and solicitude – sincerely wishing that the circumstances which she collected from Miss Bates to be now actually determined on, might be as much for Miss Fairfax's advantage and comfort as possible.

"It must be a severe trial to them all. She had understood it was to be delayed till Colonel Campbell's return."

"So very kind!" replied Miss Bates. "But you are always kind."

There was no bearing such an "always," and to break through her dreadful gratitude, Emma made the direct inquiry of –

"Where, may I ask, is Miss Fairfax going?"

"To a Mrs. Smallridge – charming woman – most superior – to have the charge of her three little girls – delightful children. Impossible that any situation could be more replete with comfort. If we except, perhaps, Mrs. Suckling's own family, and Mrs. Bragge's; but Mrs. Smallridge is acquainted with both. And in the very same neighbourhood: she lives only four miles from Maple Grove. Jane will be only four miles from Maple Grove."

"Mrs. Elton, I suppose, has been the person to whom Miss Fairfax owes – "

"Yes, our good Mrs. Elton. Such a true friend. She would not let Jane say 'No;' for when Jane first heard of it, (it was the day before yesterday, the very morning we were at Donwell), she was quite decided against accepting the offer, and for the reasons you mention; exactly as you say, she had made up her mind to decide upon nothing till Colonel Campbell's return, and nothing could convince her to enter into any engagement at present – and so she told Mrs. Elton over and over again – and I am sure I had no idea that she would change her mind! But that good Mrs. Elton, whose judgement never fails her, saw farther than I did. It is not everybody that would have stood out in such a kind way as she did, and refuse to take Jane's answer; but she positively declared she would *not* write any such denial yesterday, as Jane wished her; she would wait – and, sure enough, yesterday evening it was all settled that Jane should go. Quite a surprise to me! I had not the least idea! Jane took Mrs. Elton aside, and told her at once, that upon thinking over the advantages of Mrs. Suckling's situation, she had decided to accept it. I did not know a word of it till it was all settled."

"You spent the evening with Mrs. Elton?"

"Yes, all of us; Mrs. Elton invited us. It was settled so, upon the hill, while we were walking about with Mr. Knightley. 'You *must all* spend your evening with us,' said she – 'I positively must have you *all* come.'"

"Mr. Knightley was there too, was he?"

"No, not Mr. Knightley; he declined the invitation. Though I thought he would come, because Mrs. Elton declared she would not let him out of it, he did not. My mother and Jane and I were all there, and a very agreeable evening we had. Such kind friends, you know, Miss Woodhouse, one must always find agreeable, though everybody seemed rather tired after the morning's party. Even pleasure, you know, is fatiguing – and I cannot say that any of them seemed very much to have enjoyed it. However, *I* shall always think it a very pleasant party, and feel extremely obliged to the kind friends who included me in it."

"Miss Fairfax, I suppose, though you were not aware of it, had been making up her mind the whole day."

"I dare say she had," replied Miss Bates.

"Whenever the time may come, it must be unwelcome to her and all her friends – but I hope her new situation will offer every joy that is possible – I mean, as to the character and manners of the family."

"Thank you, dear Miss Woodhouse. Yes, indeed, there is everything in the world that can make her happy in it. Mrs. Smallridge is a most delightful woman! A style of living almost equal to Maple Grove — and as to the children, except the little Sucklings and little Bragges, there are not such elegant sweet children anywhere. Jane will be treated with such regard and kindness! It will be nothing but pleasure, a life of pleasure. And her salary! I really cannot venture to name her salary to you, Miss Woodhouse. You would hardly believe that so much could be given to a young person like Jane."

"Ah! Madam," cried Emma, "if other children are at all like what I remember to have been myself, I should think five times the amount of what I have ever yet heard named as a salary on such occasions, dearly earned."

"You are so noble in your ideas!"

"And when is Miss Fairfax to leave you?"

"Very soon, very soon indeed; that's the worst of it. Within a fortnight. Mrs. Smallridge is in a great hurry. My poor mother does not know how to bear it. I try to put it out of her thoughts and say, 'Do not let us think about it anymore.'"

"Her friends must all be sorry to lose her; and will not Colonel and Mrs. Campbell be sorry to find that she has engaged herself before their return?"

"Yes; Jane says she is sure they will. Yet this is such a situation as she cannot feel herself justified in declining. I was so astonished when she first told me, and when Mrs. Elton at the same moment came congratulating me upon it! It was just after tea that Jane spoke to Mrs. Elton."

Miss Bates then began to speak of Mr. Frank Churchill's going. A messenger had come over from Richmond soon after the return of the party from Box Hill. Mr. Churchill had sent his nephew a few lines, containing, upon the whole, a tolerable account of Mrs. Churchill, and only wishing him not to delay coming back beyond the next morning; but Mr. Frank Churchill had resolved to go home immediately, without waiting at all.

There was nothing in all this either to astonish or interest. The contrast between Mrs. Churchill's importance in the world, and Jane Fairfax's, struck her; one was everything, the other nothing — and she sat musing on the difference of woman's destiny, and quite unconscious of what was before her eyes, till roused by Miss Bates's saying,

"Ay, I see you are thinking of the piano. What is to become of that? Very true. Poor dear Jane was talking of it just now. 'You must go,' said she. 'You and I must part. You will have no business here. Let it stay, however,' said she, 'till Colonel Campbell comes back. I shall talk about it to him; he will settle for me. He will help me out of all my difficulties.' And to this day, I do believe, she knows not whether it was his present or his daughter's."

Now Emma was obliged to think of the piano and the remembrance of all her former fanciful and unfair conjectures. She soon allowed herself to believe her visit had been long enough; and, with a repetition of everything that she could venture to say of the good wishes which she really felt, took leave.

CHAPTER 45

Emma's reflections, as she walked home, were not interrupted; but on entering the parlour, she found those who must rouse her. Mr. Knightley and Harriet had arrived during her absence, and were sitting with her father. Mr. Knightley immediately got up, and in a manner decidedly graver than usual, said,

"I would not go away without seeing you, but I have no time to spare, and therefore must now be gone directly. I am going to London, to spend a few days with John and Isabella. Have you anything to say to them, besides the 'love' which is usually sent?"

"Nothing at all. But why the sudden resolution to go?"

"I have been thinking of it for some time now. I simply neglected to mention it."

Emma was sure he had not forgiven her; he looked unlike himself. Time, however, she thought, would tell him that they ought to be friends again. While he stood, as if meaning to go, but not going – her father began his inquiries.

"Well, my dear, and did you get there safely? How did you find my worthy old friend and her daughter? I dare say they must have been very much obliged to you for coming. Dear Emma has been to call on Mrs. and Miss Bates, Mr. Knightley, as I told you before. She is always so attentive to them!"

Emma's colour was heightened by this unjust praise; and with a smile, and shake of the head, which spoke much, she looked at Mr. Knightley. It seemed as if there were an instantaneous impression in her favour, as if his eyes received the truth from hers, and all that had passed of good in her feelings were at once caught and honoured. He looked at her with a glow of regard. She was warmly gratified – and in another moment still more so, by a little movement of more than common friendliness on his part. He took her hand – whether she had not herself made the first motion, she could not say – she might, perhaps, have rather offered it – but he took her hand, pressed it, and certainly was on the point of carrying it to his lips – when, from some fancy or other, he suddenly let it go. Why he should stop, why he should change his mind when it was all but done, she could not perceive. The intention, however, could not be doubted. She could not help but recall it with great satisfaction. It spoke such perfect amity. He left them immediately afterwards – gone in a moment. He always moved with the alertness of a mind which could neither be undecided nor hesitant, but now he seemed more sudden than usual in his disappearance.

Emma could not regret her having gone to Miss Bates, but she wished she had left her ten minutes earlier. It would have been a great pleasure to talk over Jane Fairfax's situation with Mr. Knightley. She did not regret that he should be going to Brunswick Square, for she knew how much his visit would be enjoyed – but it might have happened at a better time – and to have had longer notice of it would have been pleasanter. They parted thorough friends, however; she could not be deceived as to the meaning of his countenance, and his unfinished gallantry; it was all done to assure her that she had fully recovered his good opinion. He had been sitting with them half an hour, she found. It was a pity that she had not come back earlier!

In the hope of diverting her father's thoughts from the disagreeableness of Mr. Knightley's going to London; and going so suddenly, Emma communicated her news of Jane Fairfax. It served perfectly – interesting him without disturbing him. He had long made up his mind as to Jane Fairfax's becoming a governess, and could talk of it cheerfully, but Mr. Knightley's going to London had been an unexpected blow.

"I am very glad indeed, my dear, to hear she is to be so comfortably settled. Mrs. Elton is very good-natured and agreeable. I hope it is a good situation, and that Jane's health will be taken care of. It ought to be a first object, as I am sure poor Miss Taylor's always was with me. You know, my dear, she is going to be to this new lady what Miss Taylor was to us. And I hope she will be better off in one respect, and not be induced to go away after it has been her home so long."

The following day brought news from Richmond to throw everything else into the background. An express arrived at Randalls to announce the death of Mrs. Churchill. Though her nephew had had no particular reason to hasten back on her account, she had not lived above thirty-six hours after his return. A sudden stroke had carried her off after a short struggle. The great Mrs. Churchill was no more.

It was felt as such things must be felt. Everybody had a degree of gravity and sorrow; tenderness towards the departed, solicitude for the surviving friends; and, in a reasonable time, curiosity to know where she would be buried. Mrs. Churchill, after being disliked at least twenty-five years, was now spoken of with compassionate allowances. In one point, she was fully justified. She had never been admitted before to be seriously ill. The event acquitted her of all the fancifulness, and all the selfishness of imaginary complaints.

"Poor Mrs. Churchill! No doubt she had been suffering a great deal more than anybody had ever supposed – and continual pain would try the temper. It was a sad event – a great shock – with all her faults, what would Mr. Churchill do without her? Mr. Churchill's loss would be dreadful indeed. Mr. Churchill would never get over it." Even Mr. Weston shook his head, and looked solemn, and said, "Ah! Poor woman, who would have thought it!" How it would affect Frank was among his earliest thoughts. It was also a very early speculation with Emma. The character of Mrs. Churchill, the grief of her husband – her mind glanced over them both with awe and compassion – and then rested with lightened feelings on how Frank might be affected by the event, how benefited, how freed. She saw in a moment all the possible good. Now an attachment to Harriet Smith would be possible. Mr. Churchill, independent of his wife, was feared by nobody; an easy, guidable man, to be persuaded into anything by his nephew. All that remained to be wished was that the nephew should form the attachment, as Emma could feel no certainty of its being already formed.

Harriet behaved extremely well on the occasion, with great self-command. Whatever she might feel of brighter hope, she betrayed nothing. Emma was gratified to observe such a proof in her of strengthened character, and refrained from any reference that might endanger its continuance. They spoke, therefore, of Mrs. Churchill's death with mutual reserve.

Short letters from Frank were received at Randalls, communicating all that was immediately important of their state and plans. Mr.

Churchill was better than could be expected. At present, there was nothing to be done for Harriet; good wishes for the future were all that could yet be possible on Emma's side.

It was a more pressing concern to show attention to Jane Fairfax, who would very soon be leaving Highbury. Emma had a strong regret for her past coldness; and the person, whom she had been so many months neglecting, was now the very one on whom she would have lavished every distinction of regard or sympathy. She wanted to be of use to her; wanted to show a value for her society, and testify respect and consideration. She resolved to prevail on her to spend a day at Hartfield. A note was written to urge it. The invitation was refused, and when Mr. Perry called at Hartfield the same morning, it appeared that she was so much indisposed as to have been visited, though against her own consent, by himself, and that she was suffering under severe headaches, which made him doubt the possibility of her going to Mrs. Smallridge's at the time proposed. Her appetite was quite gone – and though there were no absolutely alarming symptoms, Mr. Perry was uneasy about her. He thought she had undertaken more than she was equal to, and that she felt it so herself, though she would not admit it. Her spirits seemed overcome. Emma listened with the warmest concern; grieved for her more and more, and looked around eager to discover some way of being useful. To take her – be it only an hour or two – from her aunt, to give her change of air and scene, and quiet rational conversation, even for an hour or two, might do her good; and the following morning she wrote again to say, in the most feeling language she could command, that she would call for her in the carriage at any hour that Jane would name – mentioning that she had Mr. Perry's decided opinion, in favour of such exercise for his patient. The answer was only in this short note:

"Miss Fairfax's compliments and thanks, but is quite unequal to any exercise."

Emma felt that her own note had deserved something better; but she thought only of how she might best counteract this unwillingness to be seen or assisted. In spite of the answer, therefore, she ordered the carriage, and drove to Mrs. Bates's, in the hope that Jane would be induced to join her – but it would not do. Miss Bates came to the carriage door, all gratitude, and agreeing with her most earnestly in thinking fresh air might be of the greatest service – and everything was tried – but all in vain. Miss Bates was obliged to return without success; Jane was quite unpersuadable; the mere proposal of going out seemed to make her worse. Emma wished she could have seen her, and tried her own powers; but, almost before she could speak the wish, Miss Bates made it appear that she had promised her niece on no account to let Miss Woodhouse in. "Indeed, the truth was, that poor dear Jane could not bear to see anybody – anybody at all – Mrs. Elton, indeed, could not be denied – and Mrs. Cole had made such a point – and Mrs. Perry had said so much – but, except them, Jane would really see nobody."

Emma did not want to be classed with the Mrs. Eltons, the Mrs. Perrys, and the Mrs. Coles, who would force themselves anywhere; neither could she feel any right of preference herself – she submitted, therefore, and only questioned Miss Bates farther as to her niece's appetite and diet, which she longed to be able to assist. On that subject poor Miss Bates was very unhappy, and very communicative; Jane would hardly eat anything. Mr. Perry recommended nourishing food, but everything they could command (and never had anybody such good neighbours) was distasteful.

Emma, on reaching home, called the housekeeper directly, to an examination of her stores; and some arrow-root of very superior quality was speedily dispatched to Miss Bates with a most friendly note. In half an hour the arrow-root was returned, with a thousand thanks from Miss Bates, but "dear Jane would not be satisfied without its being sent back; it was a thing she could not take – and, moreover, she insisted on her saying, that she was not at all in want of anything."

When Emma afterwards heard that Jane Fairfax had been seen wandering about the meadows, at some distance from Highbury, on the afternoon of the very day on which she had, under the plea of being unequal to any exercise, refused to go out with her in the carriage, she could have no doubt – putting everything together – that Jane was resolved to receive no kindness from *her*. She was sorry, very sorry. It mortified her that she was given so little credit for proper feeling, or esteemed so little worthy as a friend: but she had the consolation of knowing that her intentions were good, and of being able to say to herself, that could Mr. Knightley have been privy to all her attempts of assisting Jane Fairfax, he would not, on this occasion, have found anything wanting.

CHAPTER 46

One morning about ten days after Mrs. Churchill's decease, Emma was called downstairs to Mr. Weston, who "could not stay five minutes, and wanted particularly to speak with her." He met her at the parlour door, and hardly asking her how she did, in the natural key of his voice, sunk it immediately, to say, unheard by her father,

"Can you come to Randalls at any time this morning? Do, if it be possible. Mrs. Weston wants to see you. She must see you."

"Is she unwell?"

"No, no, not at all; only a little agitated. She would have ordered the carriage and come to you, but she must see you *alone*, and that, you know," (nodding towards her father) "is not possible here. Can you come?"

"Certainly. This moment, if you please. It is impossible to refuse what you ask in such a way. But what can be the matter? Is she really not ill?"

"She is not; but ask no more questions. You will know it all in time. The most unaccountable business! But hush, hush!"

To guess what all this meant was impossible, even for Emma. Something really important must have occurred; but, as her friend was well, she endeavoured not to be uneasy. Settling it with her father that she would take her walk now, she and Mr. Weston were soon out of the house together and on their way at a quick pace for Randalls.

"Now," said Emma, when they were beyond the gates, "do let me know what has happened."

"No, no," he gravely replied. "Don't ask me. I promised my wife to leave it all to her. She will break it to you better than I can. Do not be impatient, Emma; it will all come out soon."

"Break it to me," cried Emma, standing still with terror. "Good God! Mr. Weston, tell me at once. Something has happened in Brunswick Square. I know it has. Tell me this moment what it is."

"No, indeed you are mistaken."

"Mr. Weston do not trifle with me. Consider how many of my dearest friends are now in Brunswick Square. Which of them is it? I charge you by all that is sacred not to attempt concealment."

"Upon my word, Emma."

Your word! Why not your honour! Why not say upon your honour, that it has nothing to do with any of them? Good Heavens! What news can there be for me that does not relate to one of that family?"

"Upon my honour," said he very seriously, "it is not in the smallest degree connected with any human being of the name of Knightley."

Emma's courage returned, and she walked on. She asked no more questions, eventually determining to herself that it must be some money concern – something just come to light, of a disagreeable nature in the circumstances of the family, something which Mrs. Churchill's death had brought forward. Her imagination was very active indeed. Had poor Frank been cut off from his inheritance? This, though very undesirable, would be no matter of agony to her. It inspired little more than curiosity.

"Who is that gentleman on horseback?" said she, as they proceeded; speaking more to assist Mr. Weston in keeping his secret than with any other view.

"One of the Otways. Not Frank; it is not Frank, I assure you. You will not see him. He is half way to Windsor by this time."

"Has your son been with you, then?"

"Oh! Yes, did not you know? Well, well, never mind."

For a moment he was silent, and then added, in a tone much more guarded,

"Yes, Frank came over this morning, just to ask us how we were doing."

They hurried on, and were speedily at Randalls. "Well, my dear," said he, as they entered the room, "I have brought her, and now I hope you will soon be better. I shall leave you together. There is no use in delay. I shall not be far off, if you want me." Emma distinctly heard him add, in a lower tone, before he left the room, "I have been as good as my word. She has not the least idea."

Mrs. Weston was looking so ill, and had an air of so much perturbation, that Emma's uneasiness increased. The moment they were alone, she eagerly said,

"What is it my dear friend? Something of a very unpleasant nature, I find, has occurred; do let me know what it is. I have been walking all this way in complete suspense. We both abhor suspense. Do not let mine continue longer. It will do you good to speak of your distress, whatever it may be."

"Have you indeed no idea?" said Mrs. Weston in a trembling voice. "Cannot you, my dear Emma – cannot you form a guess as to what you are to hear?"

"It relates to Mr. Frank Churchill, that much seems clear."

"You are right. It does relate to him, and I will tell you directly. He has been here this very morning, on a most extraordinary errand. It is impossible to express our surprise. He came to speak to his father on a subject – to announce an attachment – "

She stopped to breathe. Emma thought first of herself, and then of Harriet.

"More than an attachment, indeed," resumed Mrs. Weston, "an engagement – a positive engagement. What will you say, Emma – what will anybody say, when it is known that Frank Churchill and Miss Fairfax are engaged – nay, that they have been long engaged!"

Emma jumped with surprise, exclaiming,

"Jane Fairfax! Good God! You are not serious? You do not mean it?"

"You may well be amazed," returned Mrs. Weston, still averting her eyes, and talking on with eagerness, that Emma might have time to recover – "You may well be amazed. But it is even so. There has been a solemn engagement between them ever since October – formed at Weymouth, and kept a secret from everybody. Not a creature knowing it but themselves – neither the Campbells, nor her family, nor his. Though perfectly convinced that it is true, I can hardly believe it myself. I thought I knew him."

Emma scarcely heard what was said. Her mind was divided between two ideas; her own former conversations with him about Miss Fairfax, and poor Harriet. For some time she could only exclaim, and require confirmation, repeated confirmation.

"Well," said she at last, trying to recover herself, "this is a circumstance which I must think of at least half a day, before I can at all comprehend it. What! Engaged to her all winter – before either of them came to Highbury?"

"Engaged since October – secretly engaged. It has hurt me, Emma, very much. It has hurt his father equally. *Some part* of his conduct we cannot excuse."

Emma pondered a moment, and then, realizing what was meant, replied, "Be assured that there has been no ill effect from his attentions to me."

Mrs. Weston looked up, afraid to believe; but Emma's countenance was as steady as her words.

"There was a period in the early part of our acquaintance, when I was very much disposed to be attached to him – nay, was attached – and how it ceased, I cannot say. Fortunately, however, it did cease. I have really for some time past, for at least these three months, cared nothing about him. You may believe me, Mrs. Weston. This is the simple truth."

Mrs. Weston shed tears of joy; and when she could find utterance assured her that this declaration had done her more good than anything else in the world could do.

"Mr. Weston will be almost as much relieved as myself," said she. "On this point we have been wretched. It was our darling wish that you were not attached to him – and we were persuaded that it was so. Imagine what we have been feeling on your account."

"I have escaped; and that I should escape may be a matter of grateful wonder to you and myself. But this does not acquit *him*, Mrs. Weston; and I must say that I think him greatly to blame. What right had he to come among us with affection engaged, and with manners so *very* disengaged? What right had he to endeavour to please, as he certainly did – to distinguish any young woman with persevering attention, as he certainly did – while he really belonged to another? How could he tell what mischief he might be doing? How could he tell that he might not be making me fall in love with him? Very wrong, very wrong indeed. And how could Jane bear such behaviour! To look on, while repeated attentions were offered to another woman before her face, and not resent it. That is a degree of reserve which I can neither comprehend nor respect."

"There were misunderstandings between them, Emma; he said so expressly. He had not time to enter into much explanation. He was here only a quarter of an hour, and in a state of agitation which did not allow the full use even of the time he could stay – but that there had been misunderstandings he decidedly said. The present crisis, indeed, seemed to be brought on by them; and those misunderstandings might very possibly arise from the impropriety of his conduct."

"Impropriety! Oh! Mrs. Weston, it is too light a censure. Much, much beyond impropriety! I cannot say how it has sunk him in my opinion. So unlike what a man should be! None of that upright integrity, that strict adherence to truth and principle which a man should display in every area of his life."

"Nay, dear Emma, now I must take his part; for though he has been wrong in this instance, I have known him long enough to answer for his having many, very many, good qualities; and – "

"Good God!" cried Emma, not hearing her. "Jane was actually on the point of becoming a governess! What could he mean by such horrible indelicacy? To suffer her to engage herself – to suffer her even to think of such a measure!"

"He knew nothing about it, Emma. On that point I can fully acquit him. It was a private resolution of hers, not communicated to him, or at least not communicated in a way to carry conviction. Till yesterday he was in the dark as to her plans. They burst on him, I do not know how, but by some letter or message – and it was the discovery of what she was doing, of this very project of hers, which determined him to come forward at once, admit everything to his uncle, throw himself on his kindness, and, in short, put an end to the miserable state of concealment that had been going on so long."

Emma began to listen better. "I am to hear from him soon," continued Mrs. Weston. "He told me at parting that he should soon write; and he spoke in a manner which seemed to promise me many particulars that could not be given now. Let us wait, therefore, for this letter. It may bring many explanations. It may make many things intelligible and excusable which cannot now be understood. Let us have patience. I am sincerely anxious for its all turning out well, and ready to hope that it may. They must both have suffered a great deal under such a system of secrecy and concealment."

"*His* sufferings," replied Emma drily, "do not appear to have done him much harm. How did Mr. Churchill take it?"

"Most favourably – gave his consent with scarcely a difficulty. Conceive what the events of a week have done in that family! While poor Mrs. Churchill lived, I suppose there could not have been a hope, a chance, a possibility; but scarcely are her remains at rest than her husband is persuaded to act exactly opposite to what she would have required. What a blessing it is when undue influence does not survive the grave! He gave his consent with very little persuasion."

"Ah!" thought Emma, "he might have done the same for Harriet."

"This was settled last night, and Frank was off with the light this morning. He stopped at Highbury, at the Bates', and then came here; but was in such a hurry to get back to his uncle, to whom he is just now more necessary than ever, that, as I tell you, he could stay with us but a quarter of an hour. He was very much agitated – very much, indeed – to a degree that made him appear quite a different creature from anything I had ever seen him before. In addition to all the rest, there had been the shock of finding her so very unwell, which he had had no previous suspicion of, and there was every appearance of his having been feeling a great deal."

"And do you really believe the affair to have been carrying on with such perfect secrecy? The Campbells, the Dixons, none of them knew of the engagement?"

"None; not one. He positively said that it had been known to no being in the world but their two selves."

"Well," said Emma, "I suppose we shall gradually grow reconciled to the idea, and I wish them very happy. But I shall always think it a very abominable sort of proceeding. What has it been but a system of hypocrisy, deceit and treachery? To come among us with professions of openness and simplicity! Here have we been, the whole winter and spring, completely duped, believing ourselves all on an equal footing of truth and honour, with two people in the midst of us who may have been sitting in judgment on sentiments and words that were never meant for both to hear. They must accept the consequences, if they have heard each other spoken of in a way not perfectly agreeable!"

"I am quite easy in that regard," replied Mrs. Weston. "I am very sure that I never said anything of either to the other, which both might not have heard."

"You are in luck. Your only blunder was confined to my ear, when you imagined a certain friend of ours in love with the lady."

"True. But as I have always had a thoroughly good opinion of Miss Fairfax, I never could, under any blunder, have spoken ill of her; and as to speaking ill of him, there I have been safe."

At this moment Mr. Weston appeared at a little distance from the window, evidently on the watch. His wife gave him a look which invited him in; and, while he was coming around, added,

"Now, dearest Emma, let me entreat you to say and look everything that may set his heart at ease, and incline him to be satisfied with the match. Let us make the best of it – and, indeed, almost everything may be fairly said in her favour. It is not a financially prudent connection; but if Mr. Churchill accepts it, why shouldn't we? It may be a very fortunate circumstance for him, for Frank, I mean, that he should have attached himself to a girl of such steadiness of character and good judgment as I have always given her credit for – and still am disposed to give her credit for, in spite of this one great deviation from the strict rule of right. And how much may be said in her situation for even that error!"

"Much indeed!" cried Emma, feelingly. "If a woman can ever be excused for thinking only of herself, it is in a situation like Jane Fairfax's. She, who nearly became a governess, shall now be the mistress of a large fortune. It is certainly a very favourable change, for her and all who are connected with her."

She met Mr. Weston on his entrance, with a smiling countenance, exclaiming,

"A very pretty trick you have been playing on me! You really frightened me. I thought you had lost half your property, at least. And here, instead of its being a matter of condolence, it turns out to be one of congratulation. I congratulate you, Mr. Weston, with all my heart, on the prospect of having one of the most lovely and accomplished young women in England for your daughter-in-law."

A glance or two between him and his wife convinced him that all was as right as this speech proclaimed, and its happy effect on his spirits was immediate. His air and voice recovered their usual briskness; he shook her heartily and gratefully by the hand, and entered on the subject in a manner to prove that he now only needed a little time to think the engagement no very bad thing. By the time they had talked it all over together, and he had talked it all over again with Emma, in their walk back to Hartfield, he had become perfectly reconciled, and was not far from thinking it the very best thing that Frank could possibly have done.

CHAPTER 47

"Harriet, poor Harriet!" Those were the words; in them lay the tormenting ideas which Emma could not get rid of, and which constituted the real misery of the business to her. Frank Churchill had behaved very ill towards herself – very ill in many ways – but it was not so much *his* behaviour as her *own* which made her so angry with him. It was the scrape which he had drawn her into on Harriet's account that gave the deepest offence. Poor Harriet! to be a second time the dupe of her misconceptions and flattery. Mr. Knightley had spoken prophetically when he said, "Emma, you have been no friend to Harriet Smith." She was afraid she had done her nothing but disservice. It was true that she was not, in this instance, the sole and original author of the mischief; with having suggested such feelings as might otherwise never have entered Harriet's imagination. Harriet had acknowledged her admiration and preference of Frank Churchill before Emma had ever given her a hint on the subject; but she felt completely guilty of having encouraged what she might have repressed. She might have prevented the indulgence and increase of such sentiments. Her influence would have been enough. And now she was very conscious that she ought to have prevented them. She felt that she had been risking her friend's happiness on most insufficient grounds. Common sense would have directed her to tell Harriet that she must not allow herself to think of him, and that there were five hundred chances to one against his ever caring for her. "But, common sense and I," she added, "have had a very strained relationship."

She was extremely angry with herself. If she could not have been angry with Frank Churchill, too, it would have been dreadful. As for Jane

Fairfax, she might at least relieve her feelings from any present concerns on her account. Harriet would be anxiety enough; she need no longer be unhappy about Jane, whose troubles and ill health having, of course, the same origin, must be equally under cure. Her days of insignificance were over. She would soon be well, and happy, and prosperous. This discovery laid many smaller matters open. In Jane's eyes she had been a rival; and well might anything she could offer of assistance or regard be rejected. A ride with her in the Hartfield carriage would have been torture, and arrow-root from the Hartfield storeroom would have been poison. She understood it all; and as far as her mind could disengage itself from the injustice and selfishness of angry feelings, she acknowledged that Jane Fairfax would have neither elevation nor happiness beyond what she deserved. But poor Harriet! There was little sympathy to be spared for anybody else. Emma was sadly fearful that this second disappointment would be more severe than the first. Considering the very superior claims of the object, it ought to; and judging by its apparently stronger effect on Harriet's mind, producing reserve and self-command, it would. She must communicate the painful truth, however, and as soon as possible. Mr. Weston, upon parting, had sworn her to secrecy. "For the present, the whole affair was to be completely unknown. Mr. Churchill had made a point of it, as a token of respect to the wife he had so very recently lost." Emma had promised; but still Harriet must be excepted. She must know the truth.

In spite of her vexation, she could not help feeling it almost ridiculous that she should have the very same distressing and delicate office to perform by Harriet, which Mrs. Weston had just gone through by herself. The intelligence, which had been so anxiously announced to her, she was now to be anxiously announcing to another. Her heart beat quickly on hearing Harriet's footstep and voice; she supposed poor Mrs. Weston had felt the same when *she* was approaching Randalls.

"Well, Miss Woodhouse!" cried Harriet, coming eagerly into the room, "is not this the oddest news that ever was?"

"What news do you mean?" replied Emma, unable to guess, by look or voice, whether Harriet could indeed have received any hint.

"About Jane Fairfax. Did you ever hear anything so strange? Oh! You need not be afraid of telling me, for Mr. Weston has told me himself. I met him just now. He told me it was to be a great secret; and, therefore, I should not think of mentioning it to anybody but you, because he said you already knew it."

"What did Mr. Weston tell you?" said Emma, still perplexed.

"Oh! He told me all about it; that Jane Fairfax and Mr. Frank Churchill are to be married, and that they have been privately engaged to one another this long while. How very odd!"

It was, indeed, so odd; Harriet's behaviour was so extremely odd, that Emma did not know how to understand it. She seemed to be showing no agitation, or disappointment, or particular concern in the discovery. Emma looked at her, quite unable to speak.

"Had you any idea," cried Harriet, "of his being in love with her? You, perhaps, might. You (blushing as she spoke) who can see into everybody's heart; but nobody else – "

"Upon my word," said Emma, "I am beginning to doubt my having any such talent. Can you seriously ask me, Harriet, whether I imagined him attached to another woman at the very time that I was – tacitly, if not openly – encouraging you to give way to your own feelings? I never had the slightest suspicion, till within the last hour, of Mr. Frank Churchill's having the least regard for Jane Fairfax. You may be very sure that if I had, I should have cautioned you accordingly."

"Me!" cried Harriet, colouring and astonished. "Why should you caution me? You think I care about Mr. Frank Churchill?"

"I am delighted to hear you speak so steadily on the subject," replied Emma, smiling; "but you do not mean to deny that there was a time – and not very distant either – when you gave me reason to understand that you did care about him?"

"Him! Never, never. Dear Miss Woodhouse, how could you so mistake me?" (turning away distressed).

"Harriet!" cried Emma, after a moment's pause – "What do you mean? Good Heaven! What do you mean?"

She could not speak another word. Her voice was lost; and she sat down, waiting in great terror till Harriet should answer.

Harriet, who was standing at some distance, and with her face turned from her, did not immediately say anything; and when she did speak, it was in a voice nearly as agitated as Emma's.

"I should not have thought it possible," she began, "that you could have misunderstood me! I know we agreed never to name him – but considering how infinitely superior he is to everybody else, I should not have thought it possible that I could be supposed to mean any other person. Mr. Frank Churchill, indeed! I do not know who would ever look at him in the company of the other. I hope I have better taste than to think of Mr. Frank Churchill. And that you should have been so mistaken is amazing! I am sure that, were it not for your encouragement, I should have considered it at first too great a presumption to dare to think of him. At first, if you had not told me that more wonderful things had happened; that there had been matches of greater disparity (those were your very words), I should not have dared to give way to – I should not have thought it possible – But if *you*, who had been always acquainted with him – "

"Harriet!" cried Emma, collecting herself resolutely, "Let us understand each other now, without the possibility of farther mistake. Are you speaking of – Mr. Knightley?"

"To be sure I am. I never could have an idea of anybody else – and so I thought you knew. When we talked about him, it was clear as possible."

"Not quite," returned Emma, with forced calmness, "for all that you then said appeared to me to relate to a different person. I could almost assert that you had *named* Mr. Frank Churchill. I am sure the service Mr. Frank Churchill rendered you, in protecting you from the gypsies, was spoken of."

"Oh! Miss Woodhouse, how you do forget!"

"My dear Harriet, I perfectly remember the substance of what I said on the occasion. I told you that I did not wonder at your attachment; that considering the service he had rendered you, it was extremely natural. You agreed to it, expressing yourself very warmly as to your sense of that service, and mentioning even what your sensations had been in seeing him come forward to your rescue. The impression of it is strong in my memory."

"Oh, dear," cried Harriet, "now I recollect what you mean; but I was thinking of something very different at the time. It was not the gypsies – it was not Mr. Frank Churchill that I meant. No! I was thinking of a much more precious circumstance – of Mr. Knightley's coming and asking me to dance, when Mr. Elton would not stand up with me; and when there was no other partner in the room. That was the kind action, the noble benevolence and generosity, the service which made me begin to feel how superior he was to every other being on earth."

"Good God!" cried Emma, "this has been a most unfortunate – most deplorable mistake! What is to be done?"

"You would not have encouraged me, then, if you had understood me. At least, however, I cannot be worse off than I should have been, if the other had been the person; and now – it *is* possible – "

She paused a few moments. Emma could not speak.

"I do not wonder, Miss Woodhouse," she resumed, "that you should feel a great difference between the two, as to me or as to anybody. You must think one five hundred million times more above me than the other. But I hope, Miss Woodhouse, that supposing – that if – strange as it may appear – But you know they were your own words, that *more* wonderful things had happened, matches of *greater* disparity had taken place than between Mr. Frank Churchill and me; and, therefore, it seems as if such a thing even as this may have occurred before – and if I should be so fortunate, beyond expression, as to – if Mr. Knightley should really – if *he* does not mind the disparity, I hope, dear Miss Woodhouse, you will not set yourself against it, and try to put difficulties in the way. But you are too good for that, I am sure."

Harriet was standing at one of the windows. Emma turned around to look at her in consternation, and hastily said,

"Have you any idea of Mr. Knightley's returning your affection?"

"Yes," replied Harriet modestly, but not fearfully – "I must say that I have."

Emma's eyes were instantly withdrawn, and she sat silently meditating for a few minutes. That brief time was sufficient for making her acquainted with her own heart. She touched – she admitted – she acknowledged the whole truth. Why was it so much worse that Harriet should be in love with Mr. Knightley, than with Frank Churchill? Why was the evil so dreadfully increased by Harriet's having some hope of a return? It darted through her, with the speed of an arrow, that Mr. Knightley must marry no one but herself!

Her own conduct, as well as her own heart, was before her in the same few minutes. She saw it all with a clearness which had never come to her before. How improperly had she been acting by Harriet! How inconsiderate, how indelicate, how irrational, how unfeeling had been her conduct! What blindness, what madness, had led her on! It struck her with dreadful force, and she was ready to give it every bad name in the world. Some portion of respect for herself, however, in spite of all these demerits – some concern for her own appearance, and a strong sense of justice by Harriet (there would be no need of *compassion* to the girl who believed herself loved by Mr. Knightley) gave Emma the resolution to sit and endure farther with calmness, with even apparent kindness. For her own advantage indeed, it was fit that the utmost extent of Harriet's hopes should be enquired into. Harriet had done nothing to forfeit the regard and interest which had been so voluntarily formed and maintained, or to deserve to be slighted by the person whose counsels had never led her right. Rousing from reflection, therefore, and subduing her emotion, she turned to Harriet again, and, in a more inviting accent, renewed the conversation. As to the subject which had first introduced it, the wonderful story of Jane Fairfax, that was quite sunk and lost. Neither of them thought but of Mr. Knightley and themselves.

Harriet then gave the history of her hopes with great, though trembling delight. Emma's tremblings as she asked, and as she listened, were better concealed than Harriet's, but they were not less. Her voice was not unsteady; but her mind was in all the perturbation that such a confusion of sudden and perplexing emotions must create. She listened with much inward suffering, but with great outward patience, to Harriet's story.

Harriet had been conscious of a difference in the behaviour of Mr. Knightley ever since those two decisive dances. Emma knew that he had, on that occasion, found her much superior to his expectation. From that evening, or at least from the time of Miss Woodhouse's encouraging her to think of him, Harriet had begun to be sensible of his talking to her much more than he had before, and of his having indeed quite a different manner towards her; a manner of kindness and sweetness! Lately she had been more and more aware of it. When they had been all walking together, he had often come and walked by her, and talked so very delightfully! He seemed to want to be acquainted with her. Emma knew it to have been very much the case. She had observed the change, to almost the same extent. Harriet repeated expressions of approval and praise from him – and Emma felt them to be in the closest agreement with what she had known of his opinion of Harriet. He praised her for being sincere, and for having simple, honest, generous, feelings. She knew that he saw such recommendations in Harriet; he had spoken of them to her more than once. Much that lived in Harriet's memory, many little particulars of the notice she had received from him, a look, a speech, a removal from one chair to another, a compliment implied, a preference inferred, had been unnoticed, because unsuspected by Emma. Circumstances that might swell to half an hour's relation, and contained multiplied proofs to her who had seen them, had passed undiscerned by her who now heard them; but the two latest occurrences to be mentioned, the two of strongest promise to Harriet, were not without some degree of witness from Emma herself. The first was his walking with her apart from the others in the lime walk at Donwell, where they had been walking sometime before Emma came. He had taken pains (as she was convinced) to draw her from the rest to himself; and at first, he had talked to her in a more particular way than he had ever done before, in a very particular way indeed! (Harriet could not recall it without a blush.) He seemed to be almost asking her whether her affections were engaged. But as soon as she (Miss Woodhouse) appeared likely to join them, he changed the subject and began talking about farming. The second was his having sat talking with her nearly half an hour before Emma came back from her visit, the very last morning of his being at Hartfield – though, when he first came in, he had said that he could not stay five minutes – and his having told her, during their conversation, that though he must go to London, it was very much against his inclination that he left home at all, which was much more (as Emma felt) than he had acknowledged to *her*. The superior degree of confidence towards Harriet, which this one article indicated, gave her severe pain.

On the subject of the first of the two circumstances, she did, after a little reflection, venture the following question. "Might he not? Is it not possible, that when enquiring, as you thought, into the state of your affections, he might be alluding to Mr. Martin – he might have Mr. Martin's interest in view?" But Harriet rejected the suspicion with spirit.

"Mr. Martin! No indeed! There was not a hint of Mr. Martin. I hope I know better now than to care for Mr. Martin, or to be suspected of it."

When Harriet had finished her story, she appealed to her dear Miss Woodhouse, to say whether she had not good ground for hope.

"I never should have presumed to think of it at first," said she, "had it not been for you. You told me to observe him carefully, and let his behaviour be the rule of mine – and so I have. But now I seem to feel that I may deserve him; and that if he does choose me, it will not be anything so very surprising."

The bitter feelings occasioned by this speech, the many bitter feelings, made the utmost exertion necessary on Emma's side, to enable her to say in reply,

"Harriet, I will only venture to declare that Mr. Knightley is the last man in the world who would intentionally give any woman the idea of his feeling for her more than he really does."

Harriet seemed ready to worship her friend for a sentence so satisfactory; and Emma was only saved from raptures and fondness, which at that moment would have been dreadful penance, by the sound of her father's footsteps. He was coming through the hall. Harriet was too much agitated to encounter him. "She could not compose herself – Mr. Woodhouse would be alarmed – she had better go" – with most ready encouragement from her friend, therefore, she passed off through another door – and the moment she was gone, this was the spontaneous burst of Emma's feelings: "Oh God! That I had never seen her!"

The rest of the day, and the following night, were hardly enough for her thoughts. She was bewildered amidst the confusion of all that had rushed at her within the last few hours. Every moment had brought a fresh surprise; and every surprise must be a matter of humiliation to her. How to understand it all! How to understand the deceptions she had been thus practising on herself, and living under! The blunders, the blindness of her own head and heart! She sat still, she walked about, she tried her own room, she tried the shrubbery – in every place, every posture, she perceived that she had acted most weakly. She had been imposed on by others in a most mortifying degree; she had been imposing on herself in a degree yet more mortifying. She was wretched, and should probably find this day but the beginning of perpetual wretchedness.

To understand, thoroughly understand her own heart, was the first endeavour. To that point went every leisure moment which her father's claims on her allowed, and every moment of involuntary absence of mind.

How long had Mr. Knightley been so dear to her, as every feeling declared him now to be? When had his influence, such influence begun? When had he succeeded to that place in her affection, which Frank Churchill had once, for a short period, occupied? She looked back; she compared the two – compared them, as they had always stood in her estimation, from the time of the latter's becoming known to her – and as they must at any time have been compared by her. She saw that there never had been a time when she did not consider Mr. Knightley as infinitely superior, or when his regard for her had not been infinitely the most dear. She saw that in persuading herself, in fancying, in acting to the contrary, she had been entirely under a delusion, totally ignorant of her own heart – and, in short, that she had never really cared for Frank Churchill at all!

This was the conclusion of the first series of reflections. This was the knowledge of herself, on the first question of inquiry, which she reached; and without being long in reaching it. She was most sorrowfully indignant; ashamed of every sensation but the one revealed to her – her affection for Mr. Knightley. Every other part of her mind was distasteful.

With insufferable vanity had she believed herself fully aware of everybody's feelings; with unpardonable arrogance proposed to arrange everybody's destiny. She was proven to have been universally mistaken; she had brought sorrow to Harriet and to herself, and she feared she had brought sorrow to Mr. Knightley as well. Were this most unequal of all connections to take place, on her must rest all the reproach of having given it a beginning, if for no other reason than that he would not have known Harriet at all but for her folly.

Mr. Knightley and Harriet Smith! It was a union to distance every wonder of the kind. The attachment of Frank Churchill and Jane Fairfax became common-place, threadbare, stale by comparison, exciting no surprise, presenting no disparity, affording nothing to be said or thought. Mr. Knightley and Harriet Smith! Such an elevation on her side! Such a debasement on his! It was horrible to Emma to think how it must sink him in the general opinion, to foresee the smiles, the sneers, and the merriment it would prompt at his expense; the mortification and disdain of his brother, the thousand inconveniences to himself. Could it be? No; it was impossible. And yet it was far, very far, from impossible. Was it a new circumstance for a man of first-rate abilities to be captivated by someone inferior? Was it new for anything in this world to be unequal, inconsistent, incongruous – or for chance and circumstance to direct human fate?

Oh! Had she never brought Harriet forward! Had she left her where she ought, and where he had told her she ought! Had she not, with a folly which no tongue could express, prevented her marrying the young man who would have made her happy and respectable in the line of life to which she ought to belong, all would have been safe; none of these dreadful events would have occurred.

How could Harriet have had the presumption to raise her thoughts to Mr. Knightley? How could she dare to fancy herself the chosen of such a man till actually assured of it! But Harriet was less humble than before. Her inferiority, whether of mind or situation, seemed little felt. She had seemed more sensible of Mr. Elton's condescension in marrying her than she now seemed of Mr. Knightley's. Alas! Was not that her own doing too? Who had been at pains to give Harriet notions of self-importance but herself? Who but herself had taught her, that she was to elevate herself if possible, and that her claims were great to a high worldly establishment? If Harriet had grown vain, Emma could look nowhere but at herself to determine the cause.

CHAPTER 48

Till now that she was threatened with its loss, Emma had never known how much of her happiness depended on being preferred by Mr. Knightley. Satisfied that she was first in interest and affection, she had taken it for granted; and only the dread of being replaced made her feel how fortunate she had been. Long, very long, she felt she had been first; for, having no female connections of his own, there had been only Isabella whose claims could be compared with hers, and she had always known exactly how far he loved and esteemed Isabella. She had herself been first with him for many years past. She had not deserved it; she had often been negligent, ignoring his advice, or even wilfully opposing him – but still, from family attachment and habit, and thorough excellence of mind, he had loved her, and watched over her from a girl, with an endeavour to improve her, and an anxiety for her doing right, which no other creature had at all shared. In spite of all her faults, she knew she was dear to him; might she not say, very dear? Harriet Smith might think herself not unworthy of being exclusively, passionately loved by Mr. Knightley. *She* could not. She could not flatter herself with any idea of blindness in his attachment to *her*. She had received a very recent proof of its impartiality. How shocked had he been by her behaviour to Miss Bates! How directly, how strongly had he expressed himself to her on the subject! She had no hope, nothing to deserve the name of hope, that he could have that sort of affection for herself which was now in question; but there was a hope (at times a slight one, at times much stronger) that Harriet might be overrating his regard for her. Could she be secure of his never marrying at all, she believed she should be perfectly satisfied. Let him but continue the same Mr. Knightley to her and her father, the same Mr. Knightley to all the world; let Donwell and Hartfield lose none of their precious exchange of friendship and confidence, and her peace would be fully secured. Marriage, in fact, would not do for her. It would be incompatible with what she owed to her father, and with what she felt for him. Nothing should separate her from her father. She would not marry, even if she were asked by Mr. Knightley.

It must be her ardent wish that Harriet might be disappointed; and she hoped, that when able to see them together again, she might at least be able to ascertain what the chances for it were. He was expected back every day. The power of observation would be soon given – frightfully soon, it appeared. In the meanwhile, she resolved against seeing Harriet. It would do neither of them good, and it would do the subject no good to be talking of it farther. She was resolved not to be convinced, as long as she could doubt, and yet had no authority for opposing Harriet's confidence. To talk would be only to irritate. She wrote to her, therefore, kindly, but decisively, to beg that she would not, at present, come to Hartfield. Harriet submitted, and approved, and was grateful.

This point was just arranged when a visitor arrived to tear Emma's thoughts a little from the one subject which had occupied them, sleeping or waking, for the last twenty-four hours – Mrs. Weston. She had been calling on Jane Fairfax, and took Hartfield in her way home, almost as much in duty to Emma as in pleasure to herself, to relate all the particulars of so interesting an interview.

Mr. Weston had accompanied her to Mrs. Bates', and gone through his share of this essential attention most handsomely; but she having then induced Miss Fairfax to join her for a carriage ride, was now returned with much more to say, and much more to say with satisfaction, than an awkward quarter of an hour spent in Mrs. Bates's parlour could have afforded.

A little curiosity Emma had; and she made the most of it while her friend related. Mrs. Weston had set off to pay the visit in a good deal of agitation herself; and in the first place had wished not to go at all at present, to be allowed merely to write to Miss Fairfax instead, and to defer this ceremonious call till a little time had passed. She thought such a visit could not be paid without leading to reports, but Mr. Weston had thought differently. He was extremely anxious to show his approval to Miss Fairfax and her family, and did not conceive that any suspicion could be excited by it. They had gone, and very great had been the evident distress and confusion of the lady. She had hardly been able to speak a word, and every look and action had shown how deeply she was suffering from self-consciousness. The quiet, heartfelt satisfaction of the old lady, and the rapturous delight of her daughter – who proved even too joyous to talk as usual, had been gratifying. They were both so truly respectable in their happiness, and thought so much of Jane; so much of everybody, and so little of themselves, that every kind feeling was at work for them. Miss Fairfax's recent illness had offered a fair plea for Mrs. Weston to invite her to get some fresh air by riding in the carriage; she had drawn back and declined at first, but on being pressed had yielded. In the course of their drive, Mrs. Weston had, by gentle encouragement, overcome so much of her embarrassment, as to bring her to converse on the important subject. She apologized for her seemingly ungracious silence in their first reception, and they talked a good deal of the present and of the future state of the engagement. Mrs. Weston was convinced that such conversation must be the greatest relief to her companion, pent up within her own mind as everything had so long been, and was very much pleased with all that she had said on the subject.

"On the misery of what she had suffered during the concealment of so many months," continued Mrs. Weston, "she was energetic. This was one of her expressions. 'I will not say, that since I entered into the engagement I have not had some happy moments; but I can say, that I have never known the blessing of one tranquil hour.'"

"Poor girl!" said Emma. "She thinks herself wrong, then, for having consented to a private engagement?"

"Wrong! No one, I believe, can blame her more than she is disposed to blame herself. 'The consequence,' said she, 'has been a state of perpetual suffering to me; and so it ought. But after all the punishment that misconduct can bring, it is still misconduct. Pain cannot atone for it. I never can be blameless. I have been acting contrary to all my sense of right; and the fortunate turn that everything has taken, and the kindness I am now receiving, is what my conscience tells me ought not to be. Do not imagine, madam,' she continued, 'that I was taught wrong. Do not let any reflection fall on the principles or the care of those who brought me up. The error has been all my own; and I do assure you that, with all the excuse that present circumstances may appear to give, I shall yet dread making the story known to Colonel Campbell.'"

"Poor girl!" said Emma again. "She loves him then excessively, I suppose. It must have been from attachment only that she could be led to form the engagement. Her affection must have overpowered her judgment."

"Yes, I have no doubt of her being extremely attached to him."

"I am afraid," returned Emma, sighing, "that I must often have contributed to make her unhappy."

"On your side, my love, it was very innocently done. But she probably had something of that in her thoughts when alluding to the misunderstandings which he had given us hints of before. One natural consequence of the unfortunate business she had involved herself in, she said, was that of making her irritable. The consciousness of having done wrong had exposed her to a thousand worries, and made her tense to a degree that must have been – that had been – hard for him to bear. She then began to speak of you, and of the great kindness you had shown her during her illness; and with a blush which showed me how it was all connected, desired me, whenever I had an opportunity, to thank you – I could not thank you too much – for every wish and every endeavour to do her good. She was aware that you had never received any proper acknowledgment from her."

"If I did not know her to be happy now," said Emma, seriously, "which, in spite of every little drawback from her conscience, she must be, I could not bear these thanks; for, oh! Mrs. Weston, if there were an account drawn up of the evil and the good I have done Miss Fairfax! Well," (checking herself, and trying to be more lively), "this is all to be forgotten. You are very kind to bring me these interesting particulars. They show her to the greatest advantage. I am sure she is very good; I hope she will be very happy. It is fit that the fortune should be on his side, for I think the merit will be all on hers."

Such a conclusion could not pass unanswered by Mrs. Weston. She thought well of Frank in almost every respect; and, what was more, she loved him very much, and her defence was, therefore, earnest. She talked with a great deal of reason, and at least equal affection – but she had too much to say to keep Emma's attention; it was soon gone to Brunswick Square or to Donwell; she forgot to attempt to listen. When Mrs. Weston ended with, "We have not yet had the letter we are so anxious for, you know, but I hope it will soon come," she was obliged to pause before she answered, and at last obliged to answer at random before she could at all recollect what letter it was which they were so anxious for.

"Are you well, my Emma?" was Mrs. Weston's parting question.

"Oh! Perfectly. I am always well, you know. Be sure to let me know as soon as the letter arrives." Mrs. Weston's communications furnished Emma with more food for unpleasant reflection by increasing her esteem and compassion, and her sense of past injustice towards Miss Fairfax. She bitterly regretted not having sought a closer acquaintance with her, and blushed for the envious feelings which had certainly been, in some measure, the cause. Had she followed Mr. Knightley's wishes in paying that attention to Miss Fairfax which was every way her due; had she tried to know her better; had she done her part towards friendship; had she endeavoured to find a friend there instead of in Harriet Smith; she must, in all probability, have been spared from every pain which afflicted her now. Birth, abilities, and education had been equally marking one as an associate for her, to be received with gratitude; and the other – what was she? In knowing her better, she must have been preserved from the abominable suspicions of an improper attachment to Mr. Dixon. Instead, she was persuaded that she must herself have been a perpetual enemy. Frank and Jane and Emma could never have been all three together without her having stabbed Jane's peace in a thousand instances; and on Box Hill, perhaps, it had been the agony of a mind that would bear no more.

The evening of this day was very long and melancholy at Hartfield. The weather added what it could of gloom. A cold stormy rain set in, and nothing of July appeared but in the trees and shrubs. The weather affected Mr. Woodhouse, and he could only be kept tolerably comfortable by almost ceaseless attention on his daughter's side, and by exertions which had never cost her half so much before. It reminded her of their first forlorn conversation on the evening of Mrs. Weston's wedding day; but Mr. Knightley had walked in then, soon after tea, and dissipated every melancholy feeling. Alas! Such delightful visits might shortly be over. The picture which she had then drawn of the privations of the approaching winter had proved erroneous; no friends had deserted them, and no pleasures had been lost. But her present forebodings she feared would experience no similar contradiction. The prospect before her now was threatening to a degree that could not be entirely dispelled. If all took place that might take place among the circle of her friends, Hartfield must be comparatively deserted; and she left to cheer her father with the spirits only of ruined happiness.

The child to be born at Randalls must be a tie there even dearer than herself; and Mrs. Weston's heart and time would be occupied by it.

They should lose her; and, probably, in great measure, her husband also. Frank Churchill would return among them no more; and Miss Fairfax, it was reasonable to suppose, would soon cease to belong to Highbury. They would be married and settled either at or near Enscombe. If to these losses, the loss of Donwell were to be added, what would remain of cheerful or of rational society within their reach? Mr. Knightley to be no longer coming there for his evening comfort! No longer walking in at all hours, as if ever willing to change his own home for theirs! How was it to be endured? And if he were to be lost to them for Harriet's sake; if he were to be thought of hereafter as finding in Harriet's company all that he wanted; if Harriet were to be the chosen, the first, the dearest, the friend, the wife to whom he looked for all the best blessings of existence; what could be increasing Emma's wretchedness but the reflection never far distant from her mind, that it was entirely her fault?

When it came to such a pitch as this, she was not able to refrain from a start, or a heavy sigh, or even from walking about the room for a few seconds. The only source from which anything like consolation or composure could be drawn was in the resolution of her own better conduct, and the hope that, however inferior in happiness might be the following and every future winter of her life when compared to the past, it would yet find her more rational, more acquainted with herself, and leave her less to regret when it was gone.

CHAPTER 49

The weather continued much the same all the following morning; and the same loneliness, and the same melancholy, seemed to reign at Hartfield. But in the afternoon it cleared; the wind changed, the clouds were carried off, the sun appeared, and it was summer again. With all the eagerness which such a transition gives, Emma resolved to be outdoors as soon as possible. Never had the exquisite sight, smell, and sensation of nature – tranquil, warm, and brilliant after a storm – been more attractive to her. She longed for the serenity they might gradually introduce, and on Mr. Perry's coming in soon after dinner with a disengaged hour to give her father, she lost no time in hurrying into the shrubbery. There, with spirits freshened, and thoughts a little relieved, she had taken a few turns when she saw Mr. Knightley passing through the garden door and coming towards her. It was the first she knew of his being returned from London. She had been thinking of him the moment before as unquestionably sixteen miles distant. She must quickly collect herself. In half a minute they were together. The greetings were quiet and restrained on each side. She asked after their family members; they were all well. When had he left them? Only that morning. He must have had a wet ride. Yes. He meant to walk with her, she found. "He had just looked into the dining room, and as he was not needed there, preferred being outdoors." She thought he neither looked nor spoke cheerfully, and the first possible cause for it, suggested by her fears, was that he had perhaps been communicating his plans to marry Harriet and was pained by the manner in which they had been received.

They walked together. He was silent. She thought he was often looking at her, and trying for a fuller view of her face than it suited her to give. This belief produced another dread. Perhaps he wanted to speak to her of his attachment to Harriet; he might be watching for encouragement to begin. She did not, could not, feel equal to lead the way to any such subject. He must do it all himself. Yet she could not bear this silence. With him it was most unnatural. She considered, resolved, and, trying to smile, began –

"You have some news to hear, now that you have returned, that will rather surprise you."

"Have I?" said he quietly, and looking at her. "Of what nature?"

"Oh! The best nature in the world – a wedding."

After waiting a moment, as if to be sure she intended to say no more, he replied,

"If you mean Miss Fairfax and Frank Churchill, I have heard that already."

"How is it possible?" cried Emma, turning her glowing cheeks towards him; for while she spoke, it occurred to her that he might have called at Mrs. Goddard's on his way.

"I had a few lines from Mr. Weston this morning, and he gave me a brief account of what had happened."

Emma was quite relieved, and could presently say, with a little more composure,

"*You* probably have been less surprised than any of us, for you have had your suspicions. I have not forgotten that you once tried to give me a caution. I wish I had attended to it, but – " (with a sinking voice and a heavy sigh) "I seem to have been doomed to blindness."

For a moment or two nothing was said, and she was unsuspicious of having excited any particular interest, till she found her arm drawn within his, and pressed against his heart, and heard him thus saying, in a tone of great sensibility, speaking low,

"Time, my dearest Emma, time will heal the wound. Your own excellent sense; your exertions for your father's sake; I know you will not allow yourself." Her arm was pressed again, as he added, in a more broken and subdued accent, "The feelings of the warmest friendship – Indignation – Abominable scoundrel!" And in a louder, steadier tone, he concluded with, "He will soon be gone. They will soon be in Yorkshire. I am sorry for *her*. She deserves a better fate."

Emma understood him; and as soon as she could recover from the flutter of pleasure excited by such tender consideration, replied,

"You are very kind, but you are mistaken, and I must set you right. I have no need of that sort of compassion. My blindness to what was going on led me to act by them in a way that I must always be ashamed of, and I was very foolishly tempted to say and do many things which may well lay me open to unpleasant assumptions, but I have no other reason to regret that I was not in the secret earlier."

"Emma!" cried he, looking eagerly at her, "are you, indeed?" – but checking himself – "No, no, I understand you – forgive me – I am pleased that you can say even so much. He is no object of regret, indeed! It will not be very long, I hope, before that becomes the acknowledgment of more than your reason. Fortunate that your affections were not farther entangled – I could never, I confess, from your manners, assure myself as to the degree of what you felt – I could only be certain that there was a preference – and a preference which I never believed him to deserve. He is a disgrace to the name of man. And is he to be rewarded with that sweet young woman? Jane, Jane, you will be a miserable creature."

"Mr. Knightley," said Emma, trying to be lively, but really confused, "I am in a very extraordinary situation. I cannot let you continue in your error; and yet, perhaps, since my manners gave such an impression, I have as much reason to be ashamed of confessing that I never have been at all attached to the person we are speaking of."

He listened in perfect silence. She wished him to speak, but he would not. Reluctantly, she went on –

"I have very little to say for my own conduct. I was tempted by his attentions, and allowed myself to appear pleased. An old story, probably – a common case – and no more than has happened to hundreds of women before. Many circumstances assisted the temptation. He was the son of Mr. Weston – he was continually here – I always found him very pleasant – and, in short," (with a sigh), "my vanity was flattered, and I allowed his attentions. Lately, however – for some time, indeed – I have had no idea of their meaning anything. I thought them a habit, a trick, nothing that called for seriousness on my side. He has imposed on me, but he has not injured me. I have never been attached to him. And now I can tolerably comprehend his behaviour. He never wished to attach me. It was merely a diversion to conceal his real situation with another. It was his object to blind all about him; and no one, I am sure, could be more effectually blinded than myself – except that I was *not* blinded – that was my good fortune."

She had hoped for an answer here – for a few words to say that her conduct was at least understandable; but he was silent, and, as far as she could judge, deep in thought. At last, and in his usual tone, he said,

"I have never had a high opinion of Frank Churchill. I can suppose, however, that I may have under-rated him. My acquaintance with him has been but trifling, but he may yet turn out well. With such a woman he has a chance. I have no motive for wishing him ill – and for her sake, whose happiness will be involved in his good character and conduct, I shall certainly wish him well."

"I have no doubt of their being happy together," said Emma. "I believe them to be very mutually and very sincerely attached."

"He is a most fortunate man!" returned Mr. Knightley, with energy. "So early in life – at three and twenty – a period when, if a man chooses a wife, he generally chooses poorly. At three and twenty to have drawn such a prize! What years of felicity that man, in all human calculation, has before him! Assured of the love of such a woman – everything in his favour – equality of situation – I mean, as far as regards society, and all the habits and manners that are important; equality in every point but one – and that one, since the purity of her heart is not to be doubted, such as must increase his felicity, for it will be his to bestow the advantage of fortune which is all that she lacks. A man would always wish to give a woman a better home than the one he takes her from; and he who can do it, where there is no doubt of *her* regard, must, I think, be the happiest of mortals. Frank Churchill is fortunate indeed. Everything turns out for his good. He meets with a young woman at a watering-place, gains her affection, cannot even weary her by negligent treatment – and had he and all his family sought round the world for a perfect wife for him, they could not have found her superior. His aunt is in the way. His aunt dies. He has only to speak. His friends are eager to promote his happiness. He has used everybody ill – and they are all delighted to forgive him. How fortune smiles upon him!"

"You speak as if you envy him."

"And I do envy him, Emma. In one respect, he is the object of my envy."

Emma could say no more. They seemed to be within half a sentence of Harriet, and her immediate feeling was to avoid the subject, if possible. She made her plan; she would speak of something totally different – the children in Brunswick Square; and she only waited for breath to begin, when Mr. Knightley startled her, by saying,

"You will not ask me what is the point of envy. You are determined, I see, to have no curiosity. You are wise – but *I* cannot be wise. Emma, I must tell what you will not ask, though I may wish it unsaid the next moment."

"Oh! Then, don't speak it, don't speak it," she eagerly cried. "Take a little time, consider, do not commit yourself."

"Thank you," said he, in an accent of deep mortification, and not another syllable followed.

Emma could not bear to give him pain. He was wishing to confide in her – perhaps to consult her – cost her what it would, she would listen. She might assist his resolution, or reconcile him to it; she might give just praise to Harriet. They had reached the house.

"You are going in, I suppose," said he.

"No," replied Emma, quite confirmed by the depressed manner in which he still spoke, "I should like to take another turn. Mr. Perry is not gone." And, after proceeding a few steps, she added – "I stopped you ungraciously, just now, Mr. Knightley, and, I am afraid I gave you pain. But if you have any wish to speak openly to me as a friend, or to ask my opinion of anything that you may have in contemplation – as a friend, indeed, you may command me. I will hear whatever you like. I will tell you exactly what I think."

"As a friend!" repeated Mr. Knightley. "Emma, that I fear is a word – No, I have no wish – Stay, yes, why should I hesitate? I have gone too far already for concealment. Emma, I accept your offer, extraordinary as it may seem, I accept it, and refer myself to you as a friend. Tell me, then, have I no chance of ever succeeding?"

He stopped in his earnestness to look the question, and the expression of his eyes overpowered her.

"My dearest Emma," said he, "for dearest you will always be, whatever the event of this hour's conversation, my dearest, most beloved Emma – tell me at once. Say 'No,' if it is to be said." She could really say nothing. "You are silent," he cried, with great animation; "absolutely silent! At present I ask no more."

Emma was almost ready to sink under the agitation of this moment. The dread of being awakened from the happiest dream, was perhaps the most prominent feeling.

"I cannot make speeches, Emma," he soon resumed; and in a tone of such sincere, decided tenderness as was tolerably convincing. "If I loved you less, I might be able to talk about it more. But you know what I am. You hear nothing but truth from me. I have blamed you, and lectured you, and you have borne it as no other woman in England would have borne it. Bear with the truths I would tell you now, dearest Emma, as well as you have borne with others. The manner, perhaps, may have as little to recommend them. God knows I have been a very indifferent lover. But you understand me. Yes, you see, you understand my feelings – and will return them if you can. At present, I ask only to hear, once to hear your voice."

While he spoke, Emma's mind was most busy, and, with all the wonderful velocity of thought, had been able – and yet without losing a word – to catch and comprehend the exact truth of the whole; to see that Harriet's hopes had been entirely groundless, a mistake, a delusion, as complete a delusion as any of her own – that Harriet was nothing to him; that she was everything herself; that what she had been saying relative to Harriet had been all taken as the language of her own feelings; and that her agitation, her doubts, her reluctance, her discouragement, had been all received as discouragement from herself. And not only was there time for these convictions, with all their glow of attendant happiness; there was time also to rejoice that Harriet's secret had not escaped her, and to resolve that it need not and should not. She felt for Harriet, with pain and with contrition. She had led her friend astray, and it would be a reproach to her forever; but her judgment was as strong as her feelings, and as strong as it had ever been before. She spoke then, on being so entreated. What did she say? Just what she ought, of course. A lady always does. She said enough to show there need not be despair – and to invite him to say more himself. He *had* despaired at one period; he had received such an injunction to caution and silence, as for the time crushed every hope; she had begun by refusing to hear him. The change had perhaps been somewhat sudden – her proposal of taking another turn, her renewing the conversation which she had just put an end to, might seem a little extraordinary! She felt its inconsistency; but Mr. Knightley was so obliging as to put up with it and seek no farther explanation.

He had, in fact, been wholly unsuspicious of his own influence. He had followed her into the shrubbery with no idea of trying it. He had come, in his anxiety to see how she bore Frank Churchill's engagement, with no selfish view, no view at all, but of endeavouring, if she allowed him an opening, to soothe or to counsel her. The rest had been the work of the moment, the immediate effect of what he heard on his feelings. The delightful assurance of her total indifference towards Frank Churchill, of her having a heart completely disengaged from him, had given birth to the hope that, in time, he might gain her affection himself. He had only, in the momentary conquest of eagerness over judgment, aspired to be told that she did not forbid his attempt to secure her attachment. The superior hopes which gradually opened were so much more enchanting. The affection which he had been asking to be allowed to create if he could was already his! Within half an hour he had passed from a thoroughly distressed state of mind to something so like perfect happiness that it could bear no other name.

Her change was equal to his. This one half hour had given to each the same precious certainty of being beloved. On his side, there had been a long-standing jealousy, old as the arrival, or even the expectation, of Frank Churchill. He had been in love with Emma, and jealous of Frank Churchill, from about the same period, one sentiment having probably triggered the other. It was his jealousy of Frank Churchill that had taken him from the country. The Box Hill party had convinced him to go away. He would save himself from witnessing again such permitted, encouraged attentions. He had gone to learn to be indifferent. But he had gone to the wrong place. There was too much domestic happiness in his brother's house; Isabella reminded him too much of Emma. He had stayed on, however, vigorously, day after day — till this very morning's letter had conveyed the history of Jane Fairfax. Then, with the gladness which must be felt, having never believed Frank Churchill to be at all deserving Emma, was there so much fond solicitude, so much keen anxiety for her, that he could stay no longer. He had ridden home through the rain, and walked up directly after dinner, to see how this sweetest and best of all creatures, faultless in spite of all her faults, bore the news.

He had found her agitated and low. Frank Churchill was a villain. He heard her declare that she had never loved him. She was his own Emma, by hand and word, when they returned into the house; and if he could have thought of Frank Churchill then, he might have deemed him a very good sort of fellow.

CHAPTER 50

What totally different feelings did Emma take back into the house from what she had brought out! She had then been only daring to hope for a little respite of suffering, and now she was in an exquisite flutter of happiness.

They sat down to tea – the same party round the same table – how often it had been collected, and how often had her eyes fallen on the same shrubs in the lawn, and observed the same beautiful effect of the western sun! But never in such a state of spirits, never in anything like it; and it was with difficulty that she could summon enough of her usual self to be the attentive lady of the house, or even the attentive daughter.

Poor Mr. Woodhouse little suspected what was being plotted against him by a man whom he was so cordially welcoming, and so anxiously hoping might not have taken cold from his ride. Could he have seen the heart, he would have cared very little for the lungs; but without the most distant imagination of the impending evil, he repeated to them very comfortably all the news he had received from Mr. Perry, and talked on with much self-contentment, totally unsuspicious of what they could have told him in return.

As long as Mr. Knightley remained with them, Emma's fever continued; but when he was gone, she began to be a little tranquillized and subdued – and in the course of the sleepless night, which was the tax for such an evening, she found one or two such very serious points to consider, as made her feel, that even her happiness must have some deterrents. Her father – and Harriet. She could not be alone without feeling the full weight of their separate claims; and how to guard the comfort of both to the utmost, was the question. With respect to her father, it was a question soon answered. She hardly knew yet what Mr. Knightley would ask; but a very short talk with her own heart produced the most solemn resolution of never leaving her father. She even wept over the idea of it, as sinful to even consider. While he lived, it must be only an engagement; but she flattered herself that if there was no danger of her being taken away, it might become an increase of comfort to him. How to do her best by Harriet, was of more difficult decision; how to spare her from any unnecessary pain, how to make her any possible atonement, and how to avoid being seen as her enemy. On these subjects her perplexity and distress were very great – and her mind had to pass again and again through every bitter reproach and sorrowful regret that had ever surrounded it. She could only resolve at last that she would still avoid a meeting with her and communicate all that need be told by letter; that it would be inexpressibly desirable to have her removed just now for a time from Highbury, and – indulging in one scheme more – nearly resolve, that it might be practicable to get an invitation for her to Brunswick Square. Isabella had been pleased with Harriet; and a few weeks spent in London must give her some amusement. She did not think it in Harriet's nature to escape being benefited by novelty and variety, by the streets, the shops, and the children. At any rate, it would be a proof of attention and kindness in herself, from whom everything was due; a separation for the present and a postponement of the day when they must all be together again.

She rose early, and wrote her letter to Harriet; an employment which left her so very serious, so nearly sad, that Mr. Knightley, in walking up to Hartfield to breakfast, did not arrive at all too soon; and half an hour stolen afterwards to go over the same ground again with him, literally and figuratively, was quite necessary for a return of the happiness she had felt the evening before.

He had not left her long, by no means long enough for her to have the slightest inclination for thinking of anybody else, when a letter was brought to her from Randalls, a very thick letter, she guessed what it must contain. She was now in perfect charity with Frank Churchill; she wanted no explanations. It must be waded through, however. She opened the packet, which began with a note from Mrs. Weston –

"I have the greatest pleasure, my dear Emma, in forwarding to you the enclosed. I know what thorough justice you will do it, and have scarcely a doubt of its happy effect. I think we shall never materially disagree about the writer again; but I will not delay you by a long preface. We are quite well, and I hope this letter finds you and your father in good health and good spirits. It has been the cure of all the little nervousness I have been feeling lately. – Yours,

"A. W."

{To Mrs. Weston.}

Windsor. – July.

"MY DEAR MADAM, – If I made myself intelligible yesterday, this letter will be expected; but expected or not, I know it will be read with understanding and indulgence. You are all goodness, and I believe there will be need of even all your goodness to forgive some parts of my past conduct. But I have been wholly acquitted by one who had still more to resent. My courage rises while I write. It is very difficult for the prosperous to be humble. I have already met with such success in two applications for pardon, that I may be in danger of thinking myself too sure of yours, and of those among your friends whom I may have offended. You must all endeavour to comprehend the exact nature of my situation when I first arrived at Randalls. You must consider me as having a secret which was to be kept at all costs. This was the fact. My right to place myself in a situation requiring such concealment is another question, one which I shall not discuss here. I dared not address Jane Fairfax openly; my difficulties in the then state of Enscombe must be too well known to require definition. I was fortunate enough, before we parted at Weymouth, to convince the most upright female mind in creation to agree to a secret engagement. Had she refused, I should have gone mad. But you will be ready to say, what was your hope in doing this? What did you look forward to? To anything, everything – to time, chance, circumstance, slow effects, sudden bursts, perseverance and weariness, health and sickness. Every possibility of good was before me, and the first of blessings secured in obtaining her promises of loyalty and correspondence. If you need farther explanation, I have the honour, my dear madam, of being your husband's son, and the advantage of inheriting a disposition to hope for good, which no inheritance of houses or lands can ever equal the value of. See me, then, under these circumstances, arriving on my first visit to Randalls; and here I am conscious of wrong, for that visit might have been sooner paid. You will look back and see that I did not come till Miss Fairfax was in Highbury; and as *you* were the person slighted, I hope you will forgive me instantly; but I must work on my father's compassion by reminding him that as long as I absented myself from his house, I could not enjoy the blessing of knowing you. My behaviour during the very happy fortnight which I spent with you, did not, I hope, lay me open to criticism, excepting on one point. And now I come to the principal, the only important part of my conduct while belonging to you, which excites my own anxiety, or requires very solicitous explanation. With the greatest respect, and the warmest friendship, do I mention Miss Woodhouse; my father perhaps will think I ought to add, with the deepest humiliation. A few words which dropped from him yesterday spoke his opinion, and some censure I acknowledge myself to deserve. My behaviour to Miss Woodhouse indicated, I believe, more than it ought. In order to assist a concealment so essential to me, I made more than an allowable use of the sort of regular contact into which we were immediately thrown. I cannot deny that Miss Woodhouse was my ostensible object – but I am sure you will believe the declaration, that had I not been convinced of her indifference, I would not have been convinced by any selfish views to go on. Amiable and delightful as Miss Woodhouse is, she never gave me the idea of a young woman likely to be attached; and that she was perfectly free from any tendency to being attached to me was as much my conviction as my wish. She received my attentions with an easy, friendly, good-humoured playfulness which exactly suited me. We seemed to understand each other. From our relative situation, those attentions were her due, and were felt to be so. Whether Miss Woodhouse began really to understand me before the expiration of that fortnight, I cannot say. When I called to take leave of her, I remember that I was within a moment of confessing the truth, and I then fancied she was not without suspicion; but I have no doubt of her having since detected me, at least in some degree. She may not have surmised the whole, but her quickness must have penetrated a part. I cannot doubt it. You will find, whenever the subject becomes freed from its present restraints, that it did not take her wholly by surprise. She frequently gave me hints of it. I remember her telling me at the ball, that I owed Mrs. Elton gratitude for her attentions to Miss Fairfax. I hope this history of my conduct towards her will be admitted by you and my father as necessary to preserve the secret I could not disclose. Please send my regards to Emma Woodhouse, for whom I feel so much brotherly affection, as to long to have her as deeply and as happily in love as myself. Whatever strange things I said or did during that fortnight, you will perhaps now understand better. My heart was in Highbury, and my business was to get myself there as often as possible, and with the least suspicion. Of the piano so much talked of, I feel it only necessary to say, that its being ordered was absolutely unknown to Miss. Fairfax, who would never have allowed me to send it, had any choice been given her. The delicacy of her mind throughout the whole engagement, my dear madam, is much beyond my power of doing justice to. You will soon, I earnestly hope, know her thoroughly yourself. No description can describe her. She must tell you herself what she is – yet not by word, for never was there a human creature who would so designedly suppress her own good qualities. Since I began this letter, which will be longer than I foresaw, I have heard from her. She gives a good account of her own health; but as she never complains, I cannot count on what she says. I want to have your opinion of her health. I know you will soon call on her; she is living in dread of the visit. Perhaps it is paid already. Let me hear from you without delay; I am impatient for a thousand particulars. Remember how few minutes I was at Randalls, and in how bewildered, how mad a state; and I am not much better yet, still insane either from happiness or misery. When I think of the kindness and favour I have met with, of her excellence and patience, and my uncle's generosity, I am mad with joy: but when I recollect all the uneasiness I caused her, and how little I deserve to be forgiven, I am mad with anger. If I could but see her again! But I must not make the attempt yet. My uncle has been too good for me to encroach. I must still add to this long letter. You have not heard all that you ought to hear. I could not give any connected detail yesterday; but the suddenness, and, in one light, the unseasonableness with which the affair burst out, needs explanation. The hasty engagement which Miss Fairfax had entered into with that woman, to be her governess, necessitated quick action. My manners to Miss Woodhouse, in being unpleasant to Miss Fairfax, were entirely to blame. *She* disapproved them, which ought to have been enough. My plea of concealing the truth she did not think sufficient. She was displeased; I thought unreasonably so; I thought her, on a thousand occasions, unnecessarily scrupulous and cautious: I thought her even cold. But she was always right. If I had followed her judgment and subdued my spirits to the level of what she deemed proper, I should have escaped the greatest unhappiness I have ever known. We quarrelled. Do you remember the morning spent at Donwell? *There* every little dissatisfaction that had occurred before came to a crisis. I was late; I met her walking home by herself, and wanted to walk with her, but she would not allow it. She absolutely refused to allow me, which I then thought most unreasonable. Now, however, I see nothing in it but a very natural and consistent degree of discretion. While I, to blind the world to our engagement, was behaving one hour with objectionable particularity to another woman, was she to be consenting the next to a proposal which might have made every previous caution useless? Had we been met walking together between Donwell and Highbury, the truth must have been suspected. But I resented her refusal and doubted her affection. I doubted it more the next day on Box Hill, when, provoked by such conduct on my side, such shameful, insolent neglect of her, and such apparent devotion to Miss Woodhouse, as it would have been impossible for any woman of sense to endure, she spoke her resentment in a form of words perfectly intelligible to me. In short, my dear madam, it was a quarrel blameless on her side, and abominable on mine. I returned the same evening to Richmond, though I might have stayed with you till the next morning, merely because I was angry with her. Even then, I was not such a fool as to plan no reconciliation in time; but I was the injured person, injured by her coldness, and I went away determined that she should make the first advances. I shall always congratulate myself that you were not of the Box Hill party. Had you witnessed my behaviour there, I can hardly suppose you would ever have thought well of me again. Its effect upon her appears in the immediate resolution it produced: as soon as she found I was really gone from Randalls, she closed with the offer of Mrs. Elton. She resolved to break with me entirely, and wrote the next day to tell me that we were never to meet again. *She felt the engagement to be a source of misery to us both, so she dissolved it.* This letter reached me on the very morning of my poor aunt's death. I answered it within an hour; but from the confusion of my mind, and the multiplicity of business falling on me at once, my answer, instead of being sent with all the many other letters of that day, was locked up in my writing desk; and I, trusting that I had written enough, though but a few lines, to satisfy her, remained without any uneasiness. I was rather disappointed that I did not hear from her again speedily; but I made excuses for her, and was too busy, and — may I add? too optimistic in my hopes to be attentive. We moved to Windsor; and two days afterwards I received a parcel from her, my own letters all returned! And a few lines at the same time by the post, stating her extreme surprise at not having had the smallest reply to her last; and adding, that as silence on such a point could not be misconstrued, and as it must be equally desirable to both to have every arrangement concluded as soon as possible, she now sent me, by a safe conveyance, all my letters, and requested, that if I could not directly access hers, to send them to Highbury within a week. Imagine the shock; imagine how, till I had actually detected my own blunder, I raved at the blunders of the post. What was to be done? One thing only. I must speak to my uncle. Without his sanction I could not hope to be listened to again. I spoke; circumstances were in my favour; the death of his wife had softened his pride, and he was, earlier than I could have anticipated, wholly reconciled and complying. With a deep sigh, he wished I might find as much happiness in the marriage state as he had done. I felt that it would be of a different sort. Are you disposed to pity me for what I must have suffered in bringing the question to him, for my suspense while all was at stake? No; do not pity me till I reached Highbury, and saw how ill I had made her. Do not pity me till I saw her pale, sick looks. I reached Highbury at the time of day when, from my knowledge of their late breakfast hour, I was certain of a good chance of finding her alone. I was not disappointed; and in the end I was not disappointed either in the object of my journey. A great deal of very reasonable, very just displeasure I had to persuade away. But it is done; we are reconciled, dearer, much dearer, than ever, and no moment's uneasiness can ever occur between us again. Now, my dear madam, I will release you; but I could not conclude before. A thousand thanks for all the kindness you have ever shown me, and ten thousand for the attentions your heart will dictate towards Miss Fairfax. If you think me in a way to be happier than I deserve, I am quite of your opinion. Miss Woodhouse calls me the child of good fortune. I hope she is right. In one respect, my good fortune is undoubted, that of being able to name myself your obliged and affectionate Son,

    F. C. WESTON CHURCHILL"

CHAPTER 51

This letter must make its way to Emma's feelings. She was obliged, in spite of her previous determination to the contrary, to do it all the justice that Mrs. Weston foretold. As soon as she came to her own name, it was irresistible. Every line relating to herself was interesting, and almost every line agreeable. When this charm ceased, the subject could still maintain itself by the natural return of her former regard for the writer, and the very strong attraction which any picture of love must have for her at that moment. Though it was impossible not to feel that he had been wrong, yet he had been less wrong than she had supposed – and he had suffered, and was very sorry, and was so grateful to Mrs. Weston, and so much in love with Miss Fairfax, and she was so happy herself, that she could not condemn. Could he have entered the room, she must have shaken hands with him as heartily as ever.

She thought so well of the letter that when Mr. Knightley came again she desired him to read it. She was sure of Mrs. Weston's wishing it to be communicated; especially to one like Mr. Knightley who had seen so much to blame in his conduct.

"I shall be very glad to look it over," said he, "but it seems long. I will take it home with me at night."

But that would not do. Mr. Weston was to call in the evening, and she must know his thoughts by then.

"I would rather be talking to you," he replied, "but as it seems a matter of urgency, it shall be done."

He began – stopping, however, almost immediately to say, "Had I been offered the sight of one of this gentleman's letters to his mother-in-law a few months ago, Emma, it would not have been taken with such indifference."

He proceeded a little farther, reading to himself; and then, with a smile, observed, "Humph! A fine complimentary opening, but it is his way. One man's style must not be the rule of another's. We will not be severe."

"It will be natural for me," he added shortly afterwards, "to speak my opinion aloud as I read. By doing it, I shall feel that I am near you. It will not be so great a loss of time: but if you dislike it – "

"Not at all. I prefer it."

Mr. Knightley returned to his reading with greater alacrity.

"He trifles here," said he, "as to the temptation. He knows he is wrong, and has nothing rational to urge. Bad. He ought not to have formed the engagement. 'His father's disposition' – he is unjust, however, to his father – Very true; he did not come till Miss Fairfax was here."

"And I have not forgotten," said Emma, "how sure you were that he might have come sooner had he wanted to do so. You were perfectly right."

"I was not quite impartial in my judgment, Emma; but yet, I think, had *you* not been involved, I should still have distrusted him."

When he came to Miss Woodhouse, he was obliged to read the whole of it aloud – all that related to her, with a smile; a look; a shake of the head; a word or two of assent, or disapproval; or merely of love, as the subject required; concluding, however, seriously, and, after steady reflection, thus –

"Very bad – though it might have been worse. Playing a most dangerous game. Always deceived by his own desires, and thinking of little besides his own convenience. Fancying you to have fathomed his secret. Natural enough! His own mind so full of intrigue that he should suspect it in others. My Emma, does not everything serve to prove more and more the beauty of truth and sincerity in all our dealings with each other?"

Emma agreed to it, and with a blush of sensibility on Harriet's account, which she could not give any sincere explanation of.

"You had better go on," said she.

He did so, but very soon stopped again to say, "The piano! Ah! That was the act of a very, very young man, one too young to consider whether the inconvenience of it might not very much exceed the pleasure. A boyish scheme, indeed! I cannot comprehend a man's wishing to give a woman any proof of affection which he knows she would rather dispense with; and he did know that she would have prevented the instrument's coming if she could."

After this, he made some progress without any pause. Frank Churchill's confession of having behaved shamefully was the first thing to call for more than a word in passing.

"I perfectly agree with you, sir," was then his remark. "You did behave very shamefully. You never wrote a truer line." And having gone through what immediately followed of the basis of their disagreement, and his persisting to act in direct opposition to Jane Fairfax's sense of right, he made a fuller pause to say, "This is very bad. He had convinced her to place herself, for his sake, in a situation of extreme difficulty and uneasiness, and it should have been his first object to prevent her from suffering unnecessarily. She must have had much more to contend with, in carrying on the correspondence, than he did. He should have respected even unreasonable scruples, had there been such; but hers were all reasonable."

Emma knew that he was now getting to the Box Hill party, and grew uncomfortable. Her own behaviour had been so very improper! She was deeply ashamed, and a little afraid of his next look. It was all read, however, steadily, attentively, and without the smallest remark; and, excepting one momentary glance at her, instantly withdrawn out of fear of giving pain, no remembrance of Box Hill seemed to exist.

"What! Actually to resolve to break with him entirely! She felt the engagement to be a source of misery to both, so she dissolved it. What a view this gives of her sense of his behaviour! Well, he must be a most extraordinary – "

"Nay, nay, read on. You will find how very much he suffers."

"I hope he does," replied Mr. Knightley coolly, resuming the letter. A governess? What does this mean? What is all this?"

"She had engaged to go as governess to a dear friend of Mrs. Elton's – a neighbour of Maple Grove; and, by the way, I wonder how Mrs. Elton bears the disappointment."

"Say nothing, my dear Emma, while you oblige me to read – not even of Mrs. Elton. Only one page more. I shall soon be done. What a letter the man writes!"

"I wish you would read it with a kinder spirit towards him."

"Well, there *is* feeling here. He does seem to have suffered in finding her ill. Certainly, I can have no doubt of his being fond of her. 'Dearer, much dearer than ever.' I hope he may long continue to feel all the value of such a reconciliation. He is a very liberal thanker, with his thousands and tens of thousands. 'Happier than I deserve.' Come, he knows himself there. 'Miss Woodhouse calls me the child of good fortune.' Those were Miss Woodhouse's words, were they? And a fine ending – and there is the letter. The child of good fortune! That was your name for him, was it?"

"You do not appear as well satisfied with his letter as I am; but still you must, at least I hope you must, think the better of him for it. I hope it does him some service with you."

"Yes, certainly it does. He has had great faults, faults of inconsideration and thoughtlessness; and I am very much of his opinion in thinking him likely to be happier than he deserves. But still he is beyond a doubt really attached to Miss Fairfax, and will soon, it may be hoped, have the advantage of being constantly with her. I am very ready to believe his character will improve, and acquire from hers the steadiness and delicacy of principle that it now lacks. And now, let me talk to you of something else. I have another person's interest at present so much at heart, that I cannot think any longer about Frank Churchill. Ever since I left you this morning, Emma, my mind has been hard at work on one subject."

The subject followed; it was in plain, unaffected, gentleman-like English such as Mr. Knightley used even to the woman he was in love with, how to be able to ask her to marry him without interrupting the happiness of her father. Emma's answer was ready at the first word. "While her dear father lived, any change of condition must be impossible for her. She could never leave him." Part only of this answer, however, was admitted. The impossibility of her leaving her father, Mr. Knightley felt as strongly as herself; but he could not agree to there being no marriage. He had been thinking it over most deeply, most intently; he had at first hoped to induce Mr. Woodhouse to move with her to Donwell. He had wanted to believe it feasible, but his knowledge of Mr. Woodhouse would not allow him to deceive himself long; and now he confessed his persuasion that such a transplantation would be a risk of her father's comfort, perhaps even of his life, which must not be attempted. Mr. Woodhouse taken from Hartfield! No, he felt that it ought not to be attempted. But the plan which had arisen on the sacrifice of this, he trusted his dearest Emma would not find in any respect objectionable. It was that he should be received at Hartfield; that so long as her father lived, it should be his home likewise.

Of their all removing to Donwell, Emma had already had her own passing thoughts. Like him, she had considered the scheme and rejected it; but such an alternative as this had not occurred to her. She felt that, in leaving Donwell, he must be sacrificing a great deal of independence of hours and habits; that in living constantly with her father, and in no house of his own, there would be much, very much, to be borne. She promised to think of it, and advised him to think of it more; but he was fully convinced that no reflection could alter his wishes or his opinion on the subject. He had given it, he could assure her, very long and calm consideration.

"Ah! there is one difficulty unprovided for," cried Emma. "I am sure William Larkins will not like it. You must get his consent before you ask mine."

She promised, however, to think of it; and pretty nearly promised, moreover, to think of it with the intention of finding it a very good scheme.

It is remarkable that Emma in the many, very many, points of view in which she was now beginning to consider Donwell Abbey, was never struck with any sense of injury to her nephew Henry, whose rights as heir had formerly been so tenaciously regarded. Think she must of the possible difference to the poor little boy; and yet she only gave herself a saucy conscious smile about it, and found amusement in detecting the real cause of that violent dislike of Mr. Knightley's marrying Jane Fairfax, or anybody else.

This proposal of his, this plan of marrying and continuing at Hartfield – the more she contemplated it, the more pleasing it became. Such a companion for herself in the periods of anxiety and cheerlessness before her! Such a partner in all those duties and cares to which time must be giving increase of melancholy!

She would have been too happy but for poor Harriet. Every blessing of her own seemed to involve and advance the sufferings of her friend, who must now be even excluded from Hartfield. Emma could not deplore her future absence as any deduction from her own enjoyment, but for the poor girl herself, it seemed a peculiarly cruel necessity that was to be placing her in such a state of unmerited punishment.

In time, of course, Mr. Knightley would be forgotten; that is, supplanted. But this could not be expected to happen very early. Mr. Knightley himself would be doing nothing to assist the cure, unlike Mr. Elton. Mr. Knightley, always so kind, so feeling, so truly considerate to everybody, would never deserve to be less worshipped than now; and it really was too much to hope even of Harriet that she could be in love with more than three men in one year.

CHAPTER 52

It was a very great relief to Emma to find Harriet as desirous as herself to avoid a meeting. Their communications were painful enough by letter. How much worse, had they been obliged to meet!

Harriet expressed herself very much as usual, and yet Emma fancied there was something of resentment beneath her words which increased the desirableness of their being separate. It might be only her own consciousness; but it seemed as if an angel only could have been quite without resentment in such circumstances.

She had no difficulty procuring Isabella's invitation; and she was fortunate in having a sufficient reason for asking it, without resorting to fabrication. Harriet wished, and had wished sometime, to consult a dentist. Mrs. John Knightley was delighted to be of use; anything of ill-health was of great interest to her, and she was quite eager to have Harriet under her care. When it was thus settled on her sister's side, Emma proposed it to her friend, and found her very persuadable. Harriet was to go; she was invited for at least a fortnight; she was to be conveyed in Mr. Woodhouse's carriage. It was all arranged, it was all completed, and Harriet was safe in Brunswick Square.

Now Emma could, indeed, enjoy Mr. Knightley's visits; now she could talk, and she could listen with true happiness, unchecked by that sense of injustice, of guilt, of something most painful, which had haunted her when remembering how disappointed a heart was near her.

The difference of Harriet at Mrs. Goddard's, or in London, was perhaps an unreasonable difference in Emma's sensations; but she could not think of her in London without objects of curiosity and employment, which must keep her from feeling the full effects of her many losses.

She would not allow any other anxiety to occupy the place in her mind which Harriet had. There was a communication before her, one which *she* only could make – the confession of her engagement to her father; but she would have nothing to do with it at present. She had resolved to defer the disclosure till after Mrs. Weston had given birth. No additional agitation should be imposed at this period upon those she loved – and she would not allow herself to be consumed by worry. A fortnight, at least, of leisure and peace of mind should be hers.

She soon resolved to employ half an hour of this holiday of spirits in calling on Miss Fairfax. She ought to go – and she was longing to see her; the resemblance of their present situations increasing every other motive of good will. It would be a *secret* satisfaction; but the consciousness of a similarity of situation would certainly add to the interest with which she should listen to anything Jane might communicate.

She went – she had driven once unsuccessfully to the door, but had not been into the house since the morning after Box Hill, when poor Jane had been in such distress as had filled her with compassion, though the real reason for her sufferings had been unsuspected. She heard Patty announcing her name, but no such bustle succeeded as before, when Jane had declined to see her. No; she heard nothing but the instant reply of, "Ask her to come up," and a moment afterwards she was met on the stairs by Jane herself, coming eagerly forward, as if no other reception was felt sufficient. Emma had never seen her look so well, so lovely, so engaging. There was consciousness, animation, and warmth; there was everything which her countenance or manner could ever have wanted. She came forward with an offered hand; and said, in a low, but very feeling tone,

"This is most kind, indeed! Miss Woodhouse, it is impossible for me to express – I hope you will believe – Excuse me for being so entirely without words."

Emma was gratified, and would soon have shown no want of words, if the sound of Mrs. Elton's voice from the sitting room had not checked her, and made it expedient to channel all her friendly and congratulatory sensations into a very, very earnest shake of the hand.

Mrs. Bates and Mrs. Elton were together, and Miss Bates was out. Emma could have wished Mrs. Elton elsewhere, but she was at present disposed to have patience with everybody. Mrs. Elton met her with unusual graciousness, and she hoped the encounter would do them no harm.

She soon believed herself to penetrate Mrs. Elton's thoughts, and understand why she was, like herself, in happy spirits; it was being in Miss Fairfax's confidence, and fancying herself acquainted with what was still a secret to other people. Emma saw symptoms of it immediately in the expression of her face; and while paying her own compliments to Mrs. Bates, she saw her with a sort of anxious parade of mystery fold up a letter which she had apparently been reading aloud to Miss Fairfax, and return it into the purple and gold purse by her side, saying, with significant nods,

"We can finish this some other time, you know. You and I shall not be without opportunities. And, in fact, you have heard the essential parts already. I only wanted to prove to you that Mrs. Smallridge accepts our apology, and is not offended. You see how delightfully she writes. Oh! She is a sweet creature! You would have loved her, had you gone. But not a word more. Let us be discreet – quite on our good behaviour."

And again, on Emma's merely turning her head to look at Mrs. Bates's knitting, she added, in a half whisper,

"I mentioned no *names*, you will observe. Oh! no; as cautious as a politician. I managed it extremely well."

Emma could not doubt. It was a palpable display, repeated on every possible occasion. When they had all talked a little while about the weather and Mrs. Weston, she found herself abruptly addressed with,

"Do you think, Miss Woodhouse, our little friend here is charmingly recovered? Do you think her cure does Perry the highest credit? (Here was a side-glance of great meaning at Jane.) Upon my word, Perry has restored her in a wonderfully short time! Oh! If you had seen her, as I did, when she was at the worst!" And when Mrs. Bates was saying something to Emma, she whispered farther, "We do not say a word of any *assistance* that Perry might have had; not a word of a certain young physician from Windsor. Oh! No; Perry shall have all the credit."

"I have scarcely had the pleasure of seeing you, Miss Woodhouse," she shortly afterwards began, "since the party to Box Hill. Very pleasant party. But yet I think there was something lacking. Things did not seem – that is, there seemed a little cloud upon the spirits of some. So it appeared to me at least, but I might be mistaken. However, what would you both think of collecting the same party and exploring to Box Hill again, while the fine weather lasts? It must be the same party, you know, quite the same party, not *one* exception."

Emma was saved from having to respond by the arrival of Miss Bates.

"Thank you, dear Miss Woodhouse, you are all kindness. It is impossible to say — Yes, indeed, I quite understand — dearest Jane's prospects – that is, I do not mean. But she is completely recovered. How is Mr. Woodhouse? I am so glad. Quite out of my power. Such a happy little circle as you find us here. Yes, indeed. Charming young man! That is — so very friendly; I mean good Mr. Perry! Such attention to Jane!" And from her great, her more than commonly thankful delight towards Mrs. Elton for being there, Emma guessed that there had been a little show of resentment towards Jane from that quarter, which was now graciously overcome. After a few whispers, indeed, which placed it beyond a guess, Mrs. Elton, speaking louder, said,

"Yes, here I am, my good friend; and here I have been so long, that anywhere else I should think it necessary to apologize: but the truth is, that I am waiting for my good husband. He promised to join me here, and pay his respects to you."

"What! Are we to have the pleasure of a call from Mr. Elton? That will be a favour indeed! For I know gentlemen do not like morning visits, and Mr. Elton is so busy."

"Upon my word it is, Miss Bates. He really is busy from morning to night. There is no end of people's coming to him, on some pretence or other. The magistrates, and overseers, and churchwardens, are always wanting his opinion. They seem unable to do anything without him. 'Upon my word, Mr. E., ' I often say, 'better you than me. I do not know what would become of my drawing and music if I had half so many visitors.' It's bad enough as it is, for I absolutely neglect them both to an unpardonable degree. I believe I have not played a single measure this fortnight. However, he is coming, I assure you; yes, indeed, to visit you all." And putting up her hand to screen her words from Emma — "A congratulatory visit, you know. Oh! Yes, quite indispensable."

Miss Bates looked about happily.

"He promised to come to me as soon as he finished talking with Knightley. Mr. E. is Knightley's right hand, you know."

Emma would not have smiled for the world, and only said, "Is Mr. Elton gone on foot to Donwell? He will have a hot walk."

"Oh! No, it is a meeting at the Crown – a regular meeting. Weston and Cole will be there too; but one is apt to speak only of those who lead. I fancy Mr. E. and Knightley have everything their own way."

"Have you possibly mistaken the day?" said Emma, "I am almost certain that the meeting at the Crown is not till tomorrow. Mr. Knightley was at Hartfield yesterday, and spoke of it as for Saturday."

"Oh! No; the meeting is certainly today," was the abrupt answer, which denoted the impossibility of any blunder on Mrs. Elton's side. "I do believe," she continued, "this is the most troublesome parish that ever was. We never heard of such things at Maple Grove."

"Your parish there was very small," said Jane.

"Upon my word, my dear, I do not know, for I never heard the subject talked of."

"But it is proved by the smallness of the school, which I have heard you speak of. Not more than five-and-twenty children, if I correctly recall."

"Ah! You clever creature, that's very true. What a mind you have! I say, Jane, what a perfect character you and I should make, if we could be mixed together. My liveliness and your steadiness would produce perfection. Not that I presume to insinuate, however, that *some* people may not think *you* perfection already."

Mr. Elton made his appearance. His lady greeted him with some of her sparkling vivacity.

"Very pretty, sir, upon my word; to send me on here, to be an encumbrance to my friends, so long before you came! But you knew what a dutiful creature you had to deal with. You knew I should not stir till you appeared."

Mr. Elton was so hot and tired that all this wit seemed to have no impact on him. His civilities to the other ladies must be paid; but his subsequent object was to lament over himself for the heat he was suffering, and the walk he had had for nothing.

"When I got to Donwell," said he, "Knightley could not be found. Very odd! Very unaccountable! after the note I sent him this morning, and the message he returned, that he should certainly be at home till one."

"Donwell!" cried his wife. "My dear Mr. E., you have not been to Donwell! You mean the Crown; you come from the meeting at the Crown."

"No, no, that's tomorrow; and I particularly wanted to see Knightley today on that very account. Such dreadful heat this morning! I assure you I am not at all pleased. And no apology left, no message for me. The housekeeper declared she knew nothing of my being expected. Very extraordinary! And nobody knew at all which way he was gone. Perhaps to Hartfield, perhaps to the Abbey Mill, perhaps into his woods. Miss Woodhouse, this is not like our friend Knightley. Can you explain it?"

Emma amused herself by protesting that it was very extraordinary indeed, and that she had not a syllable to say for him.

"I cannot imagine," cried Mrs. Elton (feeling the indignity as a wife ought to do), "I cannot imagine how he could do such a thing to you, of all people in the world! The very last person whom one should expect to be forgotten! My dear Mr. E., he must have left a message for you, I am sure he must. Not even Knightley could be so very eccentric; and his servants forgot it. Depend upon it, that was the case; and very likely to happen with the Donwell servants, who are all, I have often observed, extremely awkward and remiss."

"I met William Larkins," continued Mr. Elton, "as I got near the house, and he told me I should not find his master at home, but I did not believe him. William seemed rather out of humour. He did not know what has come over his master lately, he said, but he could hardly ever speak to him. It really is of very great importance that I should see Knightley today; and it becomes a matter, therefore, of very serious inconvenience that I should have had this hot walk for no reason."

Emma felt that she could not do better than go home immediately. In all probability, she was at this very time waited for there; and Mr. Knightley might be preserved from sinking deeper in aggression towards Mr. Elton, if not towards William Larkins.

She was pleased, on taking leave, to find Miss Fairfax determined to walk her out of the room, to go with her even downstairs; it gave her an opportunity which she immediately made use of, to say,

"It is as well, perhaps, that we could not talk privately. Had you not been surrounded by others, I might have been tempted to introduce a subject, to ask questions, to speak more openly than might have been strictly correct. I feel that I should certainly have been too forward."

"Oh!" cried Jane, with a blushing hesitation which Emma thought infinitely more becoming to her than all the elegance of her usual composure, "There would have been no danger. The danger would have been of my wearying you. Indeed, Miss Woodhouse, (speaking more collectedly), with the consciousness which I have of misconduct, very great misconduct, it is particularly consoling to me to know that those of my friends, whose good opinion is most worth preserving, are not disappointed to such a degree as to – I have not time for half that I could wish to say. I long to make apologies, excuses, to urge something for myself. I feel it so very due. But, unfortunately – "

Oh! There is no need for such things," cried Emma warmly, taking her hand. "You owe me no apologies; and everybody to whom you might be supposed to owe them, is so perfectly satisfied, so delighted even – "

"You are very kind, but I know what my manners were to you. So cold and artificial! I had always a part to act. It was a life of deceit! I know that I have treated you poorly."

"Pray say no more. I feel that all the apologies should be on my side. Let us forgive each other at once. I hope you have pleasant accounts from Windsor?"

"Very."

"And the next news, I suppose, will be, that we are to lose you – just as I begin to know you."

"Oh! As to all that, of course nothing can be thought of yet. I am here till claimed by Colonel and Mrs. Campbell."

"Nothing can be actually settled yet, perhaps," replied Emma, smiling – "but you must have some idea what will happen."

The smile was returned as Jane answered,

"You are very right; it has been thought of. And I will admit, I am sure it will be safe to tell you, that so far as our living with Mr. Churchill at Enscombe, it is settled. There must be three months, at least, of deep mourning; but when they are over, I imagine there will be nothing more to wait for."

"Thank you, thank you. This is just what I wanted to be assured of. Oh! I am so happy for you! Goodbye, goodbye."

CHAPTER 53

Mrs. Weston was now the happy mother of a little girl. Emma had been decided in wishing for a Miss Weston. She would not acknowledge that it was with any view of making a match for her, hereafter, with either of Isabella's sons; but she was convinced that a daughter would suit both father and mother best. It would be a great comfort to Mr. Weston as he grew older – and even Mr. Weston might be growing older ten years hence – to have his fireside enlivened by a daughter. As for Mrs. Weston, no one could doubt that a daughter would mean most to her. It would be quite a pity that anyone who so well knew how to teach should not have her powers to exercise again. A son would likely be sent away to school, but a daughter could be taught at home.

"She has had the advantage, you know, of practising on me," she continued, "and we shall now see her own little Anne educated more perfectly."

"Which is to say," replied Mr. Knightley, "she will indulge her even more than she did you, and believe that she does not indulge her at all."

"Poor child!" cried Emma. "At that rate, what will become of her?"

"Nothing very bad. The fate of thousands. She will be disagreeable in infancy, and correct herself as she grows older. I am losing all my bitterness against spoiled children, my dearest Emma. Since I owe all my happiness to *you*, it would be horrible ingratitude on my part if I felt anything else."

Emma laughed, and replied, "But I had the assistance of all your endeavours to counteract the indulgence of others. I doubt whether my own sense would have corrected me without it."

"Do you? I have no doubt. Nature gave you understanding; Miss Taylor gave you principles. You must have done well. My interference was quite as likely to do harm as good. It was very natural for you to say, 'What right has he to lecture me?' and I am afraid very natural for you to feel that it was done in a disagreeable manner. I do not believe I did you any good. The good was all to myself, by making you an object of the tenderest affection to me. I could not think about you so much without doting on you, faults and all."

"I am sure you were of use to me," cried Emma. "I was very often influenced rightly by you – oftener than I would admit at the time. I am very sure you did me good. And if poor little Anna Weston is to be spoiled, it will be the greatest humanity in you to do as much for her as you have done for me, except for falling in love with her when she is of age."

"How often, when you were a girl, have you said to me, with one of your saucy looks – 'Mr. Knightley, I am going to do so and so; papa says I may, or, I have Miss Taylor's leave' – something which, you knew, I did not approve. In such cases my interference was giving you two bad feelings instead of one."

"What an amiable creature I was! No wonder you hold my speeches in such affectionate remembrance."

'Mr. Knightley.' You always called me, 'Mr. Knightley,' and, from habit, it has not so very formal a sound. And yet it is formal. I want you to call me something else, but I do not know what."

"I remember once calling you 'George,' in one of my amiable fits, about ten years ago. I did it because I thought it would offend you; but, as you made no objection, I never did it again."

"And cannot you call me 'George' now?"

"Impossible! I never can call you anything but 'Mr. Knightley.' I will not promise even to equal the elegant terseness of Mrs. Elton, by calling you Mr. K. But I will promise," she added presently, laughing and blushing, "I will promise to call you once by your Christian name. I do not say when, but perhaps you may guess where; in the building in which a man and a woman promise to take each other for better or for worse."

Emma grieved that she could not be more openly just to one important service which his better sense would have rendered her, to the advice which would have saved her from the worst of all her follies – her wilful intimacy with Harriet Smith; but it was too tender a subject. She could not bring it up. Harriet was very seldom mentioned between them. This, on his side, might merely proceed from her not being thought of; but Emma was rather inclined to attribute it to delicacy, and suspicion, from some appearances, that their friendship was declining. She was aware herself, that, parting under any other circumstances, they certainly would have corresponded more, and that her intelligence would not have rested, as it now almost wholly did, on Isabella's letters. He might observe that it was so. The pain of being obliged to practise concealment towards him was nearly as poignant as the pain of having made Harriet unhappy.

Isabella sent quite as good an account of her visitor as could be expected. On her first arrival, she had thought her out of spirits, which appeared perfectly natural, as she was there to see a dentist. But, since that business had been over, she did not appear to find Harriet any different. Isabella, to be sure, was no very quick observer; yet if Harriet had not been equal to playing with the children, it would not have escaped her. Emma's comforts and hopes were most agreeably answered by Harriet's being to stay longer; her fortnight was likely to be a month at least. Mr. and Mrs. John Knightley were to come down in August, and she was invited to remain till they could bring her back.

"John does not even mention your friend," said Mr. Knightley. "Here is his answer, if you like to see it." It was the answer to the communication of his intended marriage. Emma accepted it with a very eager hand, with an impatience to know what he would say about it, and not at all checked by hearing that her friend was unmentioned.

"John enters like a brother into my happiness," continued Mr. Knightley, "but he is no complimenter. Though I well know him to have a most brotherly affection for you, he is so far from making flourishes that any other young woman might think him rather cool in her praise. But I am not afraid of your seeing what he writes."

"He writes like a sensible man," replied Emma, when she had read the letter. "I honour his sincerity. It is very plain that he considers the good fortune of the engagement as all on my side, but that he is not without hope of my growing, in time, as worthy of your affection, as you think me already. Had he said anything different, I should not have believed him."

"My Emma, he means no such thing. He only means – "

"He and I happen to agree," she interrupted, with a sort of serious smile.

"Emma, my dear Emma – "

"Oh!" she cried with more liveliness, "if you think your brother does not do me justice, only wait till my dear father is in on the secret, and listen to his opinion. Depend upon it, he will be much farther from doing *you* justice. He will think all the happiness, all the advantage, on your side; all the merit on mine. I wish I may not sink into 'poor Emma' with him at once."

"Ah!" he cried, "I wish your father might be half as easily convinced as John will be, of our having every right that equal worth can give, to be happy together. I am amused by one part of John's letter – did you notice it? The part where he says that my information did not take him wholly by surprise, that he was rather in expectation of hearing something of the kind."

"If I understand your brother, he only means so far as your having some thoughts of marrying. He had no idea of me. He seems perfectly unprepared for that."

"Yes, yes – but I am amused that he should have seen so far into my feelings. How could he have known? I am not conscious of any difference in my spirits or conversation that could prepare him at this time for my marrying any more than at another. But it was so, I suppose. I dare say there was a difference when I was staying with them the other day. I believe I did not play with the children quite as much as usual. I remember one evening the poor boys saying, 'Uncle seems always tired now.'

"The time was coming when the news must be spread farther, and other persons' reception of it tried. As soon as Mrs. Weston was sufficiently recovered to allow Mr. Woodhouse to visit, Emma had it in view that her gentle reasonings should be employed in the cause, and resolved first to announce it at home, and then at Randalls. But how to break it to her father! She had decided to do it when Mr. Knightley was away. She would have put it off, but Mr. Knightley was to join her at a certain time, and follow up the beginning she was to make. She was forced to speak, and to speak cheerfully too. She must not make it a more decided subject of misery to him by a melancholy tone herself. She must not appear to think it a misfortune. With all the spirits she could command, she prepared him first for something strange, and then, in few words, said that if his consent could be obtained – which, she trusted, would be received with no difficulty, since it was a plan to promote the happiness of all – she and Mr. Knightley meant to marry. Hartfield would then receive the constant addition of that person's company whom she knew he loved, next to his daughters and Mrs. Weston, best in the world.

Poor man! It was at first a considerable shock to him, and he tried earnestly to talk her out of it. She was reminded, more than once, of her having always said she would never marry, and assured that it would be a great deal better for her to remain single; and told of poor Isabella, and poor Miss Taylor. But it would not do. Emma hung about him affectionately, and smiled, and said it must be so; and that he must not class her with Isabella and Mrs. Weston, whose marriages taking them from Hartfield, had, indeed, made a melancholy change: but she was not going from Hartfield; she should be always there; she was introducing no change in their numbers or their comforts but for the better; and she was very sure that he would be a great deal the happier for having Mr. Knightley so near, when he got used to the idea. Did not he love Mr. Knightley very much? He would not deny that he did, she was sure. Whom did he ever want to consult on business but Mr. Knightley? Who was so useful to him, who so ready to write his letters, who so glad to assist him? Who so cheerful, so attentive, so attached to him? Would not he like to have him always on the spot? Yes. That was all very true. Mr. Knightley could not be there too often; he should be glad to see him every day; but they did see him every day as it was. Why could not they go on as before?

Mr. Woodhouse could not be soon reconciled, but the worst was overcome. The idea was given; time and continual repetition must do the rest. To Emma's entreaties and assurances were added Mr. Knightley's, whose fond praise of her gave the subject even a kind of welcome; and he was soon used to being talked to by each, whenever an opportunity presented itself. They had all the assistance which Isabella could give, by letters of the strongest approval; and Mrs. Weston was ready, on the first meeting, to consider the subject in the most serviceable light; first, as a settled, and secondly, as a good one. It was agreed upon, and everybody by whom he was used to be guided assured him that it would be for his happiness. Having some feelings himself which almost admitted it, he began to think that sometime or other, in another year or two, perhaps, it might not be so very bad if the marriage did take place.

Mrs. Weston was acting no part, feigning no feelings in all that she said to him in favour of the event. She had been extremely surprised, when Emma first told her; but she saw in it only increase of happiness to all, and had no hesitation in urging him to the utmost. She had such a regard for Mr. Knightley as to think he deserved even her dearest Emma; and it was in every respect so proper and suitable a connection that now it seemed as if Emma could not safely have attached herself to any other creature, and that she had herself been the stupidest of beings in not having thought of it sooner. How very few of those men in a rank of life to address Emma would have renounced their own home for Hartfield! And who but Mr. Knightley could know and tolerate Mr. Woodhouse, so as to make such an arrangement desirable! It was a union of the highest promise of happiness, and without one real, rational difficulty to oppose or delay it.

Mrs. Weston, with her baby on her knee, indulging in such reflections as these, was one of the happiest women in the world.

The news was universally a surprise wherever it spread, and Mr. Weston soon heard it. He quickly saw the advantages of the match, and rejoiced in them with all the constancy of his wife; but the wonder of it was very soon nothing, and by the end of an hour he was not far from believing that he had always foreseen it.

"It is to be a secret, I conclude," said he. "These matters are always a secret, till it is found out that everybody knows them. Only let me be told when I may speak out. I wonder whether Jane has any suspicion."

He went to Highbury the next morning and satisfied himself on that point. He told her the news. Was not she like a daughter, his eldest daughter? He must tell her; and Miss Bates being present, it passed, of course, to Mrs. Cole, Mrs. Perry, and Mrs. Elton, immediately afterwards. It was no more than Emma and Mr. Knightley were prepared for; they had calculated from the time of its being known at Randalls how soon it would be all over Highbury.

In general, it was a very well approved match. Some might think him, and others might think her, the more blessed. Upon the whole, there was no serious objection raised, except in one habitation: the vicarage. There the surprise was not softened by any satisfaction. Mr. Elton cared little about it. He only hoped "the young lady's pride would now be contented," and supposed "she had always meant to catch Knightley if she could." With regard to living at Hartfield, he daringly exclaimed, "Rather he than I!" – But Mrs. Elton was very unhappy indeed. "Poor Knightley! Poor fellow! Sad business for him." She was extremely concerned; for, though very eccentric, he had a thousand good qualities. How could he be so taken in? She did not think him at all in love – not in the least. Poor Knightley! There would be an end of all pleasant interaction with him. How happy he had been to come and dine with them whenever they asked him! But that would be all over now. Poor fellow! No more exploring parties to Donwell made for her. Oh! No; there would be a Mrs. Knightley to throw cold water on everything. Extremely disagreeable!

CHAPTER 54

A few more tomorrows and the party from London would be arriving. It was an alarming change, and Emma was thinking of it one morning as something that must bring a great deal to agitate and grieve her, when Mr. Knightley came in and her distressing thoughts were put aside. After the first chat of pleasure he was silent; and then, in a graver tone, began with,

"I have something to tell you, Emma; some news."

"Good or bad?" said she, quickly, looking up in his face.

"I do not know which it ought to be called."

"Oh! Good I am sure. I see it in your countenance. You are trying not to smile."

"I am afraid," said he, composing his features, "I am very much afraid, my dear Emma, that you will not smile when you hear it."

"Indeed! But why so? I can hardly imagine that anything which pleases or amuses you should not please and amuse me too."

"There is one subject," he replied, "I hope only one, on which we do not think alike." He paused a moment, again smiling, with his eyes fixed on her face. "Does nothing occur to you? Do you not recollect? Harriet Smith."

Her cheeks flushed at the name, and she felt afraid of something, though she knew not what.

"Have you heard from her yourself this morning?" cried he. "You have, I believe, and know the whole."

"No, I have not; I know nothing. Please tell me."

"You are prepared for the worst, I see; and very bad it is. Harriet Smith is engaged to marry Robert Martin."

Emma gave a start, and her eyes, in eager gaze, said, "No, this is impossible!" but her lips were closed.

"It is so, indeed," continued Mr. Knightley; "I have it from Robert Martin himself. He left me not half an hour ago."

She was still looking at him with amazement.

"You like it, my Emma, as little as I feared. I wish our opinions were the same. But time, you may be very sure, will make one or the other of us think differently; and, in the meanwhile, we need not talk much on the subject."

"You mistake me, you quite mistake me," she replied, exerting herself. "It is not that such a circumstance would now make me unhappy, but I cannot believe it. It seems an impossibility! You cannot mean to say that Harriet Smith has accepted Robert Martin. You cannot mean that he has proposed to her again. You only mean that he intends to do it."

"I mean that he has done it," answered Mr. Knightley, with smiling but determined decision, "and been accepted."

"Good God!" she cried. "Well!" Then having recourse to her needlework as an excuse for leaning down her face, and concealing all the exquisite feelings of delight and entertainment which she knew she must be expressing, she added, "Well, now tell me everything. How, where, when? Let me know it all. I never was more surprised – but it does not make me unhappy, I assure you. How – how is it even possible?"

"It is a very simple story. He went to London on business three days ago, and I got him to take charge of some papers which I was wanting to send to John. He delivered these papers to John, at his chambers, and was asked by him to join their party the same evening to see the circus. They were going to take the two eldest boys. The party was to be our brother and sister, Henry, John – and Miss Smith. My friend Robert could not resist. They called for him on their way; were all extremely entertained; and my brother asked him to dine with them the next day, which he did, and in the course of that visit (as I understand) he found an opportunity of speaking to Harriet; and certainly did not speak in vain. She made him, by her acceptance, as happy even as he is deserving. He came down by yesterday's coach, and was with me this morning immediately after breakfast, to report his proceedings, first on my affairs, and then on his own. This is all that I can relate of the how, where, and when. Your friend Harriet will probably say much more when you see her, and give you all the minute particulars. However, I must say that Robert Martin's heart seemed for *him*, and to *me*, very overflowing."

He stopped. Emma dared not attempt any immediate reply. To speak, she was sure would be to betray a most unreasonable degree of happiness. She must wait a moment, or he would think her mad. Her silence disturbed him; and after observing her a little while, he added,

"Emma, my love, you said that this circumstance would not now make you unhappy; but I am afraid it gives you more pain than you expected. He is not genteel; but you must consider this connection as something that satisfies your friend. I will answer for your thinking better and better of him as you know him more. His good sense and good principles would delight you. As far as the man is concerned, you could not wish your friend in better hands. His rank in society I would alter if I could."

He wanted her to look up and smile; and having now brought herself not to smile too broadly, she did, cheerfully answering,

"You need not be at any pains to reconcile me to the match. I think Harriet is doing extremely well. *Her* connections may be worse than *his*. In respectability of character, there can be no doubt that they are. I have been silent from surprise merely, excessive surprise. You cannot imagine how suddenly it has come on me! How unprepared I was! For I had reason to believe her very recently more determined against him, much more than she was before."

"You ought to know your friend best," replied Mr. Knightley; "but I should say she was a good-tempered, soft-hearted girl, not likely to be very, very determined against any young man who told her he loved her."

Emma could not help laughing as she answered, "Upon my word, I believe you know her quite as well as I do. But, Mr. Knightley, are you perfectly sure that she has absolutely and downright *accepted* him. I could suppose she might in time, but can she have done it already? Did not you misunderstand him? You were both talking of other things; of business, cattle, or new farming equipment; and might not you, in the confusion of so many subjects, mistake him? It was not Harriet's hand that he was certain of – it was the dimensions of some famous ox."

The contrast between the countenance and manners of Mr. Knightley and Robert Martin was, at this moment, so strong to Emma's feelings, and so strong was the recollection of all that had so recently passed on Harriet's side, so fresh the sound of those words, spoken with such emphasis, "No, I hope I know better than to think of Robert Martin," that she was really expecting the news to be proven, in some measure, premature. It could not be otherwise.

"Do you dare say this?" cried Mr. Knightley. "Do you dare to suppose me so great a blockhead as not to know what a man is talking of? He told me she had accepted him; and there was no obscurity, nothing doubtful in the words he used; and I think I can give you a proof that it must be so. He asked my opinion as to what he was now to do. He knew of no one but Mrs. Goddard to whom he could apply for information of her relations or friends. Could I mention anything more fit to be done, than to go to Mrs. Goddard? I assured him that I could not. Then, he said, he would endeavour to see her in the course of this day."

"I am perfectly satisfied," replied Emma, with the brightest smiles, "and most sincerely wish them happy."

"You are materially changed since we talked on this subject before."

"I hope so – for at that time I was a fool."

"And I am changed also; for I am now very willing to see, with you, all Harriet's good qualities. I have taken some pains for your sake, and for Robert Martin's sake (whom I have always had reason to believe as much in love with her as ever), to get acquainted with her. I have often talked to her a good deal. You must have seen that I did. Sometimes, indeed, I have thought you were half suspecting me of pleading poor Martin's cause, which was never the case; but, from all my observations, I am convinced of her being a sincere, amiable girl, with very good principles. Much of this, I have no doubt, she may thank you for."

"Me!" cried Emma, shaking her head. "Ah! Poor Harriet!"

She checked herself, however, and submitted quietly to more praise than she deserved.

Their conversation was soon afterwards closed by the entrance of her father. She was not sorry. She wanted to be alone. Her mind was in a state of flutter and wonder, which made it impossible for her to be collected. She was in a dancing, singing, and exclaiming mood; till she had moved about, and talked to herself, and laughed and reflected, she could be fit for nothing rational.

Her father's business was to announce that James had gone out to prepare the horses for their now daily drive to Randalls; and she had, therefore, an immediate excuse for disappearing.

The joy, the gratitude, the exquisite delight of her sensations may be imagined. The sole grievance thus removed in the prospect of Harriet's welfare, she was really in danger of becoming too happy for her own good. What had she to wish for? Nothing but to grow more worthy of him whose intentions and judgment had been ever so superior to her own. Nothing but that the lessons of her past folly might teach her humility and discretion in the future.

Serious she was, very serious in her gratitude; and yet there was no preventing her laughter. She must laugh at such a close! Such an end of the disappointment of five weeks back! Such a heart – such a Harriet!

Now there would be pleasure in her returning. Everything would be pleasure. It would be a great pleasure to know Robert Martin.

High in the rank of her most serious and heartfelt felicities was the reflection that all necessity of concealment from Mr. Knightley would soon be over. She could now look forward to giving him that full and perfect confidence which her disposition was most ready to welcome.

In the happiest spirits she set forward with her father; not always listening, but always agreeing to what he said.

They arrived. Mrs. Weston was alone in the drawing room. But hardly had they been told of the baby, and Mr. Woodhouse received the thanks for coming when a glimpse was caught through the blind of two figures passing near the window.

"It is Frank and Miss Fairfax," said Mrs. Weston. "I was just going to tell you of our agreeable surprise in seeing him arrive this morning. He stays till tomorrow, and Miss Fairfax has been persuaded to spend the day with us. They are coming in, I hope."

In half a minute they were in the room. Emma was extremely glad to see him – but there was a degree of confusion, a number of embarrassing recollections on each side. They met readily and smiling, but with a consciousness which at first allowed little to be said. When Mr. Weston joined the party, however, and when the baby was fetched, there was no longer a want of subject or animation, or of courage and opportunity for Frank Churchill to draw near her and say,

"I have to thank you, Miss Woodhouse, for a very kind forgiving message in one of Mrs. Weston's letters. I hope time has not made you less willing to pardon. I hope you do not retract what you then said."

"No, indeed," cried Emma, most happy to begin, "not in the least. I am particularly glad to see and shake hands with you, and to congratulate you in person."

He thanked her with all his heart, and continued some time to speak with serious feeling of his gratitude and happiness.

"Is not she looking well?" said he, turning his eyes towards Jane. "Better than before? You see how my father and Mrs. Weston dote upon her."

But his spirits were soon rising again, and with laughing eyes, after mentioning the expected return of the Campbells, he said the name of Dixon. Emma blushed, and forbade its being pronounced in her hearing.

"I can never think of it," she cried, "without extreme shame."

"The shame," he answered, "is all mine, or ought to be. But is it possible that you had no suspicion? I mean of late. Early, I know you had none."

"I never had the smallest, I assure you."

"That appears quite wonderful. I was once very near telling you — and I wish I had; it would have been better. But though I was always doing wrong things, they were very *bad* wrong things, and such as did me no service. It would have been a much better transgression had I broken the bond of secrecy and told you everything."

"It is not now worth regretting," said Emma.

"I have some hope," resumed he, "of my uncle's being persuaded to pay a visit at Randalls; he wants to be introduced to her. When the Campbells are returned, we shall meet them in London, and continue there, I trust, till we may carry her northward. But now, I am at such a distance from her — is not it hard, Miss Woodhouse? Till this morning, we have not once met since the day of reconciliation. Do you not pity me?"

Emma spoke her pity so very kindly that he suddenly cried,

"Ah! By the way," then sinking his voice, and looking serious for the moment, "I hope Mr. Knightley is well?" He paused. She coloured and laughed. "I know you saw my letter, and think you may remember my wish in your favour. Let me return your congratulations. I assure you that I have heard the news with the warmest interest and satisfaction. He is a man whom I cannot praise too highly."

Emma was delighted, and only wanted him to go on in the same style; but his mind was the next moment on his own concerns and with his own Jane, and his next words were,

"Did you ever see such skin? Such smoothness! Such delicacy! It is a most uncommon complexion, with her dark eye-lashes and hair — a most distinguishing complexion! So peculiarly the lady in it. Just colour enough for beauty."

"I have always admired her complexion," replied Emma, "but do I not remember a time when you found fault with her for being so pale? When we first began to talk of her. Have you quite forgotten?"

"Oh! No – what an arrogant dog I was! How could I dare – "

But he laughed so heartily at the recollection that Emma could not help saying,

"I do suspect that in the midst of your perplexities at that time, you had very great amusement in tricking us all. I am sure you had. I am sure it was a consolation to you."

"Oh! No, no, no! how can you suspect me of such a thing? I was the most miserable wretch!"

"Perhaps I am the readier to suspect, because, to tell you the truth, I think it might have been some amusement to myself in the same situation. I think we are more alike than you realize."

He bowed.

"If not in our dispositions," she presently added, with a look of true sensibility, "there is a likeness in our destiny; the destiny which bids us connect with someone so much superior to ourselves."

"It is not true on your side. You can have no superior, but most true on mine. She is a complete angel. Look at her. Is not she an angel in every gesture? Observe her eyes, as she is looking up at my father. You will be glad to hear (inclining his head, and whispering seriously) that my uncle means to give her all my aunt's jewels. Do you not think she will look beautiful in them?"

"Very beautiful, indeed," replied Emma, and she spoke so kindly that he gratefully burst out,

"How delighted I am to see you again! And to see you so happy! I would not have missed this meeting for the world. I should certainly have called at Hartfield, had you failed to come."

The others had been talking of the child, Mrs. Weston giving an account of a little alarm she had been under, the evening before, from the infant's appearing not quite well. She believed she had been foolish, but it had alarmed her, and she had been within half a minute of sending for Mr. Perry. Perhaps she ought to be ashamed, but Mr. Weston had been almost as uneasy as herself. In ten minutes, however, the child had been perfectly well again. This was her story; and particularly interesting it was to Mr. Woodhouse, who commended her very much for thinking of sending for Perry, and only regretted that she had not done it. "She should always send for Perry, if the child appeared in the slightest degree disordered, were it only for a moment. She could not be too soon alarmed, nor send for Perry too often. It was a pity, perhaps, that he had not come last night; for, though the child seemed well now, very well considering, it would probably have been better if Perry had seen it."

Frank Churchill caught the name.

"Perry!" said he to Emma, and trying, as he spoke, to catch Miss Fairfax's eye. "My friend Mr. Perry! What are they saying about Mr. Perry? Has he been here this morning? And how does he travel now? Has he purchased a carriage?"

Emma soon recollected, and understood him; and while she joined in the laugh, it was evident from Jane's countenance that she too was really hearing him, though trying to seem deaf.

"Such an extraordinary dream of mine!" he cried. "I can never think of it without laughing. She hears us, she hears us, Miss Woodhouse. I see it in her cheek, her smile, her vain attempt to frown. Look at her. Do not you see that, at this instant, the very passage of her own letter, which sent me the report, is passing under her eye. The whole blunder is spread before her; she can attend to nothing else, though pretending to listen to the others."

Jane was forced to smile completely, for a moment; and the smile partly remained as she turned towards him, and said in a conscious, low, yet steady voice,

"How you can bear such recollections is astonishing to me!"

He had a great deal to say in return, and very entertainingly; but Emma's feelings were chiefly with Jane, and on leaving Randalls, and falling naturally into a comparison of the two men, she felt, that pleased as she had been to see Frank Churchill, and really regarding him as she did with friendship, she had never been more sensible of Mr. Knightley's superiority of character. The happiness of this most happy day received its completion in the animated contemplation of his worth which this comparison produced.

CHAPTER 55

If Emma had still, at intervals, an anxious feeling for Harriet, a momentary doubt of its being possible for her to be really cured of her attachment to Mr. Knightley, and really able to accept another man, it was not long that she had to suffer from the recurrence of any such uncertainty. A very few days brought the party from London, and she had no sooner an opportunity of being one hour alone with Harriet, than she became perfectly satisfied – unaccountable as it was – that Robert Martin had thoroughly supplanted Mr. Knightley, and was now forming all her views of happiness.

Harriet was a little distressed – did look a little foolish at first; but having once confessed that she had been presumptuous and silly, and self-deceived, before, her pain and confusion seemed to die away with the words, and leave her without a care for the past, and with the fullest exultation in the present and future. As to her friend's approval, Emma had instantly removed every fear of that nature by meeting her with the most unqualified congratulations. Harriet was most happy to give every particular of the evening at the circus, and the dinner the next day; she could dwell on it all with the utmost delight. But what did such particulars explain? The fact was, as Emma could now acknowledge, that Harriet had always liked Robert Martin; and that his continuing to love her had been irresistible.

Harriet's parentage became known. She proved to be the daughter of a tradesman, rich enough to afford her the comfortable maintenance which had ever been hers, and decent enough to have always wished for concealment. Such was the blood of gentility which Emma had formerly been so ready to vouch for!

No objection was raised on the father's side; the young man was treated liberally; it was all as it should be. As Emma became acquainted with Robert Martin, who was now introduced at Hartfield, she fully acknowledged in him all the appearance of sense and worth which could bid fairest for her little friend. She had no doubt of Harriet's happiness with any good-tempered man; but with him, and in the home he offered, there would be the hope of security, stability, and improvement. She would be placed in the midst of those who loved her, and who had better sense than herself. She would be respectable and happy; and Emma admitted her to be the luckiest creature in the world, to have created so steady and persevering an affection in such a man; or, if not quite the luckiest, second only to herself.

Harriet, necessarily drawn away by her engagements with the Martins, was less and less at Hartfield; which was not to be regretted. The friendship between her and Emma must be lessened; it must change into a calmer sort of good will; and, fortunately, what ought to be, and must be, seemed already beginning, and in the most gradual, natural manner.

Before the end of September, Emma went with Harriet to church, and saw her hand bestowed on Robert Martin with so complete a satisfaction, that no memories, even those connected with Mr. Elton who stood before them, could intrude. Perhaps, indeed, at that time she scarcely saw Mr. Elton, but as the clergyman whose blessing at the altar might next fall on herself. Robert Martin and Harriet Smith, the last couple engaged of the three, were the first to be married.

Jane Fairfax had already left Highbury, and was restored to the comforts of her beloved home with the Campbells. The Churchills were also in London, and they were only waiting for November.

Emma and Mr. Knightley had determined that they ought to be married while John and Isabella were still at Hartfield, to allow them the fortnight's absence in a tour to the sea-side, which was the plan. John and Isabella, and every other friend, were agreed in approving it. But Mr. Woodhouse – how was Mr. Woodhouse to be convinced to consent? He, who had never yet spoken of their marriage but as a distant event.

When first told the idea, he was so miserable that they were almost hopeless. A second discussion, indeed, gave less pain. He began to think it was to be, and that he could not prevent it – a very promising step of the mind on its way to resignation. Still, however, he was not happy. Nay, he appeared so much otherwise, that his daughter's courage failed. She could not bear to see him suffering, to know him fancying himself neglected. Emma hesitated – she could not proceed.

In this state of suspense they were befriended, not by any sudden illumination of Mr. Woodhouse's mind, but by an unexpected event. Mrs. Weston's poultry house was robbed one night of all her turkeys. Other poultry yards in the neighbourhood also suffered. Mr. Woodhouse was very uneasy about his own poultry. While either of the Mr. Knightleys were there to protect, Hartfield was safe. But Mr. John Knightley must be in London again by the end of the first week in November.

The result of this distress was that, with a much more voluntary, cheerful consent than his daughter had ever hoped for, she was able to choose her wedding-day; and Mr. Elton was called on, within a month from the marriage of Mr. and Mrs. Robert Martin, to join the hands of Mr. Knightley and Miss Woodhouse.

The wedding was very much like other weddings, where the parties have no taste for finery or parade; and Mrs. Elton, from the particulars detailed by her husband, thought it all extremely shabby, and very inferior to her own. "Very little white satin, very few lace veils; a most pitiful business! Selina would stare when she heard of it." But, in spite of these deficiencies, the wishes, the hopes, the confidence, the predictions of the small band of true friends who witnessed the ceremony, were all fully answered in the perfect happiness of the union.

ABOUT THE AUTHOR

Gerry Baird lives in Utah with his wife and three children. He is an avid Jane Austen fan, and when he's not writing he spends his time playing piano and guitar. He is also the owner of Impact Self-publishing, a company that helps aspiring authors write and publish their own books. Learn more at www.impactselfpublishing.com